The Potter's Daughter

The Potter's Daughter

Jackie Ladbury

Stories that inspire emotions
www.rubyfiction.com

Copyright © 2019 Jackie Ladbury

Published 2019 by Ruby Fiction
Penrose House, Crawley Drive, Camberley, Surrey GU15 2AB, UK
www.rubyfiction.com

The right of Jackie Ladbury to be identified as the Author of this Work
has been asserted by her in accordance with the Copyright, Designs and
Patents Act 1988

A CIP catalogue record for this book is available
from the British Library

ISBN: 978-1-91255-023-4

Printed and bound in Great Britain by Clays Ltd, Elcograf S.p.A.

Acknowledgements

My childhood memories, growing up in the heart of the Potteries are the best. Home-cooked food: apple pies, thick porridge you could stand your spoon up in, and the strange 'lobby' that is particular to the Potteries. As children we had freedom to roam in wild fields, mess around in murky ponds and would make dens from reeds and sticks, and in winter the huge Aga would keep us all warm in the kitchen, although ice would form on the inside of our bedroom window and we would go to bed wearing 'sleepy socks' and balaclavas. Mum and Dad made these memories possible and I'd like to thank them with all my heart for being such wonderful parents to me and my four brothers and sisters, and I'd like to dedicate this book, the book of my heart, to both of them. Love you Mum and Dad.

I would like to say a huge thank you to Ruby Fiction for publishing *The Potter's Daughter* and for the wonderful job they have done in editing, designing, organising and promoting my book. I'd also like to thank my WriteRomantic friends who have been invaluable in my journey as a writer, especially Sharon Booth who had the dubious pleasure of reading an early version of *The Potter's Daughter*, and writer Margaret Kaine, who is also from the Potteries and provided some much-needed advice. Thanks, as always, to my lovely husband and two daughters who keep me sane, and my long-suffering friends who are probably sick to death of hearing about my make-believe worlds and the people in them.

Thank you also to the Tasting Panel who passed the manuscript and made publication possible: Isabelle D, Kirsty W, Jo O, Barbara P, Liz R, Helen C, Hilary B and Dewi C.

Chapter One

Someone was yelling at the back of Madeline Lockett's home, the voice hoarse and panicky and echoing off the grimy walls in the alleyway of China Street. Pausing in her laundry duties, Maddie tilted her head and listened to the familiar scrape of hobnail boots across the cobbles beyond the yard walls, praying it wasn't one of her neighbours coming over. There was no time in her day for idle chatter.

At fifteen years old she undertook all of the duties of an adult and felt so much older than her years. She sighed as she unpegged more washing from the line and shook the fine down of grey ash from her dad's white Sunday shirt. 'I don't know why I worry myself with trying to keep things clean,' she grumbled, instantly forgetting the commotion in the street.

She glowered at the ugly bottle kiln, visible even over the roof of her house. It spewed out its filthy poison, casting its ugly shadow into every nook and cranny, turning a perfectly good day into the gloom of night wherever it fell. She hated it, along with the brooding chimneys and the soot-stained factories that brought such easy devastation. The potteries and the pits – clay and coal – if one didn't get you the other one would.

She clamped another wooden peg between her teeth as she folded her younger brother's thin trousers, smoothing down the creases with love.

Another voice, female, louder than the first, and closer. She wondered if there might be a fight in the street, but it was a bit early in the day for brawling, and, anyway, nearly everyone who was able was at work.

The bottle kiln belched out another cloud of filth, as if to prove its superiority, taunting them that it was an easy win and it would see them all in an early grave.

There was no escaping the factories or bottle kilns. Thrown up haphazardly, regardless of location, they stole the light and disgorged fumes over the folk of the Potteries. Night and day, cups, saucers, jardinières and teapots were hauled up ladders and back down ladders, crammed into towering piles and loaded onto barrows. The endless production of supply and demand kept the inhabitants of Fenton fed and watered just enough for them to repeat the tedious actions the next day.

Someone called her name, right as the metal gate to her backyard swung open. 'Maddie, come quick.' Her neighbour, Jane, in a whirlwind of panic wheezed out the words, the condition of her lungs dictating the struggle to make herself heard.

'Whatever's wrong?' Maddie grasped her friend's arm, her ready smile fading at the terror in her eyes. 'Calm down. Tell me, slowly.'

'There's a young lad fallen in the disused marl hole, up by Irvin's old factory. Hurry. Albert's yelling up the street about it, and I'm scared it might be Tom, or Jimmy – I can't find either of them.'

Terror clutched Maddie's heart as the words sank in. *Please don't let it be Tom*, she thought, feeling immediately guilty at her selfishness. She raised her eyes briefly, begging to the God she no longer trusted, before she threw down her peg bag and hurried into the house to find her boots. 'Has Albert fetched someone?'

'He's run up to the factory, but I think they're still biscuit firing.' Jane pointed to the sky, thick with smoke. 'Look, it's still water smoke. Your dad'll be stuck in the kiln, and my dad's in bed, bad again with his lungs.'

'Don't bother your dad, Jane.' Maddie shook her head. Jane's father was always poorly of late. The Potter's rot had got to him, and if he went in the freezing water of the marl hole, there would be a funeral next week, for sure.

2

She grabbed her coat, slammed out of the front door, and rushed towards the water-filled hole with Jane barely keeping pace at her side, dreading what she would find there. 'How many times have we told them to keep away from that place, Jane?' She was close to wheezing herself beneath the effort of trying to run whilst talking.

'I heard 'em muttering about getting some newts. I should have realised what they were up to.' Jane gulped in the fetid air as she tried to keep up with Maddie.

'You find Albert and make sure he knows where to send help,' Maddie ordered Jane, and she sprinted off, quickly leaving Jane behind. She could already picture her young brother's fate as he slithered down the sticky sides of the marl hole into the icy water. 'Please don't die, please don't die,' she begged, over and over.

Her chest burned with the effort of running. The same hollow dread that had crept through her body when her mother had lain pale and still in bed, hit her like a sledgehammer, and her legs quivered as she ran. Thick mud clung to her boots, slowing her down, the recent rainfall making a mockery of the cinder-strewn street. She stopped to scrape it off, until panic filled her chest once more, and she shucked her boots off, throwing them on the ground with a clatter of hobnails splintering cinders underfoot.

She scrambled over a pile of discarded broken bricks that bled out their red dust into the surrounding oily puddles and headed towards the slight incline leading to the derelict scrubland.

Growing closer, she could see Jimmy trembling at the edge of the man-made lake. His face was white and tear-stained as he pointed towards the water.

'Tom!'

'He's out there, Maddie,' Jimmy said, his words tumbling over each other. 'I couldn't help him,' he cried.

Maddie pulled Jimmy towards her, comforting him briefly,

before rushing to the edge of the gaping marl hole, muddy slime edging its perimeter. Spotting Tom's blond head sticking up above the waterline in the middle of the lake, about all she could see of him, she called down to him. 'I'm here, Tom, hold on.' He clung to a plank of drifting wood, spluttering each time the ripples overwhelmed him. 'Stop kicking, you're heading further out.'

Jimmy stood next to her, chewing at his fingers. 'I chucked him that bit of door, Maddie. It was all I could find.'

'Well done, Jimmy. We'll get him out in a minute, don't worry.' Her confidence was forced as she scanned the ground in vain, hoping to find something to help haul her brother out of the water. There was nothing, though, just a few bits of broken twine and discarded half-bricks.

She peered over the top of the deep, dark hole. The soft, muddy sides were smooth as butter and just as slippery, worn away from years of rain, and left to erode once the useable clay had been excavated. A few scrubby, half-dead trees clung to the side and she eyed them, wondering if they would take her weight if she needed to lower herself into the water.

Jane scrambled up behind them, clutching Maddie's boots to her chest. 'Albert says they won't risk letting your dad out in case the temperature changes whilst he's gone,' she said, her words rasping and laboured. 'There'd be so many people as wouldn't eat for weeks, if the pots were ruined.'

'Oh God, I know. It's fine.' Maddie inhaled as panic gripped her once again. 'Of course, they mustn't fetch him out, Jane, but we need help.'

'I've sent Albert back to find somebody else, but who'll dare leave without permission?' Jane took in Tom's predicament, as he shivered and tried to stay afloat on the thin plank, her voice quivering as she said, 'I'm so sorry, Maddie, I should have checked on 'em, but I was peeling the veg for the lobby for our dinner an' in a world of me own.' Her hands twisted around one another, her eyes wide with fear.

'It's not your fault, Jane. They could just as easily have been playing outside my front.' Her mind scrambled as she tried to think what to do for the best. She threw off her coat and pulled down her thick wool skirt in one nimble movement, ready to lower herself down the incline and into the icy water. 'I'm going in.'

'Wait. Someone's up by Irvin's Mill. Look, on a horse. Help! Over here.' Jane jumped up and down, windmilling her arms madly. She turned to Maddie, her smile of relief disappearing as she saw that her friend was still intent on going into the water. 'Maddie, dunna go in. You can't swim.'

'I'm not going all the way in,' Maddie insisted, edging her legs over the side. 'But I have to try.'

'He's coming over. Oh, thank the Lord. Come back, Maddie. You'll drown yourself.'

As the rider turned his horse towards them Maddie tried to climb back up the incline, but her bare feet could find no purchase. She dug her fingers and toes into the soft marl trying to haul her body out, but her foot slipped, and she slithered further down, her cheek scraping over a cluster of small stones. She heard a deep voice shouting to Jane. 'Hold my horse. Hold him tight now, whilst I throw the rope.'

She jerked her head up, trying to see what was happening, but the sudden movement sent her slithering farther down toward the water's edge. Her toes touched the water, numbing them in seconds, as she knew it would, making her all too aware that Tom would not last much longer.

'Hold on, Tom, help's coming,' she yelled to her brother. As she spoke, a rope landed on the water, hitting Tom's makeshift raft, and he disappeared as the wood submerged.

'Tom!' Maddie screamed and splashed into the water, completely focused on saving her precious brother, gasping as the cold water hit. 'Tom.' She floundered near the edge and saw to her relief that he'd caught the rope and the unseen stranger was pulling him in.

'Thank God,' she breathed, as he held fast to the length of rope. She grasped at some thin bulrushes that had thrived against the odds, and tried to hoist her body back onto firm ground, but her legs were almost numb, and she hadn't enough strength in her arms to pull herself out. Her fingers curled around thin, spiky reeds that instantly snapped, and she fell back into the water with a feeble splash.

She waved her arms weakly. 'I can't … I can't get out.' Her voice was a whisper, her strength rapidly depleting. She gulped in the rank water as she slipped again, and her head disappeared under the waterline. Her eyes stung and her chest burned as she tried to hold her breath. Her mind screamed out, *no, no, I won't let this happen*, but already the water was winning. She inhaled deeply; it was impossible not to.

The explosion in her chest wasn't too bad after the first few seconds, and she opened her eyes to see the last minutes of the watery world about to take away her life. However, the water stung her eyes too much, and she closed them once more as an unlikely serenity settled on her.

Snatches of her old life passed through her mind, like a slideshow: her mother stirring a pot of soup and laughing at her brother's antics; her father, too, smiling down at a young Maddie, in the days when he had something to smile about. She opened her mouth imagining she could talk to him before it was too late.

Unexpectedly, the sensation of spiralling into a void of nothingness disappeared, and she was hauled out of the water as effortlessly as if angels had carried her to heaven. She lay on her back as her eyes refocused on a young man, a concerned frown on his brow making her think she must know him well enough for him to care. Above him, off-white, lumpy clouds hung in the overcast sky, a grey film of dust in the air making it, as always, look as if she was seeing the world through a square of muslin. It was enough to convince her that she was back in the land of the living, and, for once, she was glad to see such a sight.

Retching, she twisted on to her side as water and vomit rushed from her, the sound of it fearful to her own ears, as her saviour rubbed her back and uttered soothing words.

'I'm so cold,' she managed, between heaving up the foul water and trying to stop her chattering teeth. 'My brother?' she asked in the next breath as she collected her thoughts.

'He's okay. He's waiting for me to get you out of here. We need to move quickly. Can you sit?' The stranger put his hands under her shoulders and heaved her to a sitting position. She sat on the grey slimy ridge of mud that circled the marl hole, her head in her hands, sickness and dizziness overcoming her. Her body twitched and shook so hard, she felt like a puppet on a string, shaken by an unseen hand.

The young man tested the knotted rope around his waist. 'I'm going to get you out of here.' He hoisted her up and wrapped his arms around her, and Maddie caught a glimpse of Jane's worried face peering over the top of the crevice. 'Hold tight, now.'

Maddie closed her eyes for a moment, praying she wouldn't be sick over her saviour.

'Walk the horse now, please,' he shouted above her head, gripping Maddie tighter still, as her teeth chattered out of control. 'Just try and hold on. We'll soon be there.'

Maddie apologised constantly in between gasps of breath, for the trouble she'd caused, until the man said, 'Stop apologising and save your breath to get up the sides.'

He tugged on the rope and gathered Maddie into his chest. 'Grab the rope; we'll do it together.'

She nodded and clutched at the rope, holding on for dear life. Her face was inches away from his, and she rested her chin on his shoulder in an effort to tame her chattering teeth. She put an arm around his neck to steady herself, dimly aware that it wasn't a seemly thing for a young woman to do to a stranger, but there was something immensely comforting about surrendering to the warmth and strength of him.

Finally, heaving themselves over the edge of the marl hole and onto dry scrubland, they both collapsed, gulping in great draughts of air.

Tom launched himself towards his sister with tears rolling down his face. His trousers and shirt lay in a filthy heap on the grass, and he huddled inside the stranger's long coat, which trailed around his ankles and caught between his legs. 'I was so scared, Maddie. I'm really sorry.'

She caught him, as he almost toppled over, and hugged him so tightly that he laughed and pushed her away.

'Give over, I can't breathe.'

She pulled him close, anyway, and stroked his face and hair, unable to let him go until he squirmed out of her reach again.

'I'm all right now. Come on, let's get home.'

She nodded, but lowered her shocked body to the ground once more, unable to stand. 'Just give me a minute, will you?'

Jane hovered close by, looking solicitous as she hopped from one leg to the other. 'What can I do, Maddie, love?'

The young man turned toward her. 'Will you run home and get a fire lit and some hot water boiled? Take the other boy with you, then we'll know everyone is safe.' He nodded toward where Jimmy sat on the ground shivering, and, without waiting for an answer, he drew a rough blanket over Maddie's shoulders and pulled it under her chin, taking both of her hands in his to ensure she grasped the corners.

She clutched at the blanket and closed her eyes, trying to calm her breathing whilst praying she wouldn't be sick again. She lifted her face up to the early spring sunshine, although there was little warmth in it. Nevertheless, it gladdened her heart.

Lowering her face and lifting her eyelids, she smiled at her saviour as he tended to his horse. She imagined him to be a few years older than her fifteen years but he appeared more a man than a boy, strong and muscular. Kind, brown eyes looked back at her, and she felt a strange urge to wipe the splodge of clay from his cheek. Realising that he was studying her in return, she found herself wishing she could have presented a better image. She couldn't really have looked much worse than she did, she thought, before fleetingly wondering why she cared.

Suddenly, seeing herself through the eyes of the young man who stared at her bare limbs, pale in the glare of the afternoon, she blanched. Her legs were streaked with mud, the same colour as the long, brown woollen knickers covering her thighs. Instinctively she tried to cover herself, but it was pointless, and instead of being mortified as she ought to be, she giggled. 'Just look at the state of me.'

The man frowned. 'Are you hysterical, do you think?'

She giggled again. 'It is a rather funny situation to be in.'

He took a step towards her, his own mouth twitching into a smile as he studied her legs for a second time. 'What *are* those brown things?'

She shrugged. It didn't seem to matter that she was showing her drawers to a stranger. 'They're my winter woollies. It gets really cold in our house, even in spring.'

'Well, I've never seen anything like that at ours, and it's full of women.' He looked down at her legs again with interest.

She brought her knees up to her chest, hoping it would hide them. 'They're really itchy, so I wouldn't recommend them.'

'I don't suppose you would.' His lips turned down in distaste, but then he lowered his eyes and seemed to be taking in the rest of her legs.

Maddie followed his gaze, and as he quickly averted his eyes, a prickle of embarrassment washed over her. 'What would my mother say, if she could see me now?'

'I think we should get you home and you can find out.'

'Oh, no, my mother is dead,' Maddie said quietly. Her giggles faded as, once again, she pushed down the dreadful images of her mother's slow death.

'I'm sorry to hear that.' The man patted her shoulder, and she found she wanted to lean into his hand and cover it with her own.

A look of concern replaced the frown, as he stared down at her. 'I'm Daniel, by the way. Pleased to meet you.' He held out his hand, and she took it.

'Daniel. Me, too,' she said.

'Your name is Daniel?'

'No, I mean … my name is Madeline, although most people call me Maddie. I'm very happy to meet you.' She liked the feel of his hand, warm and strong in hers, and she held it tight as her throat constricted with emotion. 'I thank you, sir, with all my heart, for saving Tom and me.' She tried to smile, but to her consternation, her mouth didn't work, and she burst into tears instead.

Daniel wrapped his arms around her shoulders and drew her close, which made her cry even harder.

'It's the shock cutting in. No sense in trying to stop it.'

His breath warmed her neck, and Maddie allowed her body to relax, the sensation of an unfamiliar body next to hers, a new one. The only person she'd ever cuddled was Tom. Her father never hugged her, although she had dim memories of them sitting together silently, watching the crackling fire as it heated their legs, in the time before their life changed forever.

Daniel rested his chin on top of her head and didn't appear to be in a hurry to move. Maddie, shivering and wet, clung to him, enjoying his masculinity, as a sense of peace and security she rarely felt made her sigh. He pulled her closer still, and she could feel the muscles in his arms flexing and, surprisingly, the thump of his heart.

Eventually, he pulled away and cupped her face in his hands, as if inspecting it for signs of distress, before releasing her. 'Better?' he asked, his eyes full of compassion.

She nodded, the strangest sensation pulling her insides into a knot as she stared back at him, and when he smiled, it seemed as though they shared a secret, passed wordlessly through each other's eyes.

All was quiet apart from the steady chomp of the horse

pulling at the sparse grass, before Daniel swivelled around to her brother. 'Tom, what were you thinking of, playing here? It's very dangerous.'

'I've told him, over and over,' Maddie agreed. 'It's the factory owners' fault. They should fill up the hole after excavating the clay.'

'You're right. You know, I might have a word with Father about it.'

Maddie smiled at the thought that such a young man would agree with such an uneconomical proposition, let alone have recourse to deal with it. She wondered who his father was and where he lived, and found that she really cared. 'Are you far from home? Do you often ride out this way for pleasure?' As soon as the words were out, she wished she'd remained silent. She shouldn't have presumed he would want to tell her his business.

Thankfully, he laughed and seemed unoffended by her presumption. 'Oh, I wasn't riding for pleasure. I collect firewood for the workers who can't afford coal. The woodland area behind the old mill is great for logs, and dear old Algernon drags them back with me. That's why I carry a rope and other bits. You were lucky.'

'You're a potter?' Maddie knew he couldn't be. His clothes had the look of a gentleman, and she knew no one with a horse as fine as the chestnut he rode.

'No,' he said, 'but I know a few.'

'You know a few?' she repeated, trying to work out a connection. 'You charge them for the wood?' Maddie tried to suppress her disdain, blanching at the thought that he might be no better than one of the factory owners she so despised.

'Of course I don't. What would be the good in that?'

'Oh.' She was quiet for a moment, wondering, then, why he bothered, but it seemed too bold to ask for further answers, and he didn't volunteer any.

'Will you turn away, whilst I put on my skirt, please?'

The warmth in her voice cooled as she re-assessed the young man. He must be from a prosperous family, and she knew her father's boss had made his fortune at the expense of the workers' safety and welfare. If he was the son of an industrialist, then she wanted no more of his company.

'You should take your blouse off at the same time, and just put on your coat, as it is dry. You'll catch a fever, else.' His look was searching, caring.

Maddie raised an eyebrow. 'What would you know of such things?'

'I won't look,' he said, turning resolutely away without answering her question. 'Do you live close by?' he asked, once she had allowed him to turn around again. He inspected her coat, which she had buttoned up to the top, and nodded approval.

'Yes, not far from here. We can find our own way home, thank you.' She stomped her feet into her boots, hiding the wince of pain from the cuts she had sustained. The last thing she wanted was him looking at her feet. 'You'll get a fever yourself, if you stay in those wet clothes,' she said, with a hint of a smile, echoing his words.

'Nonsense. I didn't go in fully. Besides, I'm a man.'

She took in his wet clothes, disbelief written on her face, but she let his comment pass.

'My horse, Algernon, and I will be happy to escort you and your brother home.' He waved a hand in the direction of the patient horse.

Her eyes widened. 'You think I'm getting on that beast?' Despite her words, she walked over to the huge horse and patted its nose, to make sure she hadn't offended him.

'I will.' Tom ran over, his eyes full of excitement.

'Come on, then, let me help you up.'

Algernon remained still, whilst Daniel heaved Tom onto the saddle, where he sat beaming and stroking the horse's neck.

'He's a very well-behaved horse,' Maddie said politely.

'He knows a damsel in distress when he sees one. He's a very clever horse, too, aren't you?' He stroked Algernon's nose, his affection for his horse patently clear.

'You make a good rescue team.'

He waved his hand in dismissal. 'Ten a penny, damsels in distress. Now, show me a dragon, or two, to slay, and we're in business. That's what we're really waiting for, isn't it, Algernon?'

The horse whinnied and pawed the ground, and Maddie laughed once more, the distress of the last half hour already fading.

They set off towards her home, walking together amicably, but she fretted that Daniel would walk her right to her door, marking her out as a poor potter's daughter, once he took in the peeling paint and crumbling stone steps that hadn't been tended to since her mother's death. Although the inside of their house was clean and bright, and she knew she should be grateful, it still showed them up for what they were. It had never mattered to her before. All her friends existed in the same hand-to-mouth circumstances. For some reason, though, she cared that Daniel would see the shabby furniture and bare boards.

She had put down some pegged rugs in colourful patterns, to take away the starkness, and covered some old kapok-filled cushions with off-cuts of material, but it was like trying to paint a moonbeam with a tar brush, as her mother would have said.

'You don't have to take us to the door. We're perfectly well now,' she tried, but he waved her words away.

'No point in doing half a job.'

'No, I suppose not,' Maddie muttered as she trudged onwards. She half hoped the ground would swallow her up before they reached her cinder-strewn road, where neighbours' threadbare towels hung on pieces of string and blew in the soot-laden wind.

Spotting a figure over by the broken-down cart that had been dumped in front of the bit of scrubland that passed as a playing field, she almost ground to a halt. *No! Not Drunken Edith, please.* That was all she needed.

Regardless, Edith weaved her way over to them, her gap-toothed smile at the ready, and a lewd comment no doubt balancing on her lips. 'Got yerself a boyfriend, 'ave yer?'

'Hello, Edith, this is Daniel. He's a ...' What was he, exactly? She couldn't think.

Thankfully, Daniel helped her out. 'I'm a friend of Maddie's.'

She threw him a grateful smile and tried to hurry him on, but Edith swayed and put a hand out to the wall to steady herself. She pulled an old, green, woollen cardigan across her chest, the buttons having long ago fallen off, and heaved in a deep breath. The cardigan fell open again, and her gnarled fingers plucked at the fabric incessantly, attempting to keep out the spring chill.

'Is she okay?' Daniel asked as he slowed his pace, watching the woman lurch from one side of the dirt road to the other.

'Apart from being drunk, I imagine she's fine. Well, as fine as an old lady who's worked in these stinking factories all of her life can be.' She sighed and placed herself in front of Edith, legs akimbo to stop her from slipping past her. 'Have you eaten today, Edith?' Maddie asked the woman.

'I dunno, love, when did today start?' Edith's cheeks, criss-crossed with lines, her skin thin as parchment, wobbled as she spoke.

Maddie sighed. 'I'll bring you something across, if you go home directly.'

Edith's eyes lit up. 'You could fetch me a drop of gin on the way, if yer've a couple o' coppers on yer? I'm ever so thirsty.'

Maddie sighed. 'I'll make you some porridge, Edith. You need to keep your strength up.'

'Or a small beer, mebbe, that keeps yer strong, everyone knows that.' Her smile was hopeful, but it highlighted her rotting teeth, and Maddie was embarrassed that Daniel had to witness the scene. Not that Edith cared. She just wanted someone to buy her gin to numb her pain.

Maddie patted Edith on the shoulder. 'I'll come across as soon as I can.'

Daniel watched the scene unfold wordlessly, but as soon as they walked away, he pushed a hand in his pocket, took out a sixpence, and passed it to Maddie.

She stared at the coin, horrified. 'I'm not in need of money.'

'It's not for you, but for Edith.'

'She's one of ours. We'll help her.' She realised, too late, that she had just bracketed herself within the same social status as Edith, and she cursed silently.

Daniel's eyes clouded. 'We are all human beings,' he said gruffly. The coin still sat on his open palm, and his hand didn't waver as he presented it to Maddie a second time. 'I'm asking you to buy some food for Edith. Is there something wrong with that?'

'No. Thank you, although it's more than she'll need.' Maddie took it with bad grace, but she was aware of her fingertips brushing his warm skin, and the spark of awareness that accompanied it. 'I'll make her some lobby out of a mutton shank.'

He nodded, but his face creased in confusion, and she realised he wouldn't know what lobby was – would never have been in a position where leftover meat and vegetables were boiled up and thickened to provide supper for more people than it was meant for. She wasn't in the mood to enlighten him, either, suddenly resentful of his generosity. Or was she jealous of the fact that he was in a position to give away money to someone he didn't know?

She popped the sixpence in her pocket. At least she could buy something nourishing for Edith and not have to use up their own meagre resources.

The tentative friendship between her and Daniel seemed to

have shifted, somehow. The feeling that she had had earlier, that had cemented them together, had disappeared, or at least that was how it felt to Maddie. Daniel was probably desperate to dump her and Tom as soon as he could, ending the interminable walk along the cinder-strewn road.

Picturing Daniel walking up to her front door, where he would no doubt take one look at where she lived and race away on Algernon as fast as the horse could carry him, she dragged her feet, whilst praying he would do an about-turn, to save them both embarrassment, before they could reach her door. 'You can leave us now, Daniel,' she said, in an effort to guide the outcome. 'We'll be fine.'

'Nonsense. Tom is better off on Algernon.' Daniel smiled and patted Algernon's flank.

Maddie nodded in acceptance. As usual, God was not on her side.

Chapter Two

By the time they arrived at her shabby gate, more rust than iron, a small gathering had assembled. Maddie's father was at the centre of the throng. Although he'd not yet reached forty years old, his clear blue eyes were the only thing on his body that grime had left untouched and that still worked to full capacity. He still stood a foot taller than the crowd, though, despite being stooped from years of lifting heavy pots, the lines etched across his face showing the pain that it had caused.

He leaned heavily on the gate, a fixture that, bizarrely, elevated Maddie's family from the rest of the street. Their house was the last one of a row of terraces, and the builder had seen fit to ring it with a tiny patch of land, protected by a low wall and a gate. Primroses and violets used to peek out of the ground at the first sign of the spring sunshine, but since her mother's death, dusty, tangled weeds were the only offering, as neither Maddie, nor her father, had the heart to tend to the beds any more.

She tried not to see her circumstances through Daniel's eyes, as her father's calloused hand pumped Daniel's up and down in gratitude. 'Harold Lockett is me name, and I want to thank you, lad, for saving me boy – and Maddie here. Jane told me what happened. What were you thinking, Maddie, going in the water? And Tom—' His eyes scanned the road for Tom, his brows knitting together. Tears filled his eyes when he spotted his boy stroking a huge horse, and he tore his gaze away and turned back to Daniel. 'Thank you, sir, from the bottom of me heart.'

Long fingers, askew at the joints and gnarled with arthritis, grasped Daniel's hand, and Maddie wondered what Daniel would think of having to hold such a lumpy, red-raw hand. Even so, she was glad that her father had come to greet them, as it would not have been an easy thing to do.

'You managed to get away, Dad?'

'Jane fetched me out. She's gone to sort out Jimmy. I've got half an hour, Maddie. I'd a' come, anyway, if they would'na let me.' Her dad's voice was rasping and rough, his strong Potteries accent striking her, when compared to Daniel's deep and modulated tones. His chapped lips were thin, and red veins threaded across his nose and cheeks, caused by the iciness of morning walks to work and the furnace-like temperatures he endured for six days a week. Yet, she was still proud. He was her father, and she loved him, as she should.

She stood by his side, and he took her hands in his, as warm and comforting as any daughter could expect.

Tom ran to his father, who immediately knelt down and clasped his son, crushing him to his chest. Maddie saw the stark fear and unmitigated love in his eyes. If he had lost him, too, he would be a ruined man. 'I've done you some hot milk, son, and I've set the fire.' It was all he said, as he smoothed down Tom's hair and ran his hands down his son's pale arms, as if to check he was still in one piece.

Maddie knew there was no higher accolade than her father lighting a fire in the thin warmth of the morning, knowing there would be little coal left for an evening wash, or to warm his aching body when his day's work was done.

'I'll come and help you, Dad.' Their eyes locked for a second, and Maddie saw tears glistening. She dropped her gaze, not wishing to embarrass him.

'Best get in, then.' He moved towards the tiny frontage, but she hesitated to put a final distance between herself and Daniel.

She knew, however, that she must make the journey marking the vast divide between them. Taking a step forward, she pushed the dilapidated gate open, wincing at the familiar screech of complaint, as she regretfully joined her father.

Daniel had not moved from the other side. 'I'll get off, then?' It sounded like a question, but she couldn't imagine why he would want to stay.

She considered offering him a cup of tea, but then he would have to go inside and see her father's worn armchair pulled up to the fire, and the cheap table where she sat on a hardwood chair. She could visualise her overflowing sewing basket on the floor – in readiness for the evening's work ahead – giving away their status and lack of money, as if the tiny house hadn't already done that. Just like all the people in the pot-banks, she worked day and night; everyone who was able did the same.

'Yes, you must, but I would like to pay my respects to your family,' her father stated, over the top of her head.

'There's no need,' Daniel said quickly, but then he paused, as if deliberating his answer. 'The name is Daniel Davenport. I live at The Villas in Stokeville, have you heard of it?'

'I know where The Villas are, lad; very fancy.' Her father nodded, then made to turn away, signalling for Maddie to follow.

'I must see to my brother.' Maddie dragged her gaze away from Daniel, toward her father's retreating back. She hoped to get one more smile from Daniel before she left. She wanted him to look at her once more in that special way that made her stomach curl, but he looked uneasy.

He took a step away from her, then hesitantly raised his hand before letting it fall to his side. 'Maddie, your neighbour, with the lump on the side of her face – has she always had it?'

'Jane?' She was thrown, having hoped that he lingered so he could ask to see her again, fanciful though the thought was. She refocused on the question. 'Now you mention it, I think it's growing. She's been poorly for a while now – that's why she's often not at work. She finds it difficult to catch her breath, but that's common enough around here. Should I tell her to get to the doctor's, although I don't know if she's in The Friendly Society? There's no spare money for medicine around here.'

His frown deepened, and a jolt of fear passed through her.

'Shall I?' Her voice came out shrill. Everyone in Jane's family relied on Jane's income, due to her father being at home more than he was at work most weeks.

'Is she a paintress?' Daniel asked.

'Yes, she's on an evening shift, when she's well enough. She does piece work – you know, only gets paid by the piece she decorates.'

'Yes, I know how it works. Majolica, mostly?'

'Yes, I think so. I'm not very up on it. When Mum died, she made my dad promise that neither Tom, nor me, would work in a factory. She wasn't from around here, and she hated the fact that most people ended up working for one or another potter. That's why ...' She bit her lip. The last thing she wanted was to tell him she spent most of her day turning collars and lowering hems. 'I have to go, sorry.'

'Of course, but may I just say that Algernon and I were proud to have been of service today.'

The horse pawed the ground and nodded his large head once more, and Maddie laughed and curtsied to Algernon in return. 'I thank you both, and I hope that one day, I'll be able to return the favour.'

Daniel turned to go, but Maddie raised her hand to stop him, fear for her friend gnawing at her. 'Wait. Please. Why did you ask about Jane? Can you tell me more?'

'I'm interested in illnesses, that's all, especially amongst the poorer—' He stopped and seemed to collect himself. 'Where there is overcrowding and hard labour, there is often a manifestation of diseases and sickness, which are directly related to the industry prevalent in that area,' he amended.

Maddie frowned at his big words, digesting their meaning and wondering if she was included in his mass assessment of the poor people she lived amongst.

He must have thought her frown was bewilderment, as he added, 'I hope to become a doctor one day.'

'Very commendable.' She smiled, but inside she wilted. That was it, then. He was destined for great things, and someone like herself would be of no interest.

'I like to think so.' His gaze was steady, almost defiant, and then it softened as he took a step forward and held out his hand. 'Well, then, it has been a pleasure, Madeline Lockett.'

She nodded mutely as she met his outstretched hand, suddenly not wanting to let him go. But she watched him turn his horse around and walk away, folding her arms in contemplation as she considered the differences between herself and Daniel, and the unfairness of life.

As the pot-bank shot out another plume of black ash, she glanced up at the horizon, dark and sullied. Not even dusk and already she could see no farther than the gloomy factory and its outline. Black flakes of soot settled over the rooftops, and she thought of her mother's words: shooting stars straight from hell.

'This will not be my life. It will not,' she whispered, as she'd assured herself so many times.

She rubbed her arms and mentally rallied herself. Dark moods were for people who could afford the time to enjoy them, and Maddie had chores to do.

She hurried inside to check on Tom, and to rescue some coal from the fire for later on when her father would need it. Daniel's coat lay across the table where Tom had abandoned it, and she hugged it to her chest and breathed in, remembering his strength, his heat and his singular masculine smell. The fabric of his coat was so soft against her skin, as she turned it over in her hands, noting the fine stitching and the silk lining.

'He's left his coat, then?'

She turned sharply, guilty at having been caught out by her father. 'Yes, he'll have to come back for it.'

'Dunna worry. I'll tek it back when I pay my respects,' her father said briefly, eyeing her steadily.

'Of course, Dad.' She folded it carefully and, telling herself that she was afraid the sparks from the fire might damage it, carried it to her room where she tucked it next to her pillow. Stroking it once more, she smiled at the incongruity of such a fine garment in her simple room, creating a connection between her and Daniel.

A glow that needed no fire to stoke it warmed her skin as she changed out of her wet clothes and inspected her cut feet. For the first time in her life, she wondered what it might be like to kiss someone – and she knew exactly who that someone would be. Lying down in her narrow bed, she imagined a different future from the inevitable one she'd already envisaged: a future as a doctor's wife.

With a pair of warm, yet sombre, brown eyes imprinted on her mind, she promised God that she would try harder to believe in him, if he would give her this one chance.

Chapter Three

Charles Williams, Daniel's closest friend, lived in Mosely Manor, which was more of a sanctuary to Daniel than his own home. Charles's father, an editor for *The Evening Sentinel* newspaper in Stoke, mostly tended to be absent, preferring the stuffy office in the tiny building that they called headquarters to the lavish home that contained his wife and children. He spent his days turning fiction into truth, until the people of the Potteries read what he wanted them to read, assuming that none of them, in those turbulent times of political and social unrest, understood what was really happening.

The schedule he'd adopted left Charles and Daniel to their own devices – which, in the early days, consisted of overheated conversations caused by drinking the contents of the bottles in the drawing room. Alcohol was often the catalyst to their fervour in matters of the heart, religion, and the ways of the world.

Of late, however, they were too busy for such frivolities, and the temptation to drink Mr Williams' brandy until they were sick, had long ago worn off. Charles was shaping up nicely to follow in his father's footsteps as a ruthless hound dog, tweaking the flimsiest of gossip until it became fact – at least, according to *The Evening Sentinel*. He was as pliable in massaging figures and facts as any accountant, but on this occasion, he was behaving more like his mother than a cutthroat journalist.

'You left your coat on purpose, at one of those houses? You know you'll never see it again, don't you?' He ran his fingers through his blond curls and pursed his full lips. 'I'll never understand you, Daniel.'

'I should imagine trying to work each other out is what keeps our friendship lively.' Daniel laughed. 'That, and your inherent wicked streak that I am longing to change.'

'I can't be that wicked. I have given you a drink and a change of clothes,' Charles pointed out. 'Probably saved your life, you being a weakling and all.'

'I had scarlet fever when I was ten. That doesn't make me a weakling.'

'Have you reminded your mother of that, recently?'

Daniel winced. He was not yet eighteen and the mention of his mother always made him wince knowing the power she still wielded over him. Most people felt the same, especially his father. 'No, and I am not telling her about today, either. She will only go on about my heart bursting – or whatever it is she thinks will happen whenever I subject myself to any form of excitement.'

'I gathered that, or else you wouldn't have come around here, dripping slime on the hand-knotted rug.'

'And she would make a fuss that I have been into town.'

Charles held his nose and wafted an imaginary handkerchief around as he adopted a falsetto voice. 'Ooh, all of those germs, Daniel, how could you?'

'It wasn't at all like that. It was – fine.' He improvised quickly.

'I know that, stupid.'

'Sorry, of course you do. It's just that, Madeline was so—'

'Madeline? You just said you saved some riff-raff kids and now it is Madeline?'

Daniel sighed. 'She's not like the girls we know. She's interesting.'

'Ah, now we're getting somewhere. The truth will out,' Charles mocked. 'So, she is pretty, am I right?' He picked up his pen and twizzled it between his fingers like a baton.

'You can stop trying to analyse me – and stop making notes, too.' Daniel made a vain attempt to grab his pencil. 'You are not going to publish this, even though, God knows, you need the break.'

Charles pursed his finely shaped lips again, then tapped his pencil against his teeth, staring at Daniel. 'Hmm, defensive *and* aggressive. Now I *am* worried.'

'Oh, stop. And don't look at me like that, Charles. You're not getting a story from this.'

'But it's such a good story, you have to agree. See what we have here? Good old working-class gal meets the son of a dastardly, rich manufacturer, who terrorises his workers and litters the country with gaping holes for the poor saps to fall into – headfirst, of course.' He stood up, nostrils flaring and crashed his fist down onto the table, imitating the lobbyists who stood on street corners, denouncing the evils of the factory owners and their exploitation of the working classes. 'Yes, the very same factory owners who quarry clay, and pile up rubble until it crashes down on the poor disease-ridden, emaciated bodies of these bedraggled souls. Workers who barely have time to eat as the never-ending machinations of new-fangled machinery howls around their ears like banshees, scaring the babies as they sleep.'

'Okay, I get the idea.' Daniel laughed, but his brow creased. 'Did you say the slagheaps crushed someone? When did that happen?'

'It hasn't yet, sadly for me, but you get my drift. Poor people pitting against rich is always such a good storyline.' He tapped his teeth again with the pencil. 'There was that incident where a horse and cart nose-dived into a marl hole and the horse drowned. Mind you, that story was flogged to death by that dreadful little left-wing pamphlet they call a newspaper up in the damp end of town.' Pausing, he stared down at his nails with interest, before looking back up at Daniel brightly. 'We don't have to mention her by name, if you would prefer, although I do hope you're not thinking of seeing her again. Your mother would faint away to nothing.'

'Oh, Charlie, it is not an attraction that draws me. I'm interested in how they live, and the diseases they catch. There is so much that I could learn.'

'So, this pretty girl, this Madeline, she has no bearing on why you would like to embroil yourself in festering hovels full of rats and germs?'

'Her house isn't like that, Charles. Stop it.'

'Ooh, touchy with it, too?'

Daniel sighed. Sometimes, there was no getting through to his friend. 'You know, I'm still hoping that mother will allow me to become a doctor, and if I can turn my findings into a thesis, then I'll be sure to get into one of the good universities.' He warmed to his theme. 'This Madeline, she has a neighbour, a young woman who can hardly breathe. She has a growth on her jaw, which is probably related to the chemicals, or the lead at her works. I've read journals about it, and there is so much we don't know. I would love to be the one to find out exactly what's causing it. I'd be famous. There would be lots of material for you to publish, too.'

'Potter's Rot, and the arsenic, and they've passed a law to prohibit the amount of lead used in the glazes but no one takes any notice of it. Blah, blah, blah. I know, Daniel. We all know it. It's been bandied about for ages, and I'm sure you, in your medicinal zeal, will get to the bottom of it, but sadly for them, no one else really cares what befalls them.' Charles finished with a sigh. 'Why don't you just let it all go? Live your own life, worry about yourself, not everyone else?'

'I can't do that.'

Charles shook his head in despair. 'I know, and I suppose it's good that there are people like you, my friend. This world needs all the help it can get.' He laid down his pencil. 'But you're not in a position to do anything, so for now, just forget all this, *Soup, Soap and Salvation* malarkey and have some fun, can't you? It won't be long before the beautiful Fifi and her family get their poisonous talons into you and turn you into a pompous industrialist, crushing all of your visions of Utopia, so you should make the most of the time you have left.'

Daniel closed his eyes against the image of Fifi shaking her bouncy ringlets at him and offering her miniature dog for him to pet. Her own name sounded like that of a dog, and her world revolved around fashion, the minutiae of daily ablutions, and her empty-headed friends. She was, to be kind, a lady of good standing, but she had a limited intelligence and was without a shred of compassion for her fellow human beings, mostly, he suspected, because it would not have occurred to her that any of them might be in need.

'The last time I met Fifi,' Daniel said, 'she shuddered when I mentioned the Salvation Army and its mission to reform dropouts and alcoholics. I think she believed them to be some dreadful foreign cult.' He shook his head. 'I have no intention of marrying such a person. In fact, I have no intention of marrying, full stop. I will be far too busy to take a wife. Madeline is a decent, worthwhile person, Charlie, that's all I'm trying to say. I'm not suggesting I marry her, or anything ridiculous.' Charles's snobbishness burned anger in his chest, and Daniel knew it was time to leave.

'You do not *need* to say anything, my friend, it's in your eyes.' Charles picked up the pile of wet clothes and passed them across with a shake of his head. 'Go. I know you too well, and I have no intention of being drawn into an argument, when I could be having a little snooze, instead.'

'You're right. We'll just agree to differ, for now.' Daniel saluted his friend and left by the side door, throwing the sodden bundle of clothes in his saddlebag.

On his journey home, he tried to shut Charles's words out of his mind, imagining instead the weight of Maddie's shining hair sliding through his fingers, and her warm, grey eyes gazing at him. He recalled her giggle as she tried to hide her legs in those awful knicker things. He would ask his sister what sort she wore, but he knew it would be nothing like the fearful hairy-looking, woollen monstrosities on Madeline's lovely legs.

'Madeline Lockett.' He whispered her name over and over, muffling the sound against Algernon's neck, afraid that someone might hear his foolishness and report back to his mother.

Chapter Four

Daniel took his horse to the stables and wound his way up the road that led to his home, where he hovered with indecision.

Cook would catch him if he snuck in through the tradesman's entrance, and his mother would spot him if he went through the front door. Luckily, his younger sister, Hetty, was thumping out a melody on her piano in the sitting room, her eyes screwed up with concentration. He rapped on the French windows, startling her and she ceased her piano playing and let him in.

She laughed, a deep throaty laugh full of mischief. 'What on earth are you doing? What's happened to your clothes? They've shrunk since this morning, if I'm not mistaken.'

Daniel regarded his bare wrists and ankles poking out of his clothes. 'I see what you mean. They're Charles's clothes, but *shush*, I don't want Mother finding out.' He put his finger up to his lips.

'What have you been up to?' his sister hissed. She crashed the piano lid shut, eager, as usual, to hear any news that would brighten the monotony of her day. At sixteen she was bored with the life she lived and desperate for any news of life outside her four walls.

'I saved a boy from drowning in a disused marl hole. His older sister went in to save him, but she couldn't swim, so I rescued her, too.'

'Of course you did.' She rolled her eyes. 'What really happened?'

'I did, truthfully, and I'll tell you all about it once I've changed out of these clothes and washed.'

'You'd better come straight back and tell me, or else.'

Daniel grinned. 'Or else, nothing. You know you dote on me.' He chucked her under the chin, and she sighed, unable to contradict his words.

He was about to climb the stairs, but stopped, turning back. 'Hetty, what kind of drawers do you girls wear?'

'Daniel! You cannot ask a lady such a question.'

'Can I not? Sorry, but I need to know.'

'Your blunt manner will get you into trouble one day. You'd better watch out.'

'So, what are they made from?' he repeated patiently.

'Daniel!' She tutted with exasperation, shaking her head before saying, 'Oh, fine. They are a lawn material, which I think is a soft cotton, although if Mother feels extravagant, she will buy me silk.'

'So, they don't itch?' He scratched behind his ear, finding that he was, after all, somewhat uncomfortable with his line of questioning.

'No, they are beautifully comfortable. I get them from the dressmaker in Hanley. It's a very strange question to ask, Daniel. I worry about you.'

'Hanley, you say?'

'Daniel, please do not even consider buying underwear for a lady. It is far too presumptuous.'

Daniel swivelled around to fully face Hetty. 'Not yet, maybe, but one day.'

He took the stairs two at a time, thinking about soft lawn drawers on Maddie's legs, rather than the ugly brown wool she had worn. She should have the best. It seemed unfair that his sister had so much whilst Maddie had nothing.

He sighed. Of course it wasn't fair, that was what he was trying to fight against – the injustices of the world. And he would carry on fighting for it, but it would be nice if he could just help one person in the meantime – that someone being Maddie, of course.

Once he had washed the mud and stench from his body and dressed anew, he returned to the sitting room, where he found Hetty waiting for him. Two soft leather chairs had been pulled up close to the fire, a tray of tea and biscuits set out on a side table.

'I might have known you would not let me off the hook.' He eyed the scene in front of him as he spoke, grateful, after all, to have a warm fire and a drink.

'Daniel, I haven't seen you look so animated since you were ten and you found out that it was fleas and not rats that caused the plague.' She gestured for him to sit down, and he warmed his hands by the fire.

He needed a minute to work out what to tell his sister. 'Hetty, I so badly want to be a doctor. It's in my blood. You know our mother's family history, and it's only Mother who thinks I should become some bigwig factory owner because there's money in it, and there was none in her family.'

'Daniel! I don't want to hear all of this nonsense again. I want to hear about your heroism, or whatever it was that put that fervour in your eyes.'

'Yes, I suppose you do, sorry. But, Hetty, will you promise me that if a tall, careworn man turns up to pay his respects, you will not let Mother be rude to him? Please keep an eye out.'

'Daniel, whatever's got into you?'

'I met a most interesting young lady today, and I confess I am having trouble keeping her out of my thoughts.'

Hetty sat back in her chair. 'Well, I never. What about Fifi? Mother has practically booked the church, and dressed the horse and carriage in lilac voile, she is so convinced you will both marry.'

Daniel set his lips in a determined line. 'Well, Mother is wrong, and I will not marry someone because it will suit her position. I know she thinks their money will help our factory prosper, but no one marries for reasons like that any more.' He kicked petulantly at the brass fender in the hearth, gratified when sparks flew out of the logs.

Hetty grabbed her brother's hand. 'It's fine, Daniel. Don't distress yourself. Tell me about this young lady.'

Daniel sipped his tea and stared into the fire, reliving the strange tightness that Maddie brought about in his chest. 'It was odd. I held her close, and I could feel her heart beating next to mine. I could, Hetty, honestly, and I could feel her breath on my neck, and the strangest sensation came over me. It was as if we knew each other already and had a bond, as if we were made for each other, or we had met in a previous life.' He caught Hetty's sceptical eye and laughed briefly. 'Is that not the strangest thing you ever heard?'

'Yes, but it's also lovely.' His sister's gaze softened, and her eyes searched Daniel's face. 'I wish I could feel like that, just once in my life. But, why are you fretting? You'll meet her again.' She patted his hand. 'Ah, I understand. Her father is the man you are expecting to call. Now I see why you want to make sure Mother is polite. You're smitten with this young lady, and you have known her for how long? About three hours?'

'You're laughing at me.'

'No, I just want to emphasise that, for once, you are being incredibly romantic, if not slightly fanciful.'

Daniel took another sip of his drink, and then a larger one. 'I suppose I am. And I don't suppose I should make anything out of it. My desire to forge a career in medicine is more important than anything else. Anyway, Mother would hate it,' he said softly, as the truth sank home. 'Her father works in a pot-bank, firing up the ovens – at Dulton's, I think.' He shook his head sadly, before he brightened. 'But I'm eighteen soon and can do what I wish. Mother can't stop me.' He looked hopefully at Hetty for confirmation, but saw only her earlier scepticism. 'Yes, she can. Of course, I know it, too. I have no money of my own, and no way to pursue a career unless our parents allow it.' His face fell. 'I must put this woman out of my mind.'

Despite his words, he stared into the fire, and as he recalled Madeline's trusting eyes on his, he wondered how long he would have to wait before collecting his coat.

Chapter Five

Maddie trudged up the street to her home, laden down with shopping. She had been daydreaming about Daniel all week and was hoping to have a cup of tea with Jane to talk about the handsome man who'd saved Tom and herself from drowning. But as she neared her house she stopped in surprise on seeing Dolly Shanks, one of the factory's talented painters, touching her dad's arm in a tender fashion. Her heart quickened with panic, although she couldn't imagine that anything could be wrong. She picked up her speed, but, drawing closer, saw Dolly's cheeks redden as her father treated her to one of his rare smiles. Her heartbeat steadied as she realised they were just chatting and she slowed down before she neared the front gate, intrigued by this rare turn of events.

'I said I'd do you proud, didn't I?' she heard Dolly say.

Intrigue pricked at Maddie, although she didn't want to interrupt them. Her father had too few visitors as it was, and Dolly was always a breath of fresh air.

Her father still had an interest in throwing pots, and he still had a magic touch when it came to it. Everyone said he was mad to take the job as fireman, checking the kilns as they were fired up, when he was born to be a potter. But when Maddie's mother had fallen ill, anything that paid more money was the job he took. The extra money hadn't helped, of course. Her mother had died anyway.

Watching the exchange between them, for a moment Maddie saw her father transported back in time, sharing a conspiracy, or a private joke, with a woman who brought out the best in him, except it was Dolly who stood on the step, not her mother.

Dolly turned, as Maddie opened the gate. 'Hello, duck, are you all right?'

'Yes, Dolly, how are you?'

'I'm as right as rain, duck. I've bought your dad the vase I hand-painted for him. Do you want a look?' She bent down to a box set just inside the door, and pushed aside swathes of straw, lifting out a tall vase decorated in bright blocks of colour: yellows, reds and greens. She brushed off some stray pieces of straw, and held it up to the daylight. 'It's a beauty, though I say so myself. I don't believe this style won't take off. People want a bit of sunshine in their lives and now old queen Victoria's dead, Edward's injected a bit of fun back into the country and Gawd knows we could do with it.' She polished the body of the vase with her coat sleeve, pride in the vase clear by her beaming face. 'It can be tricky to get the glaze right, and the colours can run together in the kiln,' Dolly added, before glancing at her father for confirmation.

Maddie nodded. She had heard her father discussing such things with her mother in the past.

'What do you think?' Dolly's enthusiasm burned bright and it showed in her designs.

'It's beautiful, Dolly, so vibrant and modern.' Maddie knew her father admired Dolly's work greatly and now she could see why.

'I'm moving with the times, duck. No one's going to leave me behind. I've seen the way things are going.'

Harold tipped the vase upside down. 'You've signed it, I hope? I won't have them saying I bought some cheap, moulded rubbish.'

Maddie raised her eyes to her father. How were they to pay for such a desirable piece of pottery, she knew it could take weeks to hand-paint one vase? They were used to buying seconds when it came to dishes and plates and this would surely be way out of their reach.

'Don't fret, love,' her dad told her. 'I can see what you're thinking. Bert said I could use me old wheel for nowt, and Dolly kindly offered to paint it in her spare time.' He turned to Dolly. 'Maybe Maddie can make you a frock, or sommat, as

33

payment.' He seemed awkward with the exchange, unused to asking for favours.

'Aww, you're all right, Harold. Young Maddie's busy enough turning collars and darning, not to mention looking after you and Tom – and it's been my pleasure.' She looked at Maddie, her bright eyes softening in her florid face. 'I was very fond of your mum, as you know. I was just saying, I don't know why your dad doesn't come back to potting on the wheel. He was the best there was. Still is, by the looks of that vase.' Dolly turned to Harold again and took his hand. 'I won't keep you, I can see you'll be wanting your tea. Don't be a stranger, now.'

Maddie thought Dolly held on to her father's hand for a fraction too long, although he didn't appear to notice, but his eyes widened slightly when the woman winked at him.

He rubbed his hand across the back of his neck, and Maddie watched with amusement as his bemused expression grew. 'Ta-ra, love, and thanks again. You've done us proud.' He finally closed the door, frowning. He was quiet as he set the vase reverently on the mantelpiece, but he traced his finger around the gold rim, his mind obviously elsewhere.

'Dolly is very talented, but are these designs selling? They're very bold,' Maddie ventured.

Her father appeared to rouse himself from his thoughts and turned to her. 'We think so. There 'as been quite a bit of interest in the bright colours and new design shapes. People are ready for a change and a bit of sunshine, as Dolly said.'

'They are indeed,' she replied, thinking that Dolly brought the sunshine to her father, with or without her pots. 'It would be lovely to be that creative.' Maddie sighed. She longed for an outlet from mending clothes; somewhere to escape to, even if it was just inside her head. 'What's it for, anyway?' She stared at the vase, and it finally hit her that it was an incongruous piece of pottery to sit on their mantelpiece.

'It's for yon fellow's mum and dad, as a thank you for him saving you an' Tom,' he replied, nodding his satisfaction.

'It's for Daniel's parents? Oh, they'll love it.' Maddie beamed. 'What a wonderful gift.' A moment later, a frown creased her forehead. 'Are they not factory owners, themselves? Won't that be a little like carrying coals to Newcastle?' she asked.

'No. The Davenports have a long history of potting. They still own a factory but I believe most of their money now is made from financing the factories.' He headed for his chair and sat down, easing his heavy boots from his feet. 'Ah, that's better.'

Maddie took her cue and reached for the old cast iron kettle, filling it with water as her father continued.

'It's no more than I should do.' He sighed and rested his head on the back of the chair, closing his eyes.

'Can I come with you, when you take it?'

'I'd be glad of it, love. You know I'm no good, when me tongue gets tied. We'll go after church on Sunday.'

Maddie agreed with the wisdom of his words, although her stomach lurched the way it used to when she had to say a prayer in front of everyone at Sunday school. She was becoming used to unaccountable emotions when it came to Daniel, though. It was most strange.

She spooned a huge mound of tea leaves into their old brown teapot, poured boiling water over them, and started peeling potatoes, resisting the urge to fetch Daniel's coat down and make sure it hadn't become creased or damp.

After making the supper and helping Tom with his sums, she popped over to Drunken Edith's house with a bowl of mash and gravy. Edith was nowhere to be seen, probably drinking with some of her cronies, so she left the bowl and placed a plate on top of it, hoping it might still be lukewarm once the old woman returned.

Duty done, she took herself back home and sneaked upstairs, to do what she had been longing to do all day. She picked up Daniel's coat with a reverence that made her smile, and held it to her cheek, inhaling as she did so. She thought she caught a whiff of the lemony soap smell that she vaguely recalled, and it rekindled the emotions that confused her whenever she thought about him. She caressed the soft fabric, even though she felt guilty for doing such a thing. Resisting the temptation to dance around the room, holding the arms as if Daniel were inside it, she shook out the coat to check for any sign of mildew or infestation. It would be too mortifying to return a damaged coat.

As she checked each part of it, she noted the fine turn of the collar and the neatly sewn stitches. She turned it over thoughtfully, picked up a sleeve to check the cuffs, and turned it inside out to inspect the lining, which was also perfect. It was altogether a beautifully made garment that put her sewing skills to shame.

She quickly took out a scrap of spare material and copied the stitches, before checking the sewing that sealed the raw edges. She would practice her own stitches until they were as perfect as the ones on Daniel's coat. There was no reason why she could not be as good as the needlewoman who had made such a fine garment.

She headed for the stairs, unable to decide whether she should wrap the coat in brown paper, or carry it over her arm to deliver it safely back to Daniel. She thought to ask her father's advice, but she found him asleep, slumped in his chair.

She watched him fondly as she picked up her sewing basket, almost dropping it when a knock came at the door. It was past teatime, and they didn't normally have visitors in the evening. Her heart did a little somersault, as no one she knew had ever knocked, either, but just shouted their name or rattled the knob pointedly, before letting themselves in.

Breathing in, she opened the door. 'Oh, it *is* you. I mean, how lovely. I mean ...' Even though she had half hoped it would be Daniel at the door, he still took her breath away, standing in front of her as tall and broad as a Grecian god she had seen in a schoolbook. She put her hand over her chest, her heart knocking against her ribs.

Daniel took a step backwards down the step as if he hadn't realised the door opened straight into their sitting room. 'Madeline, how are you?'

She loved the way he said her name, enunciating the syllables clearly and crisply. 'I'm quite well, thank you for asking.' She pulled the door almost closed behind her, to keep the warmth in, and her father out of sight.

The setting sun behind Daniel created a misty halo around his head, framing his dark hair and casting his face in partial shadow, but his solemn eyes stared at her with intensity. She gazed back, noting the clear skin, the finely shaped eyebrows and the clean-cut jaw, and thought he was the finest looking man she had ever seen. He was certainly the cleanest man she had ever seen. She smiled at her thoughts, and Daniel smiled back.

A beat of silence balanced between them. Maddie inclined her head, waiting. She was unsure what to say, and he didn't seem in a hurry to explain why he had turned up. He continued to stare at her, an unexpected grin lighting up his face.

Maddie began to feel uncomfortable. She put her hand up to her face, wondering if she had coal dust, or a chalk mark from her sewing, on her cheek. 'Did you want something specific, or have you come to check on Tom and myself?'

'Oh, you, mostly – and Tom, of course.'

She was surprised and delighted to hear his words.

'And I need to collect my coat. I left it behind,' he added.

'Yes, you did. I gave it to the rag and bone man when he passed through. It looked a bit moth-eaten.'

'You did not!'

'No, of course not.' She grinned. 'Wait here.' She slipped back through the doorway, pulling the door closed behind her, reluctant for Daniel to see inside, where her father snored in his armchair, his belt undone and his big toe peeking through a hole in his sock. She made a mental note to darn it next time she washed his socks, as she grabbed Daniel's coat and quietly closed the front door behind her. She brushed down the coat with the back of her hand and presented it to him. 'It's a lovely coat. Where did you get it?'

'Oh, um … a place in Hanley, I think. Mother orders most of my clothes, but I did go for a fitting for this one.'

Maddie couldn't help but smile at the difference between them. She had one coat to her name, and that had been passed down from a neighbour when it had become too short. It certainly wouldn't have mattered if it fitted her, as long as it covered the bits that got cold.

She met Daniel's eye. Conversation appeared to be halted once again, but she didn't want him to go, and had a feeling that he didn't want to leave, either. However, they couldn't just stare at each other on the doorstep.

She took a breath. 'Well, now you have your coat back, we could take a walk before it gets dark?'

'I suppose we could, yes.' Daniel bowed and grinned, and she felt some of the stiffness of their meeting disappear.

They fell into step together, and Daniel glanced over at her again, as he pushed an errant lock of hair away from his eyes. 'I hope you've recovered fully from our little adventure,' he said finally.

Maddie threw him a glance, checking for any kind of subtle double-speak to his words, but the formality appeared to be genuine and it marked the difference between them more than the last time they had met. She looked down at her simple skirt, and across at his silk cravat and smart trousers, and knew that she could never hope to match him.

Not normally short of conversation, she found it difficult to find some common ground, when their complete history together consisted of approximately one hour, climbing up a slimy hill and walking home, bedraggled and cold.

She glanced over at him, thinking they must make a strange couple. He looked uncomfortable and self-conscious, and it occurred to her that he might simply have come to collect his coat, when she had badgered him into walking with her.

She bit her lip in embarrassment, as they walked to the end of the row of houses in silence, the starkness and dirtiness standing out more than she had ever noticed against the gloom of the evening. She wanted to explain that the blackness was soot from the factories and covered everything for miles around, that they were not dirty people. But she held her tongue, not wanting him to think she was ashamed of her roots. He probably had first-hand knowledge, anyway, she decided, as he didn't seem particularly surprised by the view in front of him.

They stopped walking when they reached the park that was little more than a square of scrubland. In the daytime, it was filled with squeals of laughter from the local children running around, but in the gloom of early evening, it was quiet and as forlorn looking as it truly was, a cheap make-do of wooden barrels and planks of wood, fashioned into seesaws and climbing frames.

Daniel pushed idly at a swing made out of thin wood and two bits of twine as he passed by, shaking his head at how flimsy it was. 'At least it stops anyone from building more chimneys and factories here.'

'There would be a lynching if anyone tried,' Maddie said, wishing she could sit on the swing whilst Daniel pushed her, as if they were a courting couple.

They walked aimlessly through to the allotment and picked their way through straggly cabbages and tufts of carrot tops that fought their way through the claggy soil. Daniel took Maddie's hand to help her jump over a muddy trench, and although it wasn't the first time they had touched, a spark of awareness shot through her.

'Is there somewhere else we could go?' Daniel said, as they ran out of options, ending up at the beginning of another tumbledown factory yard.

'The church is interesting enough, or we could walk to the cut – I mean the canal,' she corrected herself, although everyone called it the cut as far as she knew. She struggled to think of anywhere else to go. No one went walking around here, unless they were actually heading somewhere. 'We could visit the graveyard, if you don't mind. Mum's buried there,' she added quietly.

'Yes? Do you normally take flowers?'

'I mostly just pick some daisies on the way – holly, if it's winter ...' She trailed off, wondering if she was showing herself up again with her pitiable offerings.

'How long ago did your mother pass away?' Daniel's long fingers trailed through long, scrubby, thin grass, and Maddie's skin tingled as she wondered how they would feel trailing across her skin. 'You *can* talk about it, can't you? I don't wish to upset you.'

'I'm used to it now. Thank you for checking, though. I do still get tearful if I'm a bit down. It's been just over two years now.'

'It must be hard for you.'

'Yes, I miss her every day. It's sad for Tom, too, and Dad's a different person without her. She brought light into our lives and, goodness knows, there's precious little of that around here.' She bit back the sorrow that was never far away.

They walked in amicable silence until they reached the church grounds, where she decided to deflect the talk back to him. 'So, you mentioned that you want to be a doctor?'

He fixed his eyes, bright and speculative, on hers. 'Did I tell you that?'

'You mentioned it, but I wasn't sure how serious you were.'

'Yes, it's what I hope to do. I help out at the cottage hospital when I can, and it's opened my eyes to the inequality of rich and poor. I want to be able to help the poor people as much as the rich.'

'But how will you earn a living, if you help them for nothing?'

'Ah, you have caught on quickly. Therein lies the problem,

you see. My mother's family were doctors on her father's side, and she saw how hard they worked for so little gain. She wants me to follow in my father's unhappy footsteps, as he walks the fine line between work satisfaction and using his ill-gotten gains to escape from the very place where he makes his money.'

He sighed as he pushed an overhanging branch out of their way, and seemed to be stalling for a moment, as he inspected the overblown blossoms, pink and white. He plucked a small cluster and passed it to Maddie with a flourish.

'Thank you.' Maddie accepted the small bouquet with a shy smile, her cheeks turning the same tinted pink as the blossom. 'A doctor must bring in a good wage?' she probed.

Daniel's gaze fixed on Maddie as blossom flowers floated down from the trees and settled on her. A slow smile grew as he picked the petals out from strands of her hair, tossing them up in the air and following their descent as they drifted to the ground. 'What? Yes, sorry, I forgot the thread of our conversation for a moment.' He fell into step once more. 'Yes, but I hope to be able to treat the rich to pay for the poor, so to speak.'

'A bit like Robin Hood,' she volunteered, trying to understand his way of thinking.

He laughed. 'Yes, I suppose so. But I need Mother – or her money, more specifically. She holds a tight rein on the purse strings in our family, another throwback from years of genteel poverty.'

Maddie found his words hard to comprehend, as her father had always dealt with the finances, and surely Daniel's mother should do as his father bid her.

As if reading her mind, Daniel said, 'You haven't met my mother, have you?' He drew his eyebrows together fiercely, and Maddie smiled uncertainly.

Would it be a good thing if she met his mother? She decided, probably not.

They strolled through the churchyard, reading out some of the inscriptions on the gravestones. Sadly, Maddie knew a good few of the names, and the usual sense of sadness that washed over her competed with the fluttering of excitement that Daniel brought about.

As they paused in front of a tiny gravestone, Daniel read out the inscription. 'Sophie and Anna Dudley, beloved daughters of Edith and Jack. Taken too soon.'

'You know the lady I spoke to in the street when you walked me and Tom home?' Maddie struggled to hide the wobble in her voice. 'They were her children. They came down with something like influenza and both died on the same day. Her husband left town shortly afterwards, without telling her. She thinks he couldn't bear the constant reminders, and she never recovered, as you could see when we bumped into her. Spends her days talking to ghosts and drinking herself into an early grave.' Her voice wavered even harder at the end of her little speech. She had spent many an evening crying with Edith about their losses – she, sober in her despair, and Edith increasingly raddled by the need to blot out her memories with gin.

She bit her lip determinedly and was grateful, if surprised, when Daniel's fingers brushed hers as he reached out to take her hand. It was warm and reassuring, and she held on tightly.

With his other hand, he turned her face towards his. 'Do you want to go back?' His eyes were gentle, and once again, she was struck by how clear they were, shining with fervour and interest.

It gave her the strength she needed. 'No, not at all. We'll find Mum's grave.' She swallowed. 'It will never sound right to say those two words together.'

Daniel's hand was still firm and warm in hers, and it dawned on her that he was not going to let it go. Elation surged through her again, but she bit it back, guilty that such thoughts eclipsed a visit to her mother's grave. But then she smiled, knowing her mum would understand.

'Are you all right?' Daniel asked.

She nodded and blushed, as he inched closer as if to inspect her face.

'Your colour has certainly returned.' He smiled, and she prayed that he could not guess her thoughts.

She fizzed with expectation at the way he gazed at her, wistful and caring. She had never been looked at in such a way before, and she wondered what she would do if he tried to kiss her, but he simply brushed his finger over her burning cheeks and shook his head.

'Too sad to lose your mother at such a young age.' His eyes softened, and he threw an arm around her shoulders, hugging her into his side. As they continued the walk toward her mother's grave, Maddie clutched the pink blossom to her chest as if she were a bride heading for the altar, feeling as elated as if she was.

Silently and solemnly, she filled a glass jar with fresh water and placed the blossom inside it, nestling it into the soil at the foot of where her mother lay. Quickly, she whispered her new secret to her mother: a handsome young man named Daniel had held her hand, and it was the most thrilling feeling ever. She promised her mother she would come back soon to tell her all about him.

Chapter Six

Maddie's father looked dashing in his Sunday suit. His collar was clean, his tie was a tight knot under his throat, and, for once, he didn't look as if the world had beaten him down.

Maddie herself wore her best dress, the one with stripes on the skirt and a thick band of Petersham around the waist to emphasise her figure. She touched her curls, remembering how she used to sit still on a Sunday morning, whilst her mum brushed her long hair and tied it up with ribbons. Since growing old enough to wear a hat, she always thought of her mum as she angled it dutifully on her head.

Sitting in church, her hands fluttered as much as her heart, as she tried to turn the pages of her hymn book. The verses took forever, and the vicar appeared to know exactly what she had been up to, as he rammed home the likelihood of fire and brimstone falling on the heads of anyone indulging in the weakness of the flesh in all of its godforsaken forms.

She squirmed in her seat as she remembered how she had wanted Daniel to kiss her, and her nervous fingers flew to her neck, where she could feel a flush of shame creeping upwards.

The movement must have caught Edward Underwood's eye, because he turned and smiled at her. She had known him since they had sung childish hymns at Sunday school, but right then, his smile looked too knowing, and she turned away from him, only to be confronted by the statue of St Thomas pointing his thin, accusing finger at her.

Bowing her head, Maddie prayed in equal measure for guidance to mend her sinful ways, and that Daniel would try to kiss her the next time they met.

As she prayed, she wound her fingers around the slender chain she wore, catching hold of the cross permanently fixed around her neck. 'Mum, please let Dad do us proud today,' she whispered into the tiny silver cross.

The cross had belonged to her mother and a few days before she died she had unfastened the chain from around her neck, heaving herself upright before sinking back onto the bedclothes, her breathing ragged and laboured. Her frail fingers, thin as twigs, clutched at the cross as she kissed it and passed it over to Maddie. 'Take care of this for me, love,' was all she had said, but at that moment Maddie knew that all the bargaining in the world would not keep her mother alive.

Whilst the service washed over her, Maddie allowed the memories in. Sometimes, they offered comfort, as she imagined her mum looking down on her. She tilted her head upwards, toward the church windows, where the stained glass bestowed tongues of fiery vermillion, blue and magenta over the heads of the congregation bowed in prayer.

Maddie wondered how so many of them still managed to believe in a God who ruled as sternly and unforgivingly as the factory that doomed them. The poverty she had witnessed in her own short life was enough to send her teetering towards the edge of heresy, only the fear of being wrong the main reason for her continued worship.

'Hope Springs Eternal' had been carved above the door leading to their Sunday school room, and Maddie wondered who had had the foresight to put it there.

As the final strains of 'The Lord is my Shepherd' died down, she picked up her gloves and adjusted her hat. The congregation filed past the solemn vicar, dropping pennies they could ill afford into the collection dish, whilst watched over by his eagle-eyed wife, who looked capable of personally bringing eternal damnation onto the head of any miscreant who tried to bypass it.

As they stepped out of the chilly church and into the bright day, Maddie sighed with relief that she had not been singled out to be the sinner she so obviously was.

Her father held on tightly to the box with his precious gift inside, whilst Maddie clutched her brother's hand, all of them quiet with trepidation, unsure of the wisdom of their planned visit. Nevertheless, they caught the train that would take them to Stokeville, sitting in pensive silence as it chugged along. Soon in Stoke, they gawped at the unfamiliar shops and stalls: a tiny oatcake shop with a vast hotplate sizzling, as a round lady ladled batter out; a man selling meat pies from a big barrow; and a homemade ginger beer stand that made Tom salivate with longing.

Maddie stopped and stared in wonder as they passed a clothes shop. A shimmering green, slinky frock hung in the window, a squat hat sprouting silk leaves and peacock feathers next to it, like a brooding bird. It was the most glamorous dress she had ever seen. Taking a step backward she stood and studied it, taking in the fluid lines and the simplicity of the cut. The hat, however, was a mixture of fantastic and preposterous, and she pointed it out to Tom.

'Is it alive?' he asked.

She laughed. 'Imagine having that sitting on your head, eh?' Maybe wide brimmed hats full of feathers and vegetation will become fashionable now the century had turned? She thought not, but she tucked the design inside the back of her mind, anyway, determined to sketch its likeness when she had a minute. Fashions were changing fast, and with women participating in sports and driving motor cars, there would need to be a radical change in fashion. She pondered on this thought, barely noticing the bottle kilns interrupting every view beyond the immediate, looming up through the smog like an alien invasion. Some were small, some were huge but all of them blocked out the light and puffed out black smoke.

As they neared Stokeville, though, the proliferation of bottle kilns and pot-banks thinned, replaced by wide pavements and majestic houses with long gardens covered in green grass and exotic looking trees. The noise level decreased, and the smog all but disappeared. It was so unlike their home town that Maddie half expected to see a fairy tale blue sky emerge, with an impossibly bright orange sun lighting their way as a chorus of skylark lined up on the roof to trill out a jaunty tune. She smiled at her foolishness and soon turned back to the job in hand, wondering if Daniel's parents even knew about their son's heroic rescue. It would be a bizarre exchange if her father had to explain the reason for his visit before presenting them with the vase.

She followed her father along a road that proclaimed to be the London Road and Tom asked if that meant London wasn't far away.

Her father laughed. 'You'd 'ave most of the leather off your shoes by the time you got there,' he said, 'but I guess it must lead to London, eventually, or else they would 'ave called it sommat else.'

The more they walked, the more Maddie's stomach knotted at the thought that she might see Daniel once more. In fact, with each step, she felt more and more peculiar, until she was practically ready to faint by the time they reached their destination.

She stopped in confusion as they turned into the road via a large gate. It was as unlikely an area to find in Staffordshire as anything she had ever come across. She stared wide-eyed at the enclosed road with the pretty houses either side, and as her gaze swept its length, her heart sank. 'Daniel lives here?' she asked. If he did, it would only confirm his status as being as far removed from her way of life as she could imagine.

'He does. They're interesting houses, aren't they? I've seen something about them in *The Evening Sentinel*. The Minton china family owned some of the land, and some famous architect designed it all to look a bit Italian.'

They started up the road hesitantly, swerving past a large stone column with a lamppost fixed to the centre. Maddie's misgivings increased proportionally when she took in the size of the houses and the fancy design. It was very discreet and extremely quiet, given the hustle and bustle she was used to. 'Are you sure, Dad?'

'Aye, I'm sure. I know the surname.' He didn't look too pleased about it, and Maddie wondered if he was thinking the same as she was. How could bigwigs live in houses such as these, whilst allowing such appalling factory conditions that their workers took their lives into their hands every day?

They stopped by a lawn with colourful flower borders, chrysanthemums as big as a face and hollyhocks shooting up to the sky, making her father gawp as the gardener tending them called out in their direction.

'Good afternoon. Isn't it a fine day?' He stopped digging the earth around some leggy roses and took off his cap, wiping sweat from his forehead.

'Aye, you're right there,' her father said and stepped closer to the man. 'I've never seen such huge flowers.'

'Fertiliser's the answer,' the gardener said simply. 'Dig it over with horse muck twice a year.'

Her father nodded politely as if this was news to him.

'Look at the size of that, Dad!' Tom shook his father's hand and pointed toward an enormous worm as it wriggled up through the ground.

'It is a beauty, indeed. A lumbricus – or common earthworm, if I'm not mistaken,' the gardener said, hooking it up with his garden fork. As they watched, it slithered over the metal prongs before falling back to the soil to freedom. 'Do you like worms and insects?' he asked Tom.

Tom screwed his eyes up as if thinking hard. 'Yes. We did insects in class. Miss Byrne told us that people have found lots of new species of butterflies in foreign countries. I think they were called lepidopterists. I listen really hard,' he added proudly.

Maddie beamed with pride that Tom knew such big words, although it reminded her that an awful lot of butterflies were flapping around in her stomach at that precise moment.

Her father ruffled Tom's hair, a rare grin making an appearance.

'Well done, lad,' the gardener said approvingly.

'It's Tom,' he replied and held his hand out.

'Very pleased to meet you, Tom. My name's Geoffrey.' They shook hands politely. 'Would you like to see what else is lurking in the undergrowth, whilst your father finishes his errand?' He looked up at Harold for confirmation.

A brief frown crossed her father's brow. 'Will you stay with him?' he asked Maddie.

She nodded. 'Of course, Dad.' Although, where he thought his son might disappear to in the company of the gentlemanly gardener, she couldn't imagine. 'You go on up to the house. Will you be all right?'

He nodded as she squeezed his hand.

The gardener looked from Maddie to her father quizzically, but her father wasn't the sort to confide anything to a stranger, and he turned to Tom. 'Right then, young man, don't pester this fellow too much, all right?'

Tom nodded his agreement, but he had already found an old bucket, and was sifting through chunks of rich soil, poking it about with a trowel.

Maddie's concentration drifted as she watched her father wend his way up the large driveway. She wandered aimlessly through the garden, touching exotic flowers she had never seen before, and smelling the most potent of perfumes within their petals. Glancing up at the windows of the house, she wished she could see the front door, to gauge how her father was getting on.

I should be with him, she thought, suddenly worried that her father would need her. After a quick check on Tom, who was having a fine time with the gardener, she strolled towards the house, wondering where on earth the front door was amongst all the porches and windows. As she peered through a pair of double-fronted glass doors, one of them flew open.

'*Bonjour, comment ca va?*' said a girl who looked about the same age as Maddie, her thick coiled black hair tied in an elaborate plait over one shoulder.

Maddie blinked in surprise as the girl peered at her through large sombre brown eyes. She clutched a toy dog to her chest – at least, she thought it was a toy dog until it yapped at her. She sprang backwards, and laughed to cover her confusion when she realised the girl was talking French, although she wasn't sure how she knew that. 'I'm sorry,' she said. 'I don't understand.'

'Of course you don't understand. You're not supposed to. It will prove my superiority and confirm my capabilities as an accomplished and well-positioned lady of society.'

'Oh. I see,' Maddie said, although she did not see at all. 'That's not very kind, if you don't mind me saying.'

'No? It *is* charming, though, is it not?'

Maddie's brow furrowed.

'Oh, for goodness sake, do come inside. I'm trying to be witty and delightful. Have you never read the very scandalous Oscar Wilde? That's how he does it.' The girl placed the tiny dog on top of a piano, then flung her arms wide and threw her head back. 'This woman is a genius in the daytime and a beauty at night.' She sounded almost hysterical, and Maddie quickly retreated back toward the open windows, wishing she had not entered into conversation with the young woman, who was clearly a bit soft in the head.

'I don't think it is very charming, at all, showing off like that.' She glared at the strange girl, hoping she wasn't related to Daniel. 'I'm sorry I bothered you. I was looking for someone else.' She turned slowly, taking a tentative step through the window.

'It's an Oscar Wilde quote, silly,' the girl said, before Maddie could escape. 'Oh, stop. You are right. I'm obviously not ready for my debut into proper society.' She collapsed onto a small sofa and struck a theatrical pose, her hand reaching up to her brow. 'I have to parade myself at a dreadful party in London, and I have no idea how to act. I'm bound to make a complete fool of myself amongst all the bright young things who are used to socialising. I have no one to practice on, you see, just one brother, who will not be happy until he has changed the world and will probably die of some dreadful disease whilst trying.'

She rearranged her skirts to drape over the sofa and sighed loudly. 'There is always cook, I suppose, but she's as mad as a March hare and still thinks I am three years old. I also have an older sister who is scared of the world – and of my mother, of course, but that's no surprise – everyone is scared of Mother.' She sighed again. 'Polly is so pliable from bending over backwards to please people, she is practically Plasticine.'

'What's Plasticine?' Maddie was curious, although she still hoped to escape as soon as possible.

'I am not too sure, but it bends, I believe. Father read an article from the newspaper out to Daniel, saying it was an innovative invention and we needed to remember the name, so that is what I've done.' The girl screwed her nose up, as if in thought, and snapped her fingers, making Maddie start. 'Of course, you must be Maddie?'

'Yes, how do you know?'

'I'm Daniel's sister.'

'Oh.' *Oh, no*, she thought. 'Yes, you do look similar,' she said.

The woman pouted. 'That is too bad.'

'No, he's lovely … I mean, you have the same eyes.'

The young lady's eyebrows rose. 'So, you're keen on him, too? I had my doubts, I confess.' She stood up and peered closely at Maddie, before retrieving the little dog from the piano where it whimpered. 'I can see why he is smitten. You're almost as pretty as I am.'

Maddie smiled at her honesty and thawed slightly towards her new friend, with her quirky personality and artlessness.

The fact that she was Daniel's sister made her easier to like, of course, and maybe she was not daft in the head, after all.

'Daniel has mentioned me, then?' Maddie caught the surprise in her own voice, not thinking for one moment that she merited a mention from him.

'Yes. Come closer and shut the French windows before Father sees you and thinks you are a gypsy. Oh, Lord, there I go again. I'll never get it right.' She giggled prettily, and despite laughing along with the young woman, Maddie glanced toward the open window.

'I'd better not. I shouldn't be here, really.'

'You better had. How else are we going to become friends?' She strode past Maddie and, to her dismay, slammed the double windows firmly shut.

Her only escape route had been cut off, and she felt overawed and trapped, as her new friend ushered her inside the magnificent room.

She glanced down at her boots, unsure whether to take them off, but she didn't want the sophisticated young lady to see the ugliness of her stockings. She imagined either choice would be bad manners, so she stayed rooted to the spot as she finally gazed around the room in awe. She had never seen such a display of wealth. Everything glittered and shone in the afternoon light, and the space and opulence of the furnishings took her breath away.

A huge chandelier sparkled rainbows of colour across one wall, and the sofa in the middle of the room was almost as long as the tram they had arrived in, she was sure of that. She took three brave steps and traced a fingertip over the wallpaper, where the rainbow colours still danced. 'Oh, it feels so soft.'

'It does, does it not? I think it's called flock velvet. Morris designed the pattern. Cannot abide it myself, but Mother believes it to be fashionable.'

Maddie twirled slowly around, her gaze resting on the

piano, so highly polished she could see her reflection in it. 'Oh, is Morris a friend?'

Daniel's sister's laugh tinkled across the room. 'Priceless. You are funny.' But she didn't say why Maddie was funny, and Maddie decided she wasn't being complimentary.

'Do you play?' The young woman's fingers ran up and down the piano keys, the melodious tones filling the air as her gaze followed Maddie. 'You may try it, if you like.'

'No, I don't play. There's a piano at Sunday school, but they don't like anyone touching it.' She tested the polished top of the piano with her fingertips, not wishing to add that the piano in Sunday school was a broken-down tramp of a thing compared to the sleek work of art in front of her.

'It's one of the many talents I will put to good use when I try to snare a husband,' the young woman said.

'How are you going to do that?' Maddie had never heard such nonsense. Surely, two people fell in love and married. How hard could that be? She pressed a few of the top keys on the piano and was not surprised at the mellow, warm tones that it produced.

'I said earlier.' Hetty looked dejected. 'I just have to shine and entertain everyone in London.' She gazed at Maddie for a long moment. 'You have no idea, do you?' She threw her hands wide and tossed her hair back in another theatrical gesture, laughing. 'Look how long and white my throat is, when I laugh at my beau's jokes. Just wonderful.'

Maddie stared at her new friend's throat with a frown. Surely, she didn't expect an answer?

'I'm joking.' Hetty looked at Maddie, then crossed her eyes and pulled down her lips with her fingertips, until she looked like the gargoyle Maddie had seen on the roof of the Catholic Church. 'I could always do my *ugly face* for a party trick. It makes Daniel laugh every time.' She brought her hands away and sighed as her face returned to normal. 'I suppose I do need a husband, or else I will appear to be lacking. A brother just will not cut it.'

Maddie had never met anyone quite so contrary, and she was at a loss to know how to act, but at the mention of Daniel, she perked up. 'Is Daniel here?'

'No, sorry. I don't know where he is ... probably giving someone the shirt off his back, or whipping up a cauldron of soup for some needy family.'

Maddie bit her lip in an effort to hide her disappointment, before suddenly remembering her own brother was alone with the gardener. 'I'd better check that my brother isn't annoying the gardener.'

'The gardener? Oh, you mean my father.'

'He's your father? Oh, no.' Maddie put her hands up to her cheeks, mortified. 'I have to go. It was lovely to meet you.'

'Will you come again, Maddie, please?' Her new friend looked suddenly small and lost, and in need of cheering up.

'Of course, but I don't even know your name.'

'It's Hetty, but you can call me Hetty. Oh Lord, that's not right, is it? I have practised saying it, too.' She sighed with defeat.

Maddie laughed, as Hetty affected a deep curtsey and held out her hand towards Maddie. 'My name is Henrietta, but you may call me Hetty,' she said in a falsetto voice. 'And this is my dog, Poppy.' She lifted up one tiny paw and waved it at Maddie.

Maddie clapped and laughed as Hetty curtsied once more.

'Thank you,' Hetty said, vowels tortured, and lips pulled back in a rictus of a smile.

'It really was lovely to meet you, but I must go. Goodbye, Hetty.' Maddie pushed open the huge window onto the garden and, suddenly fearful for Tom's well-being, she hurried across the lawn.

'Madeline?' The voice could only be Daniel.

She stopped walking and spun around, unable to see him, her heart pounding erratically.

He appeared in the doorway of a summerhouse and strode over to her, greeting her like a long-lost friend, to her total surprise. He pulled her against his chest and held her, resting his chin on top of her head. 'I must have conjured you up in my thoughts,' he said, setting her away from him as if to look her over. 'Yes, as pretty as I remember.'

'You were thinking about me?'

'All of the time – I can't seem to help it – and now you're here, right in front of me. But hang on, I can't really have conjured you up, can I?' He pushed his hair out of his eyes. 'Why are you here?'

'Dad came to pay his respects to your parents.'

Daniel looked over toward the flowerbed where his father was working. 'Ah, young Tom and my father, but no sign of your father.'

'I know, we thought your dad was the gardener. I'm so sorry.'

Daniel threw his head back and laughed. 'Brilliant. Father will love it. Come on, let's go and see what they're up to.' He pulled up short. 'Oh, I've just realised, if my father is out here, your poor old dad must have been confronted by my mother.' He pulled a sad face. 'Too bad for him.'

As he spoke, Madeline's father appeared around a corner of the house, looking dazed and vaguely lost. He still clutched the parcel, and his face was bleak. Just looking at him made her sad.

Maddie rushed up to him and Daniel followed close behind. 'Dad, didn't she like the vase?'

'She didn't even look at it, love. Didn't even open the box. Thought I was some kind of tinker, I think. Your lad, here, hadn't even told her about the incident.' He acknowledged Daniel by tipping his cap and saying, 'Alright, young man.' He turned to Maddie again. 'She thought I was spinning her a yarn.' He shrugged. 'Never mind, I tried.'

He pushed the parcel under his arm and strolled over to where Tom was happily filling his bucket with soil and poking around for insects.

Maddie hurried after her father.

'Everything all right?' Mr Davenport tipped his hat backwards as if to see better, stretching out his back as he stood with his hands on his hips. 'Ah, Daniel, managed to get your nose out of a book for a few minutes, eh? Surprising what a pretty girl can do.' He winked at Maddie and grinned at his son.

'Madeline's dad brought a present for you and Mother. He had it made at his workplace, but she didn't want it,' Daniel said quickly.

'Oh?' He patted Tom absently on the head, looking from Daniel to Maddie and her dad as Daniel spoke. 'And why did you bring her a present?'

'Daniel rescued Tom and me a week ago, from drowning in a marl hole. Father had a beautiful vase made for your wife, as a thank you present.' Maddie laid emphasis on the word *wife* so that her father would understand.

'I did hear something about that, although not from Daniel. His friend, Charles, wanted to write about it in their newspaper and thought I would give my permission.' He studied Maddie and Tom, the pieces seeming to fall into place. 'And this present, may I look at it?'

'You can 'ave it. I've no use for it.'

Maddie hated to see the hurt on her father's face and held her breath as Daniel's father took the vase out of its bed of straw and held it up to the light.

'Why, it is splendid.' The man rubbed at the vase with his jacket sleeve and nodded appreciatively. 'That really is an incredible piece of work. Was it painted at your place?' He turned it over and squinted as he read the back stamp. 'Dolly Shanks. Is she new? I don't believe I know the name.'

'Yes, she's new to our factory, but she's an old friend of mine. Come from Jobson's and worked alongside a talented designer.' Her father's smile had returned to his face, and Maddie allowed herself to relax a little.

'And whoever did the firing certainly knew their stuff. I know this type of underglaze is new to us in Stoke.'

He turned it over in his hands and studied it closely. 'I will take the vase with pleasure and put it in pride of place on our sitting room mantelpiece. I do apologise for my wife's behaviour. Sometimes, she forgets her origins.' Smiling ruefully, he placed the vase carefully back in its wrapping before holding out his hand. 'Mr Davenport, at your pleasure.'

Maddie's father pulled his cap off and stuck his hand out. 'Harold Lockett, an' I'm glad you like the vase, though I'm as sorry as you can believe that I thought you were the gardener.' He beamed as he shook Mr Davenport's hand, good humour restored.

After a pause, he jerked his thumb towards the way they had come. 'Any road, we'd best be getting back. We've dinner to get ready.'

'Of course. It was a pleasure to meet you.' Mr Davenport turned to Tom. 'Maybe young Tom would like to come around next Sunday to look at my butterfly collection? He seems very interested in such things. His sister could bring him over, if that would be acceptable.'

'Thank you. I'm sure he'd like that.' Harold had already swivelled on his heels, making tracks to leave. He nodded goodbye to Mr Davenport, and Tom waved happily.

'I'll just be a moment, Dad.' Hanging back, Maddie faced Daniel, unsure what to say now they were alone again.

Daniel smiled down at her. 'So, Madeline Lockett, today was a good day for both of us. Your father's vase was a success, and I managed to spend all of ten minutes with you, which, I hasten to add, is better than nothing.' He reached out for her hand and held it loosely. 'Would I need to ask your father, if I wanted to see more of you?'

Maddie broke into a grin she could not contain. 'I have no idea. Nothing like this has ever happened before.'

'Then, I shall assume it's fine to call on you sometime soon, and if I get past the front door, I'll know I am welcome.'

Maddie's smile was fixed, but her heart sank. She hated to think of Daniel visiting her house, seeing inside it, in all its shabbiness. It would surely be enough to make him turn tail for good, but she nodded wanly and, feeling brave, stood up on tiptoes to kiss his cheek.

He pulled her closer and kissed her fleetingly on the mouth, barely catching the corner of her lips, the gesture over in seconds.

She just had time to register the pressure of his soft lips and inhale the smell that she already associated with him, and she gasped as he pulled away, her heart beating hard.

'I'm sorry. I didn't know I was going to do that myself. Have I offended you?'

'No ... not at all.' Her mouth had suddenly dried, and she moistened her lips with the tip of her tongue, anticipating another kiss. 'We have been invited over on Sunday – might you be here?'

'Try and stop me.' With that, he grinned at her. 'Until Sunday, Madeline Lockett.'

She nodded and stepped backwards, anxious to catch up with her father and Tom. She found them loitering at the end of the road, Tom swinging on the unusually big gate that kept out strangers.

He prattled on about the Latin names of insects they had seen, saying, 'Mr Davenport said he's got a book on them somewhere, and he'll look it out for me. I could become an expert on insects.'

'You can be anything you want to be.' Maddie ruffled his hair affectionately. She was finally coming back down to earth after the heady kiss, although she couldn't keep the smile from her face.

She ventured her opinion on visiting again next Sunday, deciding to keep the conversation between herself and Daniel a secret for the moment; she hadn't yet mulled over it for long enough. 'I don't know if they meant it when they invited us again. I mean, they're not really our sort, are they, Dad?'

'Of course they are. They're people, aren't they?' he said. 'My family's as good as anyone's, and dunna ever think otherwise,' he added quietly.

'I'm sure you're right, Dad.'

She had an urge to hold his hand, like in the olden days when she needed reassurance, but he would probably shrug her off. Since her mum had died, he seemed to want to distance himself from any sort of emotion, and Maddie made it easy for him, not wanting to intensify the hurt he carried.

But she knew there was a gulf as huge as the ocean between their small lives and that of the people up at The Villas, and it burned her with inexplicable shame. Her poor father had worked himself to the bone, and so had her mother, so that people like the Davenports could live in luxury. She wanted to harden her heart towards Daniel accordingly, but could find no way to dampen her feelings. And Hetty had been delightful, too, once she had got the measure of her. It was so hard to understand the workings of the world sometimes.

Maybe life was just a series of good or bad luck falling randomly, like a pack of cards delivering a good or bad hand, she thought. She certainly didn't think that God's infinite wisdom came into it anywhere along the line, as the Bible Bashers would have her believe. How could God be fair and just, when some people were too poor to have their own shoes, and others covered their walls in velvet?

She resolved to ask Daniel what he thought about it, shaking away her morose emotions. For now, she would try to enjoy the rest of the day with her father and brother.

Having eaten a fine dinner of beef stew and dumplings, her dad was now dozing by the fire grate, while her brother was in the alleyway with Jimmy, kicking a ball up the wall.

Maddie glanced out of the window, once again cursing the pot-bellied monster that heaved out its noxious poisons, as the afternoon turned dark and the smog settled in for the evening. She thought of Hetty, not too many miles away, whose lot in life was simply to play her piano and snare herself a husband, and she smiled. There were no similarities, at all, to her own life, and yet she truly believed they could be friends.

After lighting the oil lamp, she faced her basket of sewing with resignation. The little sampler she had practised on caught her eye, and she inspected the neat rows of stitching with satisfaction, although why it mattered, she didn't know.

She heaved her basket off the floor and dumped the contents onto the spare chair, picking through the pile of clothes. Maddie charged a pittance to shorten a hem, or turn a shirt collar for another year's wear. Whilst none of her customers could afford any more than a few pence, it all helped.

She imagined what it would be like to work on the soft, luxurious fabrics she had seen at the Davenports' house, rather than the washed out cottons she had in her basket. With a start it occurred to her that it could become a reality, that Hetty could help her to better her lot. That in mind, a kernel of an idea grew as she sewed, her excitement mounting as she formed a plan, until she was too fidgety to sit still.

It could work. It *would* work. She would *make* it work.

She laid down her sewing and daydreamed herself as rich and equal to Daniel's family, her own tinkling laughter matching Hetty's as she descended the sweeping staircase of her own mansion, greeting Daniel with a serene smile at the end of his working day.

She sighed. That would always just be a dream, but she could certainly do better than sewing hems for pennies. She decided that she would pay a visit to Hetty in the morning.

Chapter Seven

The next day, Maddie hurried over to the Davenports' home. Although mindful that she might not get the welcome she desired, she was too fired up with optimism to change her mind. She would earn money, and, whilst doing so, would learn how to be a lady. Her laugh would be light and tinkling, and when not laughing, she would sparkle with wit and shower everyone with nuggets of knowledge that she had gleaned from parlour room conversation.

She laughed inwardly at her foolishness, but even so could not contain the bubble of excitement in her chest.

She rattled the door of the French windows and peered inside. 'Hetty, it's me.'

One day, she vowed, *one day, I shall march up to their front door and be let in as a person of equal standing.* For now, though, she was simply grateful to be allowed into the music room, where her new friend sat at the huge piano, belting out something so fearful, Maddie worried it might invoke the wrath of the Gods, if only they were not so preoccupied heaping fire and brimstone on the good people of the Potteries who had forgotten their catechisms, or neglected to put a penny in the poor pot. It would be a difficult choice, she imagined, although she came down hard on the side of the piano playing, being as she was the one suffering right at that moment.

She kicked off her boots as she entered, desperate to blurt out the words that had been driving her insane as doubt mingled with excitement. 'I'm going to learn how to sew, and I'm going to make fine clothes for rich people and make my fortune. Hetty, I need you to teach me about fabrics. I don't know how else to find out.'

Hetty stared wide-eyed. 'You have to do a job of work? Oh,

of course you do. Sorry, I'm so sheltered in this house, miles away from the real world.'

Maddie marvelled at her friend's naivety, but hopped from foot to foot waiting for her suggestions.

'Maddie, it is simple. Just find your way to the haberdashers in Hanley. They have wonderful fabrics, and you could learn about the different textures and the best way to sew them.' She was quiet for a moment, then her face brightened. 'I know Mrs Howlett well, I could ask if you could work there, if that's what you want.' Her face fell. 'You do sew, don't you?'

'Yes, but I want to be better than just a needlewoman. I want to be the best there is, and have people ask specifically for me.'

Hetty clapped her hands. '*Bien sûr. Madame Lockett, c'est ce que vous voulez.*'

'Err, something like that, yes.'

'It will be perfect. You can be my personal dressmaker, when I marry.' Her friend laughed. 'Come upstairs with me, and I'll show you some of my dresses and tell you what I know about them.'

Maddie eyed the drawing room door with uncertainty.

'Don't worry, there is only Mother and myself at home, besides Daniel, who barely counts as his head is in a book most of the time. Mother will not mind you being here, as long as you don't tell her you're in love with my brother.'

Hetty swept Maddie through the drawing room, and they paused in a majestic hallway that was bigger than Maddie's entire house. Her toes brushed against gleaming wood floors, then sank into deep, exotically-coloured rugs as she walked.

The curved staircase they climbed made Maddie feel like a princess. 'It's like a fairy tale,' she said in wonder, as she twisted around to take it all in.

'Really?' Hetty sounded amused.

'It's the most beautiful house in the world,' she said, before falling silent, as she caught the puzzled look from Hetty.

Lesson one learned already, in her quest to become a lady: take it all in your stride and don't be transparent in your lack of breeding.

Hetty pushed open a door on the landing, and the fairy tale continued in a froth of peach, cream, and lace.

Maddie touched the eiderdown reverently, rolling the fabric between her fingers. 'This is the same material as Daniel's coat on the inside. Silk?'

'The lining of his coat is silk, yes.' Hetty sounded slightly amused again, and Maddie vowed not to let her guard drop in the future.

'He left it at my house, after he rescued us,' she explained.

'I know. Don't worry – I am not the one you have to answer to.' She frowned. 'Anyway, we won't worry about that yet. First of all, we need to get you an introduction to Mrs Howlett. I'm going to London in a couple of weeks, and will be gone for a while, so why not do it tomorrow? Shall I get my driver to pick you up?'

'No, I have transport,' Maddie lied, unwilling for Hetty to find out exactly where she lived. 'I'll see you there at ten o'clock?' She changed the subject quickly, so Hetty would not have the chance to press her for a lift. 'You must be so excited about going to London.'

Hetty screwed her nose up. 'I suppose I am, in a way, but it seems so mechanical, this securing me a husband business, and I'm scared that I will end up with a dud.'

'Surely, that would never happen?'

'I am afraid it could, all too easily, as it's all about money and status. He could be the biggest buffoon going, and Mother wouldn't care. You haven't met Mother yet, have you?' she asked cryptically.

'No, but I'm starting to realise that she has quite an influence on your lives.'

'You're right. Daniel and myself are the brave ones. Poor Polly, my sister, is totally dominated by her. Scared stiff, would be more like it. Sadly.' She lowered her voice. 'She's not the pretty one of the family. I am assured of that.' She shook her dark curls and smiled bewitchingly. 'Daniel, as you know, is handsome and clever, so he will meet no trouble in finding a wife.' She clapped her hands over her mouth. 'Oh, listen to me, when I know you are sweet on him.'

'Oh, dear.' Maddie's good humour slipped a notch as she took on board what she was up against. She longed to see Daniel, hoping that the time they had spent together meant as much to him as it did to her. 'Where is Daniel, Hetty?' she asked bravely, having expected to see him somewhere in the house.

'If I tell you, you'll leave me here on my own, and it's so good to have someone to talk to. I rattle around like a dried pea in here. In fact, that is one of the reasons I'll be happy to marry. At least I'll have company, and probably hundreds of babies, God willing.'

'I am sure you will,' Maddie said, although she wondered why God would want any more souls on this earth, which seemed very full already.

Hetty threw open her wardrobe door, revealing an array of exotic-coloured dresses and blouses, neatly arranged in a coordination of tones. 'Silk, bombazine, crepe, lawn, taffeta.' Hetty reeled off the names of the fabrics as she pulled out one dress after another.

Maddie's eyes widened. 'Goodness, how do you remember all of the fabrics?' She traced a finger down a duck egg blue dress, following a panel of lace and velvet. 'So beautiful,' she murmured.

'Would you like to try some of them on? I think we are about the same size.'

Maddie shook her head quickly. Although she would have loved to, she was more than aware, thanks to Daniel, how much her undergarments sadly lacked. 'Thank you, but I have to go. I need to prepare tea for my dad.' She looked out of the window to gauge the time of day. 'Oh, heavens, I forgot to buy the vegetables. I really must go.'

Hetty sighed and followed Maddie back down the stairs. 'I suppose I should tell you where Daniel is.' She inclined her head, an amused smile playing about her lips. 'Or did you really come here just to see my wardrobe?'

Maddie's face heated up. 'I really did, but it would be lovely to say hello to Daniel.'

Hetty's laugh was delicate and tinkling. She pointed in the direction of the rear garden, and Maddie noted her oval and pearly pink nails. 'He's in the summerhouse. You'll find it down there by the pond.'

Maddie's gaze followed the directions, but became sidetracked by Hetty's hands. She glanced at her own rough, reddened fingers and broken nails and decided that her hands would be a good starting place for the new Maddie. She would lay the fire and clean out the oven with gloves on from now on, or get Tom to do it, and she would find out how to turn her skin into a creamy colour, like Hetty's.

After saying goodbye to her friend, Maddie crept silently around the edges of the lawn feeling like an intruder, her body tensed for an expected yell of an accusing voice. However, she found the summerhouse without any kind of showdown and slowed as she neared it.

Daniel was sitting on a cane chair, studying a large book, a look of absolute concentration on his face. A stray lock of hair seemed to be tickling his nose, which he rubbed continually, pushing the hair away, only to have it flop over his face again.

Taking in the sight of him, Maddie pressed her nose up against the glass like a hungry orphan longing to be included in a family dinner.

Daniel must have felt her stare, because he glanced up from his books. It seemed to take him a moment to recognise her, before he threw down his book to greet her. 'Madeline, how lovely to see you again.'

She felt the breath leave her body with relief and allowed herself to be kissed politely on her cheek.

Daniel held her shoulders and looked down into her eyes, worry creasing his face. 'What are you doing here, is something wrong?'

'No, I came to see your sister, to talk through a plan I've hatched.'

He raised his eyebrows. 'Ah. Hetty mentioned that she'd met a beautiful dark-eyed nymph who appeared from the ether – or more likely through the French windows.'

Maddie laughed. 'Don't tease me.'

Daniel touched her cheek. 'Never. Tell me your plan. I like plans.' He rubbed his hands together. 'Go on.'

Maddie took a deep breath. 'I intend to become a professional dressmaker. Hetty says she will introduce me to the haberdashers in Hanley, where they employ dressmakers at the back of the shop.'

Daniel patted her hand. 'That's excellent news – if you are looking for a job, that is?'

'I do need to work, yes.' She didn't want to tell Daniel about the paltry job she had been doing for two years, darning and mending for the locals in exchange for a pittance.

'Well, then, that's splendid. And my plans are moving forward, too. The missionaries have been in touch and are prepared to help me.'

Maddie didn't like the sound of that, at all. Did missionaries not go to foreign lands, only to end up killed in the name of God? Her heart twisted at the thought that he might go away when she had only just met him. 'You would be as well tending to your own, wouldn't you?'

'A smart suggestion, young Maddie, one which might make me think you want to keep me here?' His tone was teasing as he took her cheeks in his hands and peered into her eyes.

She was aware that her cheeks were hot beneath his cool, smooth hands whilst his eyes mesmerised her. A rush of pleasure at his touch made her giddy, as he stepped closer, his face inches away from hers.

'It's so good to see you, Madeline. You have brightened my day.'

For a moment, she thought he might kiss her, but he let her go and waved a hand in the direction of the cane chairs. 'Take a seat. I'll get cook to bring some tea.'

'I would love to, Daniel, but I have to go. I'm late already.'

'Oh.' She was gratified to see his face fall. 'If you must, but I will see you on Sunday, will I?'

She smiled up at him. 'Yes, of course.'

'I would like to have a little more than a smile to keep me going, until we meet again,' Daniel said softly. He lifted Maddie's chin and lowered his lips to hers, delivering a firm kiss that sent vibes of tingling magic all the way down to her toes.

She gasped with shock and wonder at the touch of his lips as he set her firmly away from him.

'Until Sunday.' His voice was soft and husky and to Maddie's ear held a note of infinite promise.

'Until Sunday,' she repeated, feeling that her mind had turned into cotton wool. She couldn't think of a single coherent thing to say.

Keeping her gaze on his face, she began walking backwards, grinning inanely, until she almost walked into a tree. She giggled at her foolishness and threw him one last look.

He smiled and gave her a small wave, before pushing his hair away from his eyes once more.

Maddie didn't hear the querulous voice at first, so lost in her thoughts as she crossed the vast lawn, but finally the shouting filtered through her mind.

'You, girl, what are you doing on private property? Stop at once.'

She halted dead in her tracks, as an irrational dread filled her soul. Mrs Davenport had caught her out. She turned slowly.

A squat woman, with a head of hair like a feather duster, headed towards her, brandishing what appeared to be a fat cucumber. The woman's chest heaved as she stopped inches in front of Maddie, her arms stretched wide as if to block her route.

The incongruity of the cucumber made Maddie want to laugh, although there was a small part of her that jumped in fear. She bobbed slightly in deference to her status. 'Mrs Davenport, how lovely to meet you, at last.'

The woman's eyes narrowed, but she puffed out her chest a little and untied the apron strings around her waist. 'I am not Mrs Davenport. I am the chief housemistress, but I can appreciate your mistake.' She patted a few loose tendrils that immediately sprang upright again. 'What are you doing here?' she asked, her tone softer.

'I'm a friend of Henrietta. I've just left her.'

The woman narrowed her eyes and shook her head, her feather duster hair floating around her face a little before settling back against her scalp. 'Then, why were you coming from the direction of the summerhouse?'

'Oh, I had a quick chat with Daniel afterwards.'

Her eyes turned to slits, and Maddie could almost hear her mind whirring, putting two and two together and sadly coming up with the right equation. 'Daniel is in there, is he? Does Mrs Davenport know about this friendship?'

'We were just talking.' Maddie widened her eyes and crossed her fingers behind her back for extra luck. 'I had better be off. I have work to do.'

'Yes, I can see that you would have.' She gave Maddie the once over and, judging by the turned down lips, found her lacking.

Maddie was tempted to ask if the chief housemistress did all of the cooking, too. She was no more than a paid hand, after all.

However, determined that her newfound confidence would not let her down so soon, Maddie lifted her chin and, turning on her heel, gave a toss of her hair. 'Goodbye. Lovely to have met you.' She set off again, wishing she had stuck to the gravel drive – a squelchy lawn was near impossible to flounce upon – but she burned with indignity as she picked her way across the grass, once more aware that she had suffered *that* look again, the look that said she was of a lower class.

Maddie clenched her fists. She *would* make lots of money for her family one day, and they would live in a house as grand as the Davenports.

She would take the tram to the haberdashery on Saturday, and would not leave the store until she had an assurance that she could, at best, work for a salary, or at worst, work for nothing, until she had learned the trade.

Wondering how she would pay for her tram fare, she reworked her deal: the price of the tram fare and enough extra for a bowl of soup at dinnertime, she decided.

Her new life was about to begin.

Chapter Eight

Maddie had been firmly ensconced for a month in her new position as seamstress at Mrs Howlett's haberdashery and was learning so much – about life as much as sewing – taking in the news, and the attire of Mrs Howlett's clients as avidly as she learned about overstitching, hemming and how to choose the best fabrics for a particular style of dress. And as she sewed, her favourite occupation was to listen to the rounded vowels of the ladies from the surrounding areas of Hanley.

The ladies in question had come from Trentham to have a fitting for their autumn wardrobe and knew exactly what colours and fabrics they wanted. It seemed inconceivable to Maddie that anyone would have a new set of clothes made just for the change in the weather. Maddie herself had a coat and a pair of mittens for winter, and that was it.

They were talking about Edward, the new king, whose coronation had been put back due to illness, one of the ladies being most put out as she'd secured a house for the week of the crowning in London. Maddie, however, was more interested in how the ladies spoke rather than what they said, repeating their sentences under her breath, trying to work out why her own words did not sound the same. It didn't take a genius to work out that *at alright* was nothing like *how are you*, but their vowels were mellow and soft, not harsh and guttural. She knew her accent was far better than most of her friends and colleagues, as her mother had taught her to finish her words properly and not abbreviate when she said them, but she still had a long way to go.

'It is a lovely morning, in't it … I mean, is it not?' she said to Florence, who sat next to her.

''Tis, in't it,' Florence replied, giggling, all too aware that Maddie was mimicking the two ladies at the front of the shop.

Maddie knew Florence from church and was delighted when

she found out that she worked at the haberdashery. Florence was fifteen, and very pretty, with golden ringlets that she was rightly proud of, but Maddie knew little else about her, apart from her obedience and timidity in front of Mrs Howlett. That, and a general air of unhappiness that Maddie was trying her hardest to dispel. She was, however, an excellent needlewoman and seamstress, and a demon when it came to making dresses and blouses, managing about six a day – ready for embellishment of lace, pearls and pretty buttons, although, the newly purchased electric sewing machines had sped up the previously slow process significantly.

Maddie repeated under her breath, 'It is a lovely morning, is it not?' And then, 'That yellow dress is divine,' as she sewed, her head bowed over her machine, earning more giggles from Florence.

'When you're rich, will you employ me as a dressmaker?' Florence asked out of the blue.

'Why, do you not like your life here?'

'I've got no one who cares for me. Me mum ran off, and me dad only likes me brothers – and he's a bit too fond of the drink and using his fists.' She sighed. 'I'm not lucky like you. You'll go far, Maddie, I just know it.'

Maddie had never considered herself fortunate when compared to others, but as Florence's gaze held steady, waiting for her verdict, she knew that she did, indeed, have a lot to be thankful for. She had her family, her brains, and a determination that was lacking in many people her age. And maybe, if she was really lucky, she could have Daniel, too.

She smiled back at Florence. 'If I come up with a fail proof plan to make money, I promise I will include you in it, Florence, but it won't be an easy ride, I can tell you that.'

Florence beamed. 'Thank you, Maddie, I won't let you down.' She returned to her work, a small smile playing around her lips, as Maddie focused on listening to Mrs Howlett sucking up to her customers.

She enjoyed her work at the haberdashers, and was learning much about the trade. Mrs Howlett treated her well and was happy to answer any questions, about politics, good manners, how to eat and how to address other people – things she had barely contemplated before she met Daniel. She read *The Evening Sentinel* newspaper every day to keep abreast of local news, thinking there might come a time when she would need to be more conversant on local topics.

Most of Mrs Howlett's clients lived in the large houses on the outskirts of the smoky towns, which was no doubt the reason their complexions were so pale and smooth, and their hands creamy white and un-chapped, even when they were old. She remembered her mother's face, blotched with redness to match her hands, and how she had worked so hard, right up until her death, and it made her want to cry.

Oh, Mum, if only you were here, I would make you proud of me, she thought, blinking away a tear.

'Maddie, you're wandering.'

'What?' Her straight seams were zigzagging, and she pulled out the fabric quickly. 'Oh, no, I'll have to unpick it.' She inspected the material. 'I don't think any harm's done,' she said, thankful that it was a thick worsted wool, and not silk, or crepe de chine. She heaved out a relieved breath. 'Thank you, I was miles away.'

'Not wishing to state the obvious, but you will wish you were miles away, if you start costing her highness money,' Florence joked. 'Dreaming of lover boy, no doubt.'

'Actually, I was thinking about my mother. I haven't seen Daniel for a week.' She bit her lip, anxious once again that his feelings might have changed since she last saw him. 'I don't know what's happening between us, anyway,' she blurted out. 'His mother would never entertain the likes of me.'

Florence turned her doleful eyes on Maddie. 'The world is changing fast, Maddie. The old rules don't apply like they used to, and parents cannot make their children marry nowadays.'

Maddie sighed. 'I wish you were right, but I've heard enough about Daniel's mother to think it will be otherwise for him.'

'Love will always win out,' Florence answered solemnly.

Maddie shook her head. 'Been reading those cheap romances again, have you? Such sentiment is as likely to come true as sending a man to the moon.'

Florence laughed. 'They're to improve my reading skills, no other reason.' She blushed as she bent her head over her sewing machine again. 'Anyway, best get on, or you won't get that dress finished in time.'

'In time for what?'

'Finula Atherstone. She has an appointment this afternoon. She's the daughter of one of the richest businessmen in Hanley. She's a stuck up little madam and can do no wrong in her parents' eyes, and is apparently more-or-less betrothed to one of the bigwig's sons from over Stoke way. Must be the money talking, 'cause she's pretty thick, and he's rather a catch. Clever bloke, too, by all accounts.' Florence stopped her sewing machine and leaned her elbows on the treadle table. 'Oh, what I wouldn't give to have a man like that 'anging off me every word.' She sighed loudly. 'He came in once, and he was *that* charming. Fixed me with his lovely eyes, as if every word I spoke held great meaning. I would have thought he was in love with me, if I hadn't known better.'

She removed her elbows from the table and looked across at Mrs Howlett to make sure she had not seen her slacking. 'I dunno, us women today are fighting for freedom and respect but it still mostly boils down to whose got the money and status. What else can sway a man?'

'Love, maybe.'

'Yeah, fat chance of that around here,' Florence scoffed.

'Sounds like you are a bit jealous of this Finula.'

Florence sniffed. 'I don't suppose I will ever be wearing expensive dresses, with a rich, 'andsome 'usband to adore me.'

Fair point, thought Maddie, but she smiled as she imagined

Daniel's sister dressed to the nines, intent on finding a suitable husband even though she didn't really want one. Any animosity she felt towards the unknown Miss Atherstone died as Maddie imagined the poor thing being married off to someone she did not love, just for the status of being wed into the right sort of family.

She pulled her mind back to the present, as a pretty girl waltzed through the door, glancing from left to right, a sour expression on her face.

She stopped inches away from Mrs Howlett's worktop and swept a finger across the top of it, with a gloved hand, looking at her fingertips with distaste.

Florence rolled her eyes in the direction of the young woman and grimaced. 'Talk of the devil. Look, already she's causing trouble.'

'That's her? The one we were talking about?' Maddie whispered behind a swathe of taffeta lining she was fixing on to a particularly difficult waistband.

'Yes, and you watch yourself. Believe me, she can be vicious.'

Maddie's eyes widened with surprise. The young woman looked such an innocent little thing. However, Maddie had no chance to say anything, as Mrs Howlett swept out of her tiny office, enticed away from her ledgers, once more, by the whiff of money in the air.

'Miss Atherstone, how clever of you to make it, given the inclement weather.'

Florence rolled her eyes again. 'What's clever about climbing into a carriage and then out again?'

Maddie was used to Mrs Howlett's insincerity, and quite envied the way she managed to flatter and cajole without sounding false. She listened hard, knowing it could be a lesson worth learning.

'Needs must, Mrs Howlett. My engagement is imminent, I believe.'

'How thrilling. Has the young man in question set a date, then?'

'No, but I am led to believe it will happen. It is terribly exciting, although we have known each other since we were very young. Our families are well acquainted, and it has been an unspoken arrangement for a long time. He is very dashing, though, and we are fond of each other.'

Maddie could see no enthusiasm reflected in her eyes, and it confirmed her belief that she was probably marrying for convenience. She could not imagine spending her life and her bed with someone suitable, rather than someone she loved.

Her heart did its usual flip when she imagined sharing a bed with Daniel, before a shaft of guilt pierced her skin, prickling it with shame.

She would make an effort to be kind to the visiting young woman, who might never know what it would be like to be held in the arms of someone she loved.

Maddie walked over to the cubicle that housed the dresses and lifted a turquoise chiffon and silk dress out of its tissue paper, smoothed down the creases, and shook it until it flared out prettily. It was a beautiful dress, and having seen Miss Atherstone, she knew the colour would do her justice.

She walked confidently into the shop area, smiling warmly as she held it out towards the young woman, letting the folds of silk spread out over her splayed fingers to show off the detail in the dress. She had personally spent a week just sewing tiny pearls onto the bodice, and her fingertips were still swollen and dotted with pinpricks from the effort.

However, her smile faded, when the young woman scanned the dress briefly before nodding imperceptibly to Mrs Howlett, her face a mask of indifference. 'That is acceptable.'

Maddie readied another smile, although she was a little less sure of herself, but still she expected the young lady to finally turn and thank her. She could not help the words that tumbled out of her mouth at the young woman's attitude. 'Do you not like it?'

The woman's eyebrows shot up to her hairline, and she

looked at Maddie as if she could not quite believe that she spoke English, or even spoke, at all. She took a tiny step backwards, as if the wind had blown her off course, then she turned her back on Maddie and addressed Mrs Howlett. 'Where are the other garments I have ordered?'

'This way, Miss Atherstone,' Mrs Howlett said as she fielded Maddie away from her with a very pointed swish of her long skirt.

The young woman gave Maddie a look of utter contempt, before turning to Mrs Howlett with a sweet smile. Maddie reeled backwards at the obvious snub, letting the dress fall on to the worktop.

'You look right sneeped, you do.' Florence gawped at the retreating back of Miss Atherstone. 'What a rude little madam. I've 'alf a mind to leave a row of pins in the waistband of one of 'er gowns. She'll know about that, all right.'

Maddie took a deep breath determined not to let the young woman rattle her. 'Costs nothing to be polite, does it? Some people never learn manners, and it's not their fault, but she knows how to behave, so it's a poor show on her behalf, not mine.'

'Oh, Maddie, I don't know how you manage to be so kind. I want to smack her smug little face.'

'I suppose it's because I don't intend to live my life this way, and I don't care as long as I can learn something from people on the way.' Maddie lifted up a handkerchief to her nose and putting on a majestic voice said, 'I am just passing through on my journey to a better place, don't you know?'

Florence laughed. 'Good luck to you there, duck,' she said, before returning to her sewing.

Maddie studied the haughty lady from under her eyelashes, noting the lift of her chin, the graceful movement of her arms, and the way she managed to look down her nose at things, even though it was just a button of a nose. Maddie would never behave in such a way, but still, it was worth seeing how it was done.

She kept out of the way, as Mrs Howlett packed up Miss Atherstone's new clothes and handed them to her driver. She hoped a passing cart would spray muck up the woman's frock, or a sudden downpour would ruin her hair, but Miss Atherstone simply sailed away in her carriage, looking as pristine as when she had arrived. Maddie watched the carriage drive away and turned back to her sewing when the doorbell chimed again. She stood up on seeing Hetty bustling in through the door in a flurry of petticoat skirts, wielding a hatbox and a large bag that she tripped over as she greeted her friend.

'Maddie, dear I was so hoping you'd still be here, although the hour is late.' She dumped her boxes and bags on the floor and embraced her friend.

'Hetty, how lovely to see you.' Maddie returned the greeting with a smile realising too late that a tall, dour looking lady followed in behind her. 'Oh, I do apologise,' she said to the woman, reining back her effusive greeting and hurrying to close the door behind them. Realising that the woman was with Hetty she took a step backwards, waiting to be introduced, taking in the fashionably new velvet high-collared coat and wide-brimmed hat with a profusion of fluffy feathers that blew in the breeze caused by the door opening.

'Mother this is Maddie, a friend of mine.'

Mrs Davenport's countenance took on a puzzled expression as she glanced at her daughter and back to Maddie. 'How so?'

'I'm very pleased to meet you, Mrs Davenport.'

Maddie's words trailed off as the look Mrs Davenport gave down her regal nose said she thought the exact opposite. 'Likewise.' The eyebrows shot up slightly as if she considered Maddie too presumptuous by speaking.

Maddie pushed her hair back from her face and straightened her spine. The woman standing in front to her made her feel as if she was back at Sunday school being asked to recite her catechism in front of the adults.

'How may I help you?' She shot a look at Hetty unsure of whom she should be addressing.

'My daughter is preparing to visit London and we intend for her to wear the height of fashion. I would like to see some dress fabrics and suitable fashions for someone of her age. Please arrange to send them over.' Mrs Davenport was very much the one in command.

'Certainly, Mrs Davenport, we can have them sent to your house this evening, if that would suit.' She had no idea if it was possible to get Jack the runner to deliver them, she'd carry them there on her own if needs be now she'd made the offer.

'Would you like some tea?' Maddie ventured. 'We can discuss the styles you favour.' She turned to Hetty with a smile. Maddie remembered Hetty's wardrobe bursting with clothes and for a moment thought of suggesting that some of them could be altered and modernised, but quickly remembered Mrs Davenport knew nothing of Maddie's visit, not to mention the wrath she would face if Maddie lost Mrs Howlett money through missing a sale.

Mrs Davenport seemed to find the comment amusing as she took in Maddie's countenance and clothes and clearly found her lacking.

'No one better, Mother,' Hetty quickly put in. 'Maddie's almost my age and keeps up with all the latest fashions.'

Mrs Davenport sniffed, glanced around the shop and sighed as if acknowledging that their paltry offerings were inferior to her standards.

Maddie shot a panicked look over to Mrs Howlett's office window terrified that Mrs Davenport would leave without making a decision. Mrs Howlett caught the look and came hurrying over. 'Mrs Davenport, this is a surprise.'

Mrs Davenport bristled. 'Clearly. That's why it took you so long to leave the warmth of your counting house.' She smiled thinly.

'We do have other seamstresses,' Mrs Howlett said,

indicating Florence sitting at her sewing machine on the other side of the counter. All pairs of eyes swivelled towards Florence who, at that precise moment, sniffed loudly and wiped her cuff across her nose. Maddie winced and Mrs Howlett tried to deflect the conversation. 'You can see the new season's sumptuous fabrics have arrived if you'd like to take a look.'

Mrs Davenport strolled over to the bolts of materials lined up against one wall, her trained eyes gauging and sceptical. She took her time fingering a roll of crepe de chine and another of deep blue velvet as she pondered. 'Where does your lace come from?' She spun around directing the question to Maddie, who jumped in surprise but had no hesitation in replying.

'We have a few different price bands, the most economical being from Nottingham but if you prefer Irish, as I know the discerning ladies do, then we can cater for that.'

Mrs Davenport folded her arms. 'Very well. I shall want at least four evening dresses and the same of tea dresses. Eau de Nil, rose, midnight blue and emerald are all Hetty's colours.'

Maddie had to agree that she was correct in choosing those colours even as she wanted to ask Hetty her preference. She held her tongue until Mrs Davenport swept out of the shop with Hetty smiling and waving in her wake.

Maddie let out a sigh of relief as Mrs Howlett clapped her hands in delight. 'Well done, Maddie, I can see you are a match for our … how shall I say … more difficult customers.' She placed a hand on her shoulder and squeezed slightly. 'Right, then, I think we should call it a day.' Mrs Howlett turned the open sign to *closed* and rubbed her hands together. 'You have all earned your keep for another week.'

Florence didn't need telling twice and found their coats with alacrity, and soon they were closing up shop, happy to see the back of another working day.

Chapter Nine

'See you tomorrow,' Maddie called over her shoulder, almost bumping into a blond-haired man standing by the wall. 'Oh, I do beg your pardon.' She stepped aside for the man and thought no more of it, but as she stood in the queue at the grocer's, she spotted him through the window staring at the shop front.

She barely listened to Mrs Powell, the grocer, who talked nonstop as she weighed out her fruit and vegetables. From the rag-and-bone man to the stray dog she fed, any topic would do, as long as she didn't have to pause for one second to think about her own lot in life.

Meanwhile, Maddie's mind raced. What if her father owed money to someone and the man outside had come looking for her? It had happened to a friend of Jane's years ago, someone trying to abduct her to ensure her father paid the rent money.

With her groceries in hand, Maddie left the shop and walked away swiftly to be free of him, but she heard his footsteps speeding up behind her. She spun around decisively, squaring her shoulders, unwilling to allow anyone to intimidate her. 'What do you want from me, sir?' she snapped.

To her surprise he smiled and held out his hand. 'Charles Williams, at your pleasure. Would you care to accompany me for a pot of tea at Mrs Brown's? I don't know about you, but I am parched.'

She gaped at the man before recovering her composure. 'No, I most certainly would not.' She tried not to sound nervous. 'I don't even know you,' she added.

The man pulled out a business card and presented it to her with a disarming flourish.

Maddie glanced at it and looked at the man, concerned. '*The Evening Sentinel*? What could you possibly want with me?'

He seemed to take her question as acquiescence to join him as he placed his hand firmly under her elbow and steered her towards the teashop that was back the way she had just come. 'I am writing an article on the factory workers versus the employer and I thought you looked like a clever girl who would have a rational opinion on such a thing.'

'Oh, so you were not looking for me, in particular?' She breathed out, relieved.

'No, not at all. I am just trying to interview a broad spectrum of folk who work around here at the pot-banks.'

'Oh, I don't actually work in a factory, so I suppose I wouldn't count.' She unhooked her arm from his grip, unsure about the handsome stranger.

'No? That's even better.' He smiled disarmingly as he pushed open the door to the teashop, walked confidently to a spare table, and pulled out a chair for her to sit down. 'Allow me.'

Maddie's curiosity was roused, and thinking about it, a cup of tea in such pleasant surroundings would be just what she needed before her evening chores began.

Charles caught the waitress's eye, and within minutes, two fat pieces of cake drizzled in icing, a pot of tea, and two china cups decorated with roses around the edges sat in front of them.

Maddie turned the cup upside down, more from spending years seeing her father doing it, than having a real desire to see who made the crockery. 'Royal Albert,' she read tracing the gold crown back-stamp with her finger.

Charles smiled as he watched her. 'Why does everyone around here do that?' he asked.

'Is this part of the interview?' she asked, watching his eyes crinkle with merriment. He had beautiful, china-blue eyes, but there was a hint of something about his face. What was it? Not cruelty, but a coldness, especially around his mouth. She wouldn't like to get on the wrong side of him, she decided.

She reached for the teapot, and a shiver ran down her back as he put his hand over the top of hers, stopping her.

'I'll be Mother,' he said, his eyes meeting hers as he took the teapot from her and poured the tea. 'Right, down to work.' He tapped his teaspoon on the side of his cup and placed it on the saucer.

Maddie watched him as he spoke. He certainly was a disarming character, and his clothes were very fine – as fine as Daniel's, she thought, although maybe a little more ostentatious. As he tried to put her at ease, her mind wandered. He certainly had a flair that Daniel lacked, or was it more likely that Daniel simply wouldn't choose to dress quite so flamboyantly? There was something of the wolf about his smile, though, a smile that didn't quite reach his eyes.

The man cleared his throat.

'Sorry, I was miles away,' she said, flustered. What had he asked her?

'I said, how do you think the factory workers are treated on the whole, and how do you feel when you hear of the inequalities of the wages paid to women?'

The warmth in the café was making her drowsy, and she blinked and opened her eyes wide to concentrate on his lips. She liked the way he spoke, deep and precise. How did he sound so eloquent when he lived in the same area as she did? And he looked clean – so clean.

She had seen boys her age with coal dirt permanently etched into the premature lines on their faces, and there he was, a fresh-faced young man who smelled of flowers and newly-cut grass, pouring tea for her. She leaned towards him and breathed in, before spotting the alarm in his eyes.

She sat upright and refocused. It irked her that he knew she was working class, or else he wouldn't be asking her questions, and if he could tell, then so could everyone else. 'Erm, I do not think it's right but unless the government monitors the working conditions the injustices will go on.'

Charles nodded as he wrote down her little speech in his notebook, and Maddie was proud that she could articulate so clearly. It was her clothes and demeanour, not to mention her accent, which set her apart from the better classes.

She imagined, for a moment, that she was Hetty. How would she deal with such a situation? Probably very theatrically and beautifully vague, curling her hair around her finger in a distracted way. She lifted her hand up to her hair, noticed the pinpricked pads of her fingers from her needles, and her broken nails, and quickly hid them again.

She felt ugly and lumpish in her black wool skirt and faded blouse, and made a note to fashion a new blouse in a pretty colour when she had a spare moment. Not that moments were ever spare in her working world.

Despondency rose in her breast as she contemplated her life. And yes, some of it was because of the fat-cat factory owners, who paid their staff pennies and would happily sack them for small misdemeanours, until everyone was scared to put a foot wrong.

'If you really want my opinion, Charles, I think it's an absolute disgrace the way they get away with everything. The people get ill with sommat in the factory, I mean *something*,' she repeated slowly, pronouncing every syllable, 'and it is so obvious, but they do nothing about it, just keep them labouring until they cannot work any more, and then they sack 'em as soon as they get bad – I mean poorly.'

Charles scribbled faster, and Maddie was glad that he was taking her seriously. She was warming to her theme, having spent years pondering how they could have let her mother die without lifting a finger and not even offering to help pay for her funeral.

'Do you have first-hand knowledge of the negligence, and is it in one particular factory?'

'There's my neighbour, Jane – and her dad – both ill because of the lead and the dust. He can only work a few days, and it's nearly killing him, and Jane has something wrong with her jaw. It's a recent thing, and …' She faltered, wishing she could mention Daniel to prove she was a woman of good standing with respectable friends, but something stopped her. 'Well, we are all worried about her.'

'And have you personally suffered because of the way the factories treat their workers?' His blue eyes fixed on hers, as if demanding the truth.

Maddie clamped her lips together as images of herself and her father united in their terror tried to will her mother's lungs to work in the stuffiness of her tiny bedroom. Her strong and brave dad had tried not to cry as he rubbed his wife's back helplessly, all of them knowing it was futile.

No, she couldn't tell anyone that, it was too raw.

'Erm ...'

'There must be something. Something recent, maybe?' His voice was soft, almost tender, and he touched her hand, urging her to speak.

She felt the intimacy of the conversation almost overwhelming and suddenly wanted the interview to be over. She knew what she could tell him, though. 'My brother and me were rescued from a marl hole a month or so back. Tom, my brother, fell in, and I was daft enough to go in after him.'

'A marl hole? You mean the open pits that fill with water after they have taken all the clay? I think it's a disgrace that they are allowed to be left like that, don't you?'

'I do. And the slag heaps, too. You mark my words, there will be a disaster before too long.'

'And you think it is all because of the selfish factory owners?'

'Who else would it be? We certainly don't dig the holes out of pleasure now, do we?' Her shoulders slumped. There was no fair reason that one family worked their fingers to the bone whilst another one had everything handed to them, but talking about it wouldn't help. She rose and scraped back her chair. 'It's been nice talking to you, Charles, and I hope you find enough material for a story, but I have somewhere I need to be, so I'll bid you good day.'

Charles rose from his seat and hastily pulled her chair back for her. 'May I have your name, miss, and can I quote you?'

'Of course. It's Madeline Lockett, although why you would need to quote anything I say is beyond me. Everyone thinks the same. I'm no different.' She smiled tightly. 'Thank you for the tea.'

'My pleasure. I hope we meet again.' He inclined his head slightly, the wolfish smile back on his lips.

Don't bank on it, Maddie thought as she closed the café door behind her. She found herself wishing she had not given the young man the time of day. He was definitely a wolf in sheep's clothing and she wouldn't trust him with telling the truth if it hit him in the face, charming as he was.

She hurried home to prepare tea, fanning herself in the warmth of the evening, the suffocating heat of the bottle banks and kilns adding to the temperature. By the time she had reached her front door all uneasiness in her mind had disappeared and Charles was relegated to no more than another inconsequential incident in her day.

Chapter Ten

Maddie had arranged to meet Hetty in Hanley Park to hear a newly-formed brass band playing at the bandstand, and she was looking forward to it. She hadn't seen her friend for a while, and she was dying to hear if she had found a husband in London.

The air buzzed with gnats and the August day was humid, but Maddie didn't mind as the air at the park was so much better than the stifling smog that hung in the air over at her house.

She had made herself a new dress in stripy seersucker and satin, and bought a matching straw hat from the market that made her feel pretty. Her hopes were high that she would see Daniel who had been away for two weeks, helping out at a new branch of the Salvation Army.

They had taken to meeting up almost every day prior to that. Daniel would ride over on Algernon to Irvin's Wood, where he would collect firewood, and they would walk hand in hand along the scrubland, or sit on a bench at the church. Sometimes Maddie would manage a visit to The Villas after calling on Hetty, and they would all take tea in the summerhouse, enjoying the warm weather and listening to the birdsong. It was a world away from her own surroundings, and she always marvelled that it wasn't much more than a couple of miles away from home.

Hetty had become a firm friend during those weeks, but since her decampment to London, Daniel had seemed reluctant to invite Maddie over. She had a feeling that Mrs Davenport might be behind it, and it disturbed her, but not enough for her to ruin the day by asking Daniel.

A flutter of nerves set up in her stomach at the thought of seeing him again, and she knew she would be dreadfully upset if he didn't turn up. She sent up a silent prayer into the blue sky above her thinking that Daniel's appearance would make a beautiful day more perfect.

She soon spotted Hetty staggering under the weight of a basket she had hitched onto her hip, and she hurried forward to help her. Once they had embraced, Maddie stood back, eyeing her up and down. 'Look at you, in your finery. Already a proper lady. Did you have a lovely time?'

'Oh, it was wonderful, Maddie. I can't wait to tell you all about it, but we will wait until we get to the park. This basket is heavy.'

'Are you feeding the five hundred, my dear?' Maddie laughed as she grabbed a handle to share the weight.

'No, there's a big blanket in there – but we do have guests joining us,' Hetty said, grinning at Maddie.

Maddie's stomach lurched. It had to be Daniel. 'He's back?'

'Yes. Earned himself another few gold stars for when he gets to heaven.' She sighed. 'Oh, that boy, he has no devilment in him, at all. I despair.'

Maddie smiled to herself. She would beg to differ, as she pondered over how Daniel's caresses had become more amorous each time she saw him. She shivered in anticipation of his kisses once they were alone, as she spread out the blanket with Hetty, securing the corners with their shoes to stop it blowing in the breeze.

Glancing around the park, she saw no sign of Daniel, and so lowered herself down beside Hetty. 'Come on, then, let's hear if you put that wonderful French language to good use and wowed the boys with your piano concertos. What was London like? Did you see the king?'

Hetty peered into the basket and started lifting out bread and cheese. 'I mostly saw dusty roads, lots of urchins and very many over decorated parlours. But, you will not believe it, I have bagged myself a good one. A prospective husband! He has money, a house, and everything.'

Maddie grimaced. 'You make it sound as if you won him at the fair.' As Hetty's face fell, she added, 'No, I'm really pleased for you.'

'You will love him, honestly. He's jolly fine to look at, and has connections at Sandringham, which is something to do with royalty, I think,' Hetty said. 'But the most amazing thing is, he adores me. I didn't have to pull my funny face, or pretend to be clever, or anything.'

Maddie smiled. She was pleased for her friend, but it was a strange *to do* in their day and age, she thought. Maybe the world had not moved on as quickly as she had imagined, after all. Money and status were still the desired currency to guarantee a long and fruitful union.

She hugged Hetty, who was clearly waiting for congratulations. 'As long as you're happy, I'm thrilled for you.'

'And have you seen much of Daniel?' Hetty sent Maddie a look loaded with meaning.

'Every day, apart from these last two weeks, and I've missed him terribly.' She sighed. 'Oh, Hetty, I do believe I'm in love with your brother.'

'Maddie, I am so pleased for you – even if I cannot imagine why anyone would want to fall in love with my brother.' She laughed and pressed her friend's hand, looking suddenly serious. 'Does Mother know yet?'

'I'm not sure and I don't want to bother Daniel by asking. In truth, I would rather she didn't know about us, but I suppose she will have to find out one day.'

Hetty's smile faded. 'I am afraid that, whilst Daniel's heart is set on ridding the world of illness, Mother's heart is set on the less lofty cause of her son making money. And if he won't do it through work, Mother thinks he should do it through marriage.' Hetty's eyes were kind, but determined. 'Anyway, the less said about that, the better. Let us enjoy our day out.' Hetty looked into the distance, then waved and shouted, 'Over here.'

Maddie spotted Daniel threading his way through the throng of people, and she jumped up to greet him. 'Daniel,' she squealed, launching herself bodily at him, indifferent to decorum.

He lifted her off her feet and swung her around, whilst kissing her and holding her tight. As he set her back down on the grass, his eyes held hers, as she gazed at him, greedily drinking in the features that she had missed so much.

'Well, young Madeline, it looks as if you are pleased to see me,' Daniel said with a laugh.

She grabbed at his hand and held on tight, as they headed towards the picnic blanket. 'It's been awful without you.'

'I've missed you, too, my darling Madeline. Let's sit down.' He let go of her hand, and she lowered herself to the blanket once more and arranged her skirt around her knees. Daniel flopped down beside her and unwrapped the package he had been carrying, adding it to the cheeses and bread.

'Cherry and walnut cake, how did you manage that?' Hetty cried, her eyes lighting up. 'I only managed a crust or two, and a bit of cheese.'

'I've always been cook's favourite.' Daniel winked. 'Actually, she's used to me taking all the leftovers to the church, so it was only one more step to persuade her that I needed a delicious cake for the vicar. She's banking on her favours to ensure she gets into heaven, I suppose, and I might even take the vicar a slice if there is any left.'

His eyes flittered toward Maddie as he spoke, and he turned her way. 'You are a sight for sore eyes. How have I survived without you for so long?' He lifted a lock of her hair and twirled it around his fingers, before dropping a light kiss on the ends.

Maddie sighed happily and leaned into him lifting her face up to the sun. 'Has Hetty told you her news?' she asked.

Daniel beamed at Hetty. 'She has, and it's wonderful. Samuel is a decent sort of chap who isn't out to rob us all blind, or go off to distant lands and get shot. Good profession, too, an architect, no less. I think there is money to be made in property.'

Hetty turned to Maddie. 'I forgot to say, I am having my seventeenth birthday soon, and Samuel is coming over with his parents, so we're having a huge party. Will you make a beautiful dress for me – I will have a word with Mrs Howlett so you can do it at the shop. Oh, Maddie, I am so happy. It will be wonderful.'

Maddie patted her friend's arm. 'Of course. It will be fun dressing you, and I will make myself a frock, too, for your party, if I have the time.'

Hetty bit her lip and seemed hesitant, before brightening again. 'Yes, but it cannot be as elegant as mine, of course.'

Maddie laughed. 'I could never outshine you, Hetty.' Her smile to Daniel was full of enthusiasm, but she saw a frown cross his brow.

He plucked at a long blade of grass and wound it around his middle finger. 'Splendid,' he said.

She looked at Hetty for reassurance, but Hetty was staring hard at Daniel, her eyes demanding some kind of answer. Maddie caught a tiny movement from Daniel, a shake of the head – no more, but it was enough.

Hetty turned to Maddie, her eyes bright. 'We will have such fun – will you come with Mrs Howlett, Maddie?' Hetty didn't wait for a reply before asking, 'Shall we have cake before the sandwiches, and damn the protocol?'

Maddie took in her words, understanding dawning slowly. If she had been slapped, it would not have hurt more. It was clear that she was not invited to the party as Daniel's lady friend, or even as Hetty's companion. If she was invited at all, it would be as Mrs Howlett's little helper.

Determined not to ruin the day, she swallowed her disappointment down hard. 'Ooh, yes, please. I can't remember the last time I had cherries in a cake.'

She glanced at Daniel and found relief clear on the face she loved so much. Would she lose him, as she had always feared, because her social standing was lower than theirs?

The sun dipped behind a cloud, and a sudden chill wind made Maddie shiver as a sense of foreboding crept up on her. She could barely swallow a mouthful of food, or raise a smile, although Hetty was amusing with her acerbic comments as the ladies passed by.

It was true, a lot of the ladies were elegant and sophisticated, and although Maddie finally had some pretty clothes that she had made with surplus material from the haberdashers, she felt dowdy in her plain black shoes and unadorned hair, which hung loosely over her ears. She wondered why she ever thought Daniel would love her, the way she loved him.

Watching unhappily as the young ladies paraded by, she absorbed their style of dress, as she always did, so she could sketch them later. Hair decorations were plentiful yet small, but interesting hats were perched on top of young heads, rather than the heavy wide brimmed affairs of the older ladies. Peacock feathers and dried flowers still abounded, but it seemed to Maddie that there was a slow but significant shift in dress designs, simpler and more fluid. She gazed at more of the hat designs as an idea took hold. Hats would be far easier to make, store and transport and there would be little need for fittings and alterations that took up so much time in her working day. That in turn would make it much more lucrative, and sadly profit would be the necessary outcome of her venture.

A shadow fell over her as her thoughts crystallised, blocking out the sunlight enough for her to look up.

Daniel nudged her, seemingly unaware of her unhappiness, as he pushed himself to his feet. 'Charles, you made it.'

Maddie scrambled to her feet, as she heard Daniel say, 'This is Madeline.'

She noticed the absence of any possession, but she ignored

the slight, pleased that she would finally meet one of Daniel's friends. Her prepared smile faded, however, as the blue eyes of the newspaper reporter met hers.

He bestowed upon her the wolfish smile she remembered so well, the smile that did not quite meet his eyes, before extending his hand. He showed no sign of recognition, and she shook it in confusion, wondering if she had been mistaken about him.

What had the man said his name was again? Maybe he had not said. But the piercing blue eyes bored into hers, and she knew they were the same cold eyes that had mesmerised her when he had quizzed her in the café. She wondered why he was pretending they had not met before.

'I am very pleased to meet you,' she added. 'You're a friend of Daniel's?' She glanced over to Daniel uncertainly, hoping to be wrong, but Daniel beamed and nodded.

'Yes, we go way back, and we share *everything*.' Charles lifted her hand and kissed her fingers, running his thumb across her wrist at the same time.

A shiver of apprehension ran down her spine, but she determined not to let it show. 'Do, please, take a seat.' She rounded her vowels as Mrs Howlett did, but was a bit flummoxed because she had little more to offer him than a square of blanket to sit on.

He quirked an eyebrow, and his words dripped with sarcasm. 'Thank you, most kind.'

The mocking tone was clear as he collapsed onto the blanket next to her, too close for comfort. A steely grin directed at her confirmed that there was trouble brewing.

'So …' Charles paused and ran his gaze over her body in a leisurely fashion. 'You are the girl who my friend here thinks will make a great social study.'

Maddie blanched at his words and reddened against her will, certain she was not being paid a compliment. 'What do you mean? Daniel and myself are …' She was not exactly sure what they were, and it occurred to her that she should really know if they were officially courting. She determined to ask Daniel once they were on their own.

She eyed Charles warily, but he appeared totally unruffled, stretching out his long legs and throwing his head back to face the sun, blond curls falling around his neck. She had been unsure about him when she had taken tea with him and knew she had been right to doubt him. He was too confident – arrogant, almost. She wondered why Daniel wanted him as a friend and determined to tell Daniel about their encounter at the first possible opportunity.

Charles angled his body to block out Daniel from the conversation, his long legs effectively cutting off Daniel and Hetty from sitting near to them and his words were no more than a hissed whisper. 'I confess, I cannot see why Daniel is so taken with one of the *great unwashed*, so … tell me about yourself.' He took in her body once more, from the top of her head to her toes, and she bristled.

She looked across at Daniel who was helping Hetty to unpack the picnic, knowing she would be better off waiting to see what Daniel had told this obnoxious man about her, but nevertheless, she answered him, so he would not see how he had rattled her. 'Nothing much to tell, really. I work in a haberdashery in Hanley, and I am going to get my own shop one day and make my fortune.' She lifted her chin defiantly, meaning every word.

Charles snorted offensively. 'That is lovely, dearie. Everyone should have a dream, but let's face it, a more likely scenario will be that you marry a grubby-faced saggar maker and work in the factory until you die in the hovel you call a home.' He hissed the words into her ear, and she gasped with surprise, her fists clenching. Charles turned blithely to Daniel as if he'd not spoken the demeaning words beneath his breath. 'I say, that cake looks good. Can I have a piece, please?' He accepted a slice of cake from Daniel and took a large bite, widening his eyes innocently at her. 'Good old cook, eh?'

Maddie was horrified by Charles's rude condemnation of her life and her future. Daniel hadn't heard him, but she would bet her last shilling that he would defend her. 'Daniel, do you think my dreams are fanciful?' she demanded, remembering how interested he had been when she had mentioned her plans.

'I haven't really given it serious thought, if I'm honest. I don't suppose it is too easy, or else everyone would do it, wouldn't they? Do you have the funds, or the contacts, to start a business?' Daniel's remark was throwaway as he was still unpacking food; he could have no idea how much his words hurt.

'No, I don't … not yet, at least.' She blinked, hurt by his lack of support. 'But that doesn't mean anything. Lots of people make their fortunes from scratch. If they didn't, we would still be living in caves.'

'Darling, we know where you live, and that about sums it up.' Charles's words were muffled through a mouthful of cake.

Maddie shot a look at Daniel, expecting him to step in, but he had pulled out a small book from his pocket and was poring over it.

'When I am rich, and—' she started.

'Yes, good one,' Charles interrupted. 'Priceless.'

His words silenced Maddie, and Daniel, as if finally realising something was wrong glanced over at Charles. 'Charles, we are out for an enjoyable day. Please don't cause trouble.' His eyes darkened as he frowned, looking from one to the other.

Charles's sneer turned into a grin, as he carefully placed his slice of cake back on his plate, glancing from Daniel to Maddie and back again. He let out a suppressed chuckle. 'You have told her, surely?' he asked.

Daniel looked uncomfortable and put his book down carefully, saving the page with a bookmark.

'Told me what?' Maddie breathed steadily to calm herself. 'Told me what?' she repeated louder, but tears pricked her eyes and her throat burned. She knew it was bad, whatever it was.

'Why, Daniel, have you not mentioned that your mama has

found out that you have a little friend, and is *not* happy? Tut-tut, dear boy.' His eyes gleamed with satisfaction as he pushed his hair away from his face, and his grin grew. 'Does Madeline not know you have a real lady waiting in the wings with baited breath for you to name the day?' He huffed out a long sigh. '*Oh, Daniel, when will we be together, forever?*' he said falsetto, putting his hand on his heart.

'That's enough, Charles, we don't need to discuss this today.' Daniel reached for Maddie, but she shrank away from him, even as she craved the comfort of his arms.

Her lips wobbled as she tried to form words, but she could think of nothing to say. What did Charles mean about someone waiting in the wings? She looked wildly from Daniel to Charles, and finally to Hetty, whose eyes were huge in her head, her eyebrows almost reaching her hairline.

'Don't listen to him, Maddie. He's just stirring it up to get a reaction. He should have been a politician, not a journalist.'

Hetty's words did little to help, though, and Maddie floundered. 'If no one has the decency to tell me what you are talking about, then I shall return home.' She pushed to her feet and stood with her hands on her hips, glaring at all of them.

Hetty scrambled to her feet, followed by Daniel, who moved to slip his arm around her, but she shrugged him off. 'No, don't bother. I believe I already know the problem. I am just not posh enough, and if you don't think I am good enough, then I don't want to be here.' Her voice was louder than she had anticipated, but she meant every word.

'Well done, that girl,' Charles drawled and started a slow handclap.

'Shut up, you obnoxious man,' Maddie snarled back at him.

'Madeline!' Daniel's chin jutted with annoyance. 'What on earth is going on here?' Their eyes locked in mutual anger, but after a moment Daniel's softened, and he reached out. 'It's Hetty's party, Madeline, I can't choose who to invite. Please try to understand.'

She stared at his hand, her fists clenched, knowing and hating that her eyes glittered with unshed tears. 'Don't tell me what to do. What are we to each other, Daniel? You have never said, and it's becoming very clear why.' She slapped his hand away, furious. Her feet caught in the crumpled blanket as she stormed off, and she almost toppled over, righting herself at the last second. It would have been too mortifying, had she needed their help.

The bandstand was a blur as she dashed past it, and if she heard a faint voice shouting for her to stop, she ignored it. At footsteps behind her, she turned around, fists still clenched, ready to give Daniel another mouthful.

She stilled. 'Oh, it's you.'

She confronted Edward, the boy from church. Some kind of brass trumpet dangled from his fingers, and he huffed as he caught up with her, his breathing ragged. 'I was watching you. Are you okay? I can walk you home, if you're upset.'

'Edward, what a surprise. No, I'm fine. You're in the band?' She looked over toward the bandstand, where the band members were tuning up.

'Yes, but they can do without me for ten minutes.' He fell into step alongside her, and she smiled uncertainly. 'They're your friends?' he asked, jerking a thumb over to where Hetty and Charles still sat.

She looked back at the trio, grateful for the opportunity. Daniel, she noted, had stood up and was looking her way, but she turned away, pointedly and smiled warmly at Edward. 'Yes. Well, they were. I am not so sure—'

'That tall chap ... are you and 'im courting?'

Maddie bit her lip, trying to stop tears from falling. It seemed an odd thing to ask, and a feeling of alarm passed over her as she noted Edward's intense gaze in his clear blue eyes. 'No.' As she answered, she spotted Daniel still looking over at them. 'Edward, look, someone is waving to you. I think you are needed.' She breathed out the sentence with relief, as one of the band members gesticulated and shouted something she could not hear. 'I'm fine. Please, Edward, you need to go.'

Edward, clearly annoyed, tutted and frowned as he followed Maddie's gaze, but he turned away reluctantly. 'Some other time, maybe?'

She nodded, having no idea what he was asking, but glad to see him go. A small part of her prayed that Daniel and Charles had not seen Edward, even though she hated herself for thinking it. As the odds would have it, Edward's dad was, indeed, a saggar maker, and it seemed that he was likely to follow in his footsteps. She would hate Charles to think he had been on the right track with his insults.

Once she was sure Edward had returned to the band, she stood at the edge of the park, half hoping that Daniel would come and find her. He didn't and she stood on her own, slowly setting out along the bridle path, left to wonder how such a promising day had turned so sour.

Chapter Eleven

Maddie was no longer the happy person she had been throughout the summer and couldn't rouse herself from her lethargy as the days grew shorter and the stifling air cooled. She moped around, dragging herself to work, worrying and waiting for something indefinable to happen. She withdrew into herself at home, trying her hardest not to let her father see her unhappiness, spending her free time staring at the unlit hearth trying to empty her mind of thoughts. Her sketchbook, and its growing mountain of designer hats and dresses that had been such a source of joy, now filled her with misery.

She had spent the last three months labelling fabrics by their thickness, texture and price, whilst perfecting her sewing techniques on each one. Velvet, brocade, silk and taffeta, all had been graded and tested for their suitability. She had designed dresses in plum colours and pastel blues, soft bustles and high necks, coats in cream and black. Outrageous hats were ordained with peacock feathers and netting, simple bonnets enlivened by hand-sewn silk flowers.

It all mocked her now. She wanted to scribble all over them. She had detailed everything with such care, and for what? She would never make Daniel proud of her, and she would never own her own shop. It was nothing but a ridiculous dream.

Daniel, Daniel. His name reverberated inside her head. Did he have someone else in his life, even though he had said his career was more important? Was that the secret everyone knew about, apart from her? Her head hurt from over-thinking, and her heart ached with longing, the desperate need to hear his voice telling her everything would be fine.

It had been three weeks since she had stormed off, and

although her mind believed she wanted no more to do with him, her heart told her otherwise. It hurt whenever she thought of him – a physical pain that ached behind her ribs.

Maddie glanced up from her sewing machine as a shadow fell, to see Mrs Howlett hovering behind her. The woman passed her an expensive-looking cream envelope with a kind smile.

Maddie's name was written in thick black ink on the front, and she immediately knew what it was. She slid out the invitation to Hetty's party, and dread filled her soul as she stared at the words embossed in gold lettering.

'You are Hetty's personal dressmaker, after all,' Mrs Howlett said, mistaking Maddie's horror for astonishment. 'And it was hand-delivered to the shop. Mrs Davenport is a personal friend, remember?' She fluffed up her hair and simpered slightly.

'She's not royalty, you know?' Maddie couldn't help but say. She pushed the invitation into the envelope and placed it back on the countertop.

'I know, but she can make or break us,' Mrs Howlett said, giving her a stern look. 'It is your lifeline too, you know?'

Maddie did not doubt it, and had a horrible notion that Mrs Davenport would lean toward the breaking part if she were to discover that Maddie was the girl who she believed was trying to steal her son away.

'I'm not going,' Maddie said.

'Of course you're going. Don't worry, I will make sure you don't make any mistakes, or embarrass yourself. Stick close to me, it will be fine.'

Maddie smiled at Mrs Howlett's assumptions, but she nodded non-committedly, intending to back out of the event at a later stage.

Mrs Howlett patted Maddie's hand. 'This is important to me – and you, too.'

As Maddie opened her mouth to reply the bell over the

shop front rang. Mrs Howlett's ready smile was already forming as they both swivelled their gazes toward the customer.

Daniel strolled through the door, his eyes scanning the shop front leisurely. His gaze flickered over Mrs Howlett before settling on Maddie, who stood up in amazement.

'Mr Davenport, how lovely to see you.' Mrs Howlett swept past Maddie, who was gawping in shock. 'What can we do for you on this fine day. Have you come to collect something for your mama, or—?'

Daniel nodded in acknowledgement. 'I wanted to make sure the invitations have arrived for Hetty's party in October?'

'Why, yes, and how thoughtful of you to check.'

Daniel's eyes flittered once more to Maddie. 'And will you and Miss Lockett be attending?'

Mrs Howlett's self-assured voice faltered slightly. She glanced at Maddie and back at Daniel. 'Maddie will be coming with me, yes.' Her voice held a query to the underlying questions that were, as yet, unspoken.

There was a moment's silence when no one moved. Daniel looked uncomfortable, and Mrs Howlett looked confused.

'And you did not come to collect clothes for Miss Ath—?'

'No.' He cleared his throat. 'If I could have a moment, please, with Miss Lockett?'

'I will just be a moment, Mrs Howlett,' Maddie said, before the surprised woman could protest.

Grabbing hold of Daniel's coat sleeve, Maddie scurried to the door, dragging him with her. They escaped from the shop and hurried away from curious eyes, to the safety of an alleyway farther down the street.

Daniel faced Maddie and immediately started talking. 'Madeline, I am so sorry that I did not come to see you earlier. Father has had pneumonia, and I've had to do the rounds of the factory offices every day. We've all been terribly worried, as you can imagine.'

Maddie stared at him coldly. 'I hope your father is suitably recovered.' She was nothing, if not polite.

'I just … I just wanted to say how unforgiveable Charles was, I didn't realise what he was saying.'

Maddie blinked, momentarily surprised. He didn't know the half of it but she was so taken aback by his apology, and indeed his very appearance at her place of work, that she was having trouble processing anything.

'Hetty sends her love, too, but she has been by Mother's side since Father has been ill. She so badly wants you to come to her party. You will come, won't you?'

'I wasn't going to, Daniel. I didn't feel particularly welcome in your lives, I confess.'

Daniel grasped Maddie's arms. 'It is so hard trying to do the right thing, Madeline, but right now the right thing, in my heart, is to tell you … to show you how much you mean to me.' He pulled her close and lowered his lips to hers, kissing her gently.

'That much, eh?' Maddie smiled, forgiving him immediately.

'More,' he said and kissed her again, long and lingering. Maddie was surprised at how easy it was to kiss him back, and how much she enjoyed the strange tingling and the way her body heated up at his touch.

'Meet me when you have finished work? We can go to the park and I can get the tram back with you.'

'You came on the tram?'

'Yes, was that wrong?'

'No, but I wonder what your mother would say, with all those lower-class germs flying around?'

Daniel laughed. 'Mother is coming around to my way of thinking – I think.'

Maddie squeezed his hand. 'That's good to hear. I finish at six, and I can probably swing half an hour, or so, before I go home.'

He pressed her hand. 'Meet me by the weeping willow in the park?'

'Of course,' she agreed, relief making her acquiesce rather too readily.

As promised, Daniel was waiting by the tree, and as Maddie neared, the usual rush of excitement flipped her stomach. His smile alone was enough to make her happy.

He held out a bunch of flowers. 'For a rose amongst thorns.'

She took the pink roses, colour in her cheeks rising to match them. She'd never been given flowers before. She sniffed them appreciating the glorious scent they gave off. 'Quite the poet, Daniel, thank you.'

'Let's walk by the lake.' He took her hand and led her decisively, though his next words were hesitant. 'This party of Hetty's has become quite the formal occasion.' He breathed in. 'Hetty's meeting Samuel's parents for the first time, and is understandably nervous about it.'

'I would be, too,' Maddie said. Meeting Mrs Davenport was enough to give her a fit of the vapours, so she understood perfectly.

'The thing is, Mother has taken it into her head to do a seating arrangement.'

Light dawned. 'So, I won't be sitting with you.' It meant that she would not have to spend time with his mother, making idle conversation, and she brightened. 'That's fine. I expected to be with Mrs Howlett anyway.'

Daniel breathed out what sounded like a sigh of relief, but he turned anxious eyes towards her, and she smiled reassuringly. 'Are you sure you don't mind?'

'Honestly, I don't, Daniel.'

'Good. That's settled, then.' However, he did not look at all convinced, and Maddie wasn't as reassured as she had hoped about their relationship continuing on the same promising path as before.

'So, we're courting officially, now?' She needed to know, but she hated the pleading tone in her voice.

'As far as I am concerned, yes.' Except, his words were hesitant. 'Let's sit down.' He took her hand and led her to the boughs of the huge weeping willow, set back from the public thoroughfare. It was sheltered and discreet, and it crossed Madeline's mind that it might be an unseemly thing for a young woman to do.

She cast her eyes about. 'There's nowhere to sit.'

Daniel waved at a patch of downy grass and pulled her down beside him. 'This will do fine.'

The sunlight filtered through the long fronds of the willow, casting stretched shadows across their faces, and it was indeed sheltered away from curious eyes. Madeline tugged her dress down to her ankles, feeling inexplicably nervous as she took in Daniel's serious expression.

He ran his hands through his hair, his eyes troubled. His fingers traced a circle on her arm as he gazed at her.

'What's wrong?' Her voice sounded overloud in the quiet of the field, away from the machinery where the constant background buzz went unnoticed by the people who lived in its shadow.

'It's complicated. Father's business is not going well, according to Mother.'

'The mother I haven't yet been introduced to,' she said pointedly.

He sighed and plucked at the grass, before turning towards Maddie. 'You really do not want to meet Mother.'

'I will have to … one day, won't I?' Her eyes were steady on his face. Their conversation was not going quite the way she'd hoped.

Daniel plucked at the grass again, and Maddie waited, thinking she might die, should her heart beat any harder. Nervous flutters started in her stomach.

Finally, he said, 'I want to be with you, Madeline, but you do know that I will probably have to move away from here, eventually.'

Maddie's breath hitched at his ambiguous words, but she needed to let him know her thoughts. 'When is *eventually*? *Soon* eventually, or *years away* eventually? You know I would never stop you from becoming a doctor, surely and is it not possible that I could go with you?' Daniel was destined for greater things, she knew, but she had believed she would be included in his plans. Suddenly, she wasn't so sure. They had held hands and kissed. Wasn't that considered courting?

Forlorn, she studied the dirty grass, realising that she had been ridiculously presumptuous to hope that Daniel would, one day, ask her to be his wife. She twisted her hands around, one over the other in agitation. The hands that were finally the hands of a young lady, soft and white from the cold cream she massaged into them every night. She now wondered how pointless her efforts were. It had seemed such an achievement, another small step on the way to climbing above her working-class roots, but now it seemed rather pitiful.

'Don't look so glum, Madeline, trust me, I intend for us to be together, somehow.' Daniel shifted nearer to her, his face closer to hers. He brushed his thumbs lightly across her hot cheeks. 'You look so pretty today.'

His touch was cool and steady, and she tried to read the intent in his eyes. She thought she could see tenderness and desire, but love? Was there love in those beautiful, serious eyes?

He leaned towards her, and the soft pressure of his lips covering hers brought her soul alive once more. Mostly though, she just felt like crying. He had hurt her and shaken her belief that he would always be there for her. Even so, she returned his kisses, her body firing up at his caress. She loved him so much she couldn't bear to lose him.

Daniel groaned, as she clung on to him, and his arms tightened around her shoulders, squashing her breasts against his chest. Briefly, she wondered about the connection between her lips and the deep heat that started low down in her belly as his lips moved over hers. New sensations turned her legs weak and heated up her skin, as he probed her lips lightly with his tongue. Any common sense she had ever had disappeared, as she surrendered her body up to Daniel, hardly caring if anyone saw them.

Her whole body came to life in a startling way, hot and prickly and dizzying. The exquisite heat grew as he skimmed his tongue against her lips. She sank into his embrace and clutched at his body, fearing she would dissolve. It seemed to last a long time, before her brain re-engaged and she wondered what her father would make of such behaviour.

She pulled away, realising how incredibly forward she was being by letting Daniel be so intimate, much as she longed for it to continue. As she disentangled her arms from his embrace, he studied her questioningly.

'Don't you like me touching you?'

'I do, Daniel, too much, I'm afraid.' Her voice arrived as a breathless whisper, and she rather felt she would find out what it might be like to swoon, had she not already been sitting down. 'But we shouldn't be doing this. What are we thinking?'

'Oh, rot to that, Madeline. I am eighteen now, and you are sixteen.'

Madeline let out a short laugh. 'That doesn't make it right, Daniel.' She stopped as she registered a thought. 'Are you … are you showing me that I'm your girl?'

Daniel withdrew his hand quickly from caressing her cheek. He gave a short laugh. 'Absolutely, although at the moment, my mother—'

'Does not approve?' she finished for him. Her voice was calm, but her heart pounded as her earlier fears returned. What *was* he trying to say? She waited, barely breathing, for his answer.

'Mother will have me married off to anyone who has money and status; it's the way she thinks a marriage should be. She cares nothing for love.'

Madeline couldn't help but think she was probably a very sensible woman, but refrained from saying so. She was fearful of Daniel's vacillating, knowing how much power his mother wielded.

However, he seemed to know his mind right at that moment, and he pulled her down to the ground, holding her so close that she could feel their hearts beating together. He was impossible to resist, and she sighed with pleasure when he ran his hands across her bare arms and down around her waist, sending more exquisite sensations through her body. He slid his hand towards her breast and groaned as he touched the rounded softness.

'Dear God, Madeline, I'll never lose you.'

He looked resolute and fearful, all at the same time. She could understand his emotions. His mother would ride roughshod over any decisions he made, no matter how determined he might be, and she had power over him until he earned his own money.

His fingers closed around the fullness of her breast, and she heard a whimper of longing from her own throat, although she would never own up to uttering such a sound. Her head cried out for him to stop, even as her body begged for him to continue. Their kiss deepened, and Daniel's fingers crept up to caress the soft bare flesh above her bodice. Maddie felt as if her skin was on fire where he touched her, and she gasped with shock.

'I never dreamed that love would feel like this.'

Daniel pulled away, his hands visibly shaking. 'I'm sorry, Madeline, we must stop,' he said, getting to his feet.

She came to her senses rather quickly at Daniel's words and sat up, smoothing down her clothing, somehow feeling reprimanded. He was right, they should stop, and she should have initiated it far sooner.

She breathed in deeply, trying to slow her heart rate and stop the internal shaking that threatened to overwhelm her body. She tried to quell the thought that she had gone too far with him, and hoped he didn't think badly of her, but surely, they were both in this together.

Following Daniel's example, Maddie scrambled to her feet, trying to straighten her hair and her skirt. 'I will be for it, if anyone has seen us.' Even as she spoke the words, she regretted her colloquial dialect, and the inflection in her voice that marked her out as a Potteries girl. She sighed. Her dreams were probably just that: dreams.

Daniel heaved out a breath and brushed away a twig from her hair. 'I'm sure I can sort out these annoying complications. Just give me time.' He kissed the tip of her nose, but his eyes were still troubled. 'I didn't intend to meet someone as perfect as you.' His smile almost took away her fear, but then he added, 'I wish we hadn't kissed quite so ardently. It has given me a taste of how it could be.'

'I love you, Daniel. I will do anything for you, anything. And if that includes keeping out of your life for a while, then that is what I will do, as long as I know we will eventually be together again.'

When Daniel didn't return the sentiment, Maddie almost wished she hadn't laid her heart bare for him. There was little use in denying it, though. She did love him, and feared that she always would.

Chapter Twelve

The day of the party eventually arrived and Maddie hurried home from work, nervous, yet excited as she climbed the stairs to her meagre bedroom. She needed to try on her new gown before she could change her mind about going. Daniel had returned to being the loving, kind person that he was and she had no fears there, but it would be her first official occasion with him and she prayed that she was up to the job – in looks and decorum. He hadn't arranged to pick her up for the party, which disheartened her slightly, but he'd been so preoccupied she imagined it had simply slipped his mind.

The fashionable sage green silk dress, with a band of cream around its bosom, had hung up over her door for weeks as if challenging her, making her stomach flip in anxiety whenever she spotted it. The sleeves of the dress were fitted at the elbows and flared to the wrist in the latest fashion. It fitted beautifully, showing off her slim waist and high breasts, and she felt like a princess as she twirled around, dancing with an invisible Daniel.

The fabric alone had cost her a week's wages, although Mrs Howlett had kindly given her a bag of tiny seed pearls she'd found in the stockroom, to liven the bodice up. Occasionally, Maddie had run her fingers over the soft fabric, as if in reminder that her dreams might not yet be in tatters.

Sitting on her bed, she fidgeted as a wave of euphoric expectation overtook her. Maybe the party would be the turning point in her relationship with Daniel and she would finally be accepted in to the Davenport fold. She tried out a smile of welcome and reminded herself not to curtsey on meeting Mrs Davenport. The thought made her smile. The days of feeling inferior were gone; she was as good as anyone – her father was right.

As if on cue his cheery whistle alerted her to his return from work, and she whisked off the dress, before descending the stairs to greet him with a determined smile.

'Att alright, love. Where's Tom?'

'He's out the back with Jimmy. I'll fetch him in to have a wash.' She paused. 'And then I'm going to get ready for Hetty's party.' There, she had said it and there was no undoing it. All of her doubts and determination had vanished. Besides, she owed it to her friend, Hetty – who she had designed and made the most beautiful dress for – and to Mrs Howlett, and it would have been rude of her not to attend. Even so, a slight trepidation that she couldn't pinpoint marred her excitement.

After she had made the tea, she began to prepare for the evening, trying to quell the nerves that kept surfacing. She pushed the handmade hair clips, with the pale pink cabochons, into her thick hair, which she plaited and wound around a loose bun, leaving a few curled wisps of hair to trail around her face and neck. She dotted the tiny hairpins with silk daisies and, standing back, admired the effect. She had decided she would tell anyone who asked that she had made her entire outfit herself. No point in hiding her light under a bushel, as it said in the Bible – whatever a bushel might be.

Her new shoes fitted a treat, and she admired the button detail and the small heel, turning her foot this way and that. She had bought them on tick from the local shoemakers, but hadn't dared tell her dad, as he didn't approve of credit.

Her father hollered up the stairs. 'Jane's here. Let's have a look at you, then.'

Suddenly, she felt sick with nerves, but she walked elegantly down the stairs, nodding and curtseying to invisible guests, as Jane clapped her hands with delight.

'You'll do Daniel proud, love,' she said, stroking the material of Maddie's dress with reverence, as Maddie reached the last tread. 'Oh, my, I never appreciated how pretty you are.'

'Yer mum would be proud.' Her father's words caught in his throat, and his eyes sparkled with tears.

'Thank you, Dad.' Maddie turned to peer at her friend. 'You look pale, Jane. Are you feeling poorly again?'

'I do feel a bit queer. But I always do these days. Me dad's as bad as me, too. I dunno what'll become of our Jimmy, if we both cop it.'

'Hush, Jane, don't talk like that. You'll be fine,' she said, but was quietly alarmed at her friend's ragged breath and tiny frame. There was nothing to her, and even her apron looked too big as she stood there with her hands on her hips, her bones jutting noticeably. Maddie felt guilty for having been too wrapped up in her own problems to have noticed sooner. 'Have you seen a doctor?'

'Nah, I'll survive,' Jane said, but Maddie suspected her reluctance may have been from lack of money, rather than bravado.

She would ask Daniel what would be the best course of action. God willing, he could help.

Butterflies set up in her stomach once more at the reminder that she would finally meet Mrs Davenport as she waited until the last minute before leaving, secretly hoping that Daniel would have the foresight to call and escort her to the party. However, there was no sign of him, and she dawdled reluctantly to the tram stop, noticing to her surprise that she drew attention on the way.

Some men watched her covertly, and one actually whistled at her.

'Don't you look a picture,' an elderly lady remarked as she passed by, and Maddie threw her a grateful smile.

It boosted her confidence and convinced her that everything would be just fine.

She met Mrs Howlett at the bottom of the road by the big double gates of The Villas, which were, for once, open wide. 'You just stick by me, love,' she said. 'I will try and introduce you to the important people, although you obviously know Daniel, somehow.' She sniffed and gazed up at the long drive as if the subject was closed.

Maddie was grateful for it. Her nerves increased as she clutched the small cream evening bag to her chest on the long walk up the drive that seemed to go on forever. She had finally arrived at the front door, but was not yet the lady of standing she hoped to be, being greeted by Mr Davenport with no more accordance than that of the dressmaker she was. He stood in the hallway looking vaguely lost, as if he'd been told to greet people but was unsure what else was expected of him. Staff were dealing with the hats and coats and ushering the guests through to the drawing room so in reality there was very little for him to do.

The room was bright and the party was lively but Maddie instantly wished she could hide behind one of the huge potted plants as big as trees that must have been shipped in for the occasion. She glanced around self-consciously, hardly moving her head so as not to draw attention to herself. A riot of colour dazzled, and jewels sparkled, as ladies flitted around the room, their dresses swishing, their voices high-pitched as they conversed.

A perceptible blip in the buzz of conversation drew Maddie's attention towards the majestic staircase as Hetty and her betrothed descended the stairs. Hetty's hair and colouring worked beautifully with the lilac gown, and for once, she looked regal and sophisticated.

Maddie smiled secretly, knowing how hard she had practised being a grown up. However, her stomach twisted, when Daniel appeared behind Hetty, decked out in his finery and looking like a prince from a fairy tale, and smiled down at the crowd below. He could almost have been smiling just for her, and she sighed with relief when he headed her way.

She took a step forward to meet him, her hand raised in greeting. He smiled broadly and opened his arms but as he did so a woman glided up alongside him. Linking her arm through his, she caused him to swerve away, towards the refreshment area and Daniel could only shoot Maddie a troubled look over his shoulder. She caught a glimpse of blonde curls and a red silk dress that looked very much like the one she had recently fashioned at Mrs Howlett's shop.

Bemused she took a step behind an aspidistra, heat burning her cheeks as a trickle of sweat prickled her underarms. She recognised the young blonde as the rude woman from the shop. What was her name? Miss Atherstone, that was it. But why was Daniel allowing her to take his arm and manoeuvre him away from her?

She watched from behind her hiding place as Daniel nodded his head in greeting on being introduced to an elderly couple, his smile polite and welcoming. Maddie was rooted to the spot, anxiety filling her breast as an awful foreboding took hold.

A gong sounded out, summoning the guests to dinner, and making her jump, but she had no intention of staying that long. She should not have come and would leave immediately.

As she turned, however, a hand cupped her elbow, and Charles, his fake smile fixed, raked his gaze over her body, his blue eyes glittering with something close to triumph.

'You look ravishing tonight,' he said, without a hint of sarcasm, and she bit back the retort that sprang from her lips. 'I have nominated myself to look after you, and to ensure that you enjoy yourself, in spite of the ... ahh ... complications.'

Complications? It was a word she was learning to dread. As Charles, his hand clamped to her arm, swept her along, she briefly caught sight of Daniel.

'Yes, I am afraid things have moved on rather swiftly. Ultimatums have been given ... and accepted.' His smile was expansive, and Maddie detected the sound of victory as he spoke. 'I hope you did not go to all this trouble for Daniel.' His gaze was shameless as he looked her up and down.

Never had Maddie felt so naked in front of a man. She wanted to shake him off, but his grip was still steely as he steered her towards the vast table laid out with white china and crystal glasses. Everything sparkled beneath the light of the magnificent chandelier, which sent out its own array of spangled colours, but already, for Maddie, the shine had gone from the party.

'What if I did try to look nice for Daniel?' She sounded calm, but she could barely breathe, as she suspected that she already knew what Charles's reply would be.

'Then I am sorry you wasted your time.'

She raised her chin defiantly, although a dread cold as winter chilled her body as she was led to a table far away from Daniel's and all but pressed into her seat by Charles. Mrs Howlett, already seated on her left, greeted her warmly, as Charles settled himself down on her right, effectively hemming her in. The manoeuvre left her with no way to leave without drawing attention to herself.

'This is cosy, isn't it? Not like the other table.' Charles inclined his chin toward Daniel's table, just as Miss Atherstone, placed next to Daniel, laughed and whispered intimately to him.

As she leaned in close, her pretty blonde curls contrasted beautifully with Daniel's fine dark hair. With them, however, was Hetty, her fiancé Samuel, a plain, dark-haired girl Maddie took to be Daniel's other sister Polly, and Daniel's parents, all seated in a row, and for a moment Maddie's worry lessened slightly.

'Is Miss Atherstone related to Daniel?' That would explain their friendship, she thought.

'Not yet, dear.' Charles smirked, his eyebrows raised. He appeared to be enjoying her discomfiture, as she tried to place Miss Atherstone's role in Daniel's life.

'Is she a friend of Hetty's, then?'

'No, I do not believe so, although she does appear to know a little about you.'

'Me? Why? And why is she—?' She watched incomprehensibly as Daniel slung his arm around the back of Miss Atherstone's chair. It was too intimate and too casual a move for two people who were not well acquainted, and she shot an enquiring, yet incredulous, look at Charles.

He widened his eyes in innocence. 'Have you got it, yet?'

She glanced at Charles, and then across at Daniel, who must have known she was seated next to Charles but appeared to be avoiding her eye. A waitress placed a bowl of soup in front of her, and she picked up her spoon automatically, staring at the creamy liquid as if it were poison.

'You will be thankful to know that Daniel finally has his mother's approval to be a doctor,' Charles said conversationally, whilst looking askance at Maddie.

'Oh, that's splendid news, I must ...' She faltered as she looked over at his table miserably.

'You really *mustn't*, you know.' His frown was false, almost comical, but laughing was the last thing Maddie felt like doing. 'Of course, becoming a doctor comes at a price, I'm afraid, my little working-class dressmaker. You didn't seriously think you were invited here for Daniel's sake?' He raised a sardonic eyebrow. 'Surely not?'

Her hand flew to her mouth, and her spoon clattered into her bowl as the pieces of the puzzle finally fell into place. She closed her eyes, crushed, wanting to disappear as embarrassment engulfed her.

Charles peered at her. 'I say, are you feeling a bit poorly? Would you like to take a stroll around the garden?' His sneer made her want to slap him.

Mrs Howlett placed a placatory hand over hers and shot her a sympathetic look. 'Here take this.' She tipped up a tiny bottle of eau de cologne onto her handkerchief and passed it to Maddie. 'This sort of occasion can be a trifle overwhelming for the uninitiated. Hold it to your temples and wrists, and you will be fine in a while.' She shot Charles a filthy look, which he accepted with a thin smile and an inclination of the head.

Somehow, Maddie managed to get through dinner, barely picking at her food, whilst longing to be on her own so she could digest the bitter truth. She felt like an interloper and burned with humiliation. How could Daniel have allowed such a situation to arise?

She clenched her fists, her nails digging into her palms, and bit her cheek as hot tears of pain threatened behind her eyes.

She would not cry in public. She would not.

Finally, the interminable meal was over, and she escaped from the dining room and out of the door. She didn't think she would be missed and couldn't face bidding goodbye to Hetty or her family. She certainly wouldn't risk speaking to Daniel, not with Miss Atherstone clamped to one side, and his mother, who had ignored her completely, on the other. She was unsure if Mrs Davenport even remembered who she was.

She pushed through the nearest door and didn't slow down until she reached the outskirts of the garden, where the summerhouse sat invitingly, a dim light burning inside. The urge to enter it and breathe in the last of Daniel's world was strong, and Maddie slid the door open effortlessly. After the cacophony of noise at the house, she found it to be cool and calming, and the quietness was bliss.

She gazed around sadly. Daniel's large medical book still lay on the table, its open pages showing the workings of a heart. She smiled, in spite of herself, noting the irony of it, wondering if it could tell her how to mend a broken one. Her smile faded quickly, though, and she found tears welling up. She must leave before she was spotted, and her shame was complete.

A scrape of the door followed and a voice behind her made her jump. 'Were you really so naive? You must have known Daniel was just practising on you.'

She swung around to face Charles once more. 'Why have you followed me? Go away.'

She tried to pass him, but he caught her around the waist and held her fast, shouldering her up against the wall. 'I don't think I want to leave you alone. It's a shame to waste all of that effort you put into looking pretty for Daniel.' He dipped his face close to hers. 'Hmm, do you not agree? You smell so good, too.'

She pressed her head backwards into the wall, but there was no escaping his icy gaze and hot breath.

'Didn't you know that *rich*, educated people don't marry for love? That's not the way things are done when you add serious money into the equation. Or did you know all along and hoped you might get something out of it? Answer me, girl.' He inched closer, his chest pressing into her breasts.

She tried to push him away but he was as solid as one of the granite pillars that held up the summerhouse. 'How dare you speak to me like that, as if I was a serving maid?'

'But you are, aren't you?' He caught a rogue tear with his finger as it slid down her cheek, then licked it suggestively whilst fixing her with his stare. He positioned his elbows on either side of her head and pushed his leg in between hers, pinning her to the wall.

Fear replaced the anger, leaping hotly into her throat. She couldn't turn her face away from him as he spoke, his lips inches away from her, whisky on his breath.

'I wouldn't mind you serving me, if you know what I mean. I would be happy to take up where Daniel left off. How far did you get?' He touched his lips with hers briefly, as if testing her reaction, before pulling away. 'There, that wasn't too bad for starters, was it?' he asked, his eyes piercing hers, almost as if daring her to fight back.

She was too stunned to comment, and he bent his head again and kissed her roughly, harder and deeper, digging his fingers into her flesh. She tried to keep her lips closed, but he pried them open, thrusting his tongue inside her mouth, exploring. He pulled away again, and Maddie tried to swipe at her mouth, but he caught her hand and pinned it to her side.

'Did Daniel do this, too?' He moved his free hand up to her breast, watching as Maddie fought to break free. 'He did, I believe.'

Abruptly, he let her go and ran his fingers through his hair, staggering a bit, and Maddie realised he was quite drunk.

'Oh, Madeline Lockett, you are too intoxicating.'

'I shall tell Daniel what you did,' she stuttered, but he rounded on her savagely, his own cheeks red, with anger … or alcohol … she wasn't sure.

He thrust his face close to hers again, his hot whisky breath making her gag. 'Daniel has sold you out to pursue his dream. Why would he care?'

She fought down the bile that forced its way up her throat, making her want to vomit, and nodded, defeated. It was all the energy she had left. The fight she hadn't realised she was fighting, for Daniel's love and respect, was over.

Charles suddenly seemed to lose interest in her and threw her savagely away from him. 'He didn't care, that's the truth of it. He *was* just playing with you, my lovely.' He wiped his lips with the back of his hand, savagely, the move making him once again lose his balance. Staggering backwards, he said, 'So, why not just scuttle off back to your spider hole, or wherever it is you live, and chalk it up to another one of life's little pleasures you received for free, from someone who really counts in this world?'

He stepped away from her and swiped up his glass, still half full of whisky. Gathering up the folds of her long dress, she made for the door.

He called to her as she left. 'You can find me at my offices anytime, if you fancy a bit more of where that came from.'

Turning back to him with determination, she slapped him across the face with such force that his head smacked the wall behind him. His eyes rolled backwards for a second before he righted himself groggily, shaking his head from side to side.

He glared at Maddie, his eyes flashing and his nostrils flaring. He grabbed her wrist, twisting her arm behind her back, and raised his hand as if to strike her. Maddie, too fired up to care, readied herself to receive the blow, but unaccountably he lowered his hand.

His lips twisted and his face contorted, ugly and mean. 'You will regret that, Madeline Lockett. Oh, how you will live to rue the day,' he snarled.

She lifted her chin, determined not to lose any more pride. 'I think not.' Bestowing her most withering look on him, she swept out into the garden feeling shaken and bruised.

Chapter Thirteen

Sleep would not come to Maddie that night, as Charles's words tripped over and over in her head. She tried to find a different explanation for Daniel's behaviour, but came up with none. Charles had simply confirmed her worst fears. Finula Atherstone must have been planning her trousseau, and that was why she had so many dresses made at Mrs Howlett's. The irony of it did not escape her.

She thought she might seek out Hetty to confirm it, but really, the evidence was overwhelming. Finally, the tears she had held at bay for so long poured down her face, soaking her pillow. She sobbed for the life she had hoped to have, she sobbed for being a gullible fool, but mostly she sobbed because she had lost Daniel and she loved him so very much.

Dawn eventually broke, and she rose from her bed with swollen and bloodshot eyes, far from ready to face her old life that yawned ahead of her. She was poor, she was nobody, and the only people in the world who loved her were her father and brother. Her life would be one of mending and making do, and she wasn't sure she could face such a life now.

Kicking her basket of clothes waiting to be altered or mended she sent the contents tumbling out onto the floor. She wanted to stamp on them, tear them up, and throw them in the dirt outside hating them with all her might as she slumped down on her hard chair, limp with despair.

Why should she still have to mend clothes and sew beautiful dresses for elegant ladies when other people lived in giant houses and had servants? She sighed already knowing the answer. They needed every penny they could find to keep their little family warm and fed. Tom grew out of his clothes at an alarming rate and could eat as much as any grown man. She smiled at the thought of her beloved brother; she would lay down her life for him, so a little darning wasn't actually that much to ask.

Slowly picking up the clothes she re-folded them. Making a fuss wouldn't change anything.

She glanced out of the window watching the sun fighting its way bravely through the smog, to shine on her little patch of godforsaken garden. She wondered if Daniel was out riding Algernon in the fresh air, somewhere miles away. The thought that he might be out riding with Finula Atherstone made her weep afresh and so she put Daniel from her mind.

Examining the hem of a thin skirt to let it down, she discovered that there really was not enough material to make it worthwhile. 'It's fit for rags, for heaven's sake.' She threw it across the room, and when it landed in the fire grate, instantly becoming buried in the ashes from the previous night's fire, she put her head in her hands. It was the final straw and total despair washed over her once more, loud sobs wracking her body. Finally, she stood on shaky legs to open the back door, although what she hoped to find there to revive her spirits was anyone's guess.

The air was, as usual, pea soup thick with soot. Maddie could practically taste it, as the pot-bank shot out red sparks that turned iron grey as they hit the air. The constant dull red of burning slag over at Shelton Bar steel works lit up the sky in the distance, and the rumble of industry was all around her. *If this is what we have to do to keep body and soul alive*, she thought, *why do we bother?*

She leaned on the doorjamb, deliberating her lot in life as she ran her fingers through her hair. Feeling something sharp, she picked out one of the tiny flower hair clips she had made especially for the party. She must have missed it the night before, when she had undressed and thrown everything in an untidy heap in the corner.

She untangled it from her hair, thoughtfully, inspecting the tiny seed pearls wrapped in cream silk and organza to mimic a daisy. It was really very pretty, and if she made half a dozen and tied them onto a comb, they would look rather striking.

She twirled it around between her thumb and finger as a spark of her earlier enthusiasm lit up a tiny part of her soul, but she shrugged. What was the point? However, as she held the hairgrip, an inner fire brought back to life the body that had turned cold at the thought of living her life without Daniel.

Shutting the door on the dismal scene in front of her, Maddie instead focused on how to become a businesswoman, so that someone like Charles would never again think it acceptable to abuse her. She took out her sketchpad once more and settled it on her knees.

She heard the scrape of the front door and looked up startled. 'Dad.' She was horrified that the time had gone so quickly and she had been too busy feeling sorry for herself, to think about cooking tea. 'Goodness, where did the day go? Let me get you a cup of tea.' She stopped mid-sentence as she took in his ashen face and slumped shoulders. 'What's wrong, has there been an accident?'

'No, duck, 'tis nowt like that. Sit yersen down. Sommat's happened, and I need to talk to you.'

Maddie fell into the chair by the table, her legs buckling. She had never heard her father sound so upset. 'It's not Tom, is it?' Her hand flew to her mouth as an inner shaking set her lips trembling.

'No, love, Tom's fine.'

She heaved out a breath of relief, but still gripped onto the table, her knuckles showing white, whilst her father paced the short length of the sitting room, shaking his head. His lips moved, but no words came out.

Nerves made her clumsy, as she put the kettle on the range to boil, worried to death for her father.

Finally, he sat down, drawing his hand over his ashen face. 'Maddie, love, I've been sent home, possibly sacked.'

'What? No!' She jumped up from her chair and was beside him in a flash. 'Tell me what's happened.'

'It's sommat about an article written in *The Evening Sentinel*. They have quotes and everything, an' have said it were my doin', but I dunna know owt about it.'

Maddie went cold at his words. '*The Evening Sentinel*? Has this come out today, Dad?'

'Ah, believe so, duck, but I dunna know where it's come from. I'm at a loss.'

Maddie put her head in her hands. Charles, it had to be, paying her back for slapping him.

'Mr Dulton says the health and safety people might shut 'em down. He sent me home for my own safety. The lads were baying for me blood. Me own mates. They're talking about striking, Maddie, all because of sommat I'm supposed to 'ave said … I have no inkling where it's come from.'

She closed her eyes at the images of all those people potentially out of work, and it was all her fault.

'Dad, I need to get a copy of *The Evening Sentinel*. Can you get your own cup of tea?' She was in her boots and out of the door before her father had time to comment.

She passed the factory on her way and hurried past a huddle of men who looked as if they were working up to a fight. She heard a shout and then felt something hit her on the back of her neck. 'Hey, you buggers,' she started, until she saw a grown man poised to throw a rock at her. Unable to believe he really meant it, she strode over to give him a piece of her mind. The rock whizzed past her shoulder, landing with a crunch on the wall behind her and smashing with a loud crack. 'Oh, my God!' she said, her eyes widened with shock.

As he cursed her loudly, she spun away and hurried to the corner shop, slamming the door behind her. She eyed the stack of newspapers piled up on Mr Brassington's counter, almost fearful to pick one up.

Mr Brassington, who had run the corner shop for as long

as Maddie had been alive, watched her silently. He shook his head, then eventually said, 'What were you thinking of, when there's already unrest with the miners striking? It's like adding a match to dry kindling, Maddie. It's going to blow, if you don't make this right.'

'I didn't say anything controversial. I'm sure the journalist has made it up.'

Mr Brassington grabbed one of the papers and opened it, jabbing with his finger. 'Read it, Maddie and tell me it's a pack of lies.'

She scanned the words, and there in stark black and white was everything she had said, couched in a style that made it sound sinister and accusing. Maddie could barely breathe as she read through the interview.

Madeline Lockett, daughter of Horace Lockett, says the factory is a disgrace, and her father, who is the chief fireman at the site (he builds the fires up for the kilns, for anyone not up on Potter's speak), lost his wife three years ago to the Potter's Rot. He thinks he should be compensated, as should all of the workers who lose loved ones through overwork and the terrible conditions they endure, boiling up as they empty the too hot ovens, often covering their body in wet towels to prevent burning.

A close colleague of Mr Lockett says, 'Horace was distraught that the factory did not help out with the costs of the funeral, or even seek any medical care for his wife. Dulton's profits were up this year, and it makes you wonder how many lives it will take before they put people before profit. Madeline, Horace's precious only daughter, is seventeen and has never worked in a factory. Maybe she thinks she is above such work, work that almost everyone in her street undertakes to help their family. When asked about it, Madeline said, 'They killed my mother. Why would I want to go the same way?'

She shook her head, incredulous. 'They didn't even get Dad's name right.' She scanned the rest of the page, wondering how she would explain it to her father, when her eyes caught a name.

It was a social report on Mr and Mrs Davenport of The Villas. She held her breath as she scanned it.

Eminent factory owners of the esteemed Davenport and Company in Stoke would like to announce the engagement of their daughter Henrietta to Mr Samuel Gravestock.

Maddie exhaled with relief and read through the rest of the article.

Their son Daniel is going to study medicine. Tellingly, Finula Atherstone, daughter of the Atherstone Empire, was seated at the top table with the Davenport family during last night's social gathering. She was engaged in conversation and danced with Daniel, the Davenport's only son, until midnight, when the carriages arrived. Mr Atherstone owns the Grant Hotel chain throughout Staffordshire and has the majority share in the Burslem Colliery and several factories. We have heard rumours that Daniel and Finula will marry, and wish them all the luck in the world.

Maddie threw the paper down. The article had to be all Charles's doing, she would stake her life on it. Daniel would know what to do she was sure. He would convince Charles to retract the story or add an apology.

Marching up to the Davenport's front door she rapped hard on the large brass knocker, her anger fuelling her on. 'May I see Daniel, please?'

A housemaid she had never seen before answered the door. 'He's in the summerhouse, miss. He's only just got in. Should you be disturbing him?'

She turned on her heel. 'Yes. Thank you, I'll find him.'

Apprehension set in far too late to be useful as she marched towards the summerhouse, but her steps slowed as she neared.

She spotted Daniel through the glass, reading as usual,

frowning with concentration, his fingers threaded through the lock of hair that normally obscured his eyes.

He glanced up as she approached and sprang to his feet, his book falling to the floor. He wrenched the door open. 'Madeline!'

'What's this all about?' She brandished the newspaper at him, expecting him to take it from her, but he just looked at it, puzzled.

'It's *The Evening Sentinel*. What of it?'

'Charles has written an article about Dad and the workers at the factory – stuff I told him months ago. Dad might get the sack because of this.'

He inclined his head, his frown even deeper. 'How can that be? You didn't know Charles before last month, did you?'

'I met him for tea a while ago.'

Daniel blinked repeatedly, looking at her as if she were a stranger. He held his arms stiffly by his side and drew himself up. 'I see.'

'You do not see, at all. I did not know him then, and I certainly didn't know he was your friend.'

'So, you went for tea with a stranger and did not think to tell me of it?'

'Daniel, this has nothing to do with anything at the moment – it was unimportant at the time.'

'So you say.' His top lip set in a thin line.

Maddie sighed. 'I need you to help me. You have to tell Charles to set everyone straight about the article.'

Daniel's laugh was almost mocking as he shook his head. 'I can try, but I have to tell you that Charles is ruthless when it comes to his newspaper.' He took the article from Maddie and scanned it, a frown deepening. 'Which parts are untrue?'

'Well ...' Maddie floundered. 'None of it is completely lies, but—'

'Ahh, that's Charles's speciality.' He passed the newspaper back to her. 'As I said, I can try.' His voice was softer, concerned.

'I am so sorry about the party. Fifi heard that we were friends and said you were insolent and would get Mrs Howlett to dismiss you. I needed to deflect her from thinking about you – I think she was jealous.'

Maddie scoffed. 'Fifi?' Before adding, 'How dare she? She was a rude little madam who needs a good slapping, in my opinion.'

Daniel smiled. 'That's my girl.' He stroked her cheek gently.

Grateful for his touch, she leaned into him. 'Daniel, are you and Miss Atherstone … you know?'

Daniel sighed. 'I've known Fifi since I was little, and Mother has it in her head that we should marry as we are amalgamating our factory and some other financial nonsense with the Atherstones. I will not do it, but I just need to find the right time to tell her. Things are really difficult here. Mother is unbending and Father is unwell again.' He stammered out the words, and she could see he was not as in control as she had imagined.

'I was humiliated, Daniel,' she prompted.

'It wasn't a humiliation, Madeline, as only a few people knew about us in the first place.'

She flinched at his words and the twisted logic behind them. 'Oh, well, that's all right, then, isn't it? And I wonder why so few people knew about us, maybe because you plan on marrying someone else?' Her voice cracked as she spoke, but she bit down hard on her bottom lip to stop her emotions. She would not allow him to demean her further.

'That's ridiculous.' He ran his fingers through his hair, whilst Maddie stood her ground, waiting. 'Mother is paying for me to study to become a physician, when really she wants me to become a businessman. I am just towing the line, as Charles suggested.'

'Charles?' She spat out his name. 'Oh, please enlighten me with his words of wisdom.'

'Finula and myself are only paying lip service to it all, until everything settles down. Everyone will be happy that way.'

'Not me. I will not be happy,' she whispered. She made to leave, but Daniel grabbed her wrist.

'Madeline, my heart is with you, you know that, but I am trying to do the right thing for my family right now, and …'

'Talk is easy, Daniel. Your actions say otherwise.' She dared not move, or even breathe, as she stared steadily into his mournful eyes. She swallowed, wishing she had not been so outspoken, as she took in his harsh demeanour and his mouth pressed into a hard line.

In a moment of clarity, she knew she had been waiting for this moment since the day she first met him, and it was almost a relief to have done with the dreadful uncertainty that plagued her.

'You're taking the easy way out.'

'No, Madeline, but you are being unreasonable. I want to take care of everyone, but it's impossible.'

'Everyone?'

'You, Maddie. I want to take care of you, too.'

She looked down at where his hand held her wrist and then back up at him, and he released her. 'You have a very strange way of showing it.'

She turned on her heel and slammed the door of the summerhouse, before fleeing across the lawn.

Hetty knocked on the window from her bedroom, but after only the briefest of upward glances, Maddie put her head down and did not exhale until she had gone through the iron gates.

Chapter Fourteen

Maddie had no time to think about herself and Daniel, she had to ensure her father's job was safe and needed to appeal to the managers at his work, to tell them that the article was her doing, and that her father knew nothing about it. She would explain that she was duped, and admit that she had behaved irresponsibly.

Rifling through her clothes, she found a dress that made her look mature, and placed a bonnet on her head, tying the ribbon tightly so that her face was partially covered. She sent a prayer up to her mother to keep her safe, adding, 'I love you, Mum. Help me to do the right thing.'

After kissing the tiny cross she wore around her neck, she tucked it inside the top of her dress and put on the shoes she had recklessly bought for Hetty's party. It felt peculiar to have the soft leather so close to her wiggling toes, but the shoes made her feel more feminine and graceful, and she added more shoes to her list of requirements to become a lady. That way, she could relegate her stiff, ugly boots to wintertime only.

She ran around to Jane's house and flew in the door shouting to Jane who was in her tiny kitchen peeling potatoes. 'Thank goodness you're in. I have to go to the factory on an errand, can you watch out for Tom? He'll be back from school soon.'

'O'course I can, duck. Summat up?'

'I hope not.' She sighed and waved the newspaper in the air. 'Someone's written something bad about the factory and attributed it to my father.'

'Someone who? Sayin' what?' Jane put her hands on her hips and thrust her chin out. Scrap of a thing that she was, she still wouldn't shy away from a fight if she thought someone had been wronged.

'Oh, it's a long story but Daniel has a journalist friend who says father has criticised the factory—'

'I knew there'd be trouble brewing with that one.'

'But it's not Daniel's fault.'

Jane shifted from foot to foot. She clearly had something on her mind as she sucked in a breath, rasping and wheezy as ever. 'You should keep away from him, he'll break your heart.' Her mouth pursed and she looked past Maddie, through her front door down the dusty street as if expecting him to appear like the bad penny she had him down for.

'Oh, Jane, Daniel's a good man but he is troubled and simply trying to keep the peace.'

'He's not doin' a very good job of it, by the looks of your stricken face.' Jane sniffed and coughed into a raggedy handkerchief.

'Don't worry, Jane, I can get by on my own, I need no man for that.' Maddie straightened, stood tall.

Jane's stance relaxed and her features softened. 'Ah, Maddie, I love that you think that, and gawd knows if anyone can do it, you can.'

Maddie hugged her friend and was alarmed that she was no more than skin and bone, her slight frame clearly hidden under her friend's thin pinafore and matted wool cardigan.

'And when I'm gone, I'll be looking down on you in your finery, on me fluffy cloud, tellin' everyone up there, that you were me best mate. Don't you doubt it.' Jane started to laugh but it turned into a hacking cough. She leaned forward gasping as she thumped her chest.

Maddie rubbed Jane's back for a minute as the coughing subsided. 'Don't talk like that, Jane, you'll be better when the dust dies down a bit, come winter.' She knew that suggesting she visit a doctor would do no good and they both knew Maddie's words were just that: words.

'Give us a minute, I'll be right as rain.' She heaved in more fetid air and Maddie winced as she heard her chest rattle.

'You want me to come with you?' Jane asked finally.

'No, thanks. If you could just keep an eye out for Tom.'

Maddie gazed down the road wanting to be on her way, she had no time to waste.

'O' course I will. Go on, now,' Jane shooed her. 'Sort out what you've got to sort out. I'll still be here when you get back.'

Maddie left her resting against a wall looking completely drained. She felt so helpless, fearful for her friend but knowing that time was of the essence. 'I'll be back as quick as I can, Jane.' She backed away from her before turning and running the distance from her house towards the factory.

With a beating heart, she turned towards the factory gates on Ridgeway's Road. A few people gawked at her, and she was sure she saw a boy from her old Sunday school narrowing his eyes as she passed by. He certainly did not acknowledge her, as he normally would have.

The gates to the factory were shut tight upon her arrival, and hundreds of men gathered at the entrance, some with hands in pockets, looking dejected, whilst others were making posters to stick on the wall.

Someone started chanting when a large black car pulled up to the gates. There was a momentary hush, as if all ears tried to hear what was being discussed. The gates slid open just long enough to let the car glide through to the courtyard, before they clanged shut with a finality that was telling.

'Who was that?' she asked a young man standing next to her, his hands in his pockets and a cap pulled down low over his brow.

'Management,' the man replied, before pushing his cap away from his eyes and exclaiming, 'Blimey, it's you, Maddie Lockett.' He looked from left to right, as if wondering whether to declare his prize to all, but the man next to him pushed him away before he could say anything.

Throwing his arm around Maddie and shielding her face, he walked her determinedly away, and Maddie let out a yelp of fear, until the young man hissed in her ear. 'It's me, Edward

Underwood, from church. You need to get out of here, after the trouble you've caused. They'll be on the lookout for you, soon enough. Best get off home.'

Maddie looked into the eyes of the young man and, seeing only concern, allowed him to lead her back toward the road that would take her home. 'But it wasn't the way it's been made to look. It was months ago that the reporter spoke to me, and I had no idea he would use my words maliciously. He said he was compiling a report, and it was nothing to do with my father. Please tell them.'

'You can't tell people what they don't want to hear, love. Some are on about striking because of the newspaper article. It's brought all their injustices to the surface, and they've had enough.'

'What about those who just want to work, though?'

'They want to lynch your dad 'cause he's brought trouble where none needed to be. You just lie low and hope it will all blow over.'

'I can't do that. I have to speak to management. Please help me.' Her voice was shrill, and a few men looked at her with curiosity.

Suddenly, someone kicked the huge metal gate, and it reverberated and rattled, startling everyone. Someone else threw a brick at a window. Fortunately, it missed, but it bounced off the wall and hit someone on the rebound.

'Oi, yer bastard, what you playing at?' the unseen man shouted.

'Oo are you callin' a bastard, eh?'

'Let 'im 'ave it,' someone else shouted, and within seconds, everyone was hollering and pushing each other.

'Oh, God, what have I done?' Maddie cried.

'Keep yer voice down and put this on. We need to leave, right now.' Edward took off his over-large thick work coat and put it around her shoulders. 'Follow me.' He led her away from the factory, and she allowed herself to be pulled along. A stone hit her on the cheek and she yelped drawing attention to herself.

Someone shouted, 'Over here! It's Harold's daughter!'

'Run!' Edward ordered.

He grabbed her hand, and they raced together, out towards the myriad of houses, kilns and factories, as voices shouted, and feet pounded behind them. Blessedly, the mob was half-hearted in their chase. They must have had a preference for causing trouble nearer the factory, because they soon ceased, the jeers and swear words fading long before Maddie and Edward stopped running.

Upon realising they were no longer being chased, the two of them slowed down and eventually found themselves up by the old marl hole where Tom had almost drowned. They stopped, their breathing ragged and shallow. Edward was bent double, laughing, even as he heaved breaths deep into his lungs. 'That was fun.'

'I'm glad you thought so. I, on the other hand, feared for my life.' She leaned against a tree, her hand on her chest as her breathing steadied.

Edward straightened and gazed at Maddie for a full minute. His eyes fixed on hers. 'I would never let anyone hurt you, Maddie.'

She inclined her head. 'Thank you.'

Edward took a step towards her. 'It's lovely seeing you outside of church. I often try to catch your eye.'

'Oh.' She was lost for words. She knew what he was saying; it was far from difficult to work out, and she thought she ought to tell him she was spoken for, when, with a pang, she remembered she, in fact, wasn't.

'Don't look so sad. I meant nothing by it. Well, I did, but you can tell me to shove off, if you want.'

'Edward, I would never say such a thing. I'm far too much of a lady.' She tried to laugh it off, but couldn't raise a smile for him.

'Maybe we could take a walk along the cut sometime soon? You know, just you and me. The barges are ever so colourful, and there are some right characters that come down from Liverpool. I could bring us some butties and a bottle of tea.'

She tried to look enthusiastic about a walk along the canal whilst clutching a sandwich and swigging out of a bottle. It wasn't quite a life aspiration, but maybe she would have to re-evaluate her future and lower her expectations. 'That would be splendid, Edward ... sometime, maybe ...' She trailed off, hoping he wouldn't notice her lack of interest.

'Lovely. Do you want me to ask your dad, first?'

'No! No, really, he won't mind. He knows you.' She tried on a smile, but knew it to be weak and lacklustre. 'I suppose we should get back, should we?'

Edward beamed at her. 'Yes. I think I will ask yer dad any road, if you're all right with that?'

'Yes, do.'

Edward did not appear to notice her indifference. In fact, he looked like he had lost a penny and found sixpence. She tried not to think about the significance of their exchange, but nevertheless allowed him to walk her home.

He was surprisingly good company and kept her smiling as he made light-hearted fun of the vicar and imitated his wife's voice. 'Just a ha'penny in the collection box, Mr Brant, is that all you can spare?' He even placed imaginary spectacles on his nose and crossed his eyes.

When they reached her door, Edward loitered, fidgeting. 'I could ask your dad now, if you like.'

'He's not in yet.' She crossed her fingers against the lie. In truth her dad had nowhere to go; his life was his work. 'Now, shoo off home. I have to make supper.' She flapped her arms, waving him away whilst managing a weak smile.

'Promise me you'll walk with me after church some fine Sunday.' He leaned against the doorjamb and kicked at a lone stone. The toes on his boots were already so scuffed it looked as if it might be a daily pastime.

'Yes, I've said I will, haven't I?' She shoved him out of the gate good-naturedly and waved, when he turned around from halfway down the street. She watched him for another few seconds, as he dawdled along, zigzagging to avoid the potholes, as everyone did, wishing her heart was as light as his.

When she finally turned away, she felt unbearably sad that he wanted to go anywhere with her, when she was such a lost cause it could only end in misery.

The next morning, after a wakeful night, Maddie rose early and sat at the table drinking tea, whilst trying to marshal her thoughts into some kind of order. She still needed to see the management at her father's factory, but didn't know how she could do it if the gates were still locked.

She jumped at a knock on the door, fearful, but of what she couldn't imagine. She opened it and found a young man in a too-big suit standing on her doorstep.

He wore a grim expression, an ominous large brown envelope tucked under his arm, and he had a look in his eyes. It was the same look the undertaker had worn the day he arrived to take her mother away: pity mixed with unhappiness at being in the position he was in.

'Yes?' she said, her voice small. She tucked her hair behind her ears, aware that she presented a rather dishevelled sight.

'Can I have a moment with Mr Lockett, please?'

Her father, normally up and dressed by then, came down the stairs in his vest, looking haggard and groggy. 'Come in, our youth. Shut the door.'

He waved the man inside, and Maddie felt her skin prickle. Her father did not normally invite strangers in, and she wondered if he wanted to avoid the neighbours seeing him. 'Who is he, Dad?' she ventured.

'Maddie put the kettle on, love. No point in shooting the

messenger. Tek a seat, Jim. This is my daughter, Maddie. Maddie, this is Jim from the offices.'

Jim sat on the edge of the hard chair by the table, where Maddie usually sat. He seemed uncomfortable and pulled at his collar, as if he wasn't used to wearing a shirt. 'I won't mess about, Mr Lockett. I have been sent to tell you that we feel it's in everyone's best interest that we let you go. We've given you a generous severance, to tide you over, and we're truly sorry to lose you, but ... well ...' Jim seemed to lose his professional stance as his voice faltered. He tugged at the skin on his neck and folded his cap over and over. 'We are really sorry,' he whispered as if the walls had ears. 'There was nowt we could do. The guv'nors decided it.'

'But it was my fault. Dad, tell him.' Maddie wanted to shake the young man, to make him see sense. She clasped her hands together in a praying motion, begging him to listen. 'Please, tell management it was nothing to do with my father.'

'I think they know that, love, but they 'ave to be seen to be doing summat about it.'

'Go fetch that tea, duck. I'm sure the lad could do with a cuppa.'

Maddie never disobeyed her father and hurried to do as he asked, but inside she was panicking. What would her father do without employment, and who would take him on after he had been marked as a troublemaker? She rushed back in. 'Dad, you can't allow this to happen. It's hard enough to make ends meet, as it is.'

Jim jumped up as if he'd been scalded. 'I won't stay for tea, if it's all the same to you, miss.' He fidgeted with the envelope before holding it out. 'I just need to leave you with this, Mr Lockett.' He placed the envelope on the table and edged towards the front door.

'Go on, lad. You've no need to linger. I'm sure you must feel bad enough, without having to listen to our wench rattling on.' Her father hauled himself to his feet, to let the young man out.

His face was ashen, and he appeared to stumble as he walked. On his return, he seemed to have aged from the twenty second walk to the door and back, as if weighed down with the turn of events.

'What will we do, Dad?' Maddie fought back her tears.

'I dunno, Maddie, I just don't know.' He put his head in his hands and exhaled loudly.

'Well, I made this mess, so I'll fix it. Leave it with me.' She knew there were no other choices left. Her mind was made up.

'I don't want no charity, you hear me.'

'Don't worry, Dad. We won't need charity. I know someone who will help us.' She only prayed he would.

Chapter Fifteen

Maddie walked once more up the driveway towards the house she thought never to see again and rapped on the door. She expected the housemaid, or maybe the cook, to answer but, to her horror, Daniel opened the door. She didn't know whether she wanted to slap his face, or fall into his arms, and in the end, she did neither, just looked into his sad face as he brushed his floppy hair out of his eyes.

It was agony to see him behaving so distant and formal. He held on to a book, and she glanced at the cover, a picture of a beating heart on the front. 'Not a romance, I don't suppose?'

He smiled ruefully, following her gaze and shook his head. 'How have you been, Madeline?'

She had always loved the way he said her name, clearly and precisely, but it pained her to hear him say it now. 'I need to see your father, please.'

'My father?' He frowned, but opened the door wide. 'Come through. Would you like some tea?' She was surprised by his suggestion, but recognised that it was just inherent good manners that prompted the offer.

'No, thank you, I won't be staying long.' She stepped inside, and Daniel put his hand on her arm.

'I am going to have it out with Charles for publishing that article. I had no idea he had planned such a thing.'

She instinctively placed her own hand on top of his, and their eyes met. 'Thank you. I appreciate the thought, but I don't suppose it will help.' She removed her hand quickly, even though the mere warmth of his skin made her ache for more. She missed his touch already and didn't know how she would cope with missing it for the rest of her life.

However, there was no time for such thoughts. 'I don't think you know your friend, at all, but it doesn't matter now. We are the past, and it's the present I need to think about.' She couldn't bring herself to talk to Daniel about her father losing his job. It seemed too shameful.

Daniel nodded, ushering her in to the hall, giving nothing away. His eyes were on her, steady and unwavering, as he held out his hand, offering a truce. She looked down at his hand and then up to his face seeing sorrow and anguish. She took his hand, wanting so badly for him to offer her a way back to the way they were.

He clasped his other hand over hers. 'Madeline, let's find a way around this. We can make this work, just give me some time. Once I have qualified, we can do as we please.'

His words were balm to her tortured soul. She longed to believe him, hoping for more words of comfort, but a door slammed behind her, and she jumped, the moment gone.

'It *is* you!' There was no mistaking the imperious-looking lady who shouldered her way in between them both, a fuchsia pink hat on her head sprouting feathers.

Daniel faced the loud woman. 'Mother, this is Madeline Lockett.' His grip on her hand tightened as he pushed her forward gently. 'Madeline, this is—'

'I know who she is. You cannot see him. I will not allow it.' Mrs Davenport directed her comment to Maddie.

Maddie stepped backwards, shocked at her animosity. 'I came to talk to your husband, not Daniel, if I may.'

'Why?'

'It's private,' she whispered as her confidence crumbled under the beady eyes of the imposing lady.

'Nonsense. Nothing is private between my husband and myself. You had better come through to the sitting room.' She sighed theatrically and pulled out the pins that secured her hat to her hair, and Maddie peered at the adornment.

The hat looked as if it had a stuffed bird sitting on top of it, there were so many feathers. In spite of everything she wanted to inspect it, and her gaze tracked its resting place, as Mrs Davenport placed it on the hall table. Maddie wished she had waited ten minutes longer before knocking – at least then she may have missed the terrifying woman, but there was nothing she could do about it now.

'Daniel, go and find your father please. I believe he is ruminating on the vagaries of life in the library.'

She turned to Maddie. 'Follow me.'

Maddie jumped to attention and did as directed. She glanced around the sitting room that had once held her in such thrall and saw it for what it truly was: nothing more than chattels, paid for by working people to death in their factories, so they could live in comfort. It was a disgrace.

'Sit,' Mrs Davenport barked, indicating a well-upholstered chair, and Maddie sat quicker than any well-trained dog. 'Now, listen to me, young lady. I have no idea what you think you are playing at, trying to trap my son, but let me make one thing clear. There is no chance of you ever being together, so if you have come to try and entice my husband to your way of thinking, then I shall have none of it.'

'I have not,' Maddie said meekly. She could ill afford to upset the woman, and would beg, if necessary, to keep her family together. Any hopes she had ever harboured about marrying Daniel fled in the wake of seeing the wrath of his mother, but she would agree to anything to secure her father a job. Anything.

Mrs Davenport stared pointedly at Maddie's hands, as she twisted and turned them in on themselves, giving up the quest to find inner calm. The woman's glare was enough to melt snow, and it was clear that she had no intention of leaving Maddie alone with her husband or Daniel.

Maddie glanced over at the door, hoping to see Daniel's father walk through it, but on seeing it empty, she finally spoke. 'I am not here for myself. My father was sacked and we can't survive on my income alone, and I know your husband has a pot factory over in Tunstall. I was hoping he might consider taking him on. He is skilled at what he does – has done it since he was twelve. He threw the vase you have over your mantelpiece.'

'Ah. It is a very fine piece,' Mrs Davenport agreed, glancing at the vase, which stood in the centre of the mantelpiece.

'My father made it, especially for you, 'cause Daniel saved me brother an' me from the marl hole.' She belatedly realised she had dropped back into the Potteries vernacular and blushed.

'This is the first I have heard of it.'

Maddie wanted to answer that if she had bothered to speak to her father when he called, it would not be the first she had heard of it, but she held her tongue. 'Daniel's friend, Charles, wrote an article for *The Evening Sentinel* about the factory, and my father got the blame, but it was my fault, not his. He is not a troublemaker, never has been.'

'Ah, I did hear something about an unfortunate article published by Charles. I cannot say I am surprised by it. That boy is such a non-conformist.' She simpered at the mention of his name as if she thought he was wonderful. Pressing her lips together, she looked thoughtfully at Maddie as she clasped her hands together as if the perfect solution had just occurred to her. 'You are proficient at sewing?' she asked.

Maddie grateful that the dreadful woman had not dismissed her out of hand was prepared. 'I believe I am superior to the average needlewoman. I have been working for Mrs Howlett for a while, and she is an excellent seamstress.'

'She is, indeed.' She leaned forward in her chair. 'So, on that basis, I have a proposition for you. This is not really a choice, you understand, and is a decision that cannot be reversed. I hasten to add that this is a decision I am free to make, without the need of Mr Davenport being present, so please do not try to contact him at a later stage.' She inclined her gracious head towards Maddie and paused so that the importance of the proposition was not lost. 'We will offer your father a position – as long as you do exactly as I say.'

'Thank you, ma-am. I will do anything.'

'Good. Now we have to be quick.' It was Mrs Davenport's turn to glance over toward the door, and suspecting her suggestion would be something her husband would not be happy with, Maddie tensed in readiness.

'My offer is that you move to London to work as a dressmaker. I have contacts there, and I will find you accommodation – sharing, of course, though I imagine that would not be a hardship for you. You will leave as soon as I arrange it and if you return to live here, your father will lose his job.'

'London? But that's the other side of the world, almost. Why?'

'Because I have eyes, and I can see that you have bewitched my son, and, in doing so, have compromised our family's future. That is all I will say about the matter.'

'I must be punished for loving your son, is that what you're trying to say?' Maddie's voice trembled, but she would not let the woman see how scared her proposition made her. To leave everything she knew and loved? Daniel, too – whilst there was still a slight chance they could be together? She pushed thoughts of him firmly out of her mind.

'As I say, this is not a choice, unless you do not mind that your father is out of work. He will not find it easy to get a job after being fired.'

Maddie was already imagining being sent away like a criminal, but she forced herself to pay attention. Biting her lip, she loosened her grip on the chair arms as Mrs Davenport's words sank in, the ramifications of leaving home hitting her. Poor Tom would have to cope on his own when he was scared, or had a fever. Her father would have to prepare all the meals and buy the food, and clean, and hang the washing out. There were never enough hours in the day, as it was. She didn't know how he would cope.

Mrs Davenport opened the door, indicating that Maddie's time was up.

She sprang to her feet, following Mrs Davenport into the hallway, dazed with indecision as the woman picked up her hat and brushed an imaginary speck of dust off it. Feathers fluttered, and she looked pointedly at Maddie before placing it back on her head and pushing the long pins back into position.

'Yes, I will do it,' Maddie told her.

'A *thank you* would be appropriate.'

'Thank you – and you promise you will give my dad a job?'

'I have said I will.'

Maddie was not quite so easily convinced any more that a Davenport's word was to be believed, but she had no choice. She nodded her acceptance and allowed Mrs Davenport to walk her to the door.

She paused on the threshold. 'Why do you think I am such a bad person, Mrs Davenport?'

'I do not. On the contrary, I think you are probably a very good person, and that bothers me slightly. But you are not the person I want my son to marry. It is as simple as that.' She pulled open the front door. 'I will send instructions on what to do next. There will be no need for us to meet again. Goodbye.'

Maddie barely had the time to utter her own goodbye, before the front door was shut, and she was left on her own to contemplate a future over which she had no control.

Chapter Sixteen

Not one month had passed when Maddie stood by the front door of her home, wearing her one serviceable coat and a determined expression. She pushed her suitcase under her arm, because the handles had rotted. It was so old, she didn't even remember where it had come from.

She couldn't believe she was really leaving her family and her home. Worse still, she'd had to lie to her father about the reason.

Her father had been thrilled when Mr Davenport had said that he needed a new potter, and the first person who had sprung to mind was the man who threw the wonderful pot standing over his mantelpiece. The offer had fallen into his lap like a miracle, her father said, although he felt as if he had betrayed Maddie because of the family connection. She assured him that it was the best thing that had happened in ages, but as she paused by the door, he stood before Maddie with tears in his eyes, evidently confused and upset.

'Maddie, love, I know you're broken up over that lad you had hopes for, but it will pass. You don't have to go to the other end of the country to get over him.'

'I told you, Dad. I'm going to make my fortune. I'll come back home when I have enough money to buy a house, you wait and see.'

'Don't say that, love. I might never see you again.'

Maddie's laugh was bleak. 'Yes, you will, and sooner than you think.' She hugged her father, clinging to the warmth radiating off him. It was the only comfort she had to take with her, as she dashed away tears.

Her father took one last look at his only daughter, before he pushed his cap far down on his head and disappeared into the early dawn chill.

Alone, Maddie crept up the stairs, to kiss Tom, who was still asleep, trying to capture the image of his dear face as he slept, barely daring to stroke his downy head as she tiptoed out again, stifling her sobs.

There was nothing left to do. Her affairs were in order, not that there was much to sort out, anyway. She had a solemn promise from Drunken Edith to look out for Tom, which appeared to give Edith a renewed interest in life, transient though it may be. She had also made Tom promise to look out for Drunken Edith and Jane. Jane was to look out for all of them, poor thing, as if she didn't have enough on her plate.

Once certain she would definitely leave, Maddie had written Daniel a terse letter, explaining that she realised they had no future together and wishing him well, blotting the tears that dripped on the paper with her sleeve.

Mrs Howlett had been very understanding, and Maddie couldn't help but think she knew more about the matter than she let on. Florence, however, had cried and made Maddie promise not to go back on her word when she knew Mrs Howlett couldn't hear.

'I promise I'll send for you, Florence, as soon as I need my own staff. God willing,' she had muttered the last part under her breath.

The bus to take her to Stoke station was due to leave at seven-thirty, which gave Maddie ample time to say goodbye to Jane, who stood in the cold November dawn, shivering and crying. She covered her mouth with a handkerchief, the thick smog, combined with the cold air, making her cough. She pressed the handkerchief to her eyes. 'What am I going to do without you?' she wailed, as Maddie fought back her own tears.

Maddie had cried so much over the last few days that she didn't think any tears were left. 'I'll come back as often as I can,' she promised, but they both knew they were empty words. 'You make sure you take care of yourself, Jane. There's no point in looking after your dad and your brother, if you make yourself sick in the process. You will remember to make sure Tom has breakfast before he goes to school today?'

'I will,' she replied and clutched at Maddie's arm. 'I just don't want you to go, an' I don't know why you're doing this.' She burst into a fresh bout of tears, and Maddie pulled her to her chest carefully, afraid of how fragile she was. Her ribs were noticeable in her back as she hugged her, and her face was sickly pale. She decided to tell Jane the truth as she could think of no other story that would be believable. 'You mustn't tell anyone this, Jane, but Daniel's mother has sent me away.'

'What? Why would you go, just 'cos she said so?' The mutinous uplift of the chin was back.

'Because she gave Dad that new job he's got. I had no choice.'

Jane folded her arms, legs akimbo. 'That Daniel was wrong for you. I knew it. Didn't I say so?'

Maddie sighed. In the weeks leading up to her leaving for London she had begged to the good Lord that he would find a way around her predicament, and prayed that Daniel would find an alternative solution to her problem before she had to leave her home. But her prayers were unanswered and she knew her fate was sealed. 'I can't bring myself to blame Daniel, love, it really was my own fault for shooting my mouth off to that odious journalist. Pride comes before a fall, they say and I deserve everything I got.'

'You don't deserve this – your family doesn't deserve this.' Jane's wailing set up again as they clung wretchedly together.

Maddie hushed her friend. 'It will be fine, Jane, don't fret.' She held her as Jane's sobs subsided. Maddie wished there was more she could do, but she had no more time to comfort Jane.

Finally, she prised herself away from Jane vowing to send money home as often as possible as she began the long walk away from her old life and into her new, scarcely believing that one year of her life could have wrought about such change.

She fixed everything in her mind as she walked to the bus that would take her to Stoke Station. Her house, Jane, Drunken Edith's overflowing garden strewn with signs of her debauched life, even the old cart that lay rotting at the end of the road, with one of the children playing on it, took on a new veneer as sentimentality overcame her.

Reaching the bus, she took one last look at her hometown and gazed into the distance, still fantasising that Daniel would gallop to her rescue astride Algernon and save her from her unknown fate. However, the distance was unruffled by so much as a breeze, and she bowed her head and cried in solitude.

Chapter Seventeen

London, 1903

The months passed quickly, and Maddie enjoyed her work, although her mind was never far from Tom and her father, and sometimes homesickness overwhelmed her. It was worse at night, when she lay on her small bed, listening to the sounds of London. In the city people shouted at all hours, seemingly incapable of standing close enough for a quiet conversation. Music played well past midnight, poor folk with organs cranking out jangly music as they begged for a copper or two to feed themselves. Then the dustcarts would start before dawn, chugging out a malodorous stench, and the whole thing would start again.

Maddie had never realised that the sounds of industry in her hometown were the sounds that had soothed her to sleep all of her life. The noise of London was alien and harsh, and most nights she would wake up with a start, her heart pounding as a costermonger, or a horse and cart, clattered along the road, loud enough to wake the devil.

She had, however, been pleasantly surprised on her arrival at Shoreditch, where she was to work. Yes, there were signs of poverty: ragamuffin boys running around with no shoes on, pickpockets and poor people picking up discarded food dropped by the vendors, but the trappings of wealth overrode the outward signs of destitution. The richly embroidered clothes and garish hats overshadowed the threadbare shorts and fraying hems of the less genteel. The sumptuous carriages and, more frequently, black cars, happily overtook the people forced to go by Shanks's pony. Most of the people sounded posh, too, even if sometimes she had no idea what they were saying.

The food was overall healthier, as the London Docks brought all manner of exotic foods over from abroad, and even their home grown food seemed tastier, although she had gagged when trying jellied eels, and was unsure about oysters, having refused to even contemplate such a thing as eating a mollusc.

Every Sunday, on her day off, Maddie wrote a long and detailed letter to Tom and her father, embroidering the truth slightly to make it sound better than it was, although her accommodation actually was warm and cosy and finer than her own house, and the air was unsurprisingly cleaner.

> *Dear Dad and Tom,*
> *I told you a while ago about my idea for hats and hair ornaments and have just finished a collection for the younger person. They are called bandeaux and are a bit like a band for your hair. I've embroidered them and strewn silk daisies and buttercups about the rims to make them fun. I am hoping to show them to Mrs Parrot, my boss, and have purposefully chosen the same complementary colours for the new season. I am full of trepidation that she will not allow me to put them in the shop window, as I am not sure that I have any other recourse for selling them.*
> *Pleating the taffeta to sew into the centre of the flowers is the hardest part but I can now sew seed pearls faster than Tom can eat two oatcakes and cheese.*
> *I think you would be proud of me, Dad – I am doing well.*

She would include a present for Jane, Tom and Jimmy: a length of red ribbon for Jane's hair and a bar of chocolate or a book for the boys, sometimes Turkish Delight for Drunken Edith, although she knew she would probably trade it with someone for a gin or two.

It was normally after she'd written her letters that thoughts of Daniel surfaced unbidden. When it was really bad, she wrote him a letter, too.

Dear Daniel,
I could never have imagined meeting someone like you when I was young and impressionable. But I did meet you, and you touched every part of my life. Everything I do, I do with you in my heart, hoping that you will be proud of me, although I am not sure whether you even think of me any more. Time has passed so quickly, and I am sure you will be very busy with your studies, but I do occasionally look up at the stars and am glad that the same stars are looking down on you. Somehow, it comforts me, and I do not feel so alone.
With all my love,
Madeline

She folded it over and sealed it in an envelope with a kiss, adding it to the bulging box of letters she had written to him, though none of them were posted.

She sighed and took out a fresh sheet of paper.

Dear Edward she started. She chewed her pen, wondering what to write that sounded friendly, but not too encouraging.

Edward from Sunday school had acquired her address from her father and his letters had become increasingly personal and full of hope. She had no idea why he imagined there to be anything between them, as they'd not even made the walk along the canal together before she had been banished to London. She knew him from church, and he had saved her from being attacked by a rabble at the factory, and that was it.

She stared out of the window. The night was clear, and the stars shone brightly, creating pretty patterns in the dark sky. 'Daniel, where are you right now?' she whispered with longing.

She pushed open the sash window of her tiny attic room and let in the spring air and the odours of London: chestnuts, sewage, meat cooking in the Cock Inn across the street, and a vague scent of river water from the London Docks, which was visible in the far distance.

Down below, a few men staggered out of the inn, and she smiled at the antics of the dubious ladies, who hovered around the entrance, trying to elicit conversation, and more, from the drunken men.

The place was far from perfect, but Maddie had to admit that life in London was far healthier than her life in Fenton. The work was enjoyable and enlightening, she had made some friends, and she could afford her new tiny room, with a sink to wash in and a small gas oven where she made her own tea. There were opportunities to be had, also, and she intended to make the most of them.

She tried to concentrate on writing a letter to Edward and chewed her pen once more, then placed it alongside the piece of paper, having no inclination to tell him about her life at the moment. With a sigh, she turned out the oil lamp, knowing that, very soon, she would learn if she could be the businesswoman she had worked so hard to become. She drifted off to sleep with images of her fine house and her own shop, strangely soothed by a distant argument between two men, and the neighing of a cart horse pawing the cold ground as it waited by the road for its late-night cargo.

The following morning, Maddie was up bright and early, and at her sewing machine by seven o'clock, in the back of Parrot's Fashions, where the real work took place. Most of the girls, sitting in rows with nothing more than a sewing machine and treadle between them, ran up ready-to-wear dresses that were sold to the bigger department stores. They barely lifted their heads up from the machines all day. Mrs Parrot, however, had spotted a natural talent in Maddie and promoted her to design and make some of the made-to-measure garments, for which Maddie was grateful.

The hours were long, and Mrs Parrot, never one to miss the chance of making a few bob, had decreed that Maddie's working hours included a Saturday, where she served the clients.

Maddie didn't mind, as it gave her an opportunity to chat to the very ladies she intended to emulate, and it also allowed her to hone her selling skills at the same time. 'Oh, my, how clever of you to know that the burgundy shawl would set off your hair colour so prettily,' she cooed, having discovered very early on that flattery worked in every single case.

Mrs Parrot played the role of a sophisticated lady beautifully, but Bonnie the housekeeper, who had been with Mrs Parrot for thirty years, or so, took great delight in talking about her employer's origins. 'Get her, with the airs and graces,' she would hiss, whenever she was in a bad mood with her. 'She was born up an alley in Old Nichol, the slums, before it was razed to the ground. She only survived 'cause the whooping cough took all of her brothers and sisters, so there were enough scraps for her to eat. Spent the first three years of her life sleeping in an orange crate in an aunt's house, as her mother done a runner.'

Maddie could quite believe Mrs Parrot's life had been more colourful than she let on, as occasionally her accent would slip into unintelligible cockney, especially when a street urchin pinched something on display outside.

'Filthy little toerag. I'll cut your fingers off, if I catch you,' she would shout. 'Would you Adam an' Eve it? Bleedin' tea leaf,' she'd mutter, and Maddie would simply nod in bewilderment. However, she liked that about her. She had reinvented herself successfully, and Maddie intended to do the same.

At the end of the day, she offered to make Mrs Parrot a cup of tea. 'If you have a spare moment, Mrs Parrot, before you leave, I'd like to show you what I've been working on.'

'Let me just park me aching legs, my dear, and I'm all yours.' She heaved her bulk into a rattan chair that creaked ominously, and Maddie passed her a cup of tea in a china cup and matching saucer, as befitting the lady everyone thought she was. 'Right, what are you clutching in that bag, acting like you are guarding the crown jewels?'

'Well …' Maddie crossed metaphorical fingers and took a deep breath. It would be a momentous occasion for her, and in the next minute, or so, she would know whether she had a future as a milliner, or whether she would forever be the girl *out the back*. Not only her future hinged on her designs, but her sense of worth, and proof that she could be more than a working-class girl who was too big for her boots.

Holding her breath, she laid her designs on the large tea table. 'I was considering the growing market for matching accessories, in particular hats and similar headdresses. I have seen how quickly dresses can be made through co-ordination, and I wondered if you would consider incorporating these designs into your summer collection now spring is almost upon us.'

She spread out the drawings she had agonised over: hats covered with chiffon and organdie, decorated with silk poppies and cabbage roses, and another batch sprouting peacock feathers and silk bows. 'These are for the more mature lady.' She paused, allowing Mrs Parrot time to pore over each design. 'And these are a bit of a racy idea, but I have seen younger women wearing them. I've made several up to show you how they work.' She held out a hat bandeaux and matching hair clip, decorated with pearly seashells and tiny sprig roses, interspersed with glass jewels, which glinted in the reflection of the light. 'Look, you would wear it low over your head with a matching fastener like this.' She pinned the clip to the back of her head and pulled the bandeaux down flat, just above her hairline, and struck a theatrical pose. 'What do you think?'

Mrs Parrot's expression gave nothing away, as she examined the drawings and turned the bandeaux over in her hands, bringing them up close to her eyes to inspect.

Maddie held her breath, and as Mrs Parrot took an agonising age to pick at the stitching, the jewels, and the silk flowers, her confidence flickered, faltered, and then her hopes died. 'You don't like them.' It wasn't a question. She could see it in Mrs Parrot's expression.

'Oh, my dear.' She looked up at Maddie, shaking her head. 'You could not sell these for a profit, I'm afraid.'

'They're no good?' She dragged out the hair clip from her hair and held it limply in her hands. 'Oh, well, never mind, it was just an idea.' She dismissed her dreams in one sentence, but her throat constricted as her hopes hit the floor. 'Why do you not like them?' She could barely push the words out; her disappointment was so great.

'Not like them? My dear, I love them, they are exquisite, but the man hours you must have put into them ... Well, it would cost an exorbitant amount to reproduce them, and I would never be able to make a profit, if I set my girls to making them.'

Maddie did not know whether to be overjoyed, or deflated, by her comments. 'I never thought of that. I just wanted to make the best I could. If I made them in my spare time, though?'

'Of course, you could make them as a hobby, but to turn it into a thriving business, you would have to cut corners somewhere.'

The words were a blow to Maddie, who hadn't given that part of the equation any consideration.

'I tell you what,' Mrs Parrot said. 'If you want to see how they sell, I'll put a few of the bandeaux and matching hair accessories in the shop window, and we will wait until someone comes in and see how much they will pay.'

'Is that not dishonest?'

'Dishonest? It's business, girl, and you need to think about that, if it is the way forward for you.' She studied the items once more. 'It will be best to put just a few in the window, so the choice isn't overwhelming. It's possible to lose a sale because the customer cannot make up their mind. Leave it to me to settle on a price. I'll take just ten per cent of the profit, and if you make up a couple of those extravagant hats, we can try and sell those, too, if you like.'

'Really?' Hope sparked within Maddie's chest again, as she touched the delicate whorls made in silk, with pretty pearls nestling inside netting, all of them made with such love and determination. She chose just three of the items, which would match the colours already set out for the coming season, and laid them out alongside them in the window display.

Gnawing at her lip, she tried to decide where to place them, and re-positioned them at least half a dozen times, before rushing out of the shop to see how well they were placed for customer viewing.

Her finest hour was coming, she just knew it, and she wouldn't miss her chance this time.

Chapter Eighteen

1904

At three in the afternoon, the late summer heat was stifling, bringing forth an odour from outside that made Mrs Parrot close the door firmly shut, only to have to open it moments later, as she and the entire staff became bathed in a sheen of sweat. All of the windows were flung open, and the noise from the street competed with the noise of the sewing machines, until Mrs Parrot became quite fractious and retired to the counting house she fondly called the parlour.

Maddie watched the people of the small world where she lived go about their business: selling, buying, courting, rushing here and ambling there, and imagined another solitary evening ahead of her. She sighed. It was her second summer at Mrs Parrot's and although her status had changed radically, her personal life hadn't changed at all. She would have lived in London for two years come the winter, and although she wasn't homesick any more she did feel lonely more often than not. It wasn't right for someone as young and as full of life as herself to be sitting on her own every evening but, sadly, she had no other options.

She would try to finish off the silver and aquamarine series of hats she had been styling, and make herself a proper tea, not just bread and dripping with a hunk of cheese on the side.

She made a mental note to chase up her new contact – a parasol maker. He had agreed to trim parasols in a colour that matched her hats, so she could sell both together, or at least try. The lady she had commissioned to accessorise handbags, according to her latest design and colour, had just left, and a contract had been agreed to their mutual benefit. The velvet embroidered bags and the sturdier, silver mesh bags were ideal for evening wear, and would complement Maddie's latest hair designs for the lady who liked the finer things in life. The window display she had in mind would be fantastic, profits would increase even more, and she thought the time was right to suggest some kind of partnership with Mrs Parrot.

Mrs Parrot was proud of their new enterprise, and had made a lot of money since Maddie had first put her hats and hairpins up for sale. The business of hats was booming more than ever as they became more of a fashion statement than a necessity and Maddie thought she would be amenable to a deal of some sort, especially as Maddie did most of the work.

As her thoughts edged towards putting the kettle on and making a nice pot of tea, the bell chimed over the door. She looked up brightly, expecting to see another dowager trailing a pretty, spoiled girl behind her, intent on using up Mama's allowance for the up and coming season.

Instead, a pair of soft, brown eyes met hers, a lock of silky hair drooping over one eyebrow.

'Daniel!' she cried, so astonished that she totally forgot herself. She covered her cry with a cough, as she took in the face that haunted her nights, unable to believe he really was standing in front of her.

She reached out without thinking, before letting her arms drop to her side as she remembered her promise to Mrs Davenport. Even so, she gazed at him, devouring his clothes, his hair, looks, *everything*. He had grown taller, stronger since she had last seen him, and was more commanding than the Daniel she had left, but he was still the Daniel she fell in love with: the one she still loved.

He took a step towards her, his eyes wary and, unable to stop herself, she pitched forward and he caught her in his arms. She felt the warmth of his body and his arms holding her close and never wanted to let him go.

The smell of his clothes, of his hair – of Daniel, her Daniel, flooded back. She buried her face in the lapels of his coat, breathing him in, as his arms tightened around her shoulders. It seemed that they had both forgotten they had parted acrimoniously, and they remained meshed together for several moments, until a discreet cough alerted them to the presence of Mrs Parrot.

'I wondered what the commotion was about.' She beamed at Daniel. 'Well, young Daniel, I have not seen you for some years. Don't you look the handsome young man about town.'

'Mrs Parrot, sorry to intrude like this. Only, I wanted to see Maddie before I go.'

'How peculiar. I thought you had already gone. We were talking about it just last week.'

'I only found out a few days ago that Madeline lives close to Hetty, who I was visiting. I had no idea she worked here.'

'Hetty lives close by?' Maddie looked from Mrs Parrot to Daniel. And who had been discussing Daniel's whereabouts, exactly? 'And you're leaving? To go where?'

'Africa.'

'Africa! Why?' Thoughts tumbled around in her head. Hetty must have told Daniel that Maddie was in London, and it upset her that she had chosen not to get in touch, but she wouldn't dwell on that thought, because Daniel's appearance made everything better than all right.

Mrs Parrot bustled around the couple, as they took in the measure of each other after so much time. 'So, when are you going away, and what is your trip in aid of again?'

'I am going with the missionaries,' he replied, his gaze fixed on Maddie's face. 'There are parts of the country that suffered greatly in the Boer War, and we hope to restore some kind of faith to the indigenous people, and there are a team of medical practitioners, of which I am one – still in training, of course.'

'Well, I never thought to see you as a physician, but to be a missionary, too.' Mrs Parrot stopped talking as if finally realising that she was surplus to requirements. She waved a hand towards the door. 'Maddie, why don't you take this young man to the Glasshouse café and say your goodbyes in peace? I will be closing up shortly, anyway, as the air is too nauseating today. I would not want any of my clients to have to breathe it in.'

All thoughts of her precious designs disappeared, as Maddie gathered her hat and bag, whilst fixing her gaze on Daniel as if he were an apparition who might disappear if she blinked. Mouthing her thanks to Mrs Parrot as she left, she clanged the door shut and was finally alone with Daniel for the first time in almost two years.

They walked in companionable silence during the short distance to the café, Daniel taking hold of Maddie's hand as naturally as if it were only the other day they'd been a happy couple. They threw sideways glances at each other as if checking that it really was true: they were holding hands in London two years after Maddie upped sticks and disappeared.

They reached the café and Daniel laughed as they were shown to a table and Maddie collapsed into the squishy upholstered chairs. Red plush lamps gave off a soft glow and the chairs lent themselves to sinking into, which Maddie did appreciatively, squeezing his hand as he ordered tea for two from the waitress, who was all curls and ruddy cheeks, as she fussed over them, brandishing a large brown teapot.

Maddie poured milk into cups and asked about his mother and father, safe territory for them both. 'And Hetty? I must confess to being upset that she lives so close to me, and yet has never called into the shop.'

'Don't think that way for one minute. She has only been in London for six months since her marriage, and is tied up with all the complications of becoming the head of the household, a task I don't believe she is relishing.'

'Well, it would be rather lovely to have a friend down here. Would you ask her to contact me, please?'

'I will, when I write. I am leaving tomorrow for Southampton and shan't see her before I go.'

There was so much that was not being said that Maddie finally asked, 'Why on earth are you going to Africa, anyway, and why did you come to see me now?'

'Madeline, I need to tell you …' He sighed heavily and ran his fingers through his hair. 'It is just that …' He faltered again and closed his eyes. 'I needed to get away and my church were sending people to this place. It seemed an ideal opportunity to distance myself from home and further my career without needing mother's approval or financial backing.' He kept his eyes fixed on the table as he spoke. 'Teaming up with an experienced doctor who is heading up the expedition is a great way forward.'

'Not if you die, it isn't.' Maddie shook her head, fear for Daniel making her throat close.

He turned his gaze to Maddie, his eyes earnest and pleading as he reached across the table to grab hold of her hand. 'I want to apologise for everything that happened between us. I was in such a whirlwind of …' He shrugged. 'I should have been stronger.'

Maddie laid her free hand on his wrist. 'It's fine, Daniel, we were very young.'

'We were, and I confess, I was devastated when you left, but you were so determined. I went to see your father – did he say? He seemed as baffled as I was.'

Maddie was unsurprised that his mother had not explained what really happened. She bit her lip with indecision before deciding to tell Daniel what happened. She had no loyalty towards her but she needed to ensure her father kept his job. 'Your mother gave me an ultimatum. She promised to give Dad a job if I left you alone. There was a part of me that was terrified, but I knew it would be better for you.' She shrugged. 'I would never be good enough in your mother's eyes.'

Daniel paled at her words. 'No. You still wanted me when you sent that letter? Oh, God, this is the worst thing.'

'Daniel, do you still want us to be together? If so, I can see a way around it. We don't have to live in the Midlands. In fact, I would rather we didn't.'

Daniel put his head in his hands and groaned. 'When I come back, Maddie, I will sort everything out, I promise.'

Maddie sat up in her chair. 'Sort out what? Has something bad happened?'

His lips were thin and pale with an anger that she couldn't fathom, even as regret tinged his eyes with sadness.

'What is it, please tell me?'

Running his fingers down his face, raking the skin in an agony of indecision, he shook his head, finally saying, 'If you promise to wait for me, Maddie, nothing bad will ever happen to us again.' He paused, took her hand and held on tightly. 'Where I am going is pretty barbaric, infested with rodents and poisonous creatures, and the natives are not always friendly.'

'Then, why on earth are you going there?'

'I need to. I have this urge that I cannot shake off. It's like a calling from God. I cannot stand by and see people suffer.'

'Daniel, your family will suffer, doesn't that count?' she asked, unable to understand his reasoning.

'No, you know it does not. It's a different type of suffering, one that we all have to bear, but if you are there at the end of my journey it will be endurable.'

'You still think of me the same way?' she asked dazed. He had said the words she had dreamed of hearing and her heart sang, but still she needed more.

He leaned closer. 'Madeline, you were mine from the day we met. We both felt the connection. Everything we did together is etched on my mind. Enough time has passed for me to let you go, but I don't seem able to.'

His fingers were warm and real, and she longed for him to touch her as he used to. 'I don't want to be let go, Daniel.' She knew she should be embarrassed by her desires, but she wasn't. She needed him to make her whole again and she would never stop loving him.

Although she saw longing in his eyes, it was clouded by anguish and Maddie didn't know why. One thing she did know, however, was that his thoughts seemed to mirror her own: *Let's take this one chance of being together; it might be our last.*

Neither of them spoke the words, however. Rather, they talked of Maddie's dreams coming to fruition, they talked of Hetty – the new refined Hetty, who adored her handsome husband – and they talked of Daniel's hospital, the one he hoped to fund from rich clients so that he could help the poor.

There was no mention of Finula Atherstone and the possibility that he might never return from Africa. Their day was for the two of them – nothing could intrude.

Eventually, they could linger no longer. The tea was long gone, and neither of them could imagine wanting to eat anything.

'I'll walk you home,' Daniel said, his eyes serious.

Maddie nodded and stood up on instantly trembling legs. She tried to fasten her hat on her head with shaking hands, and Daniel took over as she fumbled unsuccessfully with her hatpin, his eyes levelling with hers the whole time, speaking volumes.

As they left the café, he took her hand and a charge surged through her body, her skin tingling with awareness. They walked towards her tiny room, weaving through the street-sellers warming potatoes and frying sausages, setting up for the evening's trade.

Street urchins were ducking and diving, hoping they might beg or steal enough food to fill their bellies before the night was over, but Maddie barely noticed the activities, lost in her thoughts, unable to contemplate leaving Daniel on the doorstep after everything he'd said.

They reached the alleyway that led to her front door and faced each other, inches apart as the moments ticked by. They each seemed unable to leave the other; their fingers incapable of untwining, and their eyes unable to unlock.

Daniel seemed rooted to the spot, and Maddie could not take the few steps that led to her door and up the stairs to her lonely room. She wanted, *needed*, more than a curt farewell to remember him by.

Wordlessly, she unlocked the door and took him by the hand up the narrow stairs, her heart racing. She knew she should not be alone with him, but she could not be without him. She pushed the door open to her room and stepped aside, allowing him to pass.

He took a decisive stride, glancing at the tiny room, taking in the battered enamel cooker, the cupboard displaying all of her worldly goods, and the small single bed pushed up against the wall. Slowly, he turned to Maddie, placed his hands on her shoulders and gazed into her eyes. His own eyes burned with hunger, and she knew what he was asking: *There will be no turning back from this – are you prepared to accept that?*

The magnitude of the unspoken dialogue made her quiver. The next moment would change her life, and she should mark it with solemnity, but she knew what she was doing. She was going to love Daniel Davenport as if her very life depended on it.

She took a step closer and placed her hands flat on his chest. He closed the gap between them, and she felt the flush of arousal flame instantly in her own body.

'My beautiful Madeline, be mine for this night,' he whispered, before placing one hand behind her head and dipping his face to cover her waiting mouth with his.

They kissed tentatively, Maddie almost forgetting the moves they used to make as timid lovers. However, the kiss deepened, and instead of pulling back, as a younger Maddie might have done, she drew him in tighter and kissed him hard, letting her tongue trace his lips.

His hands encircled her waist, and he drew her over to the tiny bed until she landed softly on top of him. He kissed her and murmured into her hair, as he stroked her arms and her shoulders, as if wanting to touch all of her, to make up for lost time.

His hands circled around her back, and his arms tightened. He wrapped her in his embrace as their hearts thudded together, their breathing shallow and rapid. They held onto each other as if they would never be parted, until their breath steadied, and they slowly discovered each other's bodies, unwrapping the delights each had to offer.

The sensations washing over Maddie were almost too glorious to bear, as she helped him to undo the buttons on her blouse, with shaking fingers. With her breasts freed from their trappings, she gasped at his touch, the intimacy shocking her. Delight, mingled with fear, caused her to tremble, but she wanted more. Anything he offered, she would take.

She knew the rudiments of having sex, but no one had told her that making love would make her feel so alive, so wanton, prepared to do anything and give as much as Daniel wanted.

They slowly found their own rhythm and matched each other's need as they touched each other, exploring and teasing until Maddie cried out in pain and wonder as Daniel entered her.

She clung to him, as he whispered words of love and endearments, whilst an explosion of heat and the most glorious sensations she had ever experienced completely engulfed her. She tried not to cry out, as Daniel gasped and, in the next moment, finally collapsed next to her, sweat sheening his body. He cradled her to his chest immediately, smoothing down her hair and entwining his legs with hers.

'I love you, Madeline Lockett,' he whispered as he held her tight enough for her to believe he would never let her go.

'I love you, Daniel Davenport. I always have and I always will,' she replied solemnly.

They laughed with happiness and enchantment at their discovery: that paradise was simply being in each other's arms. They were soon reaching out for each other once more, giving love as if it was their last night together, which they knew it very well might be.

Finally, exhausted, bathed in a sheen of sweat from the muggy air and their close proximity to one another, they fell asleep satiated and blissfully happy, as the night gently closed around them.

Maddie awoke early, a sixth sense nudging her to consciousness. It took her a moment to remember that she was not alone in her tiny three-foot bed. A rush of happiness was quickly replaced by misery, as the sensation of cool air hit her body and Daniel swung his legs over the side of the bed in preparation for his long journey to Africa.

She kept her eyes closed, sending up a prayer to the same God who had so far ignored everything she had ever asked of him. She knew He was unlikely to grant her one wish, with her having sinned so badly, but there was no one else who could help her right then. If she had prayed hard in her life before, it was nothing to the plea she sent then, to the divine God who had shaped so much of her life.

Finally opening her eyes, she watched Daniel dress. It would be her last memory of him, all she would have to treasure until his return from foreign lands. He moved around the room in the darkness, a gloomy dawn seeping through the gap in the thin curtains, as she watched and prepared to say goodbye.

She willed him with all her might to love her enough to stay, hoping against all odds that he would abandon his plans. If they married as soon as possible, maybe they could be forgiven for what they had done together. She felt a sigh of breath against her cheek and Daniel's cool fingers brushed her cheek. 'Goodbye for now, my love.'

'I love you, Daniel,' she said screwing her eyes tightly shut in case they overflowed and tears didn't stop falling, like in one of the waterfalls she seen in a book at Sunday school.

'I love you, Madeline. Stay safe for me.' She heard the

doorknob turn, felt a whoosh of air and opened her eyes in time to see Daniel slip through the door, silently, pulling it closed behind him.

'No!' The words came out involuntarily and she threw back the covers, panicking, trying to grab her clothes. Giving up, she grabbed her box of letters, and yanked open the door. Rushing out to the street, heedless of her state of undress, she hollered, 'Daniel, wait.'

He turned around startled, as she ran up to him, breathless and wearing only her nightdress.

'Take these.' She pulled a handful of her love letters from out of her precious box and thrust them at him.

He grabbed them automatically, misery clearly etched on his drawn face. 'What are they?' he asked.

'My letters to you. Keep them as close as I will hold you in my heart. Take care, my love, and come back to me.'

'Oh, Maddie.' He forced out the strangled words as he wrapped his arms around her, murmuring into her hair, 'Madeline, my love, I can't bear to do this to you ... to us. If there was a way out of this mess ...'

'Hush, just make sure you come back to me.' They swayed as one as they hugged, until finally Daniel loosened his hold, and they stared wordlessly at each other, tears glistening in both of their eyes.

'I will, I promise.' He snatched briefly at her hand once more, and her fingertips trailed across his palm, before he slowly turned and walked briskly away.

She stood shivering in the cold breeze, her thin nightdress billowing out watching him leave. A few early risers gawked at her with interest, and she turned on her bare feet, the damp cold of the pavement barely registering.

In the past twelve hours, she had changed irrevocably. Her life would never be the same again, not until Daniel returned to claim her as his wife.

Chapter Nineteen

The pain of finding and then losing Daniel was so unexpected, so numbing and traumatising, that Maddie believed herself to be ill. She dragged herself to work, her eyes red-rimmed from crying and her body aching from lack of sleep. Every day, her steps quickened as she neared her home, hoping to see Daniel, his gentle smile lighting up for her, ready and waiting to sweep her into his arms.

He never was.

Each evening, she would climb the steps to her lonely room with heavy footsteps and a heavier heart, despair replacing the optimism she had carried around since the night she felt she had finally become a woman.

Slowly, the act of love that she thought had sealed their relationship began to seem tawdry, and she wondered if she had been wrong to assume it had meant the same to Daniel. He was a decent man, and he would have realised what it meant to Maddie, surely? But the doubt had crept in and it was hard to stay positive with nothing but dreams and memories to draw on. She relived the night in every detail over and over, her body aching for him, the torture of being without him bruising her heart. She tried to remember if he had promised her anything, apart from his love, and slowly her supposed grasp of the situation blurred as fact and fiction confused her.

Yet the weeks flew by, regardless of her misery, and she found to her surprise, that customers were flocking to pay good money for her hats and hair decorations. They flew off the shelves as quickly as she sewed them. The word was well and truly out that the little boutique in a small back road in Shoreditch was the place to go if you wanted to be seen to be fashionable. It was just a shame that her earlier enthusiasm had waned since Daniel's departure from England.

'Maddie, I'd like a word, if you have a moment,' Mrs Parrot said as they closed up one Friday.

Panic immediately set in, and Maddie, expecting the worst as usual, turned fearful eyes to Mrs Parrot.

'Don't look so worried, love, I don't bite. You should know me by now.'

It was true, she was shrewd and canny – such traits were necessary to survive in business – but she was not mean-minded, or spiteful.

She invited Maddie into the back room, where she kept her ledgers and invoices and they sat down. 'I have some good news. Someone from Lawley's has been in touch, offering to sell your hats and hairpins in their store.'

'Really?' Maddie drew in a breath. 'That's wonderful.'

Mrs Parrot held up a warning hand. 'But, and it is a big but, they want them in batches of one hundred at a time.'

Maddie didn't blink. Suddenly there was a reason to be excited about life again. She could do it. She *would* do it.

'I know what you're thinking, Maddie. I have seen your determination, but you cannot do a proper day's work here *and* spend all night working, too. You could manage for a short while, of course, but not for long. It would make you ill and miserable.'

Maddie chewed her lip, wondering if it were possible to be more ill or more miserable than she already was. She knew Mrs Parrot was right, but she couldn't let such an opportunity pass her by. 'I could draft in some help, maybe?'

'And eat into your profit? You could, but I do have an alternative suggestion. You could set up your business here for a cut of the takings. I'd take on another dressmaker to replace you and we could see how it goes.'

Maddie took a minute to think about it. It sounded like a fair proposition and she could think of no better way around the problem. She nodded in acceptance. Now would be the time to get Florence down to London, if she still wanted to come. She smiled thinking of Florence's delight when she told her the news. 'I think I have just the girl, if you trust my judgement.'

'Of course I do. Excellent. Go and talk to her immediately.'

'I will, but she lives in Stoke, so I would have to send for her which might prove difficult. I thought that perhaps I could go back for a visit and bring her back with me.' She wondered briefly if Mrs Davenport would have a problem with that, but decided not, especially as Daniel was God knows where, rather than in Stokeville, being comforted by the suffocating arms of his mother.

'Yes, do. You deserve a break, and you could start your new enterprise feeling refreshed.'

Maddie grinned as she nodded her agreement. She was going home. Why hadn't she done so before?

With the upcoming journey fixed in her mind, she suddenly couldn't wait to leave and was already thinking of the treats she could take home with her; things that Tom and her father had never seen before. It would be a trip to remember, that was for sure. Jane would have a soft shawl from the market and her brother and Jimmy would have toffees in a tin with a picture of the palace on the front. She wondered what her father would make of eel pie, smiling as she planned her journey. Finally, finally, she was going home.

Chapter Twenty

Maddie breathed in the fetid air of her hometown, almost embracing the grime and asphyxiating soot in a perverse way: she was home.

She wasn't surprised to find the front door unlocked as she let herself in, running her fingertips over the worn furniture, breathing in the familiar scent that brought back so many memories. Unexpected tears pricked at her eyes as she filled the kettle and placed it on the old stove top, an action that she'd done so automatically for so many years. She had missed her family so much that she wondered how she had ever had the courage to leave. Tom's clothes and paraphernalia littered the floor of her room, when she carried her bag up. Tutting, she folded up his clothes and tidied the room, lingering for far longer than she needed. Once back downstairs, she realised there was nothing much she could do whilst she waited for Tom and her father to come home. It was a strange feeling for one used to cramming in all of the tasks she had to complete in less time than she had.

She decided to see if Jane was home. 'Yoo-hoo!' she called, rattling the doorknob and nudging the door open.

A terrible mess and a foul stench greeted her, making her gag. She reeled backwards and pushed the front door open wider, leaving it swinging. 'Jane? Mr Jones?' she called, as she stepped on the stairs, unsure whether to venture up to the top.

'Maddie? Maddie, is it really you?' The voice that greeted her was thin and reedy and sounded like it belonged to an old lady.

'Jane? Can I come up?'

''Course you can. I'm in Dad's old room.'

Maddie wondered why Jane was in her father's bedroom, when Mr Jones had occupied the larger of the two rooms for as long as Maddie had known them. She tiptoed in, fearful of what she might see.

Jane was lying in the big bed, looking as fragile as a baby bird, in the middle of a nest of grey, messy blankets.

She rushed over to her. 'Jane, how long have you been like this?'

Jane set up a bout of coughing, as she tried to push herself upright, but failed. 'I'm bad, Maddie, but I don't want to bother no one.'

'Where is your dad?'

'Me dad?' Jane's cough turned into a gasping wheeze, and she dragged out a handkerchief, soiled and grey, from the depths of her nightdress. She wiped it across her mouth. 'Don't worry, it's not contagious. It's just the Potters bad luck.'

'I don't care what it is. Why is no one looking after you?'

'There is no one. Me dad's been gone this last eight months. Did no one tell you? Jimmy's had to go and live at me auntie's, over in Bentilee. I suppose I've let things slide a bit.'

'Jane, it's not your fault. Can't you get out of bed?'

'No, I can't seem to rally like I used to. I can barely breathe, truth be told. It scares me, but there's nowt I can do about it.'

'You need help. There must be someone.'

'I can't afford medicine, Maddie. We didn't keep up with our Society payments, so no one'll come. Don't worry about me, duck, I'm pretty much done for.'

'No, Jane. I'll get someone. There must be someone.' Jane's hollowed cheeks and sunken eyes were a fright to behold, and it broke Maddie's heart. 'I'm going to make you some soup, and then I'm going to take out your rubbish and tidy up. I'll get a bowl of hot water with some eucalyptus oil in to help you breathe. We're going to make you better.' She squeezed the frail hand lying on top of the bedcovers.

'Bless you, Maddie, but you really don't have time for this. Go and see your dad and Tom. That's what you've come home for, isn't it?'

'I will, but I'm not leaving until you're better.'

She hurried back to her own house, to see if there were enough vegetables to make Jane some soup, and was pleased to find the cupboards well stocked. She set about boiling some potatoes and cabbage, before returning to Jane's house, taking out the rubbish and opening the windows to dispel the foul odour.

She lit the stove, which felt as if it hadn't been warm for some time, swept the greasy floor, and then scrubbed it with a big brush and a bucket of soapy water. She filled the large kettle to boil water to wash Jane's bedclothes, and to make her a hot drink.

She was angry with her neighbours and her father for not realising Jane had taken to her bed, but then everyone was so busy these days. There was always too much to do in one day, as it was.

She hurried home once more, to check on the soup. There was a lump of suet in the larder, and she mixed it with flour to make dumplings, praying that Jane could keep such food down. The potatoes and cabbage were mashed and thickened with a little cornstarch and gravy browning and set over the heat once more for the dumplings to cook.

As she poured the soup into a jug to take to Jane, she was suddenly overcome with dizziness and sat down with a thump on her old chair by the table. 'Oh, no, don't let me be ill,' she said into the air. She breathed slowly, and when the dizziness didn't abate, she rested her head in her hands for a few minutes.

The sound of the door latch lifting came from the back door, and Maddie raised her head weakly, a sudden nausea adding to the dizziness.

'Maddie, love, are you all right?' Her father rushed to her side, towering over her. 'What's happened?'

'Dad. It's nothing. I'm fine.' She jumped up, forgetting her dizziness, delighted to finally see her father.

'Why are you here, then? Come to buy that house, have you?'

She raised a weak smile. 'Not yet, Dad, but I haven't forgotten about it. I'm just home for a short while.' She wrapped her arms around her father, taking comfort from his bulk and unwilling to let him go. Although they didn't normally hug she was so happy to see him that she didn't care. Her father slowly enclosed his arms around his daughter in return, and they embraced, whilst Maddie inhaled the comforting smell that was home.

Quickly recalling her duties, she let go of her father. 'I've made soup. Do you want some? I can put some more dumplings in. I'm just sorting some out for Jane. Did you know she was right bad again?'

'I haven't thought about her, if I'm honest. I go out in the dark and don't get home 'til it's dark most days. Sorry, love, I should 'ave, especially with Bert being gone.'

'It doesn't matter. I'm going to make her better.' She sat down again as a bone-numbing fatigue washed over her. 'I think I'd better get myself some soup, too. I feel quite weak.' She wiped sweat from her brow. 'I'll just take this to Jane first. I won't be long.'

'Are you sure nothing's wrong, love?' His eyes softened, and his words brought a lump to Maddie's throat.

She smiled, fighting back tears. 'No, Dad, everything is very right. I'll tell you all about it, once I've sorted out Jane. Where's Tom?'

'He goes to Mr Brassington's, the newsagent's, after school. They give him his tea, in return for helping out a bit, now Iris's arthritis is so bad. It suits us both 'cause Tom doesn't have to sit on his own all evening, now Jimmy's got 'imself a little job.'

Maddie's heart contracted with love and guilt, and a longing to see her younger brother. She wished she could tell her father why she'd had to leave home, but then both of them would feel guilty. Instead, she brightened, 'I'll fetch him from the shop, shall I?'

'Yes, good idea, but have some of this soup 'fore you go. You look a bit peaky.'

Maddie dutifully ate some soup before washing up the dishes, falling back into her old routine without thinking. She ladled some out for Jane, and spent a few minutes with her, watching her eat, promising to return later.

Returning to Tom's room, she unpacked her small suitcase and chose a spotted cotton day dress to meet Tom, with tiny buttons on the cuffs and a scalloped hemline that swished as she walked. She fixed one of her best bonnets over her long hair, pushing the loose strands inside, and smoothed it down. Her ensemble was probably a bit too grand to walk down to the corner shop, but she wanted to show everyone that she was doing well, and her father should be proud of her.

Tom was leaving the shop with a cheery wave, just as she arrived, and she ran up to him, almost sweeping him off his feet.

'Maddie, is it really you?' His face was a picture of happiness, and she hugged him tightly, resting her cheek against his unruly hair. He had grown tall, but was still as thin as a lathe, and his blond hair had darkened. She couldn't take her eyes off his dear face, which had matured so much since she'd last seen him.

As they walked side by side, she ruffled his hair and touched his cheek, until he finally batted her away. Even so, he looked happy to see her, and his eyes seemed to be pleading when he asked, 'Are you home for good?'

She hated to hear the reproach in his question and see the hurt in his eyes. 'Not yet, Tom.'

'You moved away because we're poor, that's what Mrs Brassington said. She said you always did think you were better than us, and you reached too high and toppled off your pedestal.'

'Did she now?' Maddie cared little for what Mrs Brassington thought, however, she did care about what her brother and father thought, and after a moment's pondering, she decided to tell Tom the truth. 'Tom, do you remember Daniel?'

'Yes, he saved our lives.'

'He did.' She sighed. She had forgotten that she had to thank him for their lives in the turbulence he had left in his wake. 'I had to leave because of him,' she continued, hoping that would be enough. 'But when I come home, I will have enough money to buy a big house in the countryside for all of us to live in.'

'Did Daniel not love you any more?'

Maddie smiled. Tom knew more than she had realised. 'Daniel will come back to me soon.' She crossed her fingers, praying that she was right.

Tom nodded. He looked as if he'd lost interest, anyway, and she spent the rest of the journey in a reflective silence, kicking at stray leaves and stones.

A shadow fell across her path, and she tried to step aside. 'Excuse me.'

The man, covered in grime from head to foot, stood in front of her, blocking her way. He grinned and lifted his cap. 'Well, now, it's been a while.'

'Edward ...' she stammered, recognising the brown eyes fastened on hers and still full of longing after all that time. 'How are you?'

'Maddie Lockett, you came back and didn't let me know you were coming.' His voice belied his weary demeanour, as if he was suddenly pumped with a new zest for life.

'Yes, but it's just for a short while, and totally unexpected.' The fear that had jumped in her chest abated. Edward would do her no harm. 'But why are you working down the pit?' The unmistakeable garb of the pit was obvious, as was his soot-covered hands and face.

'More money, duck. Me mum's on her own now, and there's six of us kids living at home.'

'Oh, I'm sorry to hear that.' She didn't like to ask whether his father had died or just absconded, as so many men did, when the daily workload and cacophony of children became too much to bear. 'Well, it's lovely to see you.' She tried to put some enthusiasm into her voice, but she could really have done without him, right there and then.

'You, too. I couldn't believe it when I came to call for you, and you'd disappeared that Sunday. I wondered if it was something I said.' He laughed, but she detected genuine hurt in his voice.

'No, Edward, I told you in a letter. It was a spur of the moment thing. I went to make my fortune.'

Edward fell into step with her as if it was only yesterday that they had spoken. 'I reckoned it was to do with your dad losing 'is job, but I was damned if I could work out what.'

She turned to him, noting the sorrowful smile. The whites of his eyes and his teeth were almost luminous in his dusty face, but he seemed unfazed by being so filthy.

'I can see you looking at me in this state, Maddie, but I scrub up good. Never let it get deep in me skin and me nails. An' it's not really dirt, you know. Washes off in seconds.'

'Ah, that's good to know.'

'I'm just tellin' you, you know, in case you were thinking of backing out of that walk with me – like you said you would.'

Maddie laughed. 'That was two years ago.'

'You sayin' you're a girl as doesn't keep her promises?'

Maddie grinned at him. 'Edward … you are shameless.'

'So, you'll come? We can make an afternoon of it. Go to the park and along the canal with a picnic.'

Maddie sighed. She really hoped Edward was just being friendly, and he was very endearing. It wouldn't hurt, she thought. She could catch up with all the gossip at the same time. She inclined her head. 'Yes, thank you, if I can spare the time. I am rather busy.'

'Not too busy to take a walk with me, I am certain of it.' He smiled cheekily. 'Sunday, after church?'

'All right … fine.' Glancing up, she realised they had reached her door now, and she wondered how they had managed it so swiftly. 'My, that was quick,' she said.

'Good conversation, see.'

'All right, Edward, I get the picture. I shall see you on Sunday.'

'You certainly will.' He leaned over and kissed her on the cheek, then stepped back to see the effect it had.

Maddie instinctively scrubbed at her cheek, belatedly realising Edward was watching her.

'Sorry, I forgot myself for a moment. But I can't say I wouldn't do it again.' With that parting shot, he turned and walked away.

She scrubbed at her cheek some more, as soon as he disappeared. However, it wasn't the kiss that bothered her, but rather, the thought of him transferring coal dust to her face. She felt almost violated, as if he was branding her as one of his sort. And she had no intention of breathing in the suffocating air she was obliged to breathe in for any longer than was necessary.

She shook her head. She would never be part of the twilight world she had lived in again: washing clothes that became grubby whilst drying on the line, the taste of pottery dust constantly on her lips and the sunlight being gobbled up by the soot that had no shame when it came to a fight for the winner of the daylight hours.

Daniel might well be out of her life, but going for a coal miner would never be part of her plan, regardless of how friendly and endearing he was.

Chapter Twenty-One

Jane was on the mend, it seemed. At least, she was out of bed and pottering around, although she still found it hard to breathe and was stick thin. Maddie didn't think she would be capable of working for some time yet, and decided she would ask her father if he would take her in. She could at least do the housekeeping and cook, and her father could keep an eye on her health. Jane had fallen behind with her rent, due to not working, so the rent man would be after her, too.

Although it seemed the best solution, Maddie was unsure what her father would say.

In the meantime, Maddie visited Florence with the job offer. Florence was ecstatic at the chance of moving out from her tiny room above the local pub, where the creepy landlord made her fear for her chastity. She flung her arms around her old friend, her eyes gleaming. 'I knew you'd come back for me, one day, Maddie, I just knew it. Mrs Howlett is on about retiring, so it's perfect timing. But you're here for a while, are you? We can spend some time together?'

'I am here for a little while – until my neighbour is back on her feet, anyway,' Maddie answered, although in truth, she was fighting the urge to return to London sooner rather than later. She couldn't quite place why, as it was lovely to be with her father and Tom, but a sense of unease crept over her whenever she had a quiet moment. It might have been the vague worry that the pot-banks and the dust would draw her back into its grubby fold if she lingered too long. However, she also felt stifled and vaguely scared, possibly because Edward appeared to be courting her in earnest. She knew she was in a vulnerable state emotionally, and worried that she would succumb to his advances through loneliness and the need to be wanted. She had already proved she was weak in matters of the flesh, and the knowledge made her determined to keep her distance.

Even so, she had arranged to meet Edward at the park in Hanley, as a brass band was playing that afternoon, and was regretting the decision, somewhat, although she told herself it was just an innocent walk. After baking a fruitcake, which she cut in half and saved half for later, she headed out. She expected to see Edward lolling against the great tree, where most people waited to meet their friends, but he was nowhere to be seen. As the band started playing, she glanced over toward where the seats had begun to fill up in front of the bandstand, and to her surprise, she spotted Edward seated at the back of the bandstand, blowing on a brass cornet for all his worth.

Seats had been arranged in rows opposite the bandstand, and Maddie took one in the front row, giving Edward a little wave, as he looked out at the gathering crowd. He seemed inordinately pleased when he saw her, and she wished she could be the simple young girl Edward thought she was: excited to be walking out with a boy for the day.

However, she was content for the moment, or at least as happy as was possible, given what had transpired with Daniel – which, in other words, made her just one step short of miserable. Whilst she tried to warm to the idea of spending the day with Edward, her heart wasn't in it. How could it be, when she just wanted to hide away, for shame of what she and Daniel had done together, and lick the wounds that had cut deep? Even though she hadn't heard from Daniel, she still longed for him, and prayed that he would come back to her.

Sighing, she fixed her gaze on Edward once more, determined not to let him down in public, if nothing else.

It quickly became obvious that he had mentioned Maddie to his mother, who clapped madly, twisting her bulk around to grin at Maddie, as Edward stood up to play a solo. Strains of a mostly forgotten song took her back to an earlier time in her life, when her parents had danced at the church hall on a Friday, and returned home holding hands and laughing, as her father serenaded her mother with a surprisingly melodic voice. Maddie used to hug her knees to her chest, happy for her parents, whilst Tom crawled on the floor under her watchful eye. They were simple days, when even the poverty of their life had misted over with time, making her memories almost perfect.

Edward sauntered over to her, puffed up with pride at his achievement, bringing her back to the present. 'Bet you didn't know I could hold a tune like that, did you?'

'I recall that you used to lead the choir at Sunday school, so it's not a great leap of faith.' She felt mean, when his face fell. It wasn't his fault that she was unhappy, and she quickly praised him, instead. 'But what a performance. You did your mum proud, and it was lovely to hear you play.'

He grinned, his good humour restored as he took her hand. 'Come on, it's a wonderful day. I've got us a packed lunch. We'll have a lovely time.'

She smiled and wished it were true. The day was actually rather cloudy and the mild autumn weather was already turning wintry and a chill filled the air, but the time passed pleasantly enough as they strolled along the canal, swigging from a bottle of cold tea. But it just did not feel the same as being with Daniel, and Maddie experienced a twinge of guilt, knowing that Daniel might not like it.

They stopped by a lock to eat sandwiches and cake, and Edward read out the names of the barges that passed by. He seemed to know many of the people from farther up north, giving a cheery wave, and helping more than a few of the occupants to push the heavy lock gates open.

It was a pleasant enough way to pass the time, even though Maddie froze, when Edward threw his arm around her shoulders casually, and then trailed his arm to her waist. He must have picked up on her reticence towards him, as he didn't try to kiss her again, which reassured her slightly.

He seemed to have a great knowledge about the barges and their destinations, and was voluble and animated when he spoke of the boat trips that sailed up and down the country. Although the afternoon turned chilly, they lingered on a bench, watching the ducks swimming, knowing that soon they would have to return to their world of dust and grime.

Just as they were about to leave, Edward turned to Maddie and took her hand. 'Maddie, you can tell me to shut it, if you want, but we've known each other for most of our lives, haven't we?' He tugged at his collar and ran his hand around the back of his neck, his eyes having trouble focussing on Maddie's face. 'I'll just come out with it, shall I?' He nodded as if encouraging her to agree with him.

Maddie felt her eyes growing round in horror, but Edward continued.

'I always thought you were the one for me, and I was just biding me time, to be honest. But the one time I actually managed to speak to you, you disappeared. I was that upset, you wouldn't believe it. An' God knows, I'm so glad I've had another chance to tell you how I feel.'

Maddie thought it unlikely that God would want such a good Christian boy as Edward to associate with the likes of her and felt it prudent to mention Daniel, but when she opened her mouth to speak, he held up his hand to silence her.

'No, let me say me piece, love. I know sommat's gone on with you and another bloke, before me, and I'm not interested in hearing the gory details.'

Maddie bit her lip. He couldn't possibly know the half of it, and surely wouldn't want anything more to do with her, if he found out. But no one would find out – ever. Of that, she was determined.

'I'm not saying I expect us to be a couple yet, or owt like that. I'm just saying, give it a chance, eh?' He took her other hand and pressed their hands together as if they were praying. The hope in his eyes was pitiful. 'Will you, Maddie?'

She rested her head on the back of the bench as she tried to think of an evasive answer that would not destroy him. 'Edward, I don't even live here any longer. I live in London.'

'I know that, and here's the best bit. I've been offered a job on the barges. One of the lads has put in a good word for me. I know a lot of people say the trains will take over carting all our wares down to London and maybe they will, but not for years, I reckon. So I'll be pretty secure – job wise, you know.'

Maddie nodded. What did that have to do with her living in London?

Edward's eyes shone. 'I can get on any canal boat that is passing your way, as my cargo is mostly china heading to London. There's a big market for the better stuff nowadays, and the barges are miles cheaper than the train.'

'Edward, I'm flattered that you've thought this through, but I'm intending to run my own business, and I will not allow anything to get in the way of that.'

Relief, and maybe a touch of amusement, flooded Edward's eyes. 'I'm not the sort to chain you to the kitchen sink, Maddie. We're not in the Dark Ages any more. And I'm not rushing you, at all.' He seemed to inspect Maddie's face. 'Are you alright? You've come over all pale.'

'I just feel sick again. It has been happening a bit recently, whenever I've eaten. I'm sure it will pass, if we just sit here for a minute, or two. It must be something I have picked up.'

Edward patted her hand and threw his arm about her shoulder once more, pulling her to his chest as if she had just agreed to his proposition. Resting her head on his shoulder, she fought the nausea, grateful to have someone to lean on, until a steady breeze chilled them into movement. She shivered, and Edward stood up, stiff legged as he pulled Maddie to her feet. He rubbed at his knees.

'Hope I don't get arthritis as bad as me dad. It's all that

bending in the tunnels and the cold, I imagine. Still, soon be saying goodbye to all of that, I hope, an' I can start a new life on the barges an' coming down to London.'

Maddie smiled, although panic flooded her. She wanted to remind him that she had not agreed to anything, but it seemed churlish when he had been so sweet to her.

They walked back down the towpath in silence, each lost in their thoughts, until they arrived at the end of her road.

'Thanks for today. You've made me very happy,' Edward said, before taking his leave of her.

Maddie blinked in confusion, as he trudged down the street, wondering how easily happiness came to him. His mind appeared made up over his new job though, she just wasn't sure where she fitted into it all. She should have mentioned Daniel at some point, but it was done now.

Longing to sit down for a cup of tea, but knowing she had jobs to do, she diverted to Jane's house, tapping lightly on her front door before letting herself in with a cheery, 'Yoo-hoo.'

Jane was up and about, and there was colour in her cheeks and a ready smile on her face when she saw her visitor. It gladdened Maddie's heart that her friend had improved so much. 'Jane, you look so much better.'

'I know. I've rallied once more, thanks to you. I'm even cooking myself some tea. I can add some more potatoes, if you're stopping.'

'No, love. I have got to get on and cook for our Tom and Dad. I was going to ask if you wanted to have a room at Dad's, but you're looking so much like your old self again, I'm not sure you'll need to.'

'Nah, he won't want me mithering him, not when he's got Dolly coming around more times than not.'

'Dolly from his old works?'

'Yes, didn't you know? Seems she missed him more than she thought, once he moved to Blurton. I'm sorry, have I shocked you? I thought you would have known.'

'Yes, no. You're right. I should have known, but then, if Dad chose not to tell me, how would I?'

'Sit down a minute, and I'll make you a cuppa. You look white as a sheet. Not our sheets, you understand, they'll never be white.' She chuckled to herself as she busied with cups and hot water, before putting her hand to the small of her back, stretching. She rubbed at her abdomen. 'Not everything about being well again is good.'

'What's wrong?' Maddie stood up ready for another onslaught of ailments, but Jane shooed her away, wafting her teacloth in front of her. 'I'm fine. It is just me monthlies have returned with a vengeance. I've always been erratic, on account of me bad health, I guess.'

Maddie nodded, a fixed smile on her face, but Jane's words were suddenly like claws scratching at something in her memory. She gaped at Jane, her face a petrified rictus of realisation as her knees buckled. She toppled backwards into the chair she had pushed herself out of just seconds before.

'What is it?' Jane's words were like a distant echo, as her consciousness almost left her.

No, no. Her monthlies! The sickness swamped her again, as her mind raced in panic. She mustn't show her feelings. 'I just need that cuppa, Jane. I'm fine.'

'Been overworking yourself, probably. You'll be glad to get back to London at this rate.'

'Hmm? Yes, I suppose,' she replied, barely listening.

Jane placed a cup of tea in front of her and prattled on, but Maddie could not take a word in.

Picking up the cup with shaking hands, she tried to think through dates and remember exactly when she had lain with Daniel. She shook her head.

No, no, this can't be happening.

However, deep down, she knew that it already had. That was why she felt sick and dizzy. How could she have missed the signs?

Dear God, what would become of her – of them both?

She excused herself from Jane's house, promising to drop by later, even though her thoughts were in disarray. Daniel's baby, a real baby, inside her. How could she deal with that? The thought terrified her.

She leant against the wall, for fear of fainting.

What was she to do? What would become of her?

Her father would be so ashamed. She couldn't tell him, but she must tell Daniel. She needed to find him, and he would take care of her, like he promised.

The fear receded slightly. Everything would be fine. Daniel would marry her, and they would cope.

Her breathing steadied as she made it indoors, before dropping once more into her old familiar chair by the table. She put her head in her hands as a queasiness washed over her again. It seemed worse, somehow, since realising the cause of it. She put her hands to her belly, closing her eyes once more, willing the baby to disappear.

Time passed, and she didn't move. She looked out at the sky and noticed the evening drawing in, but still felt unable to do more than lift her head. Finally, she heard the door scrape open and her father's boots clatter on the tiles as he threw off his coat.

She came out of her dreamy state of denial, knowing she must behave as if everything was normal. Even if nothing would ever be the same again. She was almost twelve weeks pregnant, and although she knew little of such things, her body had already started to thicken around the waist and it was very probable that the baby would start showing very soon.

The next morning, Maddie was up early, making porridge for her father, but as soon as he left, she hurried over to Florence's, hoping to catch her before she left for work. She was in luck, as she caught her just as she rounded the street on her way to the tram.

'Oh, I'm so glad I've caught you, Florence. I have to head back to London immediately, but I promise to send for you as soon as I can.' Registering the disappointment on her friend's face, she hurried on. 'Things have changed a bit, but it's only a small setback. I'll send you a letter with the train fare, as soon as I am sorted out.'

Florence looked as if she was about to cry as she grasped Maddie's arm. 'Don't leave me here. I promise I'll be a good worker.'

'I'm not leaving you, Flo. Hand your notice in for a month's time. We don't want to upset Mrs Howlett though, so if you can, try not to tell her that you're coming to work for me.'

Florence seemed a bit dazed, so Maddie added, 'Do you understand?'

'Yes, Maddie, but I don't understand why you won't take me with you right now,' she said, her voice rising to a wail.

Maddie briefly hugged her. 'I know, love, but it will work out, trust me.'

Nodding, Florence gave her a wonky smile and shrugged her frayed knapsack onto her shoulder. She turned around once, as if checking that she was not being tricked, before heading down the road.

Maddie waved, envying her innocence and trusting nature and wondering what happened in her home life that made her so stricken at the thought of having to stay there. She hoped Florence never had cause to reconsider the trust she put in her.

Hurrying back to the house, she sent Tom off to school with a huge breakfast and the biggest hug she had ever given him. She propped the note she had written the night before on her dad's spare pair of spectacles, touching them lightly, as if she could gain courage from them. A lump formed in her throat as she took one last look at the house that was home. 'I am so sorry, Mum,' she whispered, before slamming the front door.

Sighing with relief that she had managed to flee so easily, Maddie threw her bag onto the seat next to her on the bus and, resting her heavy eyes, sank into the relative plushness of the seat. She was worn out from lying awake, worrying, for most of the night, but at least she could deal with everything on her own terms, without bringing shame on her father.

Fighting off the sickness she was becoming used to, she ate some dry bread, as the bus rattled along to Birmingham, where she would catch the train and could finally relax.

She had made a decision *and* had a backup plan, and she whispered it to her unborn baby. 'It will be all right. I know it will.' She closed her eyes once they had left all signs of the smoky towns, and the train gently rocked them both to sleep.

Chapter Twenty-Two

Unaccountable nerves bubbled under the surface as Maddie smoothed cold cream on her hands and selected another handmade dress in red velvet. After pushing two matching hair clips into her hair, she slipped on the leather shoes that she had bought for Hetty's party all that time ago, noting that they looked quite shabby, even with regular Army and Navy blacking polish. She made a note to buy some more when she had time.

She took out Hetty's calling card that she had secured from Mrs Parrott and checked the address, biting her lip. It was now, or never. She took one last look in her mirror checking there was no outward sign of the baby that refused to relinquish its hold on her, and after smoothing down her dress, she swept out of the door with a refusal to retreat, much as she wanted to.

The street where Hetty lived was much grander than she had imagined. The houses practically touched the sky, and tall poplar trees waved in the breeze. An impressive black car was parked outside, and she touched it in awe. She didn't know anyone who had a car, although she knew some of Mrs Parrot's clients arrived in such contraptions.

Taking a deep breath, she stepped onto the driveway, faltering once more as she stared at the imposing building. Surely, what stood before her wasn't just one house? If it were, Hetty's husband must have been seriously rich.

She rapped on the door using the heavy brass knocker, bypassing a large wreath, made with fir cones and various bits of greenery, hanging on the door. It made her realise that Christmas was fast approaching and she had no plans for it. It made her sad and she longed for Daniel's arms around her to reassure her that they had the rest of their lives together.

A maid answered the door bringing her back to reality, dropping a curtsey and making Maddie smile. She was escorted through to the sitting room passing huge urns filled with more leaves and evergreen branches mixed in with white lilies standing on the marbled floor of the hallway.

All Maddie hoped was that Hetty was still the same sweet girl she used to be, in spite of the trappings she had acquired, along with her fine husband.

Hetty was already seated when the maid pushed open the door to the drawing room. Her attire was muted yet elegant, her hair swept up into a coiffure.

Maddie couldn't help but smile at the transformation, as she held out her hand ready to shake Hetty's.

However, Hetty leaped up and threw herself at her old friend. 'Oh, my dear, it is so wonderful to see you.' She drew Maddie into the light. 'Let me see how you have fared since we last met,' she said, cupping her hands around her friend's cheeks. 'I do believe you might be as pretty as me now. How extraordinary.' A wide grin showed that she was joking.

Maddie relaxed. She was the same old Hetty; it would be fine. 'Your house is so beautiful, Hetty. You must love living here.'

Hetty's smile faded. 'I do. I really do.'

Hetty sounded almost as if she was convincing herself of the fact, and Maddie detected the faint whiff of wistfulness. Maddie let it pass as she sat down and peeled off her gloves.

'So, tell me all about it,' Hetty continued. 'You are still making dresses, I believe. Mrs Parrot told me all about the life you lead.' Hetty leaned forward in her chair eagerly. 'It sounds so exciting.'

'Exciting?' Silently alarmed by Hetty's words, she hoped Mrs Parrot had not been indiscreet. 'I wouldn't say so.'

The door opened, and the maid appeared again, burdened down with crockery and food held aloft on a big silver tray.

When she set the tray down, Maddie gawped at the huge

selection of sandwiches and cakes sitting next to a large pot of tea.

Hetty glanced up at the maid. 'Thank you, most kind.' She turned to Maddie. 'I hope you don't mind. I took the liberty of ordering high tea.'

'Not at all, but are you feeding half the street?' Her stomach rumbled and roiled as she took in the cream patisseries and tartlets, reminding her that the main reason for the visit was to find out the whereabouts of Daniel. But still, she could take her time and enjoy the visit. She inclined her head, determined to be as refined as Hetty. 'Most gracious.' She grinned, as Hetty looked up sharply. 'I am just copying you, Hetty. Can you not tell I have turned into a lady since you last saw me?'

'Believe me, you are more of a lady than any of the hoity-toity madams I have to deal with down here.' She sighed as she lifted the teapot and began pouring.

'Is your life not perfect now, though? You have a dashing husband, and a lovely house.'

'Dashing, he is, indeed. Dashing here, there, and everywhere. When he is at home, his mama has him running around after her all of the time. His father is dead, as you may know, and his mama seems to forget he is now a married man. He has been away almost half of the year, too.' She sighed and clutched Maddie's hands. 'I am so hoping we can renew our friendship. Mother appears to have forgotten all about you, and whilst we are down here, we can do as we please.'

'Indeed, we can.' She was warming to the idea, but she needed to get hold of Daniel first. She sipped her tea and eyed the cakes warily, wondering how soon she could mention Hetty's brother. 'Don't you have a circle of friends to call upon?'

Hetty's eyes looked troubled once more. 'They are not real friends, I'm afraid. They pretend to be, up until the Gravestocks are out of earshot, and then they just ignore me. I don't think I am fashionable enough, but they want to stay connected to the family. I also think a few of them are a little jealous that Samuel chose me to be his wife.'

'Oh, Hetty, I am sorry to hear that. I thought your life would be a whirl of socialising and fun.' She patted her friend's hand, but Hetty didn't smile. Again, she tried to lighten the mood. 'Do you still pull your funny face?'

Hetty obliged by pulling her eyes and mouth down with her fingers, laughing as she did so, but her features quickly turned back to one of sadness. 'I don't have anyone to pull my funny face for, most of the time.' She gazed out of the window and said quietly, 'I don't know when I am going to have babies and become a proper family with Samuel.'

Maddie's composure stuttered a bit at the mention of babies, and she was horrified to see tears pool in Hetty's eyes. 'It's early days, yet, Hetty. You have your whole life together. It will happen, I'm sure.'

Hetty didn't reply, but took out a handkerchief and dabbed at her eyes.

'Hetty, don't take on so. What's wrong?'

'It did happen, Maddie. I was having a baby, and then … then I was no longer. Samuel was not even here. I had no one to turn to, and I didn't know what I was supposed to do.'

'Oh, my dear, I'm so sorry for you. I'll be here for you next time it happens, and it will, I am sure of it. There are children littering the streets of England. It must be easy to manage.' She was aware of the irony of her words, but put the thought aside for the moment. She needed to make sure her friend was suitably reassured. 'You do love your husband, don't you?'

'Yes, with all my heart.' Hetty's sincerity was clear. She put away her handkerchief and smiled weakly.

'Well, then, that's a better start than most, and you are both young and healthy and in love,' Maddie added.

'I know, thank you. I didn't mean to drag this up on your first visit to me. Have a cake, and let's talk about happy things.' She picked up the plate of desserts and held it out to Maddie.

'That's what friends are for, Hetty, to listen and help each other when we are needed.' She picked up a fruit tart at random, wishing she had been offered a sandwich instead.

It would have been perfect timing to mention Daniel and her dilemma, but she couldn't confide in Hetty now, about being pregnant, not after her confession. It would be too cruel.

'I suppose you are right about being in love. Look at poor Daniel,' Hetty said, out of the blue, as if her thoughts were tuned into Maddie's.

Maddie was suddenly no longer sure she wanted to hear Daniel's name and love in the same sentence, unless her name was included. Her heart beat faster, and she placed the tart she had barely tasted back onto the plate as nausea threatened. 'Daniel is home?' she forced herself to ask.

'No, sadly not. We have heard not a peep out of him, and Mother is so worried that he has been eaten by lions, or something.'

'Oh, dear.' She hesitated, unsure whether to be relieved by the news because she had not heard from him either, or alarmed by the lion comment. 'But why do you feel sorry for him?' She feigned disinterest, but could barely swallow the tiny morsel of food she had bitten off.

'Well, he certainly does not love the beautiful Finula, does he?'

'I didn't think he ever did, but why should that matter?' She watched Hetty carefully, her pulse pounding in her throat as she spoke.

'Why? Because he is betrothed to her, of course.' She looked back at Maddie, all innocence and wide eyes. 'I thought you knew that. Wasn't that why you went away, because of Finula?'

Maddie felt the wind rush out of her chest. 'He is engaged? To that woman?' She swallowed hard as nausea turned into the distinct possibility of her vomiting on Hetty's very expensive-looking rug. She gripped the armchair, closing her eyes briefly, but that only served to increase the nausea, and she forced them open again.

Hetty rose from her seat. 'Are you alright? I didn't mean to distress you.'

Maddie waved her away. She was actually going to be sick. She wasn't imagining it. 'Where is your bathroom, Hetty?'

Hetty rang a little bell, and the maid appeared. 'Molly, show Miss Lockett to the bathroom, please?'

'Thank you. Excuse me for a moment.'

She rushed from the room and followed hard on the heels of the maid, her hand pressed to her mouth. The dizziness she had experienced returned, and she slammed the bathroom door closed behind her, running her wrists under the cold tap and willing away the nausea.

But it was in vain. She retched and vomited in the toilet, panting with the effort, and praying the maid was not close enough to hear her. Horrified, she wiped her mouth and leaned against the wall, until her breathing was under control.

Daniel was engaged? He had made love to her, but had chosen to marry someone else. She clutched at her belly. Her newborn baby would be illegitimate – forever. She was ruined. There would be no happy ending, after all.

Biting back tears, she composed herself, aware that she had already spent too long away from Hetty. There was no time for self-pity.

She checked her dress wasn't soiled and practised a smile before leaving the bathroom.

'Sorry, Hetty, I came over all strange for a moment, but I'm fine now.'

'Oh, I do hope I haven't upset you. I know you were taken with my brother, but it was a long time ago now.'

'It was,' Maddie agreed, barely hearing Hetty's words. She sat down again and tried not to look at the fruit tart still sitting on her plate. The nausea had yet to abate. 'You were saying, about Daniel being betrothed?' She attempted as normal a tone as she could manage but it was hard. 'Was it a recent engagement?' Nothing could change the fact that he would never be hers, but she needed to know how badly he had deceived her.

'If you're sure you want to know.' Hetty pressed her lips together, but continued, 'It was a very low-key affair. He bought her a pretty diamond ring and put it on her finger, and we all clapped. Darwin, Finula's dog, seemed to be the most excited one there, I have to say. He kept trying to ... well, he was most friendly with Uncle George's leg.'

Maddie smiled at her words, but really, none of it mattered any more. She had heard all she needed to know.

'Daniel left for Africa a few days afterwards. Barely seemed with it, when he came to see me on the way to Southampton.'

'You told him that I was in London?'

'Oh, let me think. It was Mrs Parrot who reminded me, so I suppose I might have. I hope that wasn't a problem.'

'Not at all.' If only you knew, Maddie thought.

'I fear Mother might have had a hand in it – in that he couldn't wait to get away from her.' Hetty's laugh was brittle. 'But has the world not been ever so. I hope they grow to love one another, in time. Anyway, enough about them, tell me how you're getting on here. Have you met a gentleman friend yet, and how is your *empire* shaping up?'

Maddie managed to relate stories of her new life to Hetty, whilst part of her mind screamed *no, no*! She needed to be alone, to think, and couldn't concentrate whilst Hetty kept on asking her questions. She answered as quickly as she could, so she could take her leave, and rose from her seat whilst her friend was still in the throes of a conversation regarding King Edward and Sandringham, where Samuel had been invited for a weekend shooting party.

'I'm so sorry, Hetty, but I have a client visiting at four. I didn't expect to be so long here.'

'That's perfectly fine, Maddie, but you must promise to visit again, when Samuel is home. I know he would love to meet you.' Hetty kissed Maddie and added, 'I will bring some of my ladies to the shop to buy your hats.'

Maddie's mind was already far removed from her hats and Mrs Parrot, as she descended the steps from Hetty's house. She had already moved on with a plan to ensure the safety of her future and that of her baby. She must leave as soon as possible so that no one knew she was pregnant. She would secure lodgings with enough room for Florence, and make enough hats to keep the Lawley's contract, so that her baby would want for nothing.

She would harden her heart towards Daniel and take control of her own life.

That part of the decision was the hardest, surprisingly. She still found it impossible to believe that Daniel had abandoned her so ruthlessly, although she had no choice but to believe the facts. And if it were true, she would make sure that no one would ever, ever suspect he was her baby's father. One thing she could guarantee was that she would trust no other man to safeguard her heart and her soul – that job would be hers alone.

Chapter Twenty-Three

London, 1905

'Florence, can you pack these up for the post tomorrow, please, love?' Maddie heaved her bulk out of her hard, wooden chair, rubbing her back as she stood. She gave the new, gold chainmail bags a final once over, before preparing them for packing.

Everything in her body ached, and every single thing she attempted to do took super human effort. Her belly was massive, her ankles swollen, and the size of her hips made her inadvertently bump into people whenever she ventured outside. She was heartily sick of it, and more than ready to give birth, terrifying as the idea was.

Months before, Maddie had moved to live on the south of the Thames, with Florence, in a small terraced house, away from anyone who might remember her as the dressmaker who worked for Mrs Parrot. The house had two bedrooms, one each for Maddie and Florence, and just enough room downstairs to make and store her handbags and hats for the Lawley's contract. Once the baby came, it would be a tight squeeze, but if she kept up the sales of her designer hats and bags, they would survive financially.

Maddie looked down at her huge bump, unable to see her feet, and completely unable to put her shoes on without contorting into shapes her body did not want to go. She had been getting twinges all day, and the baby was kicking constantly. She tried to be excited about the birth, and although she knew she would love her baby once it arrived, she was so very scared to do it all alone. Irene, a friendly neighbour was ready and waiting with the towels and hot water, but in truth Maddie had no idea why they needed such things.

She twisted her wedding ring around once more, wishing her fictitious husband could be called upon to be the proud father. Unfortunately, her brave, handsome ship's captain was riding the high seas in search of adventure, unable to be at their baby's birth. That was the concocted story, anyway.

If he were not so fictitious she would give him a piece of her mind right then, for abandoning her in her hour of need, but she would get her revenge by killing him off before he became too much of a liability. Although Maddie didn't consider herself a natural liar, her story had come easily out of sheer necessity. She just needed to ensure she had the energy to grieve and put on a good show, when the time came.

The baby gave a huge kick, and she clutched at her belly, doubling over as a long, rolling pain tightened her stomach and left her panting. She groaned; the baby was definitely coming.

She sat herself down again, only to jackknife back up as an exquisite pain sliced through her.

'Flo? I need you,' she shouted feebly, but realised Florence had returned to the back room. She could hear the sewing machine rattling along at a fierce pace downstairs, drowning out her voice. Gearing up to call again, she strained to listen as the noise suddenly stopped, and a voice sounded, deep and low, followed by footsteps on the stairs.

'Flo,' she cried. 'Thank God. The baby's coming.'

The door opened, and she gasped, sweat instantly sheening her face. 'Oh, my God.'

'Maddie, what's wrong? Oh!' Edward stood in front of her, the bunch of flowers he presented to her slowly sliding from his hand, large white daisies tangling with yellow daffodils as they landed on the linoleum floor.

'Edward?' Maddie struggled to her feet, as Edward gaped. 'What on earth are you doing here?'

Edward's eyes were wild, as if he wanted to bolt, but his feet seemed glued to the floor. He opened his mouth, but no words came out.

'Edward. Stop catching flies and help me. It's a baby, and it is not going away.' Maddie had no time for pleasantries.

Edward still gaped. 'How did this happen?'

She managed a wry smile. 'Has no one ever told you?'

'You know what I mean.' His forehead creased. 'I only saw you a few months ago.'

'Six months ago, to be precise.' She leaned against the table, rubbing her back and groaning. 'This is really not the right moment to talk about this, Edward. You can either turn around and pretend you didn't see me, or fetch Florence and knock on the door opposite. Irene is expecting a call.'

Edward gaped for another long minute, his eyes round and increasingly manic, before he found that his legs would, after all, move. He rushed toward the door. 'What number is Irene?'

'Number seven, and tell Florence to close the shop, will you?'

Edward's footsteps faded, and within seconds Florence bounded up the stairs.

'Edward's here, he's come to see you, I take it?' Florence looked perturbed. 'You and 'im, I never would have thought it.' She seemed in a world of her own as she pondered on what she'd just learned. 'You and Edward Underwood,' she repeated. 'He's a real gent, he is, one of the best.'

'Yes, he is, Florence.'

'He couldn't have timed his appearance better, could he?' She put her hands on her hips almost accusingly as she surveyed the scene in front of her.

It could not actually have been much worse, Maddie thought, tempted to put Florence right, but she truly didn't have the strength to explain right then.

Florence frowned. 'I suppose you won't have to kill off your sea captain now, will you?'

Edward does work on the barges, Maddie thought wryly, but she simply replied, 'Flo, I don't know if you have noticed, but I do believe I'm in labour.'

Florence's eyes widened. 'You mean right now – this minute?'

Maddie let out a yelp, as another pain floored her, taking away her power of speech, except for words she barely thought she knew – and were certainly not the words of a lady.

'Cripes, I'd better fetch Irene.'

Maddie waved at her. 'Don't worry. That's where Edward's gone.'

Minutes later, Irene appeared, her arms laden with towels. She immediately took control of Maddie, whilst giving Edward the once over. She sniffed once and nodded, as if she found him lacking, and then said, 'Wait outside. You can do the *proud new father pacing up and down* bit on the landing.'

Edward shot a quizzical look at Maddie, but said nothing. 'I can stay if you want. I mean, I'm not squeamish, or owt, if you want to bite on me arm, or sommat.'

'I'll let you know,' Maddie panted as Irene helped her onto the bed. Edward's eyes popped like they were on stalks, and he appeared rooted to the spot, until Maddie shouted, 'Just go. Get yourself something to eat and drink, for goodness' sake.'

Edward blinked, snapping out of his trance. His eyes locked with hers, betrayal and a flash of anger showing clearly in his eyes.

She couldn't blame him, but there was nothing she could do about it. 'Flo, get Edward a cup of tea, love, and find him some cake, or something sweet. He looks as if he needs it.' She inclined her head towards the door. 'Go. Shoo. I'll be fine.'

Dusk was drawing in, and a steady beat of rain marked the time, as Maddie laboured, listening to Edward pace outside the door, as a doting father should. One final push used up the last of her strength, and she was rewarded by a thin cry as her baby met the world.

Irene showed her how to get the baby to latch onto her breast, and by the time Edward was allowed in, Irene believing him to be the father, the baby was safely swaddled and tucked into the crook of Maddie's arm.

Irene smiled indulgently at Edward before leaving the room, and Maddie, too befuddled to think straight, allowed Edward to kiss her cheek as he rushed over to her bedside.

'So, why are you here, Edward?'

'I got your address from your dad, now I've started on the barges. It's the first time I've been down to London. I thought I'd surprise you.'

'Instead, I surprised you,' she said, cuddling her baby boy to her chest.

'What does yer dad think?'

'He doesn't know. I didn't know how to tell him, so I've said nothing. No one knows, Edward.'

'You can't hide a baby, Maddie.'

'I know. I will work it out.'

Edward was quiet for a moment. 'Can I have a little hold? I'm good with children. There are loads in our house.'

'I do know that, Edward. I only live in London, not another planet.'

'I know, love.'

She passed her baby over, and he immediately snuggled into Edward's soft cotton shirt. Edward gazed at him, a goofy smile on his face.

'You're a natural.' Maddie's heart softened as she saw the tenderness in Edward's eyes.

He didn't share his smile with Maddie, however, just looked down thoughtfully at the baby and stroked his cheek. 'What are you going to call him?'

'I thought Alfie, after my mum's dad. If it was a girl, I was going to call her Isobel, so this seems the best compromise.'

'So, you're not calling him after his dad?' he asked quietly.

She shook her head, already knowing what the next question would be. 'And I am not saying who his dad is – ever.'

'Why, 'cause you don't want anyone to know what a

coward he was for not sticking around? Do I know him?' His words were hard and flat, as if he hated the man who had inflicted the beautiful baby he held in his arms.

'No, you don't know him, and he's not around any more.'

'He's not from back home, then? You haven't been there for a year.'

His aggressive stance perturbed her; it was really none of his business, after all. 'I would rather not talk about it, and it won't change a thing.'

'If you say so,' Edward conceded.

However, Maddie had a feeling it wouldn't be the end of the matter as far as he was concerned, and it bothered her that he had assumed some kind of protective right over her. She was too tired to take issue with him, though, so she simply asked, 'How long are you in London?'

'I've got a few days' layover before we pick up the return cargo. Let me stick around and help you, until you get yourself together.' Adoration shone from his eyes, and Maddie found it strange that the inconvenient arrival of a new baby didn't seem to have fazed him, or changed his feelings.

Unexpectedly, her heart turned over with longing for Daniel. She wished he could meet his son – how proud he would be – but she steeled her mind against such thoughts. Daniel was consigned to history. 'That would be lovely, Edward, thank you.' She really didn't deserve his kindness.

'Eeh, don't go all soft on me.' He put his arm around her, and she leaned into him, grateful for his solid strength. 'I'll make us a cuppa, while you relax.'

Knowing she could trust Edward with her precious baby, Maddie felt her eyes closing and was asleep within minutes.

When Edward left her a few days later, Maddie clung to him, surprised at the strength of her dependency on his cheerful resilience and practical help. He held her close and smoothed down her hair, as she tucked her head into his shoulder.

However, when he kissed the top of her head, she stiffened. She hoped it was no more than a friendly kiss, but it was enough to make her pull away from him, realising that her neediness could be giving out the wrong signals.

Edward's eyes were quizzical, but he let her go. 'Until next time, then? It'll be about two weeks, I reckon.'

Maddie bit her lip, indecisive. She would like to see him again, and loved catching up with the news back home, but she was almost certain about the deal he was offering. He wanted a relationship with her. If not right away, then most certainly at some point. She couldn't articulate her thoughts coherently, though, so she nodded, thinking their newfound friendship too fragile to cause waves.

He beamed as he stuffed his cap on his head and grasped her hand fleetingly, before letting it go. He trailed his fingers across her palm, evidently reluctant to leave, but leave he did, and she cradled Alfie as she watched him through the window, feeling lost and fearful.

'This won't do, will it?' She kissed her son's downy head and rubbed at her eyes, squeezing away rogue tears.

Edward was a good man, and she knew that if she did right by him, he would stand by her, and her life would carry on as it was, with the added bonus of a man by her side, should she need the extra strength. She almost called him back, even had her hand on the window to throw it open, but something made her stop and she turned away. It was early days yet, and nothing needed to be decided. She had her own business and somewhere to live, to raise her son. As long as they had food and a safe house to sleep in, they would be fine.

Even so, something tugged at her. Something was missing, leaving a hollow emptiness where there used to be love and desire. She gazed at where Alfie settled to sleep in her arms, and she hoped the love of her child would be enough for now.

However, a memory of Daniel, asleep in her old bed, rose unbidden and unexpected, and as her mouth twisted with the pain of loss, she knew what was missing in her life. He had said he loved her, and she had believed him. She tried to embrace the pain, hoping that it would help to purge the love she still held for him: a love he didn't deserve.

She stroked Alfie's dark hair, thoughtfully. Maybe it was time to move forward with a different kind of love, based on mutual respect and maturity.

Her brain knew it made sense, but her heart still ached.

Chapter Twenty-Four

Maddie heard a cheery whistle that reminded her so much of her father's and she smiled. Edward was back. He kissed her cheek and enfolded her into his big arms, and she hugged him in return, pleased to see him. 'How was your trip? Come upstairs, and we can have a drink.'

'Ooh, I could murder a cuppa,' he said, bringing a waft of the canal and fresh grass with him.

Maddie remembered a time when he had smelled of stale sweat and coal dust, and she was happy for him. His complexion had grown clear, and his new life obviously suited him.

He settled by the fireplace with her, once he had crept over to the crib and stroked Alfie's cheek. 'He's so bonny, Maddie, and he's growing so quickly.' His voice was almost reverent. 'Is it not a wonder that God made such a perfect little creature?'

Maddie knew her son's conception would be considered a sin by the church, even though he looked like a cherub, so she was surprised that Edward was able to let it pass, given that he was much more religious than Maddie. 'He's not really growing quickly. It's just that you see him in fits and starts. He'll be six months old soon.' She stopped as she spoke, gazing out of the window, thinking of how much Daniel had already missed.

Edward scanned her face, anxiously. 'Penny for them?'

'Oh, nothing much, just reflecting on the vagaries of life, I suppose.' She poured boiling water into the teapot, aware that Edward still watched her.

'Maddie, I've been thinking …' he began, fiddling with his teacup and saucer.

She stilled, pot in hand, knowing that she needed to listen carefully to his words.

'We should get married. We could pretend Alfie is ours, if you wanted. No one need know.'

She sat down next to him, as an image of his robust mother clapping proudly at his trumpet playing flickered through her mind. She was a sparky woman, and Maddie could far from imagine how she might take it, if Edward declared his intentions to marry an unmarried mother.

She took his hand. 'Edward, that is such a lovely gesture, but marriage is a huge thing to contemplate, and I'm not sure I'm the right woman for you.'

'Why's that, then? I thought we rubbed along well enough.' His chin jutted out defiantly, and she knew she had hurt him.

'It's nothing to do with you, Edward. You're a good man, and I like having you in my life, but I don't think I know you well enough for such a commitment.'

His expression cleared. 'Is that all? Well, I'm in no rush, if you're not, although I don't know how you're going to explain Alfie away, when the time comes.'

'I know, but I only have my dad to answer to, you know, and he loves me well enough to cope with something like this.'

'Mebbee you're right. So, we can carry on as we are, for now?'

Tenderness filled Maggie's heart at his eager, but fearful, expression, and she smiled softly. 'Yes, Edward, you are a bright star in my dark sky.'

He beamed and nodded in agreement, tucking into the cake that Maddie placed in front of him as if a deal had been struck. 'Before I forget, your friend Jane is poorly again. I believe she's being cared for at the cottage hospital back home.'

'She's in hospital? But that means she must be really ill.' Fear flashed through her body at the news, and she sat down heavily. 'Who's paying for it? She has no money.'

'No idea,' he said, through a mouthful of cake. 'I'm guessing it must be the Co-op, or sommat. They'll have a bit of a whip round if there's a just cause.'

'She will be okay, though?' Maddie's bottom lip, trembled and she brought her fingers up to still it. 'How long has she been poorly?'

Edward shook his head. 'Couldn't tell you, sorry, love. I just heard it second-hand, like.' He looked up, finally registering her worry. 'You could come back with me, on the barge, if you're that worried. They take fares occasionally, although I could probably swing it for free. It's a bit rough and ready, though.'

She shook her head decisively. 'No, Alfie is too young.'

Edward shrugged. 'Maybe next month?'

Maddie bit her lip. She desperately wanted to see Jane, but she would have to tell her father about his grandchild first.

'Worry not, love. We'll sort sommat out. Now, sit down and drink your tea before it gets cold.'

Edward washed the dishes and kept an eye on Alfie, whilst Maddie ventured downstairs. She was slowly getting back into the swing of things, although she was desperately tired most of the time. It didn't help that Alfie was waking at least twice a night to be fed. Again, she guessed that was the nature of things and tried to be stoical about it. She often found herself to be lonely, though. Despite having Florence for company, there was, undoubtedly, a hole in her life that needed to be filled.

Since she had left Mrs Parrot's employment, Maddie had kept herself aloof from everyone, only mentioning her fictitious husband when necessary and giving little away about her origins. Irene had sniffed a bit and said Edward looked little like a seafaring captain, but that had been the end of it.

Thankfully, Maddie didn't need to be sociable in her dealings with Lawley's, but she had hoped to expand the business, and couldn't do so as long as she was living a lie. She knew, however, that more lies would be necessary before she was done with her absent husband, and once again pondered on whether she could just exchange her seafaring man for one who worked on the canals.

It was a conundrum that raised its head more frequently of late, and she knew something had to change.

After another sleepless night, Maddie had made a decision. She would ask Irene to help Florence, and she would travel home with Edward, taking Alfie. She could just about afford the return fare, and was desperate to see her family, and Jane.

She cursed herself for not insisting that Jane moved in with her dad, but the mention of Dolly had put paid to that line of thought. She heard Edward filling the kettle and guessed his night had been broken too, likely because of Alfie's crying and the hard sofa where Edward had slept.

Once more, Maddie considered his offer, more seriously than last time. It would solve so many problems, and Edward was a decent, hardworking man. But she didn't love him, and didn't think she ever would – at least, not in the way he wanted her to, anyway.

Was that a just enough cause to turn him down, though?

Alfie was snuffling in his crib, and Maddie sighed as she prepared to meet another wearying day, pausing as she heard a letter drop on her doormat. It was not a very frequent occurrence, and her heart quickened, even more so when she picked the letter up and recognised her father's spidery writing on the front of it.

Tom normally wrote the envelopes, and mostly the letters.

Without moving from the doorstep, she tore it open, her heart pounding erratically. Do not let it be Jane, *please*, she thought, as she frantically scanned the contents. Once reassured, she walked into the kitchen, intending to read it properly.

'Good news, Maddie?' Edward asked, telling Maddie her relief must have been evident.

'Erm, I think so.' She met his eye. 'Father is to marry Dolly Shanks in a couple of months.'

'Righto,' he answered, uncertainly. 'Is that good … for you, I mean?'

'Yes.' She stopped frowning. 'Definitely good news.' She sat down and concentrated on reading the letter, before grinning over at Edward. 'They're having a proper wedding. How lovely. We must go. It will be wonderful to see Dad happy again.' She grasped Edward's hand with joy, and he took the opportunity to pull her to her feet.

He grabbed her around the waist and waltzed her around the room, obviously pleased that he was included in her plans. 'I wish it was our wedding, duck,' he said. '*Here comes the bride*,' he sang over and over, as he waltzed her around the table. 'Have I convinced you, yet?'

'You have convinced me that you can't dance and you don't know the second line of the song.' She laughed, breathless and giddy.

'You'll have to make a posh frock, and wear one of your hats. You'll outshine everyone there.' He bowed with a flourish, taking off an imaginary hat of his own. 'Won't we be a couple of toffs?' He frowned for a moment. 'And baby Alfie can have a little suit, too.' He stopped larking around, suddenly serious. 'You'll have to tell everyone, Maddie. You can't keep him a secret forever.'

She sat down. 'And I don't want to, either. I've already decided I need to tell my father about him. I know it was wrong of me to keep it quiet.'

'My offer still stands. It always will, Maddie. I'll never stop loving you.' He suddenly pulled her towards his chest and kissed her.

Caught off guard, Maddie grabbed hold of him to steady herself, but Edward appeared to take it as a sign that she wanted more, and he pulled her tighter and deepened the kiss.

She let him kiss her, waiting, once again in vain, for the tingle to begin. Nothing happened in any part of her body, except her mind, which drifted to wondering how long the kiss would last and that Alfie would need feeding soon.

Chapter Twenty-Five

Tom charged through the front door of their family home, but stopped in his tracks, backing away from the baby curled up on a makeshift bed on the floor, with pillows cushioned around him. 'Dad, there's a baby in the front room,' he shouted, his confused gaze glued to the small bundle.

Watching him from the kitchen doorway, Maddie pursed her lips. It would not be easy to explain a baby away, but for then she just needed to hug her brother. 'Tom?' She was by his side in an instant.

Tom turned and allowed himself to be mauled by his sister, but he soon pushed her aside. 'Maddie, there's a baby on the floor. Didn't you see it?'

'It's my baby, Tom.'

His eyes widened. 'Where did you get it?'

'Umm, in London.'

'Wow. They sell everything there.' He tiptoed towards Alfie and peered over at him. 'What does it do?'

'Erm, cries and wees, and waves his arms and legs around, mostly.'

Tom seemed unimpressed by the description. 'I wouldn't have bothered, if I was you.' He crept away from Alfie, losing interest immediately. 'What's for tea? I'm starving.'

Maddie smiled to herself. It had all turned out so much easier than she had imagined. She had turned up with Edward, Alfie tight in her arms, praying her father would understand.

Although he had glared at Edward for a second, looking like he might deck him, the moment he had seen Alfie's cute little face, the gleam of anger had disappeared, replaced by a tender look. 'Ah, love, what've we got here, then?' He reached out a hand and stroked Alfie's head, his eyes filling. 'You'd best come in.' As he had turned away, he wiped his eyes, and

Maddie wanted to throw herself into his arms and beg for forgiveness.

However, he had surprised her again, by lifting Alfie tenderly out of her arms and folding him into the crook of his own as if he had been doing it all his life.

'I will put the kettle on, Dad, and you can get to know your grandson properly.'

Her dad nodded, looking choked. He wasn't angry with her; everything would be fine.

They settled around the hearth, and Maddie poured tea whilst watching her father, whose eyes never once left Alfie's face. 'So, Dad, you and Dolly? That is a surprise.'

She caught a look from Edward that said *not half as much as your surprise*, and stifled a giggle.

Her dad looked sheepish for a moment, then reached out for Maddie's hand. 'You know, no one will ever replace your mum, duck. Dolly knows it, too, but we care for each other and, well, you only get one shot at this life, don't you?'

Maddie squeezed his hand. 'You do, Dad and I'm pleased for you both.'

'When did you get wed, you and Edward?' he asked, out of nowhere.

Panic rose in Maddie's throat as she shot a look at Edward.

'We're not yet, Mr Lockett, but we hope to, once we've sorted out the whys and wherefores,' Edward said, the perfect gentleman.

'Ah.' Her father sipped his tea, holding the teacup away from little Alfie's head, and the silence recommenced.

'Dad, I want to see Jane as soon as I can. Do you want to look after Alfie for a while, or should Edward take him?'

'Jane's proper bad this time, Maddie. I'm sure she could do with your company. She's over at the cottage hospital. I'll look after little 'un. Dolly's coming around soon. She'll be over the moon, I know it.'

Edward looked slightly put out, but Maddie knew he would

be expected home, and it would surely be better if he turned up without a 'spare baby', as her mother would have called Alfie.

She kissed him on his cheek as they parted, thinking how they were behaving like a regular couple of late. Sadly, it did little to reassure her, but she decided not to think too deeply about it and, instead, focus on Jane. The rest could wait.

Fenton Cottage Hospital was forbidding and not at all cottage-like from the outside. Maddie was comforted, however, when she entered, and a cheerful lady, wearing a starched apron, bustled up to her. She explained about Jane, and the nurse led her along a corridor to a small room.

'Such a polite wee thing,' she said as she guided Maddie into a room furnished with one solitary bed and a small bedside table.

Jane lay in the bed, so still and thin that she looked as if the bedsheet she lay beneath had flattened her. Maddie crept closer, unable to believe her friend had deteriorated so much since she had last seen her. Her cheeks were sunken in her stone white face, and her lips were almost blue and cracked with dryness.

'Jane?' she cried, stifling a sob as she reached for her friend, a lump forming in her throat as she spoke.

Jane opened her eyes. 'Well, I never. Fancy seeing you here.' She tried to raise her head, but fell back onto the pillow weakly.

'Jane,' Maddie repeated, as the full horror of her condition hit her.

Jane's breath sighed with a slight hiss as she tried to speak. 'I can sit up, Maddie, if you just help me a bit.'

She raised her hand, and Maddie grasped her twig-like fingers, tears springing unbidden in her eyes. She stroked Jane's cheek and smoothed her hair, embracing her gently, trying not to squeeze too hard. 'Oh, Jane, Jane.' It seemed all she could say. Nothing else came to her mind. There were no words of comfort. Jane was dying, it was clear.

Maddie had seen people with the wasting disease before, and although Jane had always said it was not that, whatever it was called, it was definitely death calling to her.

She buried her face in Jane's hair as she held her, anxious that she would see her crying.

Jane must have noticed, as she said, 'There, there, don't take on so, Maddie. It'll be fine. Jesus will take care of me.' That only brought about a fresh bout of tears from Maddie, until Jane patted her hand. 'Fine visitor you are. You're supposed to cheer me up. Tell me all about the latest fashions and fripperies in London.'

'I'm that sorry, Jane. Just give us a min.' She bit her lip as she realised she had slipped back into the Potteries dialect again, but then felt bad for caring. She cast her gaze around for a chair, but ended up sitting gingerly on the end of Jane's bed. Unable to see much of Jane's legs beneath the bedclothes, Maddie prayed she would not hurt her as she sat down.

She swallowed. 'London. Right. Well, you've never seen anything like the fashion show I went to a short while ago. The colours and the fabrics, real diamonds glittering on capes and shoes and ostrich feathers, white soft feathers – everywhere plumes of feathers ...' She wafted imaginary feathers away from her nose as she made up story after story, until she realised Jane was no longer listening and stopped mid-sentence. For one terrifying moment, she thought her friend had died, but when she touched Jane's pale cheek, she found warmth there and breathed out with relief.

As she watched her friend sleeping, she wondered how it could have come to this. Life was so unfair. In the quiet, still room, just looking at Jane, she found herself reliving old memories, wiping tears away as they dripped off her chin.

At a cough behind her, she twisted around.

'I'm sorry, am I in the way?' She swiped at her cheeks, rising as she spoke, then lurched to her feet as a feeling akin to being punched in the stomach hit her so hard she could barely breathe. 'Daniel?'

Daniel blanched, almost dropping his notes. 'Maddie? Is it really you?' He flung the notes on the end of Jane's bed and simply stared at Maddie as if unable to believe his eyes. 'I've waited so long to see you. You look—' He clasped her hands and gazed into her eyes. 'You look beautiful.'

Maddie's mouth was suddenly dry, and she moistened her lips with the tip of her tongue, as she drank in the man she had dreamed about for so long.

His hair was still overlong at the front, his smile still broad, but he looked world weary and tired. She couldn't believe he was standing in front of her, but unlike the last time, when she had thrown herself into his arms, she didn't move.

Finally, she found her voice. 'Yes, it's really me. Not an altogether pleasant surprise, I imagine.' A bitterness she didn't know she harboured forced out the words, which belied Daniel's actions.

'Madeline?' He shook his head in confusion, letting go of her hands.

'I came to see Jane.' She turned back to her friend, fumbling for something to say beyond stating the obvious, to fill the awkward silence.

'Ah, yes.' Daniel looked over at Jane with sadness. 'I was coming to check on her, but it can wait, if she's asleep.'

'Are you looking after her? Did you sort this out?'

'Yes,' he said simply. If for nothing else, she would be eternally grateful to Daniel for that one act of selflessness.

'She needs specialist care, really, but there are no places. I've offered to look after her and pay her keep, until ...'

Maddie knew what he meant. 'How long?' She pressed her lips together, trying to stem the tears.

'Ah, not long, maybe a week.'

'A week!' Her fingers flew to her lips as she realised how loud she had spoken.

Daniel's eyes widened in warning as he grabbed her elbow and led her away. 'There's a waiting room along the corridor. We can have a cup of tea.'

She almost shook him off, determined to stay with Jane, but allowed herself to be walked into a small room where cups and saucers were laid out. Daniel poured her a cup of tea from a hissing tea urn and passed it to her. She took it with shaking hands and smiled weakly as the cup rattled in the saucer, before placing it quickly on a side table.

'Here, take a seat. I am sorry. I shouldn't have been so blunt but it was such a shock to see you here.'

'It's fine.' She sat down and put her hand up to her trembling lips as he hunkered down in front of her, peering into her face.

'You're pale.' He stroked her cheek, brushing back her hair and she had to force herself not to lean into his warm hand. 'Might you faint?'

'I do feel a little …' She was going to say overwhelmed, but the word did not come out, as her throat closed. She shook her head, unable to speak. She really didn't want to break down in front of Daniel, but he reached out for her hand, and the last of her reserve broke.

She choked out a sob as she fumbled for her handkerchief, and Daniel sat next to her and put his arm around her shoulders. She bowed her head with sorrow, unable to stop the wracking sobs that escaped her, and when he pulled her close, she turned into him, burying her face into his chest. As he stroked her shoulders, smoothing her hair as her body shook with grief, she clung on to him, her breath hitching and heaving, her tears overwhelming her.

Daniel kissed her forehead and framed her face with his hands. 'Please don't fret so. I hate to see you so upset.'

'She was … she *is* my best friend, and I left her alone to die,' she wailed, quite beside herself.

'No, you did not. You know you didn't.' He tightened his arms around her shoulders, and slowly, she controlled her crying, but her heart was breaking for her poor, dear friend. Eventually, Daniel drew her up gently from the chair and led her out of the room. 'Let's take a walk outside. It will help you to compose yourself.'

He took her hand firmly, and once again, she allowed herself to be led outside. It felt natural to be holding his hand, and she didn't want to question the rights, or wrongs, of it. She needed him right there and then, and no one else would be a decent substitute.

Glad to be away from the smell of carbolic and antiseptic she breathed in deeply, dubious though the Fenton air was. Tall oak trees broke through the murky smog, and the sky, for once, was a clear blue. 'It's just so unfair. She's never hurt anyone in her life.'

Daniel squeezed her hand. 'Life isn't fair, Maddie. I think we both know that by now, but you must be strong for Jane. Come and see her whenever you can.' His eyes were full of compassion. 'Will you be returning to London, shortly?'

'Not immediately. I can ... wait.' It sounded too harsh to voice the truth, but she would stay with Jane until the end came. Her breath hitched again, but that time she won the battle and remained calm.

'Would you care for another cup of tea?' Daniel having dropped his professional demeanour looked more like the man she had known so intimately. Hopeful and vulnerable.

However, Maddie shook her head. 'I must return home. I'll be missed.' As she said the words, though, she faltered, suddenly wanting to talk. Surely, she and Daniel needed to speak of the last time she saw him. He owed her an apology, at the very least, for deceiving her so and neglecting to contact her when he had promised he would. She thought of her precious Alfie, waiting to be fed, and for a fleeting moment wanted to blurt out the truth about their child, but Daniel had made his choice, and in her book, he didn't deserve to have any part of Alfie's life.

She closed her eyes as the rawness she'd harboured for so long simmered. She had been wronged by this man and she shouldn't have even let him comfort her. Her resolve hardened. 'I must go. Tell Jane I shall return tomorrow.'

'Maddie, don't go, please.'

She heard the desperation in his voice, and it gave her a small satisfaction, but it was too little and too late. She swept down the steps and did not turn around once to see if he watched her departure.

Chapter Twenty-Six

When Maddie returned to her old house, Dolly was sitting in the big armchair reserved for her father, jiggling Alfie on her lap. He was fretful and whiney, but stopped as soon as Maddie took him from Dolly.

'Someone needs feeding, I'd say.' She hugged her son, relieved that nothing untoward had happened whilst she was absent. 'Dolly, how lovely to see you, and congratulations.' She hugged Dolly with her free arm, and they beamed at each other.

'I think I should be saying that to you, shouldn't I? A new baby, and a husband on the horizon? You kept that quiet, all right, didn't you?'

Maddie tried to smile back. She wished Edward hadn't said anything about getting married, but he was probably only trying to help. She gave Dolly a wan smile.

'Oh, dear. You look a bit like you lost sixpence and found a penny.'

'I've been to see Jane, Dolly, she's not at all well.'

'Oh, that's right, poor girl. It's very sad.'

'It is.' They stood together for a moment in silent contemplation until Maddie pulled herself together. 'I'll just sort out Alfie and we can have a nice chinwag.' She whisked Alfie into the kitchen, to feed him and to be alone with her thoughts.

Seeing Daniel had unsettled her, and talk of marrying Edward even more so. She needed to remember that she was her own person. She would not be pushed into doing anything she didn't want to. Those days were long gone.

Letting her eyelids close for a moment, she recalled Daniel's concerned eyes seeking out hers. She had forgotten how long his dark lashes were and would never forget his crooked smile that changed his face from angelic to roguish. Although, he could never be a rogue, even though he had let Maddie down badly. It just wasn't in his nature.

Knowing her father would be returning soon, Maddie walked back into the tiny sitting room.

'Your dad is surprisingly pleased about Alfie, you know,' Dolly said, and Maddie tried to refocus her mind.

'So it seems, but I shall speak to him about it, now Edward has gone.' She was ready to face the consequences of bringing Alfie into the world, but it made it so much easier knowing that her father had fallen instantly in love with Alfie and wouldn't let her down.

'You've no need, love.'

The rattle of the door she remembered so well told her that her father had returned. He took off his cap and coat, and hung them on a hook by the door, before turning around to face Maddie and Dolly. 'You've sprung a surprise on us, Maddie, I won't say you haven't, but all I know is, I value anything that lives. Since Isobel died, I won't even kill a fly. Some might say that makes me a weak man, but I disagree, and I don't hold with the notion of it being shameful to bring a new life into the world. Although, I would question the wisdom of it.'

Maddie had never heard her father be so voluble, or eloquent, and stared at him, blinking.

Dolly intervened, as she tied on a pinafore ready to prepare supper and put the kettle on to boil. 'The minister might have something to say about that, but then, he's on God's side to start with.'

'I've heard there's some chap who says we weren't even made by God, but evolved over time, and I think there are others who agree with him. I think he's as unsure about this Adam and Eve stuff as I am. Any road, Dolly, let's be over and done with this. Tell Maddie your news.'

Dolly turned away from the sink and wiped her hands on her pinafore. 'Well, I've been offered a partnership in an exclusive pottery works in Stoke – but near Trent Vale, and there's a small house attached to the deal. It's a very nice area, away from the smog around here, that's for sure, so your dad's moving out of this house to be with me. Jimmy's coming, too, of course, he can share a room with Tom. I hope that's all right with you, Maddie. I know this has always been your home, but we'll be happy to see the back of it and its life-sucking kilns.'

'Once me an' Dolly are married, you can tell the minister to get stuffed, as far as I'm concerned. You don't have to get married, or owt, and no one will be any the wiser about – you know, you and Edward living over the brush. It'll be a new beginning for all of us.'

'I think your dad's trying to tell you that your baby and whoever you include in your life, will be loved by us – wherever they come from.' Her look was shrewd, and Maddie heavily suspected Dolly had doubts about Edward being Alfie's father.

Tears welled once more, but they were tears of happiness, not misery. It made a nice change, Maddie thought. 'Thank you, Dad … and Dolly.'

Dolly patted her hand. 'Early night for you, I think. Would you like me to get up with Alfie in the night, to give you a break? I've got an old pap jug somewhere. I can give him a drop of milk with some sugar in, if you'd like, or a bit of bread crust-might help his gums?'

Maddie was so drained from all of the travelling, and the emotions that she had been subjected to, that she nodded, although she had never let anyone feed Alfie before. 'Milk would be great.'

'You need a break, love. Your nerves are shot. Look at your hands, they're shaking.'

It was true, her hands hadn't been steady since she'd seen Daniel, and her mind seemed unable to focus on anything for long. She twisted the wedding ring around her finger, wondering if Daniel had noticed it. He'd made no mention of it, if he had, but then he didn't say much at all to indicate they were anything more than two people who cared about Jane.

It had been as if they were strangers, apart from the thumping of her heart matching his as she had cried her heart out on his chest. He was probably used to having people soaking him with their tears, but he had kissed her forehead, she was sure of it, and that would not be usual, surely?

He had changed so much in such a short space of time. He had become so authoritative and steadfast, she would barely have known him as the boy she had met, who was scared of his mother. Perhaps he was finally strong enough to stand up to her, although Maddie imagined that not many managed that feat. She had quaked in her own boots when she had been confronted by her, and had bent to her demands readily enough.

Dolly rose with a sigh and a moan, bringing Maddie back to the present. 'Ooh, me old bones need their bed.' She stood up, working her fingers into the small of her back, as she walked with Maddie to the bottom of the stairs.

As if reading Maddie's mind, she said, 'Maddie, love, I know you left home because you were let down by your young man, but all that's behind you now, and you'll need some help with the little 'un. Why not come home? Your dad misses you, and Tom's growing up so fast, and you're not here to answer his awkward questions.' She raised her eyebrows. 'There's only so much a stepmother can cope with. I mean, who knows why Jesus is a fully-grown man at Easter and a baby by Christmas?'

Maddie smiled. Tom had always been inquisitive.

'You could live with us, if you wanted, if Edward's not the right one for you,' Dolly continued gently. 'Your dad misses you so much, Maddie. You're so much like Isobel, he must feel he's lost her all over again.'

Maddie paused at the foot of the stairs. 'I've never thought of it that way, Dolly. I do intend to come home, just not yet.'

'Is there something bothering you, another reason, because

from where I'm standing you don't look so happy, and I can't see the pull of London being enough to keep you there? You've said yourself that most of your hats and bags are sent out as parcels.'

Maddie bit her lip, wondering whether to confide in Dolly about her promise to Mrs Davenport. But Dolly might tell her dad, and she didn't want him to think he'd been given a position because of her. He was far too proud to be accepting of that.

She closed her eyes, struggling with the urge to unburden her worries. Daniel had once said that nothing would come between them, and in her naivety, she had believed him. Well, a whole heap of life had come between them, and most of the problems were unsolvable.

She shook her head. 'I'm fine, Dolly. It's best that I stay in London for now, but don't worry, I don't intend to stay there much longer.'

Dolly brushed her cheek with her fingers. 'It's all right. You don't have to tell me anything you don't want to, but I'm here if you need me, duck. You can trust me.'

'Thank you, Dolly.' She gave her a smile and turned towards the stairs, before she could say something she might regret.

Back in her old room, her thoughts returned to Jane once more. She kneeled by her old bed and bowed her head in earnest, for the first time since her mother had died.

She knew nothing could save Jane, but she prayed that her journey to heaven would be easy and painless. She thanked God for keeping her family safe, before she crossed herself and finished with, 'Amen.'

It couldn't hurt to keep on the right side of Him, after all. Just in case.

Chapter Twenty-Seven

Jane had begun drifting in and out of consciousness, mumbling and agitated one minute, still as a corpse the next, causing Maddie to cry out for a nurse on more than one occasion.

Dolly turned up as Maddie was about to leave. 'I've brought Jane some egg custard. My mother always swore by it,' she said, before she took in the sight of Jane, still as death under the bedclothes, her breath barely a whisper. 'Oh, dear God,' she murmured, crossing herself. 'I had no idea she was this bad.' She sat down with a thump, her eyes taking in Jane's emaciated body. 'Your dad wanted to come and see her soon, but I think I'd better tell him to come today, don't you?'

Maddie nodded, her eyes filling with tears, and Dolly squeezed her hand. She looked up, as someone approached, and her heart fluttered when she saw it was Daniel.

'How is our patient today?' He addressed Maddie, but his eyes drifted towards Dolly.

'Hello, Daniel. Allow me to introduce my mother-to-be, Dolly Shanks,' Maddie said, rising to greet Daniel.

Dolly raised her eyebrows, her eyes quizzical and interested as she met Maddie's.

Maddie's smile faded when she turned back to Daniel, who shook Dolly's hand.

'Congratulations, Miss Shanks.' He looked at Maddie. 'I didn't know your father was re-marrying.'

'Why would you?' she said sharply, gratified to see his face fall. She intended to let him know there would not be a repeat of the demonstrative hugs and hair stroking, regardless of the situation.

'Quite so,' he replied stiffly, drawing himself up, before stepping towards Jane's bed.

'She's barely woken up since I got here.' Maddie's voice quivered.

'May I speak candidly, Maddie? Miss Shanks, you might like to take a moment out, if you don't mind.'

It was not a question, and Maddie quickly directed Dolly to the waiting room for a cup of tea.

With just the two of them left in Jane's room, Daniel placed a hand under Maddie's elbow and they moved out of earshot. Maddie barely dared to meet Daniel's eyes as he sought out hers. He lifted a hand towards her shoulder, as if he meant to comfort her, but then he seemed to think better of it and looked down at Jane's notes instead. 'Maddie, we need to make a decision on whether Jimmy ought to see her. He's with his auntie, as I think you know. Jane said she didn't want to distress him whilst she was ill, but now ...' He trailed off.

'No. I don't want his last memory of his sister to be like this. I shall tell him when the ...' She swallowed. 'When the time comes, I shall go and see him.'

'I would like to come with you.' Daniel's voice was gentle, his eyes meltingly kind, but she steeled her heart against him.

'No, I'll be fine, thank you.' Her voice was clipped and dismissive.

Daniel stared a moment longer before nodding curtly and Maddie knew she had hurt him by her refusal.

'What will happen?' Maddie asked, turning her attention to Jane to halt that line of discussion. 'Will she just slip away?'

'She will. She'll not know anything much from now on, I'm afraid, but it is a merciful end. I have seen some horrible deaths.'

Maddie glanced up at him. 'You followed your dream, Daniel, and it was the right thing to do.' She wanted to ask if it was worth it, but it was hardly the time, or place.

'Yes.' He paused. 'Maddie, can we meet ... when this is all over? There are things I would like to say.'

He might have finally acknowledged their past, but Maddie

didn't want to hear his excuses. He could never be forgiven for abandoning her. 'I don't think there's any point. I always knew that you would put your career over anything else – me included. Best to follow our own dreams, I think.' She sighed. 'Let's just focus on Jane, shall we?' She moved across to Jane's bed and took her wasted hand once more, the skin mottled and tinged with blue, the bones of her fingers clearly defined.

'But I didn't, Maddie, you must believe me. It was only when I found out that you married—'

Both sets of eyes swivelled as Dolly returned, cup in hand to stand over the bed, her eyes troubled as she took in the scene in front of her. She eyed them both up steadily before saying, 'I won't stop any longer, duck.' She kissed Jane softly on her forehead and, dabbing at her eyes, patted Maddie on the shoulder. 'I'll tell your dad to come over when he's back from work.'

'Thank you, Dolly.' She gave her a brave smile, while her mind was whirling over Daniel's comment about her marrying and why he believed such a thing. But there was no time to mull over it as he continued to speak.

'I have to go, too, Maddie. I have to give a talk at Stoke Hall about our charity funding for the hospital. I'll come back as soon as I can. If you could just keep talking to Jane, I find it soothes patients when their other functions fail.'

She nodded sadly, and once left alone with her friend, turned back to Jane, preparing to dredge up more old memories of their early life, to divert them both from Jane's dire situation. Daniel's comment, troubling as it was, would have to wait. She spoke softly to Jane smiling as she recounted the trouble they'd caused when they let out Mrs Beasley's chickens and had to chase all over town to capture them, and how they had decided to cut a fringe into Jane's hair, making it far too short. Jane had worn a man's cap day and night to hide it, making them both giggle at the strange glances she'd received.

She spoke of the old pond freezing over, and them skating

on it for a whole afternoon, until loutish boys came along and stamped on the ice. She kept her eyes on Jane throughout, noting her excessively shallow breathing and the sporadic twitching of her hands.

Her lungs began to rattle when she breathed, and Maddie had to steel herself to carry on talking and not run for a nurse. She just kept reminiscing, staring at the window above Jane's bed to stop from crying. When she ran out of stories, she told Jane how envious she had been of her curly auburn hair and her confidence. Finally, she told Jane, her best friend from the day she was born, that she had a son.

She glanced around to check no one was listening as she spoke, glad to have shared the news with someone she loved, whilst sad that Jane would never get to tickle his toes and count his perfect fingers.

Jane's eyes flickered, and Maddie leaned forward, hoping she would speak, but she didn't rouse herself, although her middle finger lifted slightly.

'He's such a sweet thing, Jane. I wish you could see him.' She studied her face, wanting a sign, anything, to show she had heard Maddie's special news and was happy for her. But somewhere along the last sentence Maddie uttered, Jane had slipped away. Her breath simply ceased, and her face relaxed into a semblance of the old Jane. She seemed to be at peace.

'No. No, please, Jane, don't die.' Maddie had become so used to crying that when the time finally arrived, there was nothing left, apart from disbelief that her friend had really gone. She didn't call anyone over and couldn't be sure how long she sat there for, until she felt a hand on her shoulder.

'I need to call a doctor to confirm her death. I'm so sorry. She was a good girl, and far too young to be taken.' It was the kindly nurse, whose long skirt was so starched it didn't move when she walked, making it seem as if she was hovering over the floor wherever she walked. Jane had mentioned her, saying it was enough to scare her to death when she turned up at night, floating like a ghost. Had that really only been three days ago?

Maddie stroked Jane's cheek before rising. 'Goodbye, my dear friend, sleep tight.' She turned to the nurse. 'Can you let Dr Davenport know, please? Jane was a friend of his, and I'm sure he would like to be informed.'

'I'm sure *Mr* Davenport will be upset that he wasn't there for Jane. He's not qualified yet, but he will make an excellent doctor when he is.' She patted Maddie's shoulder.

'Oh, I thought he …' Maddie said before falling silent and shrugging. It didn't really matter if he was qualified or not. He was nothing to her and she needed to remind herself of the fact.

'Help yourself to some tea before you go, dear. It will help you to remember the good times,' the nurse said as she departed down the wide corridor.

Maddie managed a weak smile, unable to believe that she could think a nice cup of tea would negate the awfulness of seeing her friend die, but she merely said, 'Thank you, I will,' and headed off to the waiting room.

After two cups of tea, and a bout of silent tears, she felt composed enough for the journey home. She had drained her teacup, but for some reason was reluctant to leave. Her gaze wavered between the corridor, where poor Jane lay, and the main door, dreading that Daniel might turn up whilst simultaneously praying that he would. She felt bone weary, when she finally heaved herself to her feet and made her way home, inevitably reluctant to return to the everyday tasks of life.

Dusk had arrived by the time she walked up the street to home. She heard an off-key voice singing heartily as she neared her house, and she knew immediately that it was Drunken Edith. She steeled her mind, as indeed Drunken Edith appeared before her, waving a half empty bottle in the air.

'She's gone, 'ant she?' she hollered, as if Maddie was three streets away. Edith hardly ever slurred her words, though, and Jane was astounded by her capacity for alcohol without it rendering her unconscious.

'She has, Edith. How did you know?'

Edith tapped the side of her nose. 'Ah knows these things, an' I know I wunna be long after her, neither. And about bloody time.' She lifted her face up to the sky and shook her fist in the air to the unseen God who had left her too long on this earth.

'Don't say such a thing. That's blasphemy.'

'Bah, I'll be 'aving words with 'im when I get up there. Taking a lovely, young girl like Jane for no good reason. "All Things Bright and Beautiful", they'll be singing at her funeral, as if God took her for her beauty. Hypocritical old buggers. I didn't see them cooking her nourishing food, or paying her bills when she was ill. I left 'er me house, you know. Told the vicar to sort it out. Miserly old git he is, too. Bet he wished I left it to the church.' She lurched away, but then stopped and turned once more. 'You've been good to her, though, you an' your dad. Will you take Jimmy in, now? I hate to think of 'im in that hovel with half a dozen other rammels they call kids. I knew his aunty. She was no better than she should be, an' a right mardy arse to boot.'

She waved her fist in the air again and staggered away, before Maddie had a chance to reply, and she watched her go, intrigued.

'Well, I never, who'd have thought it?' she said to Edith's retreating back. She hadn't imagined that Edith owned her own house, but then, she had never seen the rent man knock on her door, either.

'Who'd have thought what?' Edward's voice made her jump.

'Nothing. Just that … you think you know someone.' She turned towards him, and on seeing the concern in his face, said, 'Jane's gone.' At that, her grief returned, along with a lump in her throat.

Edward put his arm around her shoulder, and she leaned into him, laden down with sorrow. She wanted no more than to be held, and he obliged until her aching heart steadied, and for that she loved him. She wasn't sure it was the way he wanted to be loved, but it was the best she could do for the moment.

Edward drew her close and kissed her cheek, whispering into her ear that he would look after her and make it all right. And she wept all over again, because she didn't deserve his love, and wanted Jane back again, just to say goodbye properly, if nothing else.

Knowing such a thing was impossible, however, she allowed Edward to lead her indoors, where she shared the grim news with her family.

Chapter Twenty-Eight

Daniel knew he had handled the unexpected meeting with Maddie badly, but it had been such a shock to see her again that he had still not quite recovered. What had shocked him even more was the way his hands had trembled, his heart had beat erratically, and his eyes had constantly focused on her lips. He knew he should have been concentrating on Jane, and he had been, as much as could be expected, but Maddie being so close had shaken him profoundly.

It was as if his thoughts had conjured her there. Of course, she was never far from his mind, even after all this time, but tending to Jane had brought her to the forefront of his thoughts. That she was cross with him saddened him. Maybe she was even more than cross, but he didn't know what else he was supposed to have done; the sanctity of marriage was not to be taken lightly and she surely wouldn't have wanted him to make contact knowing she was a married woman.

Hearing his name once more, he returned to the here and now and the social commitment he should've prepared for.

'Daniel, for someone who is supposed to be the star turn at this event, you are lamentably absent of mind, even if your body is in fine fettle.' Charles flicked Daniel's cravat playfully and made big eyes at him.

'I'm not quite with it, you're right. I need to be at Jane's bedside, really, but I know I committed to this a long time ago.'

'Is that all that's bothering you?' His friend peered at him.

Daniel ran his fingers through his hair. 'No, I'm quite out of sorts. I … I met Madeline Lockett again, at the hospital. It's her friend, Jane, who is poorly. Do you remember her?'

'Ah, your little Potteries Maid. How could I forget you mooning all over her? Mind you, those delicious breasts are not easy to forget.'

'Charles, I find that remark very disagreeable.'

'Which bit? The mooning over her, or the luscious breasts? Anyway, I thought you were long over her. You have the delectable Finula to drool over now.'

'Please don't be so crass, Charles. And you know how I feel about Finula.'

'I know you were practically blackmailed into becoming betrothed and I'm not exactly sure how your dear mother managed it, knowing how much you were against such a union.'

Daniel sighed. 'Jane is no better. Thank you for asking.'

'Oh, don't pull that one on me. There's no point in trying to make me feel guilty. You know I am heartless, through and through. So, how was she, she of the pert breasts?'

'She was unhappy, rather aloof, I felt. All totally understandable, given the circumstances.'

'You don't think she ever truly expected you to marry, do you? You were so young. It was just exuberant lust on your part, she must have understood that?'

'I don't think she did. And I'm not sure I did ... at the time, anyway.'

Daniel was uncomfortable with the way the conversation was heading, but there was a part of him that wanted to share his guilty secret. He had never told Charles of his visit to London, but seeing Maddie again had brought it all back. The sweet pain of being with her, knowing it was transient, and the exquisitely short time he had held her in his arms, subsequently finding out that she had married in his absence. That he would never again make love to her had tortured him, still did. How could Charles possibly understand that?

He felt the familiar cloak of shame wrap around him, heavy and oppressive, whenever he thought about his shabby behaviour. He wanted to tell Maddie that he still loved her. He knew it, as soon as he saw her at the hospital, but it was totally impossible. She had a husband and he would do well to remember it. 'Charles, have you ever really made love with someone you cared for, someone other than the Sexy Susan's and Merry Mary's you take in grubby rooms that you pay for by the hour?'

'Yes, of course I have.' Charles narrowed his eyes, the journalist in him sniffing out a story. 'Where is this leading?'

'I do not sleep with Finula, if that is what you are thinking.'

'No, of course not.'

'Why do you say that? People do – all of the time, in spite of what they say.'

Charles looked slightly uncomfortable before he answered, his eyes sliding away from Daniel. 'Because you are far too honourable.'

Daniel laughed inwardly at that, but it was enough for him to say what was on his mind. 'I called on Madeline before I went to the missionary last year, intending to tell her of my engagement.'

'Oh. Why?'

'I thought it only fair to let her know, even though she had shunned me. It always felt as if we'd not said goodbye properly. I also think it was an excuse to see her. You see I did it all the wrong way around. I should have found Maddie earlier and discovered why she left me. If I'd done that I wouldn't have become engaged to Finula.'

'Ah, so you still hold a torch for the young maid.'

'The thing is, we ended up sleeping together,' Daniel blurted out.

Charles's eyes widened, and annoyingly, so did his grin. 'Wow, you dark horse. You had sex with the Potteries Maid?'

'Stop calling her that, Charles.'

A rumble of laughter started in Charles's throat, and Daniel was already regretting his decision to confide in his friend.

'Don't laugh. It has eaten away at me for almost two years.'

'But this is priceless.'

'Do you think it would be enough to disengage myself from Finula, if I told her?'

'Why would you do that? Do you really think no other man carries on a relationship whilst they are engaged? Do grow up, Daniel. It was just a small aberration, and you were probably not the first man the maid lay with.'

For the first time in his life, Daniel wanted to punch his friend. He unclenched his fingers as the urge became almost irresistible. 'Were I not a man of peace, I would enjoy clouting you one.'

'Ooh, no!' Charles covered his nose, exaggerating the gesture whilst laughing at Daniel.

'I don't know why I thought you would understand,' Daniel said. He squeezed the bridge of his nose and closed his eyes briefly, sighing. 'The business is tied up with Finula's family now, and it will be a dreadful mess, but I think I will ask to end the engagement.'

'You have no idea of the ways of the world, do you?' Charles's words were hard, his eyes flinty. He almost sneered. 'Do what you think best. In my opinion, you need to let go of your guilt and get on with the business of living, instead of behaving like a monk, flagellating yourself after the slightest aberration.'

Daniel's eyes narrowed as he stared at his friend, digesting his little speech. He was missing some vital part of this whole conversation, he was sure. Gazing at his old friend dispassionately he wondered what had ever kept them together? His shoulders slumped as the fight left him. He checked the time, he would have to ponder on it later. 'I must go to the hospital and look in on Jane. Will you meet Finula for luncheon in my place, please? I told her we would all go to the Victoria Hotel after this event, but back then I didn't know Jane was quite so near the end.'

Charles pulled a face. 'Only you, Daniel, would prefer to go and a see a sick pauper, rather than enjoy a delicious luncheon with your fiancée. Only you.' He shook his head.

'Send her my apologies.'

'I frequently do,' Charles replied, and Daniel thought he saw the hint of a smirk on his friend's lips.

He pursed his own lips and rose, wishing to be far away from him and their distasteful conversation.

By the time he arrived at the hospital, Jane's body had already been taken away and an orderly was stripping the bed, readying it for the next unfortunate soul to inhabit the space. He thumped the wall, angry and upset that he'd not been there for her. He'd not been there for Maddie, either, and it upset him almost as much. There were things that needed to be said, but finding the right moment would be hard to do, given that she wasn't exactly well disposed towards him.

He sighed. He would just have to badger her until she did listen to him, he couldn't let it slide any longer.

Chapter Twenty-Nine

Daniel arrived a little late to the church where Jane and most of her neighbours had always worshipped, and the service had already started.

'There Is a Green Hill Far Away' was being played very badly on a rickety piano, the enthusiasm of the pianist far outweighing his, and the piano's, capabilities.

Daniel was glad he had paid for a decent casket for Jane and flowers at the entrance to the church. It seemed a small thing to do, but it pleased him that it looked like someone cared. He *had* cared, he realised, a lump in his throat making him cough.

His gaze flickered over the congregation as he searched for Maddie. It wasn't hard; she shone like a beacon, beautiful and composed amidst the dusty girls from the factory, who sobbed quietly as they tried to join in with a song most of them had probably never heard before. The dreaded potteries dust was still causing deaths as directly as tuberculosis, and many of the young ladies lining the church held handkerchiefs to their mouths as they coughed discreetly. Daniel reckoned that half of them would be following Jane before they reached middle age, but thankfully they seemed oblivious of it as they mourned their friend.

Maddie held tight to a young lad he assumed must be Jane's brother, Jimmy, with Tom standing next to him, his head bowed and his shoulder pressed up against Jimmy in solidarity. Harold clasped Tom's hand, and Maddie glanced at her father with concern as he sniffed and wiped his eyes. There was no sign of Dolly, which Daniel thought slightly strange, but she had hardly known Jane, so maybe it was to be expected.

An unreasonable jealousy shot through Daniel as he acknowledged that he, too, wanted to be enfolded in the love that so patently united the Lockett family. He hesitated for a moment wondering if it would be presumptuous to join them on their wooden pew. In the end, someone shoved a prayer book at him and indicated a free space, so he contented himself with slipping into a side row.

He found it hard to concentrate on the service. His gaze constantly drifted over to Maddie, and he seemed quite unable to tear it away. He had a bird's eye view of every movement she made, every nuance of her face as the light from the stained-glass window danced on her hair.

Occasionally, she would attend to Jimmy who wasn't faring too well. Daniel willed her to turn around and spot him, but she didn't do so once. He was mesmerised, remembering how he used to love the soft silkiness of her hair as it slipped through his fingers, and out of nowhere an image of her popped into his head: of her naked, her head resting on his chest as she traced circles on his abdomen, discussing a future he had prayed would come true.

The disgust he felt towards himself rose up once more, but the image of Maddie's body would not disappear as he glanced over to her again, his wicked thoughts conjuring up memories that had no place in a house of God.

After crossing himself at the figure of Jesus on the crucifix hung from the wall, he slipped out of the church as the last verse of 'Lead, Kindly Light' died down. He found his way to the open grave, reading a few inscriptions on other gravestones as he went, sad to see how many young people had died in the town, barely starting their lives before they were taken from their family. Such a terrible waste of life brought on by malnutrition, bacteria, cold, and the infernal soot from the bottle kilns.

He stared vacantly into the freshly dug hole that awaited Jane's body entombed in its small coffin. The sight of it almost brought him to tears, and he looked up to Heaven, praying for God to give him fortitude until the service was over.

Behind him, the church door scraped open, and Jane's coffin

was wheeled out and along the pathway towards her final resting place. The congregation appeared, shuffling out of the church, and he retreated to the shade of a huge copper beech tree as leaves crackled underfoot. He thought he might wait until everyone had left before seeking out Maddie's undivided attention. He was becoming desperate to speak to her.

He watched from a distance, as the vicar chanted a prayer and spoke soothing words about Jane being in a better place. He prayed that it was true, because Daniel could not see the point of suffering on this earth if there was no such thing as salvation in the next.

He wanted to comfort Maddie as she threw a clod of earth on Jane's coffin, pain twisting her features. He longed to kiss away her hurt and wipe her tears, as she dropped to her knees, folding Jimmy into her chest when he joined her, crumpled up on the cold earth.

There were no more than half a dozen people left at the graveside when Daniel took a step towards Maddie, the urge to speak to her unstoppable. Would she allow him to comfort her once more? He dearly wanted to put his arms around her and draw as much comfort from her warmth as he might give himself.

He knew it was too late for more, but if he could at least make his peace with her, he would be satisfied. Despite leaving the cover of the tree with determination, on catching sight of a sturdily set man heading towards Maddie, he stopped in his tracks. He tried to place the man, but didn't believe he had ever seen him before.

Maddie scrambled from her knees and helped Jimmy to his feet. The man opened his arms, and she walked into them, enfolded into the depths of his coat, Jimmy following in her wake.

Daniel witnessed the pleasure in the man's face and was struck by a pain so physical he had to hold onto the trunk of the tree, retreating once more to the safety of its cover.

As he watched, Maddie allowed her head to sink into the man's chest, and he rested his hand on her hip and led her away. Daniel took in the scene with absolute clarity as it played out, unable to drag his gaze away. As if to annihilate any secret hopes Daniel had harboured, the wedding ring on Maddie's left hand glinted in the sun, mocking him. He had to confess the man she had married resembled no sea captain, although why Daniel thought they should all be tall, handsome and muscular, he didn't know. She was obviously happy, and that was what mattered.

The sun dipped over the church spire, casting a sinister shadow across the graveyard, and still Daniel did not move. The gravediggers started to fill in the grave, and the air had turned cold. It was time to say his final goodbye to Jane.

The gravediggers stepped back a few paces when they saw him walking towards the grave, as if allowing him some privacy. He stood stiffly by her grave, murmuring a prayer that he had learned especially, to ensure Jane's successful route to heaven.

Jane had said that Maddie still loved him and asked him to keep an eye out for her, even if he could not see it in his heart to love her in return. She had made him see that he had never stopped loving Maddie, and he had believed that, finally, he had a chance to make amends. Seeing Maddie at the church today, however, he realised that Jane must have been confused.

'I hope I did right by you, Jane, but I don't think Madeline needs me any longer.' His voice cracked as he spoke, but he was done. 'May God bless you, Jane, and I hope He looks after you better than we managed it here on earth.'

Maddie had asked Edward to check that Dolly was still coping with Alfie at her house. She wanted some time on her own to think about Jane, and also to tend her mother's grave and talk to her about her son.

She had sat by her mother's grave and told her all about

Alfie, and how much she would have loved him, had she met him. Despite the coolness of the air chilling Maddie's bones, she found it soothing to sit silently in the growing gloom, reluctant to return to her home and the normality of living people, demanding and vibrant. It was as if she waited for some kind of sign, as she fiddled with the flowers she had placed in the glass jar and listened to the chirping sparrows, unaware of the solemnity of the occasion.

Sighing, she heaved herself up. It was just a graveyard. She would find no divine intervention there. However, as she was leaving she spotted Daniel emerging from the shadow of a large tree, tall and aloof. She hadn't known that he was at the church, and as usual, her heart lurched at the sight of him. She wanted to join him as he stood over Jane's coffin, but instead she observed from her vantage point, as he bowed his head in prayer.

When he turned to leave, nodding for the gravediggers to continue, Maddie impulsively called out to him.

'Daniel, thank you for coming. I didn't realise you were here.' She narrowed her eyes as a thought hit her. 'Did you buy the casket and the flowers?'

'Yes, it was the least I could do.'

'That's very kind of you. I tried to find out who it was, but the funeral parlour wouldn't say.' She smiled uncertainly. They were being terribly proper with each other, and she was unsure how to alter the level of formality they both observed.

Daniel's facial expressions changed, as she watched him, from worried and pained, to contrite and resigned. Finally, he spoke. 'Madeline, might I take this opportunity to apologise for the way things worked out between us.'

'Or didn't work out.' Maddie tried a laugh, but it came out strangled.

'Yes, quite.' He smiled ruefully. 'I fell in love with you as soon as we met, I think, but we were so young and, I suppose, very naive in the ways of the world.'

'I can accept that, Daniel, but when you came to London we were not children.'

'And I am so sorry for that, Maddie. I came with the best of intentions, to tell you I was engaged to be married. It seemed only right that you should know after … well, after all we meant to each other, but once I saw you again, I couldn't leave you.'

'I believed you loved me, and that we could overcome whatever obstacles were put before us.'

'So did I.' He cleared his throat. 'The night we spent together was the best—'

Maddie raised her palm up to him. 'No, just stop it right there. I have no wish to discuss that night.'

'Sorry.' He looked abashed and was silenced for a moment, his eyes searching out hers. 'But you are happy now?'

She nodded. It was all he needed to know. Unless?

Daniel frowned. 'Madeline?'

She thought quickly. It might be the last chance she would ever have to tell him about Alfie, and it wasn't right to keep a son from his father. Yet, as she tried to find the right words, an image of his mother brow-beating her into submission crossed her mind. She was a force to be reckoned with and might even try to take Alfie away from her. Such stories were always being bandied around and Mrs Davenport would definitely have the wherewithal to do such a thing. To keep the Davenports away from Alfie she'd have to keep quiet, at all costs.

'Yes, I am happy,' she echoed, trying to inject some levity into her voice and not sound bitter.

He shuffled his hat around in his hands, looking uncomfortable, and his gaze slid away from her. 'Madeline, I …'

'Yes?'

'I saw you with your husband.' He swallowed and continued slowly, stumbling over his words. 'So, my good wishes will always be with you. I hope you will do me the same courtesy.'

He bowed his head, and although she could not see his face, he sounded so very unhappy.

She put her hand on his arm, and he glanced up. The sadness in his eyes mirrored her own, and on instinct, she stood on her tiptoes and kissed him gently on the lips. In a flash, his arms were around hers, and she clutched at his coat as his lips crushed hers.

She lost herself in the kiss before pulling away, determined to hide the love she felt for him and the desire that she would never admit. 'I have to go. This isn't right.'

Daniel raked his fingers through his hair. 'I know. I never seem to get it right when I'm around you. Might I see you again?'

Bending down, she picked up his hat from where it had fallen on the grass, and passed it to him. 'No, I was just saying goodbye.'

'Wait, please.' He shook his head and took her hand. 'That was not a goodbye kiss.'

She snatched her hand away. If she gave in now, the whole cycle of pain and disappointment would start again, and she couldn't afford to let that happen. She had her son, and she had Edward, and that would have to be enough.

'Yes, it was,' she whispered before turning to hurry away, breathless, with barely a taste of his lips on her own to remember him by.

Chapter Thirty

There was no reason for Maddie to stay any longer, and in many ways, she was relieved. Although sad to be leaving her family, and Dolly, who she had grown to love, she finally thought she could erase Daniel from her mind; theirs was never going to be the happy ever after she'd dreamed of, and it was better to leave the memories behind.

She slowed in her packing as she recalled their last conversation. Yes, it was finally goodbye, and they had both recognised it, but the pain still weighed her down like a millstone around her neck.

A cart pulled up outside and she pushed open the window to see the commotion as a gang of noisy lads hired by the local church started piling Jane's pitiful furniture into it. Maddie could have cried as they chucked piles of clothes, crockery, and the trappings of a whole family life onto the cart, joking as one on the boys held up a pair of Jane's father's scruffy work trousers, dancing as he draped them around his hips.

The new people were waiting to move in, their furniture stacked up by the side of the road and looking as shabby as Jane's. Maddie thought she should go downstairs to greet them, but couldn't summon the enthusiasm.

And the world just keeps on turning, she thought, staring out of the window before returning to her packing.

She finally dragged her case down the stairs to say goodbye to Dolly.

'You'd better make sure you know how to find us in our new home, when you next come back. Let me see if I can draw you a map. Have you made any firm plans with Edward yet?' Dolly bustled around, picking Alfie's clothes off the settle, where she had been airing them, and folded them neatly.

'No, Dolly, if I'm honest, I try not to think about it. We are all right as we are, me and Alfie, but I know Edward thinks I need a man about the house.' She sighed, feeling bad for Edward, who had never done anything but his best for her and Alfie. 'Don't worry about a map, Dolly. I can find Dad at the Davenport factory, and he can take me there.'

Dolly's forehead creased. 'But your dad won't be there, duck, will he?'

Fear shot through her. 'Why, what's happened?' Surely, Daniel's mother hadn't got wind of her coming home and sacked her father.

'He's moving, with me. Didn't I tell you as much?'

'House, yes, but job, also?'

'Well, it'd be a bloomin' long way to walk from Trent Vale to work every day, don't you think? I managed to get him a job throwing pots with me, just like old times.'

'But that's fantastic news. How did I miss this?'

'You've had a lot to put up with since you came home, and your mind was probably on other things.'

She nodded in agreement, but the only thing on her mind right then was the promise she had made to Mrs Davenport. 'So, I *could* move back home, then?'

Dolly's eyebrows shot upward. 'Am I being thick, or am I missing a piece of the puzzle here?'

'It doesn't matter any more.' Maddie could hardly keep the grin from her face. *I'm free. I can move home whenever I want to.*

She hugged Dolly, who returned the gesture as she passed her a wrapped parcel. 'Oatcakes and bacon, to keep your strength up for the journey. Now don't forget our wedding date, will you?'

'Am I likely to?' She laughed as she tucked the food parcel into her voluminous bag.

'I should hope not. I'm relying on you to keep Drunken Edith out of the way – or at least keep her semi sober, if she turns up.'

'You can't not invite her. She's part of the furniture.'

'I know, duck, don't worry.' Her brow creased. 'You *do* know this is the last time you'll be returning here, don't you?'

'Yes, but it's fine. It's time we all moved on.' Here she was, almost twenty-one saying goodbye to the house where she grew up, tracing the faded peonies on the wallpaper, running her fingers across the old coal-fired settle that had not let them down in all her years of living there.

As she walked out of the front door for the last time, with Dolly in tow, her gaze landed on the small patch of garden. 'Did you plant these?' She stooped down to the green shrubs that fought their way through the poor soil.

'I did. You don't mind, do you? Only, I know your mum was fond of this little patch of garden. It seems a shame to let it go to seed, and it will encourage the new owners to keep it going.'

Maddie's eyes filled with tears, and she rushed back to hug Dolly once more. 'Thank you. We didn't have the enthusiasm to do it after Mum died, but she would love it.'

'Let's hope she's looking down now and seeing that we're all getting on fine.' Dolly wiped her eyes with the back of her hand.

Maddie kissed Dolly's cheek, suddenly appreciating how hard she had worked to integrate with her new family. 'It's time for all of us to move on, and I'm sure Mum would give us her blessing. She loved my dad, and I think she would approve of you to take her place.'

'I'll never take her place, Maddie, you know that, but I hope you'll come to see me as more than a stepmum. Now, give us a last hug, you, and this gorgeous child of yours.'

Maddie passed Alfie over to Dolly and watched patiently as she hugged him to her chest and kissed his head. As she passed Alfie back, she drew Maddie into an embrace, wiping a tear from her eyes 'Safe journey, duck, and let's hope next time you'll be home for good.'

Chapter Thirty-One

1906

Winter turned into spring and Maddie had mulled over her future for long enough. It was time to take action and the lethargy that indecision and the cold winter weather had bought about dissipated, bringing new vigour to Maddie.

But she neglected to clarify her plan to Florence who was horrified when Maddie said they were moving.

'You're sending me home, Maddie?'

The look of dismay on Florence's face was enough to make Maddie explain faster than she had intended. 'No, not just you. All three of us. We're moving back home, but don't tell anyone yet.'

'Are we doing a moonlight flit?' Florence's eyes grew wide. 'Have we gone bankrupt?'

Maddie laughed. 'Don't be daft. I've secured us a better contract, that's all, and due to a change in circumstances, we can go home. We just need to find somewhere to live that has enough space for our business.'

'Our business? I like the sound of that.' Florence brightened quickly and she preened flicking her curls over her shoulder.

Maddie smiled. She couldn't have done half of what they had achieved without Florence, and she was glad that the day was drawing close when she could show her gratitude. 'I'm going back for Dad and Dolly's wedding soon, and hope to find us somewhere then.'

'Oh, that soon?' Florence's mouth stayed slack, and she didn't look particularly overjoyed by the news.

'What's wrong? Don't you want to go back home?'

'Got no one who cares about me there,' Florence muttered into her sewing machine, keeping her head down. 'And I hoped

I'd got away from my rotten family, once and for all, and the blooming factories and their foul air.'

Maddie was surprised at Florence's outburst, so unlike her usual meek acquiescence, but she had to agree, she was rather reluctant to bring Alfie up in such a climate. 'I've been mulling over an idea, Florence, and when I go home, I shall look into living somewhere different, somewhere clean and healthy, away from the pot-banks.'

'Really?' Florence's face lit up instantly. 'Why didn't you say so? *Our business*, eh,' she repeated grinning. 'When are we off?'

'Soon.' She nodded in agreement and felt as if already a weight had lifted from her shoulders. With Florence placing the seed in her mind, to live somewhere out of the reach of the pot-banks and factories, Maddie was impatient to find out if it was at all practical. She remembered a pretty town called Stone that she had passed through, when she had travelled on the barge with Edward and stopped at a lock with an overnight pub. She wished she had taken more of an interest in the houses and shops, but it had seemed like a thriving town, and the air was certainly clean enough to bring up healthy children.

'We'd be best off getting a little shop with rooms above it, if we could manage it, and we could make clothes for the passing trade, like Mrs Howlett used to do before she retired,' Florence said, as if reading her mind.

'That's an excellent idea, although I'm more inclined to simply make hats and such paraphernalia.'

'I could make dresses, though, couldn't I? And we could move somewhere out of the reach of the Potter's Rot,' Florence said, hammering home her opinion of the factories and pot-banks.

Maddie paused for a moment mulling it over. 'You know, I think it might work, if I can raise enough funds. You can dedicate yourself to making clothes and I can make contrasting hats.'

'Will you be marrying Edward when we return home?' Florence's voice held a note of restraint that Maddie had noticed before and she wondered if Florence disliked Edward for some reason.

Maddie sighed at the constant merry-go-round of thoughts that assailed her whenever she thought of Edward and marriage. 'Why does everyone think I will be better off married? I can survive on my own, you know.' It came out more forceful than she intended, and she felt guilty when Florence blanched.

'I was only asking,' Florence huffed, looking put out. 'Edward's a good man and sometimes ... sometimes ...' She closed her mouth, looking mutinous.

Maddie was more than startled by Florence's outburst. 'Sometimes what?' But Florence simply sniffed loudly and resumed sewing, the noise of the machine almost putting paid to further talk.

'I mean ... I don't know. He hasn't asked me recently.' Maddie raised her voice over the thrum of the treadle, surprised by her own confusion and Florence's obvious disapproval. A year ago, she would have put money on her not marrying Edward, but the dynamics of their relationship had shifted since then. It would solve all of her financial problems, too, but that was far from a good enough reason to marry. She had always expected to wed for love, and didn't see why she should have to forsake her ideals to make a happy marriage.

Oh, Daniel, she thought, as she often did, *why did it have to be like this*?

Maybe that was still the problem. If she couldn't have Daniel, she didn't want anyone.

How silly she had been over him, with her big, sorrowful eyes and desperation to please. But she had loved him and had been a willing participant in the events that had formed her life. However, did she still want to spend her life lying about an absent husband every time someone commented on Alfie? A good alternative would be to marry Edward.

She shook her head as if she had spoken out loud before saying, 'We are doing just fine on our own, don't you think, and we can all choose our own destiny.' She smiled at her grandiose words, not quite believing them, but enjoying the confidence they brought her.

Florence nodded enthusiastically, her earlier surliness evaporating. 'I'm happy, as long as I'm tagging along when you change the world.' She smiled briefly at Maddie, who felt quite choked at her words.

'Right, then, let's put our best foot forward and see what happens.'

Her eagerness was only slightly marred by Edward telling her that he was coming down once more. He took it for granted that he would stay with them, and she was aware that their relationship had changed. They were edging towards more of a commitment, but her judgement was clouded because of the way she had loved Daniel. She had believed that all relationships were the same, but had since concluded that the passion and all-encompassing love she had felt for Daniel just wouldn't happen with Edward.

Edward expected more intimacy of late, too, but she knew she couldn't give it in the way he wanted.

She was so weary of going around in circles, she would just have to wait and see, but the clock was ticking and Edward would not wait forever.

Chapter Thirty-Two

Edward appeared on time, as he always did, which often amazed Maddie, considering the vagaries of the waterways. He produced a large bunch of wild daffodils, claiming he had picked them by the side of the river. 'There were hundreds of them – no one would miss a handful,' he said, as she reached up for a vase and filled it with water.

He edged up to her, as she stood at the sink, wrapped his arms around her waist and nuzzled the back of her neck. 'Ooh, you do things to me when you smell so delicious.'

'Edward!' She turned, annoyed by his presumption, but found herself pinned against the sink, her lips level with his.

'Come on, I've missed you, so give us a kiss.'

Without asking any further, he lowered his mouth onto hers, and she found herself in a clinch that was none of her doing.

He pulled away briefly. 'I've been thinking about doing this all the way here.' His hand crept up from her waist, and he groaned as he fondled her, feeling the weight of her breast in his hands.

Maddie was alarmed at his actions, behaving so raucously. 'Edward, no.'

'Why not?'

'Because …'

'Because what?' As if he believed she was teasing him, he began fumbling with the buttons on her top.

'Edward, it's not appropriate for you to behave this way.' She tried to disentangle herself from him, but his legs were firmly enclosing hers.

'But we're practically engaged, aren't we?'

'That has nothing to do with it.'

He let her go as quickly as he had grabbed her, his face a mask of suppressed anger. 'Make us a cup of tea, then, will you?'

She looked at him suspiciously. 'Have you been drinking?'

'I've 'ad a few. It's thirsty work on them boats, but that's got nowt to do with the way I feel about you, and well you know it.' He stared at her for a second, as if he was weighing up the wisdom of pursuing the conversation, but instead he settled into a chair and rested his head against the back of it.

Maddie felt churlish for acting the way she had. 'Yes, take the weight off. You deserve a rest. I've made some bread and butter pudding. I can slice some to go with your tea, if you fancy it.' She turned back to the sink to refill the kettle, telling herself that she had overreacted, but her hands shook at his unexpected behaviour, and fear jumped in her chest.

As she busied herself making the drinks, she mentally calmed herself. It was just Edward, after all. He would never harm her in any way.

She wondered if it was the right time to tell him she was moving back home, but something stopped her. She was becoming inextricably tied up with Edward, and she worried that the decision would be taken out of her hands if she told him of her plans.

Sitting down across from him, she balanced her cup and saucer warily, sizing him up.

He smiled disarmingly as if he knew he had rattled her. 'I'll bet you've tipped that one upside down already, but even from here, I can tell you it's a Minton's.' He indicated the new cup and saucer Maddie had bought from a market stall. 'Me mum worked there for years – got a cupboard full of seconds. Can't get enough of it in London. Mind you, they *are* well made, and it's a pretty pattern for the ladies.'

Maddie smiled in agreement. She had, indeed, tipped the crockery upside down when she had first bought it, although she, too, already knew who had made it. It had a scrawl of indecipherable writing underneath the glaze, a mark that said it was sub-standard. Why else would it be on a market stall?

She held the handle of the cup delicately, between thumb

and forefinger, appreciating the fine china and the pretty pattern. 'Still tastes the same – the tea.' She waved her cup at him.

'You're right there. There's nowt that can beat tea in a good china cup.' He smacked his lips together and picked up his slice of bread pudding. 'It's good to be home.'

His comment was yet another confirmation of the change in their status. She hadn't, for one minute, thought that Edward considered her home to be his own, and she certainly didn't think it, even if he did have a smattering of clothes and various chattels hanging around. She felt a flush of nerves creep up her neck. Something had certainly changed between them.

'I thought we could go out tonight, just you and me. You could get dressed up, look pretty for me. I'll bet Florence would look after little 'un, for a penny or two.'

Her sense of foreboding grew as she sipped her tea. 'Aren't you too tired?'

'No, I'm never too tired when I see you. Although, I'll tell you what I am tired of.' He nudged her foot with his toe, his sock full of holes. 'I'm tired of that sofa, and that's no word of a lie.' He grinned, as if to take away the full force of the rebuke, but the inference was clear.

Maddie glanced over at the sofa, hoping it might answer Edward back, telling him that it was as comfortable as her bed, and he had no need to think otherwise.

It seemed to Maddie that the time had come to make a decision. Edward had had enough of playing the doting beau and wanted more. She bit her lip. 'All right, I shall ask Florence. I'm sure she won't mind.'

Maddie made an effort for Edward, pulling on gloves and tipping one of her hats jauntily over her curls before they left. No one had ever asked her where she acquired her hats, but she was ready with an answer and a business card, all the same, just in case anyone ever did.

Edward crooked his arm, and she slid her hand through it, as if accepting that she was his woman. They strolled along the docks, admiring the boats and commenting on the hustle and bustle around them. Edward bought some hot chestnuts and jiggled them around. They laughed as they tried to peel them, the heat warming their hands in the cold night air.

He put his arm around her shoulders and drew her close. It felt good to be part of a couple, despite her misgivings, and she leaned into him, enjoying the solidarity it brought. She knew she was being silly about his presumption earlier, and determined to make it up to him.

As she put her arm around his waist, he smiled down at her. 'There's a turn up for the books, eh? I'm glad to see this relationship isn't as one-sided as I was starting to believe.'

'I'm sorry, Edward. I've been pre-occupied. In fact, I have some news.' This was as good a time as ever, she decided, and drew in a breath. 'I've decided to return home, as the business no longer needs to be in London, with freight being so easy now. A good deal has been struck with a few department stores, and if things carry on the way they are, we should be able to take someone else on.'

'But that's fantastic. Why did you wait 'til now to tell me? Your dad won't want you back, once he's married, though, will he?'

Maddie was a bit put out by his triumphant tone. 'I don't see why not, but I wasn't intending to move in with them, anyway.'

'I've still got me old room when I go home. We could all move in with me mum.'

Maddie tried not to look too horrified at the suggestion. She would never live in his mother's house, which was already full to bursting with children and elderly relations. 'That's very kind of you, but I'm going to find somewhere suitable – for Florence, as well as myself and Alfie.'

Edward frowned. 'Just for a while, though, until we get settled?'

Maddie stalled. 'Settled?'

'When we are wed? I assume you do know what this is all about, Maddie. You wouldn't be leading me on, now, would you?'

There was an edge to his voice that she had not heard before, and the disquiet she had felt earlier returned. She had known how Edward felt about her from the beginning, and she should have known it would come to this, but she had let it go on, regardless.

She refrained from speaking until they arrived back at her house, where they both made a show of stamping their feet, removing their coats and warming up, but the unspoken words were still there.

Did she want to marry Edward, or not?

She filled the kettle once more, as Edward said goodnight to Florence, who retired to her small room. They sat down with a pot of tea between them, and Maddie fussed with some biscuits and fiddled with saucers, until there was nothing left to do. She looked at Edward, whose face was granite. 'What's wrong, Edward?'

'You don't know?'

'I can see you're upset over something.'

'Maddie, I know you're in two minds over us getting married, but I don't know what you think you'll do if you don't marry me. Spend a lifetime lying about Alfie's father, making up stories about him being on a boat somewhere?'

'Actually, I was going to kill him off after a suitable amount of time.' She smiled wanly, but Edward didn't join in.

'I'm just telling you how it is.'

'I'm well aware of my situation, but I would not have thought you'd be crass enough to state it so bluntly.'

'People are still pretty narrow-minded, when it comes to living over the brush, or having children out of wedlock, and I don't like to think of us doing either of those things. We can get married tomorrow, for all I care. Just say the word, and I'm yours.' He smiled, but it was a mournful, half derisive smile that looked as if he realised the odds were pretty unlikely.

'I do want you in my life,' she floundered, unsure how to make it sound more loving.

He gave her a measured look. 'That's good enough for me. At least for now.' Except, he didn't look any happier. 'Is it 'cause of the fellow … you know, Alfie's dad. He's not around still, is he? I mean, I wouldn't know if he was coming around when I'm not here.' Edward ran his hand across his face wearily.

Maddie shook her head at how unlikely that was, hating that she was hurting Edward. 'I'd never do such a thing to anyone, least of all to you.'

He nodded, fixing her with his stare, until she turned away. He took a deep breath, and she turned back, waiting.

'You might say no, but can we be together tonight, Maddie?'

'Edward, what are you asking?'

'You know what I'm asking, love, and it's not as uncommon as people like to make out.' He reached out and placed his upturned hand on the table between them.

She took it automatically, as her mind searched for excuses, none of them plausible. 'I don't feel that the time is right, Edward.'

'If it's not right now, when will it be? We'll be good together, Maddie, I know it.' He lifted hopeful eyes to hers. There was no doubt that there was love in them, but then he added, 'It's not as if you haven't done it before.'

Maddie felt her cheeks burn instantly as anger rose within her. She stood up, knocking over her chair, and the slap she gave him was so unexpected that even she didn't know she was going to do it until she heard the crack.

He stood up, shocked, holding his cheek. 'What was that for?'

'Don't you dare presume that my being no longer a virgin will make it easier for me to sleep with someone again. It was once, Edward, just once.'

'I'm sorry, love, truly I am. I wasn't thinking clearly. It's hard when you're just a few feet away from where I sleep. I want to hold you in my arms. I long for it, in fact.' Edward covered his face with both hands. 'Oh, God. I'd hoped I would make this so right, and I've done it all wrong.'

Hearing the anguish in his voice, Maddie softened and put her arms around him. 'Don't worry, Edward, please.'

He stifled a sob before resting his head on her chest. 'I'm so scared I'll lose you, Maddie. I can't bear the thought of it.'

She knew that he'd never had her, anyway. A part of her heart had been locked away for Daniel, and it would never be set free, but it was time to start loving again, if it were possible. Even so, she still heard herself say, 'Let's wait until I move, and we can see how things go, shall we?'

Edward sighed and pulled away, searching her face. 'Are you sure?'

'Yes, Edward. It will be all right, you wait and see.'

He nodded and resumed sipping his tea, watching her warily over the rim of his Minton's teacup.

Once she had made up the sofa into a comfortable bed, she left him alone with his thoughts and climbed into her bed feeling miserable and guilty.

She was being cruel to Edward, knowing she had never loved him and, after all this time, probably never would. But it was yet another problem to add to her list, so she pushed it firmly to the back of her mind and fell into an exhausted sleep.

Chapter Thirty-Three

1907

Finally, after months of preparations Maddie, Florence and Alfie made the journey up from London – made painless, by sending their luggage separately, so all Maddie had to worry about was Alfie's well-being.

Although excited to be home, Maddie was even more eager to see the premises she had rented in the market town of Stone. She had taken a huge gamble in renting the small shop on the high street, as she'd not even seen it, or the accommodation above it, but she had been assured it was in a thriving part of the town. There was an indoor produce market, and a cattle market, which would be exciting for Alfie, and Stone was renowned for shoe making. Maddie thought that might come in handy to make contacts and boost sales.

Her decision to settle there was doubly enticing, as she knew she could start afresh. No one from her old life would venture as far as Stone, with it being twelve miles from her old home. Daniel, for instance, would never know she was but a short journey away, and whilst she ought to be pleased with that knowledge, it simply filled her with sadness and regret.

She stepped down from the train, and Florence passed Alfie down after her. He wriggled in her hands, itching to be set free – as he always did, since he'd been able to walk – and full of energy. The long journey had made him fractious and fidgety, and Maddie hoped to find somewhere he could run around safely, to burn off his liveliness.

Alfie had turned into a typical toddler, into everything and inquisitive about the world around him. Each day the likeness to Daniel struck Maddie more forcefully. His facial expressions were similar, and he had a black lick of hair that fell forward in the same way as Daniel's. In fact, it broke her heart afresh every day, watching him shove that rogue piece of hair away from his eyes, but she couldn't quite summon up the courage to change his hairstyle and chop it off.

She set him down on the cobblestones. 'Stay here. Don't dare to run away.' As a familiar voice called her son's name, she started and turned, to see Edward coming toward them. 'Edward, what are you doing here?'

'Meeting you. What, do you think I'd let you unpack on your own?'

She smiled uncertainly. His constant attention had begun to grow stifling, and she'd hoped that she would be able to get to know her new neighbours without them assuming Edward was her husband and, therefore, Alfie's father. She hadn't formulated a plan yet regarding her son's parentage, hoping that no one would be impolite enough to ask.

She gazed up at her new home and her new premises. A sign over the shop declared, in brass letters: M and F Milliner and Dressmaker. She had paid a good few pounds for the sign and was pleased to see it was money well spent.

Florence had been more than delighted to be included in the name. 'Bloody hell. Who'd a thought it? Me own name in lights.'

'Hardly, Flo, but it *is* rather splendid, I agree.' She clutched Florence's arm, squeezing it briefly, before turning back to Edward when he spoke.

'Ooh, it is rather splendid,' he parodied, falsetto. 'You can drop your affected accent, now yer back home for good.'

Maddie scowled at him. 'It's who I am, Edward. I'm not putting it on.'

Edward snorted rudely, picked up her case, and lugged it across the street, looking moody and resentful. If she didn't know better, she would have thought him jealous of her new start. Every time she saw him of late, he made a derisive comment about how she would never make it on her own, or he would belittle her on her lack of business acumen.

In her worst moments, she wanted to remind him that he was a coal miner before he became a canal boat hand, which was hardly the pinnacle of anyone's career. She would have to talk to him about it, once they were settled. He was either with her, or not. She would not allow him to make her feel small.

Despite his attitude, she smiled when he returned from dropping off her bag and kissed him on the cheek. 'How lovely of you to be here. I'm so looking forward to settling in. I hope there's a kettle. I'm gasping.'

'I'll brew you the best cuppa you ever had, made from God's honest water,' Edward said, and Maddie wondered who then had supplied the water she drank in London, if it was not from God.

No matter, that part of her life was over. It was time to start afresh, and there was little time to waste, if she wanted to make sure her business would be a success.

Just as she finished inspecting the rooms above the shop, finding, thankfully, that they were exactly what she had hoped for, she heard a cheery, 'Aye up, anyone there?'

She flew down the stairs. 'Dolly, you're here. Dad!' She launched herself at her father, almost toppling him into the stairwell.

'Give over, love, I'm about to get married. I don't want to be in me box anytime soon. I've got a future again.'

'Oh, Dad, I can't believe you're here.' Tears welled as she embraced her father, before turning back to Dolly and hugging her tightly.

Tom peeked out from under a cloth cap. 'You're not going to slobber on me, are you?' But he ran towards Maddie, clearly as excited as she was. Jimmy trailed in his wake, a shy smile on his lips.

'Tom, you've grown so much, you've almost overtaken me.' She tousled his hair before turning to Jimmy her arms outstretched. 'Jimmy, my, you're more handsome than ever.' She just about refrained from mentioning that he looked the spitting image of his sister, Jane, as she took in his countenance, for a second transported back in time seeing a thin, doe eyed Jane in place of Jimmy. She hugged the boys, and they all grinned at each other, before Maddie realised Edward stood still, in the shadows, watching. 'Edward is here, too. Look!' She waved at Edward, who raised his hand briefly, but his expression was sullen.

Dolly raised her eyebrows, but said not a word.

Maddie had spotted his evident bad mood, but wasn't prepared to let him ruin her reunion. 'Come and see the flat. It's wonderful.'

Edward joined them, the corners of his mouth lifting with reluctance. 'I didn't expect your whole family to turn up. I thought it was our special day?'

'Edward, don't do this. Be happy for me.'

'I'm sorry, love, but I hope they're not going to make a habit of this. We'll give 'em a cuppa and send 'em on their way.'

Maddie bit back her retort, incensed that Edward presumed she would rather be with him than with her family. Up until then, it had been the two of them together with Alfie, making a cosy little family, but he would have to get used to taking a back seat in her life from then on. There was no room for jealousy and possessiveness.

She beamed at everyone. 'Who would like a cup of tea? If we have enough cups, that is. Tom would you and Jimmy run to the bakers and get a Victoria sandwich cake, there's a love? It's down that way.' She pointed out of the window to where she had seen a baker's shop.

She fished around in her purse and passed Tom some coins, making it clear to Edward that she would not be bundling her family home any time soon. When they were ready to catch the train back, they would let her know, but until then, if he valued their relationship, he had better behave.

Still beside herself with excitement that she had her name above the shop, Florence kept hopping down the stairs and out of the main door, to see if anyone was showing interest. She would rush back upstairs at intervals, exclaiming that this or that person of good standing lingered long enough to be given a business card.

After tea was drunk, and the rooms upstairs, where Maddie, Florence and Alfie would be living, were commented on and peered into, Maddie's father declared it was time to catch the train home.

Edward collected the plates and cups and ran a bowl of water to wash them up.

'Got him well trained already, I see.' Dolly nodded over at Edward, who laughed, his bad mood seemingly disappeared.

'You walk with them to the train station, and I'll start on these. Goodbye, Dolly, Tom, Jimmy, Mr Lockett.' He nodded briefly and turned back to the sink.

As they approached the train station, Dolly rooted in her voluminous bag. 'I almost forgot, I have an exhibition in October, showing me wares.' She elbowed Maddie and sniggered. 'If you know what I mean.'

Her father raised his eyes. 'Enough of that lewdness, Dolly Shanks. Not in front of the children.'

Maddie laughed. 'I know what you mean, Dolly. How exciting, though. Is it your new range?'

'Yes, it's still the sinuous flowers and elongated shapes, but I'm edging toward brighter colours and a little more geometry when I'm given the freedom to choose. It's doing great, and I love it.'

'And I'm sure everyone else will, too.'

'My *do* is invitation only, so don't forget to bring this with you. I thought I'd give you fair warning because I know you're going to be so busy with your new venture.' She handed Maddie a cream envelope. 'Will Edward come, too? Florence will look after Alfie, will she?'

'Edward? Oh, I suppose so.'

Dolly narrowed her eyes. 'Is that a problem?'

'No, not at all. I suppose I'm not used to being considered Edward's partner. We shall be there.' She slid the invitation out of the envelope and scanned the words. 'Oh, Hanley Town Hall, eh? Gone up in the world, have you?'

Dolly preened slightly. 'It'll be posh, so dress up in one of your best frocks.'

'I certainly will, Dolly. What a good start to celebrate my return. I promise we'll do you proud.'

They beamed at each other, until Dolly spotted Alfie attempting to blow a dandelion clock he had picked, but had ended up with most of it in his mouth. 'Look at him, bless his little heart.'

'No, Alfie.' Maddie scooped him up, tickling him until he dropped the flower.

Dolly looked on lovingly. 'You'll have your work cut out, now he's walking. Harold, take the lad for a walk along the tracks, eh?'

Her father obliged, taking Alfie by the hand.

Dolly watched them for a moment before continuing, 'I don't mean to press you, but what is the story on Alfie?' She held up her hand. 'Tell me whatever you want, duck, I don't need the truth of it, but we all need to be clear, as people will ask.'

Maddie bit her lip, wondering if then was the right time to confide a small amount of truth to Dolly. She prevaricated, before deciding that half a story would do for now. 'The thing is, Dolly, I didn't leave home of my own accord.'

Dolly peered along the train track at the sound of a train, but soon turned her attention back to Maddie. 'I did wonder, duck. It seemed so unlike you, to take off like you did.'

'I had to leave ... so that Dad could be given a job, after he was sacked from Dulton's.' She wavered. She had never expected to tell anyone what she had done, but the words were finally out, and the emotions she had felt at the time returned, churning her stomach: bitterness and anger mixed with the helplessness she felt over Daniel. 'It wasn't that I wanted a job in London, Dolly, I had a good job in Hanley, but ...'

'Are you telling me you were sent away?'

'Kind of. Yes, I suppose it was a trade-off, and I promised I wouldn't come back.'

'Why not? What had you done that was so bad?'

'It was just something ... nothing, really, to be honest. It's a part of my life I would rather forget. Don't tell Dad, will you?'

'Of course not, duck. But you've got nothing to feel bad about, whereas whoever sent you away should be thoroughly ashamed of themselves.'

Maddie could see Dolly's mind whirring, trying to work out where Alfie fitted into the scheme of it all. The big question was still hanging in the air: who was Alfie's father?

Dolly would probably think it was someone in London, Maddie was convinced. It was a reasonable assumption as she had been in London for some time before she became pregnant. Maddie was happy to encourage the idea. 'It's old news now, anyway, and I wouldn't change any of it. It's stood me in good stead, to be honest.'

She allowed herself a moment's reflection on the parts she would change, if she had to do it all again. The terror of finding out she was pregnant and alone in London being one. She tamped down the fleeting wish she'd had, that she would miscarry, closing her mind against that thought, never wanting it to return.

No, she would not let her memories get the better of her. She had started a new chapter in her life, without Daniel. No one would ever guess about his part in bringing Alfie into the world. She decided right there and then that she would never tell anyone, either. Not Daniel, and certainly not Edward.

'It *has* stood you in good stead,' Dolly agreed, 'but what story are we to tell?'

Maddie worked a smile onto her face. 'I think it's inevitable that Edward and I will marry, so I think that answers your question.' She blinked away the tears that pricked at her eyes, brightening at the thought that her family were a mere half an hour journey away. She could cope with marrying Edward and whatever life threw at her, since she was back where she belonged.

Dolly patted her arm. 'It's all looking good from where I'm standing, but you know you don't have to marry Edward to make things legitimate.'

'It's fine, really. My priorities are towards Alfie, and the business. I shall be a success in Stone, I just know it. There's some money around here. I can sniff it out like old Mrs Howlett used to.'

'Right enough,' her dad cut in, coming up behind them. 'But you just make sure you direct it into your own coffers.' He grasped Alfie's shoulder as the train pulled up, huffing and wheezing its arrival.

Her father produced a sixpence from his pocket and held it out to Alfie, who grabbed at it and promptly tried to put it in his mouth. Maddie snatched it off him just in time.

'Oops, must remember not to do that again,' her father said, but Maddie merely laughed.

'Thanks, Dad. I'll make sure he buys a treat with it.' She put it in her pocket, remembering a time when a couple of pence would have been a lifesaver to them all.

As the train pulled away with her family on board, she waved them off cheerily, knowing that she could see them whenever she wanted. Alfie copied her, his podgy arms going ten to the dozen.

'Right, then.' She waited until the train had disappeared before walking back along the platform. 'Home, Alfie, shall we? You can have a nice splash around in the sink before bedtime, and I'll unpack your clothes and toys ready for the morning.'

She delighted in the thought of getting to know her new home, but her heart sank when she remembered that Edward would still be there, and she would be obliged to play happy families for a bit longer. She knew he would be expecting a decision from her very soon, and she wanted to stall for more time, although there was no good reason for it. Life might have been pretty close to being perfect, but there was always one thorn to niggle her.

Chapter Thirty-Four

'Daniel?' She looked up from her invoice book in amazement and the usual telltale blush heated Maddie's face in seconds, She lifted her hands, which shook of their own accord, to cool her cheeks.

'Madeline, how are you?'

'I'm well, thank you, and you?'

'Yes, yes. I'm well, too.'

'Ah, that's good.' Her fingers fluttered to her throat, and she clutched at the silver cross and chain nestling there. She had no idea of the reason for his visit to her little shop, and to see him appear like the vision she had longed for was a little disconcerting.

He didn't, however, look at all well. He looked careworn, ruffled and self-conscious, his eyes darting around the shop as if to find a bolthole, before fastening on her face.

He gazed at her wordlessly for so long that she felt obliged to break the silence. 'What brings you here? I'm quite sure you have no desire to purchase a new dress, or a hat – but if you do, we need to have a serious talk.' She expected him to laugh, or at least smile at her words, but he simply reached out to grasp her hands, his eyes steady on hers. 'I came to see you, of course.'

His words were unexpected, his demeanour concerning. His eyes were rather wild and sunken in their sockets, and he ran his fingers through his hair repeatedly. There was something very wrong with him.

'Would you like some tea, Daniel? Are you sure you're quite well?'

'Ah, yes, sorry, I am very tired. I have been at the hospital all night.'

'Oh?' A flash of fear swept through her, but she stilled

it. Daniel was not the bearer of bad news. Preoccupied and troubled he undoubtedly was, but not in despair. 'Come through. I'll get Flo to watch the shop.' She lifted the wooden countertop and led Daniel up the stairs through to her little flat, calling to Flo at the same time.

'Just give me a moment, will you?' she said to Daniel, before sprinting up the stairs ahead of him. Casting her gaze quickly around the sitting room, she reached for the few toys lying around, and grabbed Alfie's trousers that were drying on a chair. After bundling them all in his toy box, she sighed with relief, glad that she was a naturally tidy person. Quickly checking that her darling boy was still asleep in their tiny bedroom, she closed the door on him, almost bumping into Daniel who had followed her into the sitting room.

Daniel glanced around, taking in the comfortable looking room, before sinking into her squashy sofa. 'Ah, that's better.'

He looked, Maddie thought, as if he would fall asleep right there and then.

'I didn't know you had moved back, Madeline until Hetty informed me.' His words sounded wistful, by no means accusing, but still she felt the old resentments surface.

'No? It's been two months now, but I don't suppose we move in the same circles, so how would you have known?' She didn't mean her words to sound harsh but Daniel looked pained as if she was slighting him. As if to hide his emotions he closed his eyes and rested his head on the back of the chair.

Maddie's heart quickened with fear. 'Are you ill, Daniel, is that why you've come to see me?' As she uttered the words, a terror she had forgotten filled her chest, making her incapable of breathing properly. She still loved him, after all this time – her heart told her it was true, even if her head pretended otherwise.

'No, Maddie, I'm not ill. I just cannot think straight. I'm so very tired. I was at the Salvation Army before my hospital shift, tending to a dying woman who should never have to endure such a death.' He squeezed his eyes shut as if trying to block out the images.

'You're clearly overwrought, Daniel – through overwork, I imagine. You can't be all things to all people, you know.' She sighed, as Daniel showed no sign of listening to her words. 'Stay and rest a while.' It was the least she would do for anyone who needed tending. She disappeared into her kitchen, and reappeared with a mug of tea and some hot toast with beef dripping smeared over it.

Daniel accepted it with a grateful smile.

'You must look after yourself. I know that's a little like telling your grandmother how to suck eggs, but you can't help others if you are in no fit state yourself.' Maddie stood over Daniel, her hands on her hips, making sure that he ate and drank.

'I know, and thank you for caring.' He smiled, but it wilted quickly, as if his last reserves of energy had emptied in that one smile.

She waited, still puzzled as to the reason for his visit. It was difficult for her to drag her eyes away from him. It had been so long. Too long. She wanted to reach out and smooth his hair and his troubled countenance, ease whatever pain he was carrying. Clearly, there was something on his mind.

'Is your mother well ... and Hetty?' she ventured finally. 'I have written to her but have yet to receive a reply.'

'Yes, all quite well.'

There was a pause and more silence, which Maddie filled thoughtlessly. 'Your father ... and Algernon?'

There was a ghost of a smile from Daniel. 'Both well and I'm sure my horse would send his regards if he could.'

Maddie nodded and continued to watch Daniel in silence as he bolted down a second piece of toast, and sipped at the cup of tea he cradled, as if it was nectar. Finally he spoke. 'One of the reasons I came over was to tell you that Mrs Dudley has died.'

'Mrs Dudley? Do I know her?' Maddie frowned, trying to recall the name, which sounded slightly familiar.

'Edith. Edith Dudley?'

'Oh, no.' Her hand flew to her mouth. 'Drunken Edith, of course. Poor thing.'

'It was probably for the best. She's at peace now.'

'You may be right. She wasn't a happy woman and was quite elderly when I was a neighbour.' She took a moment to remember Drunken Edith and crossed herself automatically, praying she was in a better place. She waited as Daniel sipped his tea, seeming to thaw out with each sip. 'Is that all you came to tell me?'

He sat up straight, blinking. 'Sorry, trying to keep awake here. This sofa is far too comfortable.'

'I shall make you more tea.' Maddie held her hand out for his mug, and as he passed it to her, their fingers touched. Her eyes shot to his face, to see if he had felt the same jolt of awareness that she had, and their eyes met. Unspoken words hung in the air as they gazed at each other. She swallowed. Nothing had changed, Daniel's eyes told her that much.

A lock of his hair fell softly to his brow, and he pushed it away. 'Edith, yes,' he continued. 'If she was lucid by the time of her death, it appears she has left her house to you. She was staying at the Salvation Army. No one knew who she was. It was only because I remembered seeing her with you that I found out. She asked me to visit your father to tell him, when … when the time came.'

Maddie put her hand to her mouth. 'She owned her own house, I remember now. She left it to poor Jane.'

'She seemed very bothered that the church would take it, and said she had left a letter with the Salvation Army, adamant that the church would not have a penny of her money.'

'Yes, she was very bitter towards the church. The vicar wouldn't christen her children because they were born out of wedlock. Terribly sad.' She shook her head in sorrow.

'You don't appear to be particularly pleased that you now own a house,' Daniel said carefully.

'I don't want it. I could never go back there.' She folded her arms and lifted her chin as if she expected a fight over it.

'Of course. You could sell it and buy somewhere else, though.'

'That would be up to Dad,' she said after a moment's deliberation.

'Edith was quite clear that she wanted you, not your family to have the house,' Daniel said.

'Oh.' Suddenly a new world of possibilities opened up to her. She bit her lip, holding back her excitement. However, her second thought was that if Edward caught wind of it, he would be all for moving into it, so they could marry and settle down. There would be no reason to wait if they had their own home; the thought did little to cheer her up.

She put such decisions aside as her thoughts turned to Alfie who would be waking from his afternoon nap soon. She must ask Daniel to leave, before Alfie cried out for her, but she was reluctant to send him on his way.

Glancing over to her bedroom door she said, 'Excuse me for a moment, will you?' She crossed the floor and quickly slipped into the bedroom, pulling the door closed behind her. Alfie was still asleep, and she stroked his pink cheek, her love for him spilling over. It was so tempting to pick him up and present him to Daniel. She bit her lip and folded her arms, staring down at her son. The likeness to Daniel was uncanny.

With a heavy sigh, she steeled her resolve, thinking once again of the formidable Mrs Davenport, before creeping out again.

Daniel was exactly where she had left him, except that he too had fallen fast asleep. She took in his smoothed-out face, peaceful in sleep, happy that she could gaze at him at her leisure. She sighed. How could she wake him, when he was so exhausted?

She pulled off a blanket from her bed and plumped up a pillow. 'Daniel, stay a while. Lift up your head.' She patted the arm of the sofa where she had placed the pillow. 'Swing your legs around, it's quite comfortable.' In spite of what Edward thought, she smiled to herself.

Daniel sounded groggy with sleep. 'Just an hour, then,' he muttered sighing as he lay down on the sofa.

Maddie covered him with the blanket, resisting the urge to kiss his cheek, as she would Alfie. She gazed at him once more, and as her heart swelled with love, it was in that precise moment that she knew she had to end her relationship with Edward. It wasn't fair of her to lead him on any longer. Her feelings for him were a paltry imitation of real love, and he deserved better.

She hoped Miss Finula Atherstone realised what a wonderful husband she would have in Daniel. She had never met anyone so caring and hard-working, dogmatic maybe, but for all the right reasons. He would try to save the whole world of illness and poverty, if he thought he could.

She sat on an armchair and simply stared at him. Tears pricked at the back of her eyes, and she shrugged her thoughts away. Daniel would never be hers, and that was that.

Finally, she headed down the stairs to speak to Florence. 'Will you take Alfie out for a long walk along the canal, please? I'll wake him up in a minute and give him something to eat.'

Florence gave her a measured look. She had seen Daniel come in, and Maddie could see she was trying to work out a connection. 'That's Daniel Davenport, isn't it? Wasn't he engaged to that little madam Finula Atherstone?'

'Still is, as far as I know. He came to give me some news, that's all, but he's worn out – he fell asleep on the sofa. I simply don't want Alfie bothering him.' Maddie knew her words were lame, but knew also that, although Florence's thoughts must be buzzing, she was too polite to ask outright what the young man thought he was doing, falling asleep in their front room.

She crept back up the stairs to wake Alfie, who looked at the sleeping man on their sofa with interest. She dressed him up warm and bundled him out of the room with a wrapped sandwich in case he was hungry, leaving him in the safe hands of Florence.

Alone once more with Daniel, she sat on the floor next to him and woke him by tracing her fingers on his cheek and saying his name softly, enjoying the moment of false intimacy.

His eyes opened and then clouded, as he took in Maddie and his surroundings. He jumped up before clutching at his head. 'Goodness, did I fall asleep.' He eased himself back onto the sofa, closing his eyes briefly, before opening them again and glancing blearily at Maddie. 'It wasn't a dream, then?' His smile was the slow burn she remembered so well, the one that made her heart flip, but it quickly faded as he sat up again. 'I'm so sorry about this. I shouldn't have come really, but once I had found your address, I couldn't resist.' He seemed flustered as he jumped up, brushing down his trousers and straightening his collar.

Maddie couldn't understand why he suddenly seemed in such a rush, not when she wanted him to stay a while. 'Let me make you something to eat before you leave.'

However, he seemed determined, and she was at a loss to work out what could have happened since his arrival, to make him so jumpy.

'I really must go,' he said. 'I do hope my visit won't cause any trouble between you and your husband, but I'm sure when you explain the reason why he will understand.'

They made it to the door, but she stopped at his words, doorknob in hand. 'My husband?'

'The ship's captain.' Daniel glanced down at her hand, and sure enough, there was the thin band of gold circling her ring finger.

Maddie's hand flew to her throat. She had completely forgotten that Daniel believed she was married and had grown so used to wearing the ring she hadn't given it a thought. 'Oh, I don't … I'm not …' Stumbling over her words, she wished she had, after all, prepared a speech about her errant husband to trot out when needed, as Dolly had suggested, but Daniel was already clattering down the stairs, running his fingers through his hair.

'Goodbye, Madeline. Take care,' he called over his shoulder, as he left.

'Bye, Daniel,' she said, and then added to thin air, 'I love you.'

Chapter Thirty-Five

The day of Dolly's exhibition loomed, and Maddie's thoughts were in turmoil. In her mind, she was already one step removed from Edward, and found she could no longer abide him touching her. He must have noticed the change, she was sure, but he'd said nothing.

He was always so thrilled to see her and Alfie, treating Alfie like his son, and it wrung her out to see them fooling around together, knowing that she had made a decision that would shatter Edward's world.

She knew how much a broken heart hurt and wouldn't wish it on anyone, but she felt she had no choice. Settling for second best was cruel and unfair to Edward, and it had taken her too long to decide, allowing Edward to become entrenched in their life. Although it would be difficult, she knew it was the right thing to do.

He was meeting her at the exhibition, coming straight from his mother's house after work. He had kissed her the night before, declaring that he was looking forward to showing her off, and she had smiled thinly, putting aside their relationship for the moment. She needed to focus on Dolly's big night and make sure she was there for her.

She dressed carefully in her newly-designed burgundy dress, which was silky and fluid, with a hidden vent at the back to help her walk. She felt very glamorous in it, and knew it would give her the much-needed confidence to shine, for Dolly's sake. With her contrasting bag in hand, designed and made in the shop, of course, she caught the train to Hanley.

The event was, as Dolly said, a very grand affair. A handsome doorman bowed as he opened the door, and she stepped inside the large hall that was buzzing with people, sweeping the room with her dressmaker's eye. A few dresses were obviously the height of fashion, with fish tails and trains that pooled around their feet but none of the ladies wore any outfits that she couldn't make, and make them better. It was a good feeling with which to begin the evening.

The hall was decked out with fabric panels hung from the walls in bright patterns of geometric colours, the look softened with swathes of cream lilies in huge vases on podiums. Maddie recognised the patterns as Dolly's designs and on inspecting closer found that vases and bowls lined the walls on trellis tables, discreet price tags placed next to them. Her eyes widened when she took in the amount that was being asked; Dolly had indeed found her niche market.

Spotting Dolly, she was about to greet her, when she saw, to her horror, that Mrs Davenport was bearing down on her also. Although the woman might not recognise her – after all, Maddie was no longer the meek, unfashionable teenager she had been – she nevertheless slowed her pace and helped herself to a drink she didn't want, to avoid an embarrassing introduction.

Mrs Davenport's booming voice cut through the chattering crowds, making Maddie wince. 'Miss Shanks, how lovely to finally meet you. I have been a supporter of your work for many years.' She towered over Dolly, who beamed at her with pleasure.

In spite of her newfound determination, Maddie's stomach clenched nervously as she watched them converse.

'Hello, lovely to meet you, too. You are?' Dolly extended her hand benevolently.

'Mrs Davenport. Yes, from Davenport's factory in Blurton.' She obviously expected Dolly to have heard of them, but was left floundering, as Dolly's enquiring expression didn't change. Maddie smiled to herself as, of course, Dolly knew the Davenport factory because that is where her dad had worked. She marvelled at Dolly's acting skills.

Mrs Davenport's patronising smile faded when the

adoration she thought she deserved was not forthcoming, but she pressed on. 'I have one of your very early pieces, you know. I have a keen eye for new talent.'

'Really, which one of the series is it?'

'Oh, it was a very early piece. Very desirable.'

Dolly's eyes strayed, as Mrs Davenport tried to recall how the vase had arrived on her mantelpiece, and she spotted Maddie, who cursed under her breath.

'It was a gift, I believe ... yes, it was a gift.' Mrs Davenport's brow furrowed at her memory lapse, but Dolly had already lost interest.

'Maddie, over here,' she called. 'Let me introduce you to a Mrs Davenport, eminent owner of Davenport's factory.' She winked conspiratorially, a faint smile about her lips.

It gave Maddie renewed confidence as she held her hand out to Mrs Davenport.

'How do you—'

'You!' Mrs Davenport stuttered as recognition hit her. She recovered quickly, but dropped Maddie's hand as if it still contained the contaminating dust of the Potteries that she so feared.

'You know each other?' Dolly still fixed on a smile.

'We met once, but it was a long time ago.' Mrs Davenport looked Maddie up and down, shock registering on her face.

'Ah.' Dolly seemed to be expecting them to elaborate, but Mrs Davenport's nostrils flared, and her smile turned into a pained rictus. As if realising something was amiss, Dolly frowned. 'Maddie is my daughter to be. It is her father I'm marrying,' she said.

Mrs Davenport rallied surprisingly quickly, but she paled under her make-up. 'Yes, I recall, we gave him a position at our factory.'

'Ah, that's right. I knew the name Davenport sounded familiar. He's moving over to Trent Vale with me, shortly, to take up a superior position.' Dolly winked secretly to Maddie.

She obviously had no intention of allowing Mrs Davenport the upper hand.

However, Mrs Davenport was already glancing over Dolly's head as if seeking escape. 'Please excuse me, I do hope we'll keep in touch.' She threw Maddie a guarded look and sailed off.

'Now, that's one lady who thinks she's better than she is. How do you know her?'

'Oh, it's a long story. I will tell you one day. Look, here's Dad with some champagne.' Maddie accepted a glass from her father, making a big deal of it in the hope that Dolly would forget about Mrs Davenport. However, it quickly dawned on her that Daniel might turn up, also, and she sipped her drink rather too quickly as nerves got the better of her.

'I'd better take my wrap to the cloakroom, it's getting rather warm in here.' She fanned her face for emphasis and hurried off, running her wrists under the cold tap once she had found the cloakroom.

The surprise meeting with Mrs Davenport had thrown her, and Maddie was not sure if she could behave as coolly should she bump into Daniel again. The world was turning out to be much smaller than she had thought, having naively imagined there would be little chance of bumping into old friends – or otherwise – from her old life. However, this was Dolly's night, and Maddie would do her proud, as she had promised and forget about the obnoxious Mrs Davenport.

She checked the time. Edward would be arriving soon. In the past, she would have been shored up by his steady presence, but right now, she had only a feeling of foreboding. He had been determined to make a big deal of the event, had bought a new suit and shoes, and every time the evening was mentioned, he would smile a secretive smile.

Returning from the cloakroom, Maddie stopped in shock at Daniel pushing through the double-doored entrance of the building, twisting a cravat in his hands before throwing it around his neck, absent-mindedly. She just had time to take in his pale, strained face, before she turned away quickly, her heart thumping. She was tempted to disappear beyond the doors through which Daniel had just stepped, but knew she would have to face up to seeing him. She briefly wondered about having to introduce him to Edward, and the temptation to run was overpowering.

She exhaled loudly and composed herself, but just as her heart stopped thumping, it appeared things were going to get worse. Her heart almost stopped completely, when Charles staggered into the vestibule with a pretty girl in tow. It took merely a second for Maddie to remember the spoilt, pretty face of Finula Atherstone, Daniel's fiancée. Except, by the way the obnoxious Charles held her, it appeared more as if *he* was engaged to her, not Daniel. He had obviously been drinking, and she knew what Charles was like when he'd had a drink.

She held her breath, hoping it might render her invisible, as she stood, helpless, unable to make a decision on whether to stay, or go, knowing she would be spotted whatever choice she made. She had not seen the odious Charles since he had tried to kiss her, and she would never forgive him for publishing that dreadful newspaper article. She hated him for what he had done to her father, and vowed to not even give him the time of day, if he tried to speak to her.

Luckily, they headed into a different part of the room, and Maddie managed to steal back into the large hall, rattled and dejected that what had promised to be a wonderful evening was already tarnished. By the noise level, however, it sounded as if everyone else was having a great time, the merriment no doubt being helped along by the free flowing wine. Taking it all in, Maddie wished she had stayed at home with her darling Alfie, but it was no good wishing, she was there and must make the best of it, until she could creep away, hopefully avoiding Daniel and Charles.

'Madeline?'

She closed her eyes at the mention of her name, said in the soft way that could only be Daniel's voice. She turned around slowly, to find herself inches away from his face. Reeling backwards at his close proximity, she almost slammed into another guest, and Daniel shot out a hand to steady her.

'Steady on there, Mrs ... Mrs ... Madeline. What is your married name, by the way?'

'It is, ah ... I do not have a married name. My ... erm ... my husband is dead.'

'Dead?' Daniel's eyes rounded as his voice rang out, overloud.

A few people turned to stare, and Maddie grabbed at his sleeve, pulling him into a quiet corner.

Daniel blinked. 'Your husband died? I am so, so sorry, Madeline.'

'Not now, Daniel, please. What are you doing here?'

'But what about your husband? What happened?'

Another voice she recognised boomed out. 'Ah, Daniel, you have found the working-class maid again, I see.'

Maddie stiffened. *Charles*.

She turned slowly, to see him lurching towards her. He was clutching at Finula's sleeve. Whether he was guiding her, or she was helping him, Maddie couldn't tell. When she had a quiet moment, she would try to understand why they had arrived together, but right then, she had more urgent business to deal with.

The colour in Daniel's cheeks deepened and his eyes flashed. 'Do *not* call Madeline that, Charles. I will not have it.'

'Oh, you always were protective of her and her common ways. Liked a bit of rough, he did, Finula, before you came along.'

'I hardly think either of you are in a position to judge. I'm surprised I didn't thump you, to be honest, when I caught you two out,' Daniel said in a tightly controlled voice.

Maddie looked from Daniel to Charles, and then across to Finula, who had paled under her rouge and lipstick.

'Daniel, what's happened?'

Daniel shook his head. 'It doesn't matter and it's history now.'

'What? You don't want your pretty maid to know that your beautiful fiancée could not bear your chaste ways and the faint whiff of carbolic soap you carried with you – you and your Salvation Army dropouts.' He pointed a finger at Daniel and staggered sideways as Finula's hold on him loosened. 'You would rather spend time with your grubby sinners than with your friends. It's no wonder she turned to me. I did you a favour in reality, you wanted to break off the engagement anyway,' he sneered.

Daniel's lips turned down. 'I blame myself, Charles, for not being stronger, for not wanting to hurt Finula, you know that.'

'And that makes it worse, somehow. Why are you always so bloody saintly?'

'You feel guilty, Charles, that's why you try to turn it on me. I always considered you my greatest friend. I asked you if I could disentangle myself from Finula, and you said I was being naive, when all along you were—' He shut his mouth abruptly and ran a hand over his face. 'I confided in you, and you repaid me by being a lying, deceitful cad.'

'I was helping you out!' Heads began turning as Charles's voice rose. 'Don't you see?' His words slurred into one, and he plucked at Daniel's sleeve ineffectively.

'And you preferred this cheap tart over me,' Finula butted in, her gaze sweeping over Maddie.

'Don't talk about Madeline like that. She's a woman of good standing and integrity.'

'Yes, so much integrity that you managed to sleep with her whilst shunning your own fiancée,' Charles rasped, leaning against a handy wall whilst trying to snag a glass from a passing waiter. By all intents, he seemed to be enjoying the set to, even if he was wobbling on his feet.

Maddie gasped and reeled, realising that Charles had just announced the biggest secret of her life to all and sundry.

Daniel looked stricken, as his gaze flitted from Charles to Maddie. 'How dare you do this to her?' His voice was low and even, but he clenched his fists and took a step toward Charles.

'Yes, come on, then. Peace loving man like you? You wouldn't know how to hit someone, let alone have the gumption to do it,' Charles sneered.

The sound of Daniel's fist cracking Charles's cheek brought Maddie to her senses.

Charles staggered backwards, his drink shattering on the floor. Gasps rang around the gathering crowd, as he fell into one of the flower arrangements, sending it crashing down, and all heads turned to see what the kerfuffle was about. It seemed that a live show was much more appealing than still works of art.

Maddie sprang towards Daniel to prevent him from hitting Charles again. 'Don't damage your hands. He's not worth it.' Not that her efforts mattered. Charles's cheek was cut and bleeding, and Daniel's knuckles were already swelling.

Maddie took his hand in hers, cradling it close to her chest, mostly because she still didn't trust him to refrain from hitting Charles again. Considering he said he was a man of peace, Daniel looked very satisfied with the outcome.

Charles, on the other hand, looked stunned, but he was still upright, holding his cheek and cursing.

Finula cooed around him, but had the foresight to keep her dress away from any blood. All in all she did a marvellous job of being completely ineffective whilst appearing to be very productive.

Charles sneered once more, looking past Daniel and Maddie. 'Oh, yippee, here comes the cavalry. Or should I say the cuckold.'

The silence that spread across the room was deafening.

Edward, in his new suit, clip-clopped across the wooden floor in his shiny shoes, clutching a single rose, as he edged forward to see what all the commotion was about.

'Edward, here you are. Let me get you a drink.' Maddie's voice was too bright and her smile false.

'No, you're all right, love.' He glanced briefly at Maddie, before turning his attention to Charles. 'What was that you just said about my Maddie?'

'Your Maddie? Don't make me laugh. She has always belonged to Daniel, and he has always been her one and only love. It makes me sick.'

'Okay, that's fair enough. Just run by me again what it was you said, will you?'

Charles crooked his finger at a dumbstruck waiter, who held a tray of drinks aloft, as if poised for another round of fighting. He gingerly lowered his tray, and Charles snatched at a glass of champagne, downing it in one. He would have been the picture of composed arrogance, if not for his cheek swelling to twice the size it should have been. 'That would be the part where I said he made love to the delectable Madeline when he visited her in London, a few years ago, would it?' His smile was back, albeit wonky and swollen.

Maddie closed her eyes. *Dear God, let this be a terrible dream.* She prayed Edward would not understand the enormity of what was being relayed.

However, once again, it appeared to be payback time from the God she'd had a love and hate relationship with for all of her life.

Edward's gaze flicked to Daniel's hand, caught in Maddie's grasp, and then up to meet Maddie's eyes. She dropped Daniel's hand and stepped towards Edward, but he simply shook his head sadly, his lips conveying his bitter disappointment. The red rose fell from his grasp, the outside petals shedding, symbolic and final as it hit the ground.

Edward thrust his chin out. 'It was 'im all along, the tall chap from the picnic day. Alfie?' He squared his shoulders. 'All this time, I'd been thinking it were some chap off the ships, or sommat, and it was '*im*, right under my nose.'

Charles regained his equilibrium, folding his arms as he watched Edward's emotions play out for everyone to see. His eyes narrowed as he took in his words and Maddie flinched, wondering if Edward's breathy 'Alfie' would set Charles's clever mind whirring.

Edward's mouth twisted, ugly and grief-laden, as he briefly lifted his hand to his brow, running his hand over his face.

Maddie thought he might cry.

'I never knew I was up against a gent such as yourself.'

Daniel drew himself up tall. 'I'm sorry, but I don't quite understand what is playing out here. Besides which, I thought you were dead.'

'Well …' Edward spoke slowly and deliberately. 'As you can see, I'm not dead, and I'll tell you what's happening. This evening, I was going to ask this young lady if she'd do me the honour of being my wife, but I can see I'd be wasting me time. Have been wasting me time, in fact, this last couple of years, or more. Never knew what the competition was, you see. But I'll tell you one thing. I'd never have treated Maddie the way you did.'

He turned as if to walk away, but stopped mid-track, briefly pinching the bridge of his nose. He closed his eyes and nodded, as if coming to a decision, then whirled back around. He lifted his fist up and, as if in slow motion, swung it at Daniel's face. 'That is for treating the lass I loved so shabbily.'

Daniel, incredibly, did not fall over, but Edward's chest heaved with the effort of trying not to lose control.

On seeing that Daniel had not crumpled to the floor, he took another swipe. 'And this is because she loves you, against all odds, and you don't bleedin' well deserve her.' He huffed out a satisfied breath before turning to Maddie. 'Sorry, love, I tried to be what you wanted. I hope he comes to his senses, that's all.' He picked up his cap from where it had fallen and carelessly trampled on the rose as he slammed out of the door.

Mrs Davenport crashed through the double doors into the

vestibule. 'What is going on? Who did this to my son?' she demanded, her voice shrill, as she glided over to Daniel like a ship in full sail.

'Mother, stop.' Daniel put one hand out, the other one trying to staunch the flow of blood.

But Mrs Davenport, it seemed, still had the power to terrify mere mortals and the sea of people parted as she passed through them. The audience, riveted up until that moment, suddenly slunk away.

Dolly hurried over. 'What's all the fuss, then?' She took in Maddie's dishevelled dress and pale face. 'Maddie, are you all right, duck?'

'Don't worry about her. Look at my son.' Mrs Davenport was indignant, as Daniel held a no-longer-white handkerchief to his bleeding nose and was waving his mother away.

Dolly took in the scene, her eyes swivelling towards Maddie. 'Where did Edward go?'

'He left, Dolly. I think he was trying to avenge my honour, or something …' She trailed off, concerned for Daniel and Edward, but helpless to support either.

'This is your doing, is it?' Mrs Davenport demanded of Maddie. 'I knew as soon as you were back that there would be trouble.'

Maddie winced as Dolly's eyes narrowed to slits. She was far too shrewd not to work out the relationship between Maddie and Daniel. She could practically see Dolly's mind putting two and two together.

She looked at Maddie, before peering at Daniel. Maddie was glad a handkerchief obscured most of his face as the jigsaw pieces in Dolly's mind fitted together. Dolly faced Mrs Davenport, her anger rising as she came to the right conclusion. 'It was you who sent my poor girl away. You!' She poked at Mrs Davenport with her index finger, and Mrs Davenport flinched as if it were a hot poker. 'You' – she poked her again – 'should be ashamed of yourself. Now I know why you don't remember where my vase came from. Oh, yes, it's all falling into place now. Turned my poor Harold away from your door and banished Maddie to London.' She flung her hand wide as if to indicate the huge distance poor Maddie had travelled.

Maddie could not help but smile at Dolly. She knew how to put on a good show, all right.

'And you?' Dolly almost spat out the words as she stared Daniel down.

He looked perplexed by the diatribe but was clearly expecting to be next in line for the finger poking.

'You need to sort this out and become the partner Maddie needs in her life.' She swivelled on her heel and a few people applauded. 'Right, let's get this party back on track,' she said and marched back into the main hall.

Maddie caught her father's eye, and he raised his eyebrows and grinned. He had seen Dolly in fights down at the factory when she had been a teenager and knew she could stand up for herself. He took Dolly by the elbow and passed her a drink, which she downed in one go, smacking her lips in satisfaction as she glared at the crowd in case anyone else felt like taking her on.

A very puzzled Daniel, his eyes wary but interested, said, 'I confess I'm utterly at sea here. Will you please tell me what's going on?'

'Not now, Daniel. You need to get yourself looked at. I think your lip might need stitches.'

'Oh, I can sort that out later.'

'Physician, heal thyself?' Maddie smiled.

Daniel tried to smile, but winced instead. 'Yes, something like that.'

They eyed each other guardedly, before a subdued Mrs Davenport returned from fetching her coat. 'Daniel, you need to get some medication.'

'And you need to pipe down, Mother.' He took his mother

by the elbow indicating the exit. 'Let's go.' He turned to Maddie. 'I'm afraid I have outstayed my welcome, and I'm dripping blood onto the floor. On the positive side, I shall spirit Mother away with me – if I allow her to fuss over me, she might, with a bit of luck, forget this whole conversation.'

'It might work,' Maddie agreed, but both their smiles were doubtful. They locked gazes, and it seemed as if they shared the same unspoken secret they had shared on that fateful day they met.

'So, no husband, then?' he asked.

'Sorry, no.'

'Don't be sorry.' His smile reached his eyes, still locked on hers. 'We *will* sort this out.' He brushed her cheek with the back of his hand. 'Until later, my Madeline.'

His mother, who had planted herself firmly next to Daniel, nodded a curt farewell to them both. 'Goodbye, Miss Lockett.' Mrs Davenport threw Maddie a weak smile, surprising her almost more than any of the startling events that had played out that evening.

'Goodbye, Mrs Davenport,' she said. She breathed a sigh of relief on watching her disappear out of the door almost smiling as she fussed over Daniel, whilst he ineffectually tried to bat her probing fingers away.

Chapter Thirty-Six

The next day Maddie was polishing the glass countertop in the shop absent-mindedly. The same patch had already been cleaned to within an inch of its life, over and over. She could see her face through the glass, but the repetitive action helped to stop her thoughts from veering wildly from Daniel to Edward, and back again.

Edward had called on Maddie early in the morning, to collect the few things he had left at her place. He was sad and angry in equal measure, and she felt incredibly sorry about the way she had treated him, letting their relationship drag on when she was clearly still in love with Daniel. Such was life, she thought, sadly. Were people not living out such lies all over the world?

Edward had stood at the front door, looking as if he didn't want to leave, as if he wanted to barrel his way back into the hallway and refuse to accept that it was all over. He had treated Alfie as his own, and he was a good man who hadn't deserved such a publicly embarrassing end to their relationship, or such a shabby treatment of the love he had shown her.

'You can come and see Alfie whenever you want,' Maddie had told him, hoping to take some of the pain away.

However, his lips had turned down, his tone bitter as he said, 'I'd rather spend time with kids that were my own, thanks all the same.'

She knew it was a deep hurt that made him say it, and although she wished she could ease his pain, she agreed that it would be for the best to make a clean break of it.

Although they had stared at each other in the doorway for seconds, tears glistening in both their eyes, there was nothing much left to say, and in the end Edward just doffed his cap and turned on his heel. A tear or two had escaped her eyes as she polished and she dashed at her wet cheeks when the bell over the door jingled, bringing Maddie out of her reverie. She looked up brightly, as she always did, although it was hard to find anything to be cheerful about.

Her eyes widened on seeing Mrs Davenport bustling through the door, bringing in a draught of air as cold as the iciness that ran down Maddie's spine. 'Mrs Davenport?' She would not have been more amazed if the king himself had marched in. 'What a surprise.' She could not quite bring herself to label it a lovely one.

'Yes, well, needs must,' Mrs Davenport said cryptically as she took in her surroundings. 'This is impressive,' she added, sliding hairpins out of her hat and setting it on the counter. She glanced down at a midnight-blue velvet turban with an impressive ruby stone in the centre, which was under the countertop in pride of place. 'I say, that is rather lovely. May I see it?'

Robbed of speech at the appearance of Mrs Davenport perusing hats in her shop, as if it was an everyday occurrence, Maddie mutely reached under the counter and brought out the hat. She placed it on the shiny countertop, and they both stared at it, Maddie still too stunned to speak.

The hat was rather daring in its style, but Maddie had seen something similar in a magazine and had copied it, just to see if it would sell. The result was exquisite, but the price did not come cheap, with its semi-precious jewels and peacock feathers standing proudly at the back. It was not a hat for the fainthearted and would suit Mrs Davenport to the ground.

Mrs Davenport picked it up and rotated it, touching the scalloped edges and soft velvet. 'Who made this?'

'I did.' Maddie could not keep the pride from her voice, although she wished Mrs Davenport would tell her what it was she wanted and be on her way. She thought she ought to invite her upstairs, but Florence was out with Alfie, and there was no one to mind the shop. She also wanted Mrs Davenport gone before Florence returned, and so asked her as politely as possible, 'Might I ask the reason for your call today?'

'You might, indeed.' She waited as if expecting Maddie to take them somewhere more private.

'I'm sorry, but we will have to conduct our business here, as I have no one to mind the shop at the moment. Florence is out at the … err, the shops,' she improvised quickly. Her skin prickled with apprehension, as fat raindrops hit the window. The park trip would be curtailed, and Alfie might charge through the door at any moment, pushing at the flop of dark hair, identical to Daniel's, out of his eyes.

Mrs Davenport seemed to hesitate before speaking, as if choosing her words carefully. 'I think I have come to apologise, Madeline – if I might be permitted to call you that.'

'You can … with pleasure.' She imagined that Mrs Davenport had called her some choice names in the past. Madeline would be a big improvement.

'Thank you.' Mrs Davenport inclined her head and continued, 'I have come to believe that my behaviour over your relationship with Daniel was unacceptable and am sorry for what I did to you and your family.' She took a deep breath; her little speech was clearly costing her.

Maddie took in the grooves etched into her face and wondered why she had not noticed earlier how much the woman had aged in five years.

Mrs Davenport continued, 'I am afraid I have always been too careful with my son, as his health was precarious when he was younger, but having seen you and Daniel together, I can see that you will take as much care of him as I do.' She faltered as her mouth wobbled and her words appeared to stick in her throat, but her emotion was clearly heartfelt. 'You are clearly in love with my son and that means everything to me.'

She took out a handkerchief and dabbed at her nose. 'I am afraid I pushed Daniel to become engaged to Finula. No, I did more than that – I lied to him about his father's financial position to convince him that marrying Finula would be the only way out of our mess. He did the best he could, until it became too obvious that it was not going to work.'

She pursed her trembling lips. 'What I am trying to say, is that I now believe the love of a good person is everything, and I would be happy for you to marry my son.'

Maddie shook her head, puzzled by Mrs Davenport's speech. She didn't exactly consider it Mrs Davenport's place any more to approve or disapprove of her. She also had a sneaking suspicion that it was more to do with her desire to be seen to do right by Dolly, rather than having a fit of remorse.

She pondered her response before speaking, not wanting to sound ungrateful. 'Do you not think it would be better for Daniel and myself to make such a decision?'

'No, not at all.' Panic was clear in her voice, and her eyes widened.

'Why not?'

Unexpectedly, Mrs Davenport's face collapsed. Her cheeks sagged, and her chin quivered. 'Daniel has made plans to work in Africa again, and I cannot let him do that. He will die amongst the savages, and he is my only son.' Her voice rose alarmingly. 'You can put a stop to it, I know you can, because you love him, and he loves you. He does not feel he can change his plans at such a late stage. You know what he is like, far too honourable a man.' She put her hand to her mouth. 'You have to help me, please.' Her eyes were beseeching, and she looked utterly defeated.

Maddie's heart went out to her. She didn't appear intimidating any more. She was just a mother, wanting the best for her son. 'Ah, so I'm the lesser of two evils, am I?' Maddie smiled to take away the sting of her words.

Mrs Davenport, eyes full of unshed tears, looked perilously close to losing the battle against full on weeping.

'Let me get you some tea.' Maddie did not want to prolong the woman's visit, but couldn't let her leave as distressed as she was. She indicated a chintz-covered seat by a rail of dresses, usually reserved for the long-suffering husbands of the fashion world. 'Take a seat, and I'll bring it down.'

As Mrs Davenport sat down heavily, fumbling for a handkerchief, the door opened again, bringing a fresh gust of wind.

Florence blew in, bringing the rain and squally weather with her. 'It's pouring down so bad, we had to cut our trip short. Alfie's not happy, but what could we do?' She drew in an equally windswept Alfie behind her. 'Oh, sorry, ma'am.' She nodded at Mrs Davenport and squinted at Maddie, who waved her arms in a shooing gesture, eyes wide and frantic. 'What are you on about, Maddie? We can't go out again. It's pouring down.' Florence pulled Alfie's cap off and ruffled his hair. 'Alfie, I'll come upstairs with you and get you changed, as your mum's busy.'

Mrs Davenport's polite smile faded in bewilderment.

Maddie froze.

Mrs Davenport glanced at her, before swivelling around to focus on Alfie. Her eyes grew huge in her rapidly paling face, her mouth gaping open as she stared in astonishment.

She stood up, took a step, faltered, and then, putting her fingers to her mouth, staggered backwards. Losing her balance, she crumpled into the rail of dresses with a resounding crash.

The rail looked as if it might hold out for a second, before it folded in on itself and collapsed on top of her. Silk, brocade, tulle and velvet dresses, in a multitude of colours, smothered her completely. She raised one arm half-heartedly, before she exhaled weakly and passed out cold.

Maddie rushed over. 'Oh, Lord, what am I to do now?'

'What's wrong with her?' Flo joined Maddie to stare at the prone Mrs Davenport. 'Is she dead?' She bent down and prodded the still form of Mrs Davenport, who groaned.

Maddie fell to her knees beside the woman, wringing her hands before proceeding to disentangle silk arms and taffeta bows from the unconscious form of Mrs Davenport. 'It's Daniel's mother. She saw Alfie.'

Florence was not the quickest person on the uptake, but Maddie knew her words had sunk in. Florence had never come out with it, but Maddie had an inkling that she had put two and two together some time ago. 'Alfie looks like Daniel, I'm thinking.'

'He's the double of a photograph I saw on Hetty's piano of when Daniel was around three years old.' She wrung her hands again, as Mrs Davenport stirred. 'Let me help you up. I'm afraid you fainted.'

Mrs Davenport put her hand up to her forehead and pushed herself to a sitting position. 'I am fine, but where is the little boy?' She struggled to her feet, frantically looking for Alfie, as Maddie signalled for Florence to fetch some water. 'The boy, can I see him?' she pleaded, as she extricated herself from the riotous dresses that appeared to have a life of their own. 'What is his name?'

'His name is Alfie, after my grandfather, who was called Alfred.'

'He is your son?'

Maddie nodded reluctantly. It seemed the game was well and truly up.

'Maddie, you must tell me the truth … Is he …?' She placed her hands together, palms inwards in a praying gesture, her eyes pleading.

Maddie sighed. There was no point in prevaricating. It was too late for that. She kissed Alfie's head and took his hand. 'Alfie, would you like to say hello to your gran?'

Alfie looked doubtful as he looked at the older woman but nevertheless took a polite step forward. He looked up at his mother and then over at Mrs Davenport, whose eyes filled with tears as she opened her arms wide in hope.

'Will I like having a gran?' Alfie spoke hesitatingly as he took a tentative step forward.

Mrs Davenport crouched down in front of Alfie. 'I give you my word that you will like it, Alfie, because I have already vowed to never again make the mistake of putting money and status in place of family love.'

'Then … hello, Gran,' Alfie said formally.

Mrs Davenport whipped out her handkerchief again, using it to dab at her nose and swipe at her eyes. 'It is very nice to meet you, Alfie. Indeed, you cannot imagine how truly wonderful it is to meet you.' She took his hand, tears finally spilling over her eyelashes, before drawing him to her chest. 'Oh, you sweet, dear boy. You sweet boy,' she mumbled into his hair, unable to release him, even as he struggled to escape from her grip.

Tears pricked Maddie's own eyes, the warm glow she felt at the touching scene surprising her. She was humbled at seeing the softer side to Daniel's mother and thought that, maybe, it was protective instincts that had turned her against Maddie. It would not be easy to forgive her, but it suddenly seemed easier to understand.

She smiled warmly when Mrs Davenport grasped her hand. 'This is the most wonderful gift ever, my dear.'

Maddie's eyebrows lifted slightly at hearing the endearment. Was a higher accolade possible?

It was only when she thought of Daniel that her happy bubble burst. She had no idea how he would take the news and if he went to Africa, she and Alfie might never see him again.

However, if Mrs Davenport had her way, Daniel would not be going anywhere, and she did seem to be better than most at getting what she wanted.

'Would you come to the house tonight, after you have shut your shop. Daniel is still not himself. As you know, he has suffered from his nerves, due to overwork and, I suspect, seeing too many horrors that this world has to offer. I do not want to upset him, but this will be a wonderful tonic.'

Mrs Davenport appeared to be back on track, doing what she did best: bossing people around.

Maddie smiled, thinking she now had more of the measure of Daniel's mother. Daniel would soon know that he was a father, and that would surely convince him to stay in England. She could finally admit the truth of Alfie's parentage, and resume her friendship with Hetty, with Mrs Davenport on her side.

'I shall get Florence, my co-worker, to look after the shop. I think we should go sooner, rather than later, don't you agree?' She ruffled Alfie's hair and reached for her bag and hat.

'Oh, my goodness, dear, that would be wonderful. Give it an hour, or so, and we will be ready.'

Maddie nodded in acceptance. It would never do for the Davenport household to be caught by unexpected visitors turning up, even if one of them was a Davenport himself.

Mrs Davenport pressed Maddie's hand as she left the shop. 'I always knew you were a good girl.' She almost winked. 'Put that turban to one side for me, by the way. It will be perfect for church.'

'Of course, Mrs Davenport.'

Things were, indeed, looking up.

Chapter Thirty-Seven

Maddie studied the house she had never expected to see again, as she walked up the driveway, clutching Alfie's hand. It had appeared so imposing only five short years ago, but really, it was not so grand, at all. Even so, she liked the idea of ringing the doorbell and entering as an invited guest, just as she had promised she would, as a much younger and trusting girl.

Although Alfie knew he had another granddad, Maddie had yet to mention his real father. He still asked about Edward, and she didn't want to spoil the memory of the time they had spent together. He had been an excellent role model for Alfie, and she was sorry she hadn't had the chance to tell him how much that had meant to her.

Butterflies set up in her stomach as she rang the bell, even as she repeated to herself that she was equal to the Davenports.

Mrs Davenport answered the door, and Maddie's heart hammered so hard she felt sure the cook would be able to hear it in the kitchen. 'Maddie, come in. Let me take your coat.' She ushered Maddie inside, but immediately turned her attention to Alfie. 'And how is my precious grandson?'

Maddie stepped inside, dragging Alfie along as he hid behind her skirts, his arms wrapped around her legs.

'A grandchild. I still cannot believe it.' Mrs Davenport's eyes softened, and she bent down and hugged her grandson. She straightened with a groan, and her hand pressed in to the small of her back. 'You shall keep me young, won't you, darling?' She waved a stuffed rabbit in front of Alfie and threw it down the hallway.

Maddie blinked. Did she think Alfie would chase it?

However, almost immediately, a Labrador puppy appeared, wagging its tail, ready for the fun to start.

'A puppy, how lovely,' Maddie said, her smile widening.

'We got Treacle here to keep Geoffrey's spirits up. Since he gave up work, he seems a bit lost. As you know, Daniel did not want to follow in his father's footsteps ...' She trailed off, as if not wanting to open up that particular can of worms. Even more signs that Mrs Davenport was, after all, a human being.

Alfie detached himself from Maddie's legs and clapped his hands. Maddie watched affectionately, as the enthusiastic dog bounded after Alfie, to follow the tantalising toy he scooped up.

Maddie was happy to let Alfie run around the garden with him. After all, if Mrs Davenport protected Alfie as devotedly as she had protected Daniel, then all would be well.

Mrs Davenport inclined her head towards the summerhouse, Daniel's favourite place of old. 'Daniel is out in his den.'

'Thank you,' Maddie said simply, as once again an unrecognisably gentle Mrs Davenport gave her a soft smile.

Maddie walked steadily to the summerhouse, her hands clasped in front of her, as she steeled her nerves. She took a calming breath, as old memories surfaced. The summerhouse looked the same, and even smelled the same, but Daniel, his head in his hands, seemed troubled, no longer the vibrant young man, with big enough ideals to save the world twice over.

He stood up quickly when Maddie entered the room, and stared at her with tormented eyes. His face was pale, apart from the angry bruise on his cheek. The cut on his lip looked painful, and he certainly didn't look his best, but she had never loved him more.

Whilst her heart went out to him, she felt awkward, trying to conjure up appropriate words, when she had no idea what he expected to hear.

He exhaled loudly, his finger and thumb pressed into the bridge of his nose, as if he, too, was trying and failing, to say the things he should. His fingers trembled as he groped for Maddie's hand.

She reached out to him, holding on tight, and the returned squeeze was better than any words of explanation. She took a step towards him, and he gripped her shoulders, pulling her into his chest.

He buried his face into her hair and simply held her, his heart beating against hers. After a few long moments, he released her. As his gaze landed on something beyond the window, Maddie turned to see Alfie running around outside chasing Treacle. Daniel took a few strides forward and pressed his hands flat against the glass, resting his forehead on the pane, just staring at Alfie as if transfixed. His lips moved as he watched his son running around, and a smile spread across his face.

He stayed by the window for so long that, finally, Maddie stole over to him and touched his shoulder. 'He's full of energy, isn't he?'

Daniel swung his head around slowly, as if he had forgotten that she was there. He gazed at Maddie, running his fingers through his hair until it stood up on end. 'He's wonderful.' He rubbed his hand over his face, as tears glistened in his eyes. 'Maddie … I don't know how you can bear to see me. I am so, so sorry. Please try and find it in your heart to forgive me.'

He looked so anguished that Maddie felt only concern for him. 'Daniel, you're still not well, I can see. But it's fine. We are perfectly happy, and I would not change anything that happened between us, so please don't upset yourself.'

He put his head in his hands, shoulders heaving. Maddie stroked his arm, but he buried his face further into his hands. 'All this time, I didn't know. How could that be?'

She gathered him into her arms. 'I'm sorry, Daniel. I should have told you, but we can make up for lost time. You can be as much of a father as you wish – or as little,' she added, wondering if she had missed the part of the equation that was making him so unhappy.

Mrs Davenport crept in and quietly placed a tray of tea on

the low table behind them. She locked eyes with Maddie's, hers full of hope and compassion, surprising Maddie once again at the difference in her demeanour.

She smiled reassuringly, as Mrs Davenport silently retreated.

Maddie relaxed her hold on Daniel. 'Shall we take some tea now?' she asked as she led him to the sofa.

'Yes, thank you.' Daniel twisted around once more, to see Alfie playing with the puppy. 'He is really mine. I have a son.' His eyes held wonder and instant adoration.

'Yes, you do, but the news seems to be upsetting you.'

'It's not upsetting me, and I'm sorry if it appears that way. I'm so astonished by it, that's all. Mother thinks I am ill, too. She says I need a rest, but there is so much to do. I can't afford to rest.'

'You will be of no help to anyone if you become incapacitated yourself, Daniel. I think you're overwrought, working too many hours and taking on problems you can't solve. You need a break from it all, and then you'll be able to see clearly.'

'Yes, yes,' he agreed, but still he seemed distracted. 'I'll do whatever you want, where Alfie is concerned. I have a feeling he might be the making of me.'

Maddie smiled and sipped her tea. That was all she needed to hear – for now.

'Of course, I'm going away shortly, but if I could have the opportunity to get to know Alfie before I go.'

Maddie's face fell. She placed her teacup very carefully back on its saucer, thinking fast. 'You've made your mind up, then?' She forced the words out as her mouth dried. Alfie might have discovered he had a father, only to have him snatched away again.

'All the people I would let down … but what am I thinking?' Daniel ran his fingers through his hair once again, and the pain he carried with him was laid bare in his distracted state of mind. 'I can't believe that I didn't know I had a son. On some level, one would think I might sense it, surely?' His self-loathing was clear. 'I need to atone for my lapse, and what better way than to help others less fortunate than myself?'

'But you don't have to atone for anything, and you certainly don't have to go to Africa to do so,' Maddie blurted out. 'You haven't sinned. I'm sorry, Daniel, but I don't understand your logic.'

'Look at the evidence playing on the lawn.' He glanced over at Alfie, whose cheeks were ruddy and lent a healthy glow about him.

Maddie, hands on hips, launched herself in front of Daniel, to shield her son. 'Now, you stop right there. I will not have you alluding to any kind of sin, when it comes to my – *our* son. He is pure and beautiful, and I won't have you tainting him with your religious-ridden guilt.' She fought down the urge to call Alfie in from the garden and take her leave immediately. Rather, she sighed and rubbed at her forehead. 'You know, Daniel, I don't know why you believe in this God who is full of spite, bringing down fire and brimstone and allowing people to feel shame and the need to be cleansed. The God I want to believe in is kind, and proud of any achievement that one human being manages to accomplish in this hard, cold world of ours. You should think the same. It will make you a happier person.'

Daniel nodded. 'Yes, you're right, of course.'

But Maddie had a feeling he wasn't even listening; he simply gazed out of the window staring at his son. However, she had said her piece and that was all she intended to say on the matter. She stood up. 'Right, let's introduce you to Alfie, shall we?'

She caught hold of Daniel's hand as she pushed open the double doors to the garden and called to Alfie. Her son seemed to be in two minds about whether to ignore her as he tore around the big garden in delight, the puppy's ears flying upwards in the wind as it raced after him.

Finally managing to calm him down Maddie carefully introduced him to Daniel, expecting a barrage of questions, but Alfie took the news of having a father with less interest than expected.

'Can we stay for tea, then?' he asked, barely taking his doting eyes off the dog.

Daniel laughed, looking more like his old self for a few moments. 'Yes, and I will make sure there is cake.'

'Great.' Alfie nodded before turning his back and returning to the garden.

They headed back inside, and Maddie took Daniel's hands in hers, trading her warmth for Daniel's cold hands as they watched Alfie together. Daniel threaded his fingers through hers and the old tingling she used to feel whenever he touched her set up once more.

However, sadness still radiated off him, and she wished she could understand his melancholy. For now, though, she was content to simply be with him whilst he grew used to the idea of being a father.

Alfie finally crashed through the doors, laughing, his cheeks and ears pink with cold. 'That was such fun, but I think I have tired Treacle out.'

The dog flopped down at Daniel's feet, and he stroked his ears, distractedly. 'Tired yourself out, too, I shouldn't wonder. I'll call for some tea, shall I?'

Alfie nodded enthusiastically and ripped off his coat, throwing it carelessly on the back of a chair.

Daniel picked it up and folded it carefully, before hugging it to his chest. It reminded Maddie of her younger self, when she had done the same with Daniel's coat, so long ago.

The longer she spent there, the more she lost hope that Daniel wanted to re-kindle their relationship, as he'd not mentioned a future together, but whatever happened, she knew Daniel would be a good father, and if that was the best she could hope for, then that would have to do.

Tea arrived, courtesy of Mrs Davenport, once again. She took a seat opposite Maddie and beamed at them all, as Daniel's father arrived and took his place next to her.

He had hugged Daniel and Maddie, congratulating them and clapping them on the back, as Treacle bounced around his legs. He asked after Tom and her father, all whilst staring at Alfie adoringly.

Mrs Davenport plied Alfie with food as if it were his last meal on earth, and Geoffrey started to discuss a savings fund for him, pulling out a notebook and a pen to jot down figures.

Maddie truly felt that she had finally been welcomed into the fold, but Daniel's illness, and the fact that he might go abroad, still clouded the day.

'You were right, Mum. I do like it here,' Alfie said, through a mouthful of chicken sandwich. 'Why don't we live here, though? My friends' mums and dads all live in the same house.'

Daniel looked startled and opened his mouth as if to say something, before glancing at Maddie and closing it again.

Mrs Davenport looked pointedly at Geoffrey, who cleared his throat.

'These things have a way of sorting themselves out, but we are here if you need us.'

Maddie smiled at the cryptic sentence as she held out her hand to Alfie. She had no intention of accepting handouts, and the very last thing on earth she would want to do would be to live in the Davenports' household. Besides, Drunken Edith's house had been sold and Maddie might very well buy herself a little house of her own. She turned to Daniel. 'We need to be going, but you know where I am.'

Daniel jumped up on cue. 'I shall see you out.'

Maddie thanked Mr and Mrs Davenport, finishing with, 'I do hope we shall see you soon.'

'Yes, of course. Bring your brother over. He must be looking for some sort of office apprentice work, do you think? We can have a chat,' Geoffrey offered, although understandably he couldn't recall her brother's name.

'Tom? Thank you, I shall do that.'

She took her leave of Mr and Mrs Davenport and stood at the front door with Daniel. He caught hold of Maddie's hand, toying with her fingers. 'I do … need you, Maddie, you and Alfie.' He swallowed, and his lips flattened as he struggled to regain his composure. 'May I see Alfie again?'

'He's your son. You can see him whenever you wish.'

The smile he gave her seemed genuine – if painful. He winced and put his fingers up to his lips. 'And his mother?'

'Daniel, you have always held my heart …' Her throat constricted, and she ran out of words. She smiled weakly, willing him to say more, but he didn't.

'Yes … yes.' The distracted air was back as he ran his fingers through his hair. 'Leave it with me.'

Unsure as to what she was leaving to him she nodded half-heartedly, slightly let down. Bundling Alfie into his coat she kissed Daniel's cheek wishing she was brave enough to kiss him on the mouth. 'I shall leave you to it, Daniel. Take your time in deciding what you want. But I would appreciate it if you let me know your decision.' She didn't mean a word of it; she would do her utmost to stop him from going off to Africa. The man was clearly unwell and his state of mind was questionable right at that moment.

Daniel stooped down and hugged Alfie as if his life depended on it, kissing the top of his head and ruffling his hair. 'See you soon, son.' He stood up and embraced Maddie briefly. 'I don't want to lose you again, Madeline.'

Her smile was sorrowful as he released her. 'The answer is in your hands.' As she turned to leave, she caught a glance of Mrs Davenport standing in the doorway of the sitting room, wiping away a rogue tear.

Chapter Thirty-Eight

The weeks passed by and Maddie, although thinking about Daniel constantly, was caught up in the excitement of Dolly and her father's imminent wedding. She gazed at herself in the long mirror in her old room, a recent addition no doubt brought on by Dolly, liking what she saw. Her face and body shape had changed so much from the young girl that had fallen for Daniel, and here she was, now a fully-fledged adult with a child and her own business.

She pushed down a sudden sadness on thinking of her dear mother, her friend Jane, and now Edith Dudley, all cold under the ground in the church graveyard. Edith and her children might never have existed: just gravestones lined up in a row to mark their sad lives.

She knew that soon it wouldn't be quite so easy to visit the church and its occupants, who meant so much, but it was time to move on. Jane and her mum would be happy for her, she knew – and Edith. She could never repay Edith's kindness and sent up a silent prayer of thanks to her.

Maddie brought herself back to the present and forced out a smile. No matter, she was heading for a celebration and celebrate she would. She checked her dress from all angles in the mirror, ensuring she had done as good a job as she had hoped from the design she'd copied. Fashions were changing so quickly that she had begun having a magazine delivered all the way from London each month, to make sure she stayed on top of new trends.

The midnight-blue, fluidly fitting silk dress she had designed loosely skimmed her kid leather buttoned cream shoes and was a far cry from the fussy dresses she was making three years ago, shored up with whale-bone and frills. The new style emphasised her natural figure and she enjoyed the frisson of freedom it gave her. It was an elegant but simple style devoid of embroidery and contrasting insets as she had spent so long creating a perfect winter wedding dress for Dolly that she'd quite forgotten about her own outfit.

Picking up the winter flowers she had bought from the market she divided them into three: one for Jane, one for Edith, and one for her mother. With her hair piled up on top of her head and threaded with tiny pearls, she set out, wishing her heart felt lighter on what should be a happy occasion.

The day was cold, and frost edged the bare trees and grass with the magic of winter. She tried not to feel lonely as she walked to the church with Alfie, who kicked at the shrubs until the ice clinging onto the branches showered his legs. There was an air of desolation in the wind as it whistled mournfully through the gravestones adding to her morose mood.

Alfie was soon engrossed in cracking the ice on top of the frozen puddles around the graveyard, leaving her free to crouch down by her mother's grave. The water in the vase was half-frozen, and Maddie held out little hope for the new flowers as she placed them in the vase.

She blew on her hands, glad that Dolly had considered the weather when she had asked her to design her wedding dress. Marrying the love of your life would be no fun if you were freezing. Dolly's thick lace dress, with an ostrich-feathered capelet, matched by long, kid leather gloves trimmed with white rabbit fur, would keep her nice and warm in the church. The bone-chilling cold of their church was something that Maddie would remember all of her life, frozen toes and fingers adding to the misery of interminable gospels and prayers that had meant little to her simple soul.

Her thoughts returned to her own mother, remembering all the occasions she had missed. 'Oh, Mum, I wish you could meet Alfie. You would adore him, and I would love to know what you would make of Daniel. He has a beautiful soul, but a tortured mind.' She sighed. 'But I love him, regardless.'

She heard a cough behind her and scrambled to her feet, dusting down her dress. 'Daniel?' Alarmed to see him, she wondered if he had heard her telling her mother that she loved him.

'I was hoping I might find you here,' he said.

'You know Dolly and Dad are marrying today?' Maddie asked.

'Yes. Dolly came to see me.'

That was news to Maddie. 'Why?'

'I think she wanted to give me a piece of her mind.' Daniel looked abashed and ran a hand around his neck self-consciously. 'And she certainly did that.'

Maddie smiled. She could well imagine Dolly giving Daniel a tongue-lashing. Part of Maddie thought he deserved it, too. 'What did she want to talk about?'

'My misplaced obligations, mostly.' He paused. 'You look beautiful, by the way, if I'm allowed to say that.'

'Thank you. Anyone who thinks I look beautiful can say whatever they like.'

He inclined his head. 'Dolly explained about Edward not being your ship's captain.' He smiled gently. 'It doesn't take a genius to work out why you invented a husband, although it's a little disconcerting to find I had been jealous of a man who didn't exist.'

Maddie found herself blushing. 'It's still not easy to have a child without a husband, even in this day and age.'

They both looked at Alfie who was now inspecting an old tin can that was full of frozen water, poking the icy top layer with a stick and laughing when icy water jumped out at him.

'You've done a remarkable job, so far.' Daniel smoothed Alfie's hair down affectionately.

'Thank you.' She gathered Alfie in to her side to stop him from getting his trousers messy and faced Daniel, taking in the unfamiliar lines of worry that had somehow become etched on his face. She loved the way he listened intently whenever she spoke, his kind eyes becoming serious, even though the infernal lock of hair obscured them half of the time. She loved his hands and his long fingers with the square nails, knowing that they were healer's hands. She loved the way he was so self-deprecating and would always stand in the background, unless someone needed his help, and then he would be first on the scene. She loved everything about him, and she hoped that, maybe, it was not too late for that love to be returned.

She took in his suit and cravat, briefly wondering if he was attending a funeral, before she put two and two together. 'You look very smart. Are you going somewhere special?' she teased.

'Yes, very funny. I'm not sure how welcome I will be, though.'

'Believe me, Dolly wouldn't invite any old person to her wedding unless they were welcome.'

'I'm not sure I'm your father's idea of a perfect guest.'

'You'll be fine, as long as you don't drip blood on the flagstones.'

'And if I don't have to fight for someone's honour.' Daniel laughed, and it warmed her heart to hear it. 'Charles, by the way, is no longer a friend,' he added.

Maddie nodded, her eyes bright. 'What's changed? You seem so different from the last time I saw you.'

'You can thank Dolly for that. She has made me see that I can serve God in a different way and I must say I am very relieved by it.'

Maddie held her breath. 'Meaning?' He was going to become a monk or something, she just knew it.

'I can't bear the thought of going to Africa without you and Alfie.'

'You want us to come with you to Africa?' She failed to keep the horror from her voice, instantly imagining a life of man-eating beasts and blood-curdling natives trying to spear them.

'No, I don't want to go to Africa at all.' He tried to take her hands in his, but the church bells started ringing interrupting his chain of thought.

Maddie glanced over at the church where guests had started to arrive for the service.

'I'm sorry, I've intruded on your personal time.' Daniel made to leave but Maddie stopped him.

'Not at all. I visit Mum every week. I'm quite sure she would understand, anyway.'

'Do you think you might have time to talk to me, after this. I mean, properly talk, so we can discuss our future?'

'I'd like that,' she whispered.

Alfie who had escaped his mother's grasp once more ran up to them both. 'Mum, Mum, they're here. Dolly has a white dress and looks like a princess.' Alfie tugged at her arm as he stared up at Daniel. 'Are you coming to see Granddad get married?'

'Yes, and I wonder if you would hold my hand, so I don't get lost.' Daniel smiled down at his son, holding out his hand.

Alfie looked at Maddie, who nodded towards Daniel's outstretched hand and Alfie shyly took it. Maddie took his other hand, and they walked towards the church as a small unit of three, the epitome of a happy family.

Alfie dragged them both along, looking from one to the other, unaware of the undercurrent of unspoken words between his parents. 'Come on, Mum and ... err, Dad, we don't want to miss the best bits.'

'We certainly don't.' Maddie laughed, wondering if Alfie thought the wedding was some kind of show.

They joined Jimmy – who was already seated and decked out in a smart suit – and moments later Dolly walked gracefully down the aisle, linking arm's with her brother, whilst the pianist once again tried valiantly to play a decent tune on the beaten-up piano.

Tom stood next to his father at the altar, Dolly's wedding

band safely in his pocket as the strains of the wedding march played out.

Maddie's heart swelled. It was wonderful to see her father happy, and Dolly would make a wonderful wife and stepmother.

A tear of happiness slid down her cheek and Daniel passed his handkerchief over to her. She wiped her eyes, and he put his arm around her shoulders, squeezing Alfie in between them both. She leaned into Daniel, praying that the time had come for them to finally be together unable to bear the thought of him leaving her again.

When the service was over, the congregation trooped out, but Daniel kept a firm hold on Maddie's hand. He caught Tom's eye and asked him to look after Alfie for a short while.

Anxiety made Maddie's breath hitch as she wondered what Daniel was going to say, but the puzzled smile she loved so much spread across his face and she knew everything would be fine.

'I think I heard you say you still loved me, Madeline Lockett, over in the graveyard?' He waited, the smile still playing around his lips.

Maddie swallowed. She had to say the words she had wanted to say for so long, and if he didn't love her in return, well, so be it. 'I do love you, Daniel. I've never stopped loving you.'

'In that case, stay where you are. My timing could probably be better, but the venue is ideal for what I have in mind. I ... have a ring.' He produced a small box from his pocket and opened it, to reveal a sparkling ring, diamonds circling a ruby red stone. 'Hetty says it's in the latest fashion, but if you don't like it ...'

Maddie glanced down at the ring glinting in the box, and then back up at the dear face of the man she loved so very much. 'Daniel, I would wear a brass curtain ring if it was given with your love,' she answered.

'Then, Madeline Lockett, will you do me the honour of becoming my wife?'

It took her less than a second to make up her mind. She held out her left hand. 'I will, Daniel Davenport, indeed I will.'

There was a clatter of running feet on the flagstones as Tom, followed closely by Alfie, raced out of the church door, yelling, 'Dad, Dad, Maddie and Daniel just got married, too.'

Maddie laughed, and Daniel winced. 'I think I'd better go and put them straight.' He kissed Maddie briefly. 'Don't go away.' He snapped the box shut, keeping the precious ring safe.

She grabbed his hand. 'I'll come with you.'

They pushed open the church doors to a round of applause and a shower of rice that had them spluttering and shaking off the grains from their hair.

'She said *yes*,' Daniel shouted. He held up his hand, and the crowd quietened as Daniel took out the engagement ring from its box once more slipping it onto Maddie's finger. He turned to the crowd, beaming as he stated, 'I am the luckiest man on earth to be given this second chance.' Lifting Maddie off her feet, he swung her around, kissing her, as the guests cheered and clapped again.

Dolly rushed over to Maddie and hugged her, tears brimming. 'Oh, duck, I'm that happy for you.'

Alfie sidled up to them and tugged on Maddie's dress.

'What is it?' She bent down to hear him better.

'Does Grandma know about this?' he asked, frowning.

Maddie laughed. Even Alfie knew his gran's ways. 'No, but I think your grandma will be very happy to hear the news.'

'That's good. And will we all live in the same house?'

'You, me and your dad will live in a new house, probably. Just us three.'

'Good. With a dog?'

'With a dog,' Maddie agreed.

'And Algernon?' Daniel said, joining in.

'How could I forget Algernon?' Maddie rolled her eyes.

'Who is Algernon?'

'You wait and see.' Daniel winked at Alfie.

'Will I like him?'

'Absolutely.'

Alfie smiled with satisfaction. 'Then, that's … everything.'

Daniel knelt down to double check that Alfie was not troubled by the changes in his small world. 'So, it's all right with you?'

'It's great,' he agreed, nodding manically.

Daniel looked from Alfie, up to Maddie, his brows lifted in question.

'It certainly is,' Maddie said. She took Daniel and Alfie by the hand, and they walked down the path together. Maddie suddenly had a thought. She veered off the pathway towards the graveyard. 'Let's tell Mum the good news, shall we?' She swallowed as a lump formed in her throat.

Daniel squeezed her hand. 'I'll introduce myself.'

'Oh, she knows all about you already.' Maddie smiled up into Daniel's face.

'Then she knows that I love you, that you have been my salvation, and that I will cherish you and our children until the day I die.'

'She does, but it won't hurt you to say it again,' she said, her eyes twinkling.

They reached the small grave and bowed their heads, silent in prayer and contemplation. Eventually Maddie kissed her fingers and touched her mother's headstone. 'We're off now, Mum, but I'll come back next week and keep you up to date with everything. Love you.'

She wiped away a tear and clasped Alfie's small hand in hers. Daniel took her other hand and together, as one, they walked out of the churchyard and into a better life.

Thank you!

Dear Reader

As a writer I love to hear from readers who have enjoyed my books and am thrilled when someone takes time to leave an online comment or review. I grew up in the Potteries and love to hear stories of potters and painters and the idiosyncrasies that capture the essence of my part of the country.

I hope you enjoyed reading about Daniel and Maddie's journey as much as I enjoyed writing about them, and if you would like to get in touch you will find my author details below.

Thank you once again for spending time with my characters and me.

My very best wishes
Jackie xx

About the Author

Jackie Ladbury writes heart-warming contemporary and historical women's fiction that is nearly always guaranteed a happy ever after. From spending many years as an air-stewardess and seeing first-hand that it really is love that makes the world go around, she determined to put the same sparkle and emotion into her stories. Her life is no longer as exotic (or chaotic) as it was in those heady days of flying, and she now lives a quiet life in Hertfordshire with her family and two cats, spending most of her time making up stories and thinking up reasons not to go to the gym.

For more information on Jackie visit:
www.twitter.com/jackieladbury
https://www.facebook.com/jackie.ladbury

More from Ruby Fiction

Why not try something else from our selection:

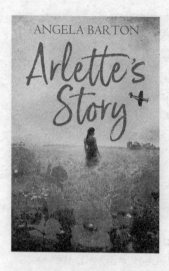

Arlette's Story
Angela Barton

One woman's struggle to fight back against the enemy in order to protect the ones she loves.

When Arlette Blaise sees a German plane fly over the family farm in 1940, she's comforted by the fact that the occupying forces are far away in the north of the country. Surely the war will not reach her family in the idyllic French countryside near to the small town of Oradour-sur-Glane?

But then Saul Epstein, a young Jewish man driven from his home by the Nazis, arrives at the farm and Arlette begins to realise that her peaceful existence might be gone for good …

Available in paperback from all good bookshops and online stores. Also available as an eBook on all platforms and in audio. Visit www.rubyfiction.com for details.

The Best Boomerville Hotel
Caroline James

Let the shenanigans begin at the Best Boomerville Hotel …

Jo Docherty and Hattie Contaldo have a vision – a holiday retreat in the heart of the Lake District exclusively for guests of 'a certain age' wishing to stimulate both mind and body with new creative experiences. One hotel refurbishment later and the Best Boomerville Hotel is open for business!

Perhaps not surprisingly Boomerville attracts more than its fair share of eccentric clientele: there's fun-loving Sir Henry Mulberry and his brother Hugo; Lucinda Brown, an impoverished artist with more ego than talent; Andy Mack, a charming Porsche-driving James Bond lookalike, as well as Kate Simmons, a woman who made her fortune from an internet dating agency but still hasn't found 'the One' herself.

With such an array of colourful individuals there's bound to be laughs aplenty, but could there be tears and heartbreak too and will the residents get more than they bargained for at Boomerville?

The Purrfect Pet Sitter
Carol Thomas

**Introducing Lisa Blake,
the purrfect pet sitter!**

When Lisa Blake's life in
London falls apart, she returns
to her hometown rebranding
herself as 'the purrfect
petsitter' – which may or may
not be false advertising as she
has a rather unfortunate habit
of (temporarily) losing dogs!

But being back where she grew up, Lisa can't escape her
past. There's her estranged best friend Flick who she bumps
into in an embarrassing encounter in a local supermarket.
And her first love, Nathan Baker, who, considering their
history, is sure to be even more surprised by her drunken
Facebook friend request than Lisa is.

As she becomes involved in the lives of her old friends Lisa
must confront the hurt she has caused, discover the truth
about her mysterious leather-clad admirer, and learn how to
move forward when the things she wants most are affected
by the decisions of her past.

Available in paperback from all good
bookshops and online stores. Also available
as an eBook on all platforms and in audio.
Visit www.rubyfiction.com for details.

Who Cares if They Die
Wendy Dranfield

Did she jump or was she pushed?

It starts with the hanging woman in the Maple Valley woods; the woman with no shoes, no car and no name. On paper it's an obvious case of suicide – but to Officer Dean Matheson, something doesn't add up.

Then there are the other deaths, deaths that also look like suicides – but are they? The victims are all women living on the fringes of society, addicts and criminals. Who will miss them? Does anyone really care if they die?

Dean Matheson is making it his business to care, even if it means he becomes the target …

Introducing Ruby Fiction

Ruby Fiction is an imprint of Choc Lit Publishing.
We're an award-winning independent publisher,
creating a delicious selection of fiction.

See our selection here:
www.rubyfiction.com

Ruby Fiction brings you stories that inspire emotions.

We'd love to hear how you enjoyed
The Potter's Daughter. Please visit
www.rubyfiction.com and give your feedback or
leave a review where you purchased this novel.

Ruby novels are selected by genuine readers like yourself.
We only publish stories our Tasting Panel want to see in
print. Our reviews and awards speak for themselves.

Could you be a Star Selector and join our Tasting Panel?
Would you like to play a role in choosing which novels
we decide to publish? Do you enjoy reading women's
fiction? Then you could be perfect for our Tasting Panel.

Visit here for more details …
www.choc-lit.com/join-the-choc-lit-tasting-panel

Keep in touch:
Sign up for our monthly newsletter Spread for all the latest
news and offers: www.spread.choc-lit.com. Follow us on
Twitter: @RubyFiction and Facebook: RubyFiction.

Stories that inspire emotions